"The LitRPG aspects are  d sheet type text. The system works and it makes sense and feels like it being the story and is not an afterthought. And when the MC isn't swinging his axe like the Chad barbarian warrior he is and gaining levels, the drama and the slice of life parts of the story are a great respite and help flush out all the characters. The world itself is filled with an interesting mixture of creatures of the cat variety that can't help but make you chuckle. I'm very much looking forward to exploring the future zones of this story."

— *Ranger Frank, Author of Deathworld Commando: Reborn*

"I was genuinely surprised that what at first seemed to be an egregious lowest common denominator bait actually turned out to have surprising depth. It takes a premise that is typically used for self-insert fiction and applies Fridge Logic to the setting to come up with some rather uncomfortable and genuinely unsettling directions for the plot to go, which was treated with the seriousness it deserved."

— *ShneekeyTheLost, Author of Don't Poke the Humans*

"How dare this story be so good. I'm filing a complaint with the author—it oughta be against the rules to hit me in the feels with a story like this. I love it so much. 'Matt, you moron,' I laughed over and over again. This story has no right to be full of entertaining characters, an actual plot and worldbuilding, and remarkably good writing. How dare this story get me invested in Ravyn's history and traumas, and Yomi's decisions and dilemmas. How dare all of the lurid descriptions of outfits be totally right up my interest-alley. How dare."

— *Pastafarian, Author of Quill and Still*

"Every character simply feels real. Even Matt, despite all his flaws, is entirely believable. So, pick up your iPaw and get to reading!"

- Notorious

"I didn't expect fun characters to become fun people, I didn't expect the tonal shift, I didn't expect a more meaningful look at what being a man and being a father means, I didn't expect rotating themed chapter-naming schemes, and I didn't expect to want to keep reading this all the way through. But all that happened, and here I am."

- Golden Brown

"The story is well-paced, with a plethora of relatable characters and realistic responses. The world of Nyarlea is detailed and interesting, and I'm looking forward to getting to explore it more in future volumes. Equal parts heartwarming, exciting, and disturbing, it's a breath of fresh air in a genre that is increasingly crowded with shallow characters and cookie-cutter plots."

- Skade

"Everyone's a Catgirl!" has absolutely exceeded expectations in just about every way I can think of. The author addresses serious real-world issues, characters develop in deep and meaningful ways, there are gritty scenes with consequences attached where appropriate, and amazingly enough, the author has done this without losing any of the initial cute humor from the earliest chapters. Kudos to DoubleBlind; well done indeed."

- Kenny Celican

"This is an enjoyable fantasy romp in an unlikely world that's lots of fun."

- Stan Hutchings

Volume Three

Written by
DoubleBlind

Illustrated by
Comt216

Cover Art by
GBSArtworks

Edited and Formatted by
Catherine LaCroix

Copyright © 2024 DoubleBlind

All rights reserved. No part of this book may be produced or used in any manner without the prior written permission of the copyright owner, except for the use of brief quotations in a book review.

To request permissions, contact the author at ddoubleblindd@gmail.com

Paperback: 979-8-9881624-5-2
eBook: 979-8-9881624-4-5
First paperback edition: February 2024

Cover art by GBSArtworks
Illustrations by Comt216
Editing and Formatting by Catherine LaCroix
Title Logo by Racknar Teyssier

For Naomí Barrios, Leah Sutton, and Kiora.
For every Patron and Reader
Thank you.

Chapter 1

Blue Screen

[Initiate ping: USER MATTHEW KELMER...]

[USER MATTHEW is not responding.]

[VITAL SIGNS: STABLE]

[Initiate ping: USER TRISTAN ERATO...]

[Connection successful.]

[Transmitting feed...]

There were already a thousand questions clouding Tristan's head, and a hundred more joined them when Matt disappeared from the tavern.

"What just happened?" He looked around at the girls' blanched faces. Ara sat closest to him, rotating her jaw as if chewing on the event itself. Ceres, the newest warrior to apparently join their ranks, gave Tristan a slight shake of her head.

Jazz stood from her table and sauntered to theirs. Without asking permission, she slid into the seat beside Tristan, forcing him to scoot over. Ara frowned but silently did the same.

"I'll go check on him," Keke said, butting her shoulder against Ravyn so she could escape the booth.

"I don't recommend that," Jazz replied, twining her fingers together and leaning her elbows on the table. "I can't imagine he's in a fit state to speak to any of you."

"What do you want, bitch?" Ravyn snarled.

Tristan flinched. His eyes wandered to the dark red streaks on Jazz's fingers.

"Ravyn," Ceres warned.

"No. Fuck that," Ravyn snapped. "Speak plain, Jazz, or go back to your hole."

Ceres sat back, recognition flickering in her eyes, and her stare hardened.

Jazz only smiled. "I would think you would all show more compassion to a leader who'd lost six of her tribe." The smile widened, and Tristan shivered. "Especially when it's your fault."

Cannoli, who'd sat watching the exchange with watering eyes and lowered ears, held her blazard close to her chest. Her mouth formed a tiny 'o'-shape, and she blinked in confusion. "That...couldn't be, though," she murmured in her angelic voice. She looked to Keke, Ravyn, Ara, and then Tristan for clarity. "Could it?"

Jazz reached across the table and took a tendril of Keke's long brown hair between her fingers. "Why did you do it, hm? What is it you're trying to prove?"

All eyes turned to the [Scout]. Tristan replayed the dangerous walk from Catania to Sorentina again in his head and could tell the others were doing the same. They'd stalked between tall grass and thickets, shying away from uncovered areas. They'd fought the slime and avoided a number of Encroacher nests and Defiled approaches. So, when could Keke have possibly shifted the attention of a monster to another group?

"I-I don't understand," Keke stammered.

Ball Gag hopped from Ravyn's shoulder to Keke's, snapping his sharp beak in warning mere inches from Jazz's fingertips.

"Hands to yourself, cunt! Squaaawk!"

"Naughty bird." Jazz tapped the top of his beak, and the blue parrot yawped in anger. "You ignored my signal, then threw that rock where Marianne's group was hiding. You saved your own skins in exchange for six of mine."

Tristan had seen Keke's terror when facing the skeleton and the [Necromancer]. How her skin lost its color to the point where her lips turned gray. But the look on her face now was worse than either situation. Her mouth hung open, and her eyes glistened. Her whole body slumped as if the strings holding her up had suddenly snapped.

"Keke wouldn't have done that if she saw them!" Cannoli protested.

Buttons nodded his enthusiastic agreement, though Tristan was certain the blazard would agree with anything his master said. "She was just keeping us safe!"

"Oh? Is that all?" Jazz's smile vanished, replaced by the fearsome façade they'd witnessed their first night in Catania. "Not out of spite? Jealousy, perhaps? As I understand it, Marianne so recently enjoyed the pleasure of his company."

Keke's ears flattened, and she shook her head. "No. No, no. I didn't know. Please," she begged. "I had no idea. I'm so sorry."

"If only apologies were enough to bring them back," Jazz mused. "I can't imagine Matt is taking the death of an unborn kitten well, either."

"Enough!" Ceres slammed her armored hands against the table, her long braid bouncing against her shoulder. "I trust my lord and his companions with my life. If Keke says it was unintentional, then it must be true. Your provocations are unnecessary and unwelcome."

"And what is it that I win in this exchange, hm?" Jazz replied. "From where I'm sitting, the only ones who have gained anything are your allies."

Silent tears streamed down Keke's cheeks. "I…I didn't see you…"

Cannoli clasped Keke's shoulder and murmured words of assurance in her ear. Ravyn pushed two fingers beneath Ball's feet, encouraging him back to her hand, and looked behind her in the direction Matt had disappeared. The sounds of comfort and merriment from the other girls grated against Tristan's ears.

Tristan traced the familiar shape of Desiree in his lap. Ever since they'd removed him from Venicia's School of Etiquette, he'd felt out of place. Like he'd just entered Nyarlea for the first time all over again. Matt had served as their Party leader and face, and right now, he was completely out of the picture. *I have to show them I'm not worthless. Matt can't do this alone.*

"You're right, Jazz. You've risked and lost a lot." The surety of his tone surprised him. Ara's stunned gaze emboldened him. "But you came here for farmers and foragers, right? And you still have plenty of girls willing to stay."

"Young master is correct. There's still much you can do for Catania. Their deaths will not be in vain," Ara added.

Ceres clasped her hands together and looked from Tristan to Jazz. "Please allow me to clarify. You wish to leave girls here and take ours back with you?"

"Ah, she does listen. Yes, little warrior. We leave a few fighters to train with you and help guard your precious Sorentina in exchange for your knowledge of farming and foraging."

Ceres frowned. "For lawful purposes, I assume?"

"So, you've heard of me," Jazz laughed. "I'm flattered."

"Just answer the fucking question," Ravyn groaned. "This isn't Nyarlean Court intrigue, for fuck's sake."

"None of Sorentina's people will be subject to anything unlawful. You have my word," Tristan said.

"And as we all know, Tristan's word is *gold*," Jazz teased.

Tristan locked her gaze. "Jazz. Please." He'd seen a side of her that he was sure very few had before. All he could do was hope that gave him some weight in the conversation.

Jazz held her silence for a few heartbeats, then relented at last. "Yes. You have my word."

Tristan sighed in relief.

Keke wiped the tears from her cheeks and touched Ravyn's arm. "Excuse me," she whispered.

"Yeah. Sure," Ravyn said, stepping away from the booth to let Keke free. Cannoli moved to follow, but Ravyn touched her shoulder and shook her head. "Let her go."

Cannoli chewed her lower lip, and Tristan couldn't imagine the war she was fighting with herself. But she conceded to Ravyn and slid back into the booth next to Ceres.

"I'm close with the captain of the guard. I can arrange the exchange and have the girls ready in two days," Ceres continued. "If your girls are comfortable sharing room arrangements, we can split them between the inn and the Guild Hall."

"We've lived in cramped spaces for years. They'll appreciate the change of scenery, I think," Jazz said.

That's an interesting 'we' considering your gigantic room, Tristan thought but bit his tongue.

"Right. I will help pay for food and medicine for your injured. The guard should be able to assist me with the remaining bill. And," Ceres gestured to the revealing garments that hugged Jazz's lithe body, "we will find you more suitable attire."

"Back to playing servants, are we? What a glorious day." Jazz gestured grandly.

"*Mattaku!* Just thank her, you ungrateful twat!" Ravyn shouted.

It was Cannoli's turn to flinch.

"Yes. Thank you. Saoirse bless you." Jazz tapped Ceres's forehead. A piece of dried blood flecked away from her finger and clung to Ceres's yellow hair. "Now, if you'll excuse me, I have six rites of death to organize."

Jazz stepped away from the table and looked over her shoulder one last time. "Oh, I forgot, Happy Cherishing Day." She smirked and returned to her table. Cannoli carefully plucked the blood from Ceres's hair.

"Thank you," Ceres bowed her head toward Cannoli. "She is more terrifying than I ever imagined."

"I'm surprised Tristan escaped her gross clutches alive," Ravyn noted.

Tristan blushed. Ara saved him from having to reply.

"I take it the aim was to retrieve you all along?" Ara said, staring straight at Ceres.

"I don't understand what you are insinuating," Ceres replied levelly.

"Your comrades dragged us through every hell on this island under the guise of showing the young master the poor conditions of the cities." Ara's hands moved the sheaths of her daggers. "No one thought to mention that we suffered so Matt could steal another girl from this island?"

"'Steal another girl?'" Ceres scoffed. "How could you say such a thing after my lord saved my life?"

"No, Ceres, hang on. She doesn't mean it." Tristan rested a hand on Ara's wrist and shook his head. "I don't think the whole thing was a lie, Ara. I needed to see what Shi Island looked like. It's really bad."

"Yeah, no shit," Ravyn spat.

Tristan ignored Ravyn's comment, focusing only on Ara. "Don't you think we should fix it?"

Ara paused but dropped her hand away from her weapon. "It is my purpose to ensure your safety."

"I know. But what do you want?"

Cannoli let Buttons roam free on the table. He dove into a bowl filled with peanuts and wrestled two into his mouth.

"You have some time to decide," Cannoli said softly. "But the original reason we came here was to find Tristan so all of Nyarlea's men could meet safely in one place."

"Why?" Ara asked.

"Because the Defiled are fucking everywhere, and it's getting worse," Ravyn supplied. "And as much as I *hate* agreeing with a waste of good air, the man who suggested it has the right idea."

Ceres nodded. "A united front will be much more powerful than, well, being locked away in a school."

"I don't want that. Ever again," Tristan said. Resolve heated his words. "I will never close my eyes to this again."

"Young master, we must return to Venicia—" Ara began.

"Eventually, yes. But we'll meet with the others first and then decide where to go from there." Tristan crossed his arms. "If you'd rather go back alone, I'm sure we can find someone to go with you."

"No. My place is at your side."

"Then come with me. Please."

Ara's cheeks reddened, and she placed a hand on her chest. "O- of course. You can always count on me."

"*Mou ii*," Ravyn whined. For the first time that afternoon, Cannoli giggled.

Please be okay, Matt. I can't do this without you.

Cannoli Pro Tip: You're doing a great job, Tristan. I know this is hard, but thank you.

Chapter 2

Black Mamba

[Initiate ping: USER CAILU RALOQUEN...]

[Connection successful.]

[Transmitting feed...]

Nyarlothep was known for its many luxuries the smaller islands could never afford. Parlors that traded pampering for coin, restaurants that served rare ingredients and dishes, theaters with nightly performances. It was obvious that those born in the capital were destined for affluence and indulgence, and the men who made it this far were rewarded with the same.

While the constant travel was bothersome, Cailu had grown quite fond of the grander lifestyles offered in Nyarlothep. It was like coming home each time he was called back—despite San being his designated island. The girls here were of a more refined breed, and they treated him like a king. At least, for the duration of his stay, he felt adequately remunerated for the grueling work he put into this world.

One comfort he enjoyed immensely was the large private bathhouses offered near many of the inns. A few extra Bells ensured no prying ears on confidential conversations. He and Naeemah were so often known to meet in the later hours at these establishments that owners rarely batted an eye.

"What did the queen have to say?" Naeemah leaned her head back against the smooth ivory stones of the bath's rim. Her dark hair was loosened from its tight hold and fell around her shoulders.

Steam drifted from the water's surface, tracing her bare throat and outlining the sharp line of her jaw.

Cailu breathed in the steam and exhaled slowly, enjoying the rapid surrender of tension in his body to the bath. "As always, Queen Nehalennia regaled me with many words that carried little meaning."

"Just a friendly visit today, then?" Naeemah asked, still staring at the ceiling. The small lump in her throat bobbed with her words. "That's unlike you."

"Not all useless court gossip. A messenger brought word that a second man had arrived on Shi Island. It caused quite a stir, as I am to understand."

Naeemah's head lolled to the side, her serpentine eyes widening but a fraction. "Matt made it, then?"

"So it seems. He was a wise gamble, after all." Cailu rolled his shoulders and slid deeper into the water. "It is impossible to gauge the Defiled threat he'll face there and on Ichi. I've not been to either in years."

"With Magni ruling? Ichi's surely gone to hell," Naeemah chuckled, but it didn't warm the sad gleam in her gaze.

"You know I am a man of my word," Cailu replied.

"Mhm. And so I keep my patience." She breathed deeply, and her breasts hovered near the surface.

Cailu drank in the sight of her as he did each time they shared a similar moment. However, they had never engaged in anything more intimate—they never would. It was an unspoken rule of trust between them. It would stain his spotless opinion of her, and she was well aware of what the others that prostrated themselves at his feet meant to him.

"Anything else you learned in your plays at politics?" Naeemah stretched her arms to either side and crossed one shapely leg over the other. "Or in the queen's bedroom, perhaps?"

You will never stop tempting me, though. Will you? "We're needed back on San Island. Shulan and the outlying cities are having a difficult time fighting off both Encroachers and Defiled."

She frowned. "That's a shame. We've only just arrived."

"Some weeks ago now," Cailu laughed. They'd shifted back and forth between Nyarlothep and the outlying islands so often that it would make a lesser man's head spin. The Defiled threat was too much for the Royal Guard and Queen's Knights to handle by themselves anymore. As much as he and Naeemah could use a reprieve, the fall of the queen would throw the world into chaos. "But it is welcome knowledge that I am not the only one to miss this place."

"Not in the least. You know that I'm more accustomed to the palace games and administrative work that comes with it. Traveling and fighting are still newer to my repertoire."

"No one would ever believe that if they'd borne witness to your skills in combat." He shrugged and ran a hand through his hair. "You learn quickly."

"A compliment? Are you feeling sentimental?" A tiny smile tugged at the corners of her lips.

"Perhaps."

Naeemah hummed. She tilted her head and eyed him knowingly. "So, should we expect the announcement of another princess in Nyarlea soon? You *were* in her company for a painfully long time."

Cailu chuckled. "What happened to your patience?"

Naeemah sighed. "You order me to remain in [Combat Mode] for the duration of your visits. Staring down nobility in their finery from behind a mask loses its charm after a while."

"There may be such an announcement soon, yes." Cailu rolled his shoulders and glanced at the ceiling. "There's something else we should consider."

"And what would that be?" Naeemah searched for the line of scented oils along the water's edge and selected her two favorite bottles.

Lavender and cedar. Cailu didn't have to look to know. "Yomi's replacement."

Naeemah paused, fingers curling around each bottle. "We've managed well so far without her."

"We need another healer." He shook his head. "As much as I loathe the thought of finding and grooming yet another Party member, if the worst should come, we should be prepared."

"Only for them to couple with another man and leave us out to dry once more?" Naeemah said sourly.

Whether she'd intended it or not, Naeemah's words struck a still-live wire of anger with Cailu. "I will give him the benefit of ignorance just once. But I will ensure that Matt never does something so brash again."

Naeemah sighed and uncapped the first bottle, tipping its contents free into her palm. She looked at him with lowered lids and a skeptical sneer. "I can say that's more than you offer your catgirls."

"Should I have turned you in after I found you trying to poison Magni?" he growled.

"You were different then," she mused, ignoring the blatant annoyance in his voice. "But it seems as if the topic of Yomi still aggravates you."

Cailu leaned his temples against two fingers. Naeemah was the only woman in this world that he would allow this extent of emotional probing. At times it felt as if she abused her power knowingly. However, he found it difficult to fault her. "Even with his shortcomings, I find it difficult to believe he would have done something to so blatantly hinder my group."

Dabbing the ointment beneath her jaw and across her chest, Naeemah slowly nodded. "Just from my observations, I agree with you. He had nothing to gain from slighting you, and in a fight, it was clear who would triumph."

"That leaves a second, more disturbing option." The ringing sound of Yomi's staff echoed in Cailu's ears, and he frowned. That girl was the devil incarnate. In his world before Nyarlea, they would have burned her at the stake at the first sign of her Enchantments.

"You believe she forced herself on him?" Naeemah murmured.

The disgust on his face must have been more evident than he'd intended. "Yes."

"She– would she–?" Naeemah stammered in a rare loss for words. "That's tantamount to suicide."

"It is. Should a man report it to the right people," Cailu agreed. "However, should Ravyn have discovered it first, I could see her persuading him to keep it to himself."

"Ravyn? That foul-mouthed [Sorcerer] who abandoned us after a month? I thought she and Yomi had fallen out years ago."

Cailu grimaced as the picture came together. "Ravyn was a sentimental type. Her memories are often more important to her than the present." He shook his head. "Gods above, I think she would still protect Yomi."

"This is a heavy accusation. What will you do?" Naeemah slid her lathered fingers through her thick tendrils, but her rigid spine belayed that she was still attentively listening.

"There is nothing I *can* do. Yomi is gone. She can use that foul door to travel wherever her heart may take her. The kingdom does not have the resources to use to track her down and apprehend her, should my suspicions prove correct."

"You could have let me cut her down on the spot," she suggested nonchalantly.

You have fallen as far as I, Naeemah. "While the world would not mourn the loss of one kittengirl, I fear it would have severed all ties I have built with Matt."

"Then our only option is to find a new healer and let matters lie until you can speak with him." She separated her hair into halves, pulling one section over each shoulder. "She may try to return to him."

"Let her. I don't believe she will find the sanctuary she seeks." He traced the scar beneath her right eye with his gaze. One of their first Defiled battles had earned her that mark. "When we return to Shi, I need you to utilize your diplomacy and gather a group of potential healers while I work with the Guild Hall. Interview them, take your favorites into the field, and don't bring them to me unless you believe they will stay."

Naeemah blinked and worked her jaw. It was a menial task, but there was no one better suited for it. After the span of a few heartbeats, she nodded. "Consider it done." She hoisted herself up over the edge of the bath. The droplets clung against her dark skin, shimmering in the light.

"What can I give you in exchange?"

"The same thing I have always wanted, Cailu." She stood,

wringing the water from her tail in one dexterous movement. "Keep your promise to me."

Naeemah Pro Tip: You will have my blade as long as you require. So long as I have yours.

Chapter 3

Haunted By Gold

[Initiate ping: USER MATTHEW KELMER…]

[Connection successful.]

[Transmitting feed…]

By the time I came to, it was dawn. I couldn't recall falling asleep or waking up. I wasn't sure where the time had gone ever since Jazz dropped the news on what had become of Marianne's group. It was a bewildering feeling—like someone plucked a period of time out of my memory. No matter how I struggled to recall the events of her tactful announcement, I just couldn't put the pieces together.

I guess I should go downstairs and see what's going on.

Just as I opened the door, a figure with long hair and golden eyes stared back at me, her hand poised to knock.

"Keke?" I whispered. My stomach twisted into knots.

Keke blinked, then bowed her head. Her ears drooped with the bend of her neck. "Matt… I'm so sorry."

I should have figured that Jazz would tell her what happened. She'd worn her loss like a crown. Still, I didn't know what to say. I could only trust that Keke had honestly missed Jazz's signal and was doing what she thought was right. And that was a hard pill to swallow.

She shuffled from one foot to the other, then continued, "I understand if you're not in the mood. But I wanted to see if we could talk for a bit."

I wasn't sure how to respond. To say that I wasn't in the mood to talk would be putting it lightly.

Avoiding the issue would get us nowhere. "Sure. Yeah. Come in." I stepped to one side so she could pass.

"Thanks."

I shut the door and steeled myself for a rough conversation.

Keke turned around and approached me, tipping her chin to look me in the eye. I avoided meeting her gaze. "Oh, Saoirse," Keke said, resting a hand on my cheek. "Have you even slept? Your eyes look dreadful."

I shrugged. "Not sure. I don't remember sleeping, so it's anyone's guess." My voice sounded so automated. Like a damn pre-recorded message on the other end of the line. At least, to me, it did. I hated myself for the way I was acting. Like a petulant child who wanted help, but the only way they knew how to garner attention was by acting like a sad puppy who needed their master's care. It was a weird sensation that left me wanting to be coddled, but I was too proud and upset to admit it.

Keke reached for my hand. I tried to jerk it away, but she was faster. She had it in a firm grip. I didn't fight back once she had a hold of it. She took it into both of her hands and held it against her chest. "Remember that I'm here for you. We all are. You know that, right?"

"Yeah, I know."

"Then talk to me," Keke pleaded, shaking her head. Her lips and eyes moved, but no words came. "It may be difficult to believe, but I…have an idea what you're going through—"

"Look, I just need some sleep." I sighed. "Clear my head is all. Tonight will be a better night, I'm sure."

"Matt, if you need time—"

"We don't have time." I snapped, furrowing my brow. The words tumbled out before I could stop them. "The Defiled threat is growing bigger every day. We came here to make a trade, so we're going to trade. That's all there is to it." I tried to meet her in the eye, but it just got harder and harder to commit each time I tried. "We can always talk later. We have a job to do, right?"

"Matt, *listen to me,*" Keke pleaded. "You were right. I shouldn't have thrown the rock. I should have just watched for Jazz's signal. I'm so sorry—"

"Stop." The images of Keke throwing the rock, Jazz's team not far from ours, the clouds of adrenaline covering the finer details of the forest and its denizens. It was all coming back to me, and I absolutely despised it. As more and more memories resurfaced, I fought harder to suppress them. How ironic it was that fighting back seemed only to strengthen the memories as they struggled to become as fresh as the day it occurred.

They compounded onto the reflections of Marianne's face in the hot spring. Her hot breath against my hand and her soft skin on mine. Her laugh, her murmurs, her lips…

"They were there, we saw them. The whole group." Tears streamed down Keke's face. "You and I both knew what was going to happen if we didn't intervene. I was so sure I was doing the right thing—"

"Keke. Just stop." I could feel tears of my own threatening to fall.

The skin around my left eye twitched, and the corner of my mouth twitched with it. I felt a newfound fury rise from within me. My own emotions loomed over me with the promise of impending doom. And at last, I felt what I knew was inevitable—the eventual loss of Keke, Cannoli, Ravyn, and now Ceres.

They would all fall under my command at some point. It was impossible to protect them all. Time is all that stood in my way— time I didn't have.

"I… Matt, I…" Her words trailed into something unintelligible.

Countless scenarios of losing Keke and the others played in my head as Keke's voice grew more and more distant and muddied. I felt as if someone was drowning me. And yet I breathed.

Then I looked at her. I drank in every detail of her body, every word out of her mouth, the intricacies of her skin, her mannerisms, all of it. I even pictured how she looked after we'd made love and cuddled together as we laughed about when I'd next be shot by one of her arrows. Maybe plenty of catgirls acted the way she did, were [Scout]s like she was, spoke how she did. I'm sure there'd be plenty like her in my journey.

But they weren't Keke.

"Keke," I whispered, interrupting something she was saying that I couldn't understand.

"Matt!" I finally heard her say. "I'm not asking for forgiveness. I acted rashly, a-and I ca-can't do anything to take it back. B-but I don't want to lose you. The thought of it is just too much to bear." Keke buried her face in her hands with muffled sobs. She fell to her knees in a slump. "I'm so sorry. This isn't fair to you."

I took the spot next to her and leaned up against her, shoulder to shoulder. "I don't know what to say."

Keke shook her head vigorously, then took her hands away from her face. "I've felt how you're feeling—" Keke coughed and sniffled. "L-lost, angry, empty, n-numb. And no m-matter what anyone says, it doesn't h-help." Her words were chopped up between gasps and whimpers, but she forced each one out like she was fighting against herself. "I never would've wished that on you, and there's *nothing* I can do about it! I want to take away your pain, and I can't even do that!"

"You're right. I do feel that way," I whispered. "But I won't be able to get through this without you." I put my hand on top of hers. "There's still so much to do. And now with Marianne and my—my daugh— *God damn it.*" I couldn't say it. There was no way I could vocalize what I thought. What I knew to be true yet was unable to say.

Keke took her free hand and covered my mouth. "D-don't say it. You don't have to." She took a deep, trembling breath. "You don't owe m-me or anyone else those words." She removed her hand and wiped away one of my tears.

Wait, when did I start crying?

"I don't understand anything about the men from where you're from, or—" Keke chuckled weakly, "—or I guess any men for that matter. But…you can tell me when you're upset about something or if you just want to talk. But you never have to force these things."

I still wasn't sure what to say, so I just let her keep going. It felt as if a single word out of my mouth would crush my entire self-esteem, wipe away the bravado, and destroy the sense of accomplishment I'd saved up until now. So… I just let her keep talking. I listened—well, tried to anyway. Sometimes, it took a lot of my concentration. Hell, all of it.

Guess I didn't sleep after all.

"You don't have to shoulder the entire burden. We're here for you," Keke put a hand to her chest. "*I'm* here for you."

I nodded. Some far-off memory reminded me that I'd said the same thing to her multiple times. And to the rest of our Party.

My Party... "The others are going to wonder where we are."

Keke wrapped her fingers around my hand and squeezed. "I've taken care of everything I can. Remember, there's another man here, too. I think Tristan is starting to understand what he has to do."

I set my jaw and drew a deep breath. "I hope so."

"Just rest." Keke ran her free hand through my hair. "I'll sing you a song to help you sleep."

"You sing?" My eyelids drooped.

"I used to." Keke's voice seemed distant, like she was reflecting on an old memory. "Years ago. For you, though, I'll...I'll sing the song my mom sang to me when I was upset."

"...Alright."

I curled up in the tavern bed, and Keke perched comfortably beside me. My eyes felt heavy. My body felt heavy. Everything felt so damn heavy. But her sweet voice lulled me to sleep while she stroked a hand through my hair.

For a few perfect seconds, it was just us in the world.

Keke Pro Tip: Cares you not, therefore sleep, while over you a watch I'll keep...

Side Quest
Keke's Promise

Elona and Keke perched at the end of the dock, both holding fishing rods cast far into the ocean. While Elona held hers with the comfort of experience, Keke gripped the handle and reel with clammy fingers. Her miscast that very morning had summoned an angry Defiled to the surface. Luckily, her mother had dealt with it quickly, reacting to her [Fisherman's Sense of Danger]. Even so, the experience had encouraged Keke to keep a much closer eye on her line.

"The fish aren't going to come out of your rod. You don't have to squeeze it that hard," Elona laughed and ruffled the hair between Keke's ears. "Relax, love. Not all is lost."

Keke sighed and flexed her fingers around the handle. Thirteen years old, and she was still scared out of her mind of the Defiled. "Does... does it ever get easier?"

"Hmm?" Elona hummed, glancing at her daughter. "Does what get easier?"

"Seeing the Defiled? Coming face-to-face with them?" Keke still remembered the day she'd faced off against the fox-tailed beast that had nearly claimed her mother. Many nights, it reappeared in her nightmares, finishing the job it had begun. She shuddered with the thought.

"I don't think 'easier' is the right word," Elona began. "However, one day, you'll have others you care for and want to protect. Facing them will become necessary. You'll experience something greater than fear—obligation."

"Is that what you felt this morning?" When the fish-faced Defiled's roar had churned the waves above it, Elona had shot to her feet, [Combat Mode] enabled, and her bow nocked and drawn.

Keke had barely had enough time to snatch their rods and move behind her before the first arrows pierced into the Defiled's scaly head.

"It is. It's what I feel every day." Elona nodded. "I'm certain you'll understand someday. Especially if you have kittens of your own."

Keke flushed at the thought. "But there needs to be a man around for that, right? Like Dad?"

"Mhm."

A tall wave crashed against the pier's posts, splashing a thin mist over Keke's bare calves. "There hasn't been one in a long time, it seems."

"Not since your father. That's right." Elona gently tugged on her line in idle thought. "Some islands are more fortunate than others with the appearance of men."

"You mean, like, they don't have to wait as long?"

"That's exactly what I mean." Elona stretched her legs and tail, allowing the latter to settle behind Keke. "But, who are we to question Saoirse's interventions?"

"I think we should be allowed to question her methods," Keke grumbled.

Elona raised an eyebrow. "Don't let too many people hear you say that out loud."

Keke frowned. "Well, it's not really fair, is it? You've said some of the other islands have huge cities brimming with catgirls. Ni Island doesn't have anywhere like that. Shouldn't we be first in line, then?"

"Perhaps. But we have less people to protect and fewer mouths to feed. Our way of life is simpler than the other islands, and so, it doesn't require as many hands to maintain our balance." Elona shrugged. "We have a Party here that can take care of the Defiled and the Encroachers."

"You mean you, Cannoli's mom, and the others," Keke said flatly. "But is it enough?"

"They have names, you know," Elona chuckled.

Keke blushed. "I know, I'm sorry."

"You should always do your best with what you have. Strengthen what you can control and let go of what you can't. We can't force another man to appear, so we must be enough."

Keke chewed on her mother's advice in silence for a time. Elona reeled in a sizeable fish and added it to the dangling chain attached to the post.

I still haven't caught anything, Keke thought sourly. She exhaled her frustration and continued on with the next string of thoughts that addled her young mind. "If a man does show up, what will it be like?"

"Well, that's impossible to say. He could be tall or short, funny or serious, smart or slow."

"I know *that!*" Keke giggled. "What I mean is, what do I do?"

"Be yourself, sweet. He may take you into his Party, or if you find that isn't for you, you can raise your very own kitten."

The thought of not following in her mother's path sparked an excitement in Keke that overwhelmed her words. "I want to travel! And fight! I want to be strong and brave like you!"

"There's more than one way to be strong and brave, Keke. Being a mother is strong and brave, too."

"Yeah, but I want to see the world!" Keke gestured out to sea, imagining the outlines of Ichi, San, Shi, and Nyarlothep just there in the distance. "I want to meet new people and help them like you did. And then, maybe, I'll have a kitten. Maybe two." She kicked her feet out, and her ears stood high on her head, reaching for the sunlight. "I have to make sure he likes me! So I can be in his Party!"

Elona tipped Keke's chin, bringing their gazes together. "Don't be anyone other than yourself, Keke. Promise me."

Keke hissed in a quick breath of air, the elation pounding in her chest slowing with her mother's stern gaze. "But—"

"No, Keke. No 'but.' Promise me you'll always be true to yourself."

"Okay. I promise," Keke whispered. If it was that important to her mother, how could she say otherwise? The weight of her stare was enough to quell her dreams of grandeur.

"Good." Elona released Keke's chin and smiled. "He'd be a fool not to choose you, love. You're one of the finest shots on the island with a bow; you've taken to tracking and foraging like a bird takes wing, and you've a wise head on your shoulders." She stroked Keke's back before turning back to the ocean. "Not to mention, you're cute as a button."

"Mom!" Keke laughed, the tension evaporating from her shoulders. "Please don't introduce us when he gets here. I'll die of embarrassment."

"Oh? You don't want me to tell him you're afraid of eight-legged roaches? Or that you cuddle a stuffed doll when you have nightmares?" Elona's grin widened. "What about your love of singing? Surely, he'll hear your beautiful voice through the walls when you think no one is listening."

"I had no idea you could hear me!" Keke squeaked. "No! No, no, no! You can't say any of that!"

"Ruin all of my fun, then," Elona sighed, rolling her eyes. "I suppose he'll have to discover all of these things on his own."

"Absolutely not. I'll never tell!" Keke cried. "And Cannoli wouldn't, either. She's my best friend, and we'll always keep each other's secrets."

"I'm surprised Cannoli isn't here with us right now. You two are inseparable." Elona quickly reeled in another fish. "A violet ryba! We're in for a treat tonight."

Keke's mouth watered at the thought of her favorite fish cooked by her mother's expert hands. But her confidence was quick to override her excitement as she realized she *still* hadn't pulled in a fish. "The last time we took Cannoli with us, she lost two fishing rods."

"They were just glorified branches, really. No harm done." Elona dismissed Keke's remark with a wave of her hand. "It may take her longer to learn how to fish than it did for us."

"*If* she learns."

Elona shrugged. "Even if she doesn't, there are other things Cannoli's good at. She's been a quick study in the kitchen. She can help me cook our catch tonight."

They sat in companionable silence when another pressing thought gnawed at the back of Keke's mind. A confession that had plagued her for days now. "There was, um, something else I wanted to ask you about." As the words left her lips, her mouth went dry, and her heart sped.

"What's that?"

Her face burned, and the sun suddenly felt exceptionally hot on her dark hair. "You know Bellini?"

"Of course. That's Jaclyn's daughter. She's come to the house a few times before."

Keke rubbed the back of her neck and focused her eyes on the very edge of her fishing rod. Butterflies fluttered in turbulent patterns inside her stomach, and she chewed her lower lip. "I…I kissed her."

Elona was the picture of patience, her features placid and her posture unchanging. "You're attracted to her, then?"

The red in Keke's face and chest deepened. She leaned forward so her hair covered her cheeks. "I think so."

"Does she feel the same way about you?"

The memory flooded her senses. Bellini's soft lips and her warm, cerulean gaze. Keke had been so afraid she'd crossed a line that friends should never cross. But to her surprise, Bellini had touched her cheek and leaned in for another. "I think so."

"Then invite her over more often," Elona said easily.

Keke's jaw dropped, and she gawked silently at her mother.

"Why do you look so surprised?"

"I-I thought you would be mad! Or disappointed. I don't know. I was so afraid to tell you."

"If you care for each other, then take care of one another. Your feelings are perfectly normal, love." She kissed Keke's forehead.

"Is this the 'obligation' feeling you were talking about?"

"That's for you to answer for yourself. But I would gamble that this may be a little different. Regardless, showing affection to the ones you care about is normal. So long as it's reciprocated, of course."

Keke narrowed her gaze. "You're not going to tell her all of those embarrassing things, are you?"

"Hmm." A wry smile tugged at Elona's lips. Then her eyes flew wide, and she pointed at Keke's bouncing fishing pole. "Hey! You've got one!"

Keke's rod dipped, nearly knocking her over the dock. She squealed in surprise and leaped to her feet. She steadily reeled in the catch, cutting slack only when absolutely necessary. Her tongue poked between her lips as she concentrated on the jerking line. At last, a sizable violet ryba emerged from the surface, and Elona snatched it with her net.

"That's the biggest fish we've caught all day!" Elona exclaimed. "Great job, sweet!"

Keke beamed with pride as Elona hooked her catch to the chain. Her thoughts returned to Bellini. "Mom, you *can't* tell Bellini about Baby." Her stuffed rabbit was one of the only things she had left of her father. But big girls didn't sleep with stuffed dolls.

Elona's grin returned. "I won't make a promise I can't keep."

Keke Pro Tip: I always want to protect those closest to me. Just like my mom did.

Chapter 4
Shades of Gray

I was lucky to sleep without any dreams. I could only assume that Keke being by my side helped. I felt a little bit better the next morning, but I'd be lying if I said I didn't find myself still searching for Marianne's face in the crowd of people downstairs the next morning.

She's not coming back, man.

I buried the thought while we pushed several tables together to form long, narrow lines. Reminded me a lot of the school cafeterias back when I was a kid.

The trade wasn't as simple and easy as we'd hoped. It took us a long time to work up the chain of command with Ceres's urging until we got someone high enough to make the deal.

Sorentina didn't lack for crafters or gatherers, and they were certainly stretched thin for their combat efficiency. But as it turned out, they weren't too happy with the prospect of losing some of their girls with tradecrafts to their name, especially those who knew how to farm or cook. And training new military recruits was on the lower end of their priorities.

"I'm just saying, wouldn't it be a better idea just to bring the rest of your gang to Sorentina?" Mercy snapped. She was the girl who'd been arguing with Jazz and the rest of us for the last hour. Pretty sure she had no understanding of her namesake.

"You wish for us to abandon everything we've done thus far, go back, and then return with dozens more girls with minimal combat training?" Jazz replied with an incredulous stare. "I've lost six already; how many more must be torn apart for you to understand? A pox on you."

"You wench!" Mercy pounded the table. Ale dribbled from the tankards on the surface. "We cannot simply give away our people at your beck and call! We've spent the better part of a year fighting against the Defiled, and now that we're finally starting to gain some ground, you want us to part with our livelihoods?"

"That's not what we're saying," Tristan said before Jazz could reply. "You aren't losing people. What we're proposing is a one-to-one trade."

"I heard the terms just fine the first time, fool," Mercy spat back.

We weren't getting anywhere. Each attempt at diplomacy felt like it was just surrendering every chance we had to get on their good side. I still thought it sounded like a great deal. Clearly, they were not in agreement.

"My time is precious, so I'm not going to waste much more of it on you if you aren't willing to listen," Jazz said. "If you're gaining so much ground, then why the hell did you go crawling to Badyron for reinforcements in your previous scuffle?" She tapped at her elbow, awaiting an answer.

Mercy went silent.

"How did you hear about that?" asked one of the girls behind Mercy.

Jazz gestured over to where the rest of my Party and I sat. I opened my mouth to deny it, but it was already too late.

Mercy sourly eyed the girl behind her. "Catania is a lost cause," Mercy said in a gentler tone. Well, gentle for her, anyway. "I can't throw away good arms just because you all thought it was a great idea to trade bodies."

"You keep saying that, but what exactly do you think it is you're doing here?" Ravyn unfolded one of her slender legs and stood. "You can bottleneck them for now. But without the proper training, the proper plans, and more soldiers, it's not going to go well. For now, why doesn't your little group—"

"Don't talk down to me!" Mercy pounded her fist against the table. "I've been leading these girls for years!"

"Don't interrupt me, cunt!" Ravyn shouted back. "You're just a wrinkly old nyapple who can't get with the times!"

"Say that again, you insolent girl!" Mercy stood up, and the bench behind her screeched backward from her weight. She drew a cutlass from its sheathe on her belt, then pointed it at our snappy [Sorcerer]. "I'll *cut you down.*"

"You won't lay a finger on her," I growled and rose to my feet. "We all want the same thing, but all you've done so far is yell at my girls and point weapons at them."

"I've nothing to say to an idiot!" The candlelight flickered against Mercy's eyepatch. She was built a lot like Espada, but if she kept on like this, I had no problems coming to blows.

Ceres, who'd perfected interjecting only when there were more than three seconds of silence, held up one armored hand. "Mercy, you agreed that you would hear them out and consider their offer."

"Heard. Considered. Found wanting," Mercy snapped.

"Right. So, then keep barking like a dog," Jazz said, smooth as a cucumber. She was seemingly incapable of succumbing to anger. "It suits you." Before Mercy could spout another word, Jazz looked over the crowd of Sorentina citizens witnessing the conversation and called out to them. "Do you tire of holding up in one area? Being imprisoned in your own city?"

A few sheepish nods followed. As the seconds passed, however, more and more girls joined in and voiced their agreement.

"I've heard your leader say that she sees progress," Jazz continued, her stare scanning the room like an apex predator. "Yet the walls are no less chipped, the homes vacant, the roads torn asunder. I've seen only a handful of kittengirls running around, and the looks in their eyes tell me a different story from the one your leader speaks of."

"There's much we can do!" Cannoli added her sweet voice to the chorus. "I've seen it! I've cooked for these girls! I watched how my friend, Keke, helped teach them to hunt and trap!" She put a hand to her chest and looked several of the girls directly in the eye. "It can be done! There is fertile soil, Encroachers to hunt, reliable water sources, and sanctuary!"

"Way to show me up," Ravyn whispered with a scoff.

Cannoli didn't seem to notice and instead pressed on. "We can take back the rest of Shi Island! I've seen Jazz and her girls do great work!" Her voice came down a few notches, but she continued to speak loudly enough for all to hear. "I know it's tough. I was scared, too. I still am. But even someone like me who can't fight very well or come up with great ideas found a way to contribute."

"U-um," one of Jazz's tribe, a dark-skinned girl with a scar beneath her left eye, spoke with her hand raised, "she's actually made the best meals I've had in a long time. Maybe since ever." Tears threatened to fall from her eyes. I couldn't imagine how she felt if a home-cooked meal could stir such emotions in a person.

Cannoli blushed. "Th-thank you! *Ehehehe.*" She smiled wide and curtsied.

"You want me to give up six of my girls based on some foreigner's cooking?" Mercy raised an eyebrow. "You're all daft."

Ceres cleared her throat. "You divert from the heart of the matter on purpose, Mercy. We are trapped in Sorentina until the surrounding cities improve, not ours alone. This trade benefits everyone. Your name would go down in history as a savior of Shi Island."

Shouts of approval from the Sorentina crowd backed Ceres's statement.

Mercy clicked her tongue and let the cutlass fall to her side. She turned to the group of witnesses. "None of you understand what they're asking for! The grass is no greener over there than it is here."

"No one ever claimed it was," Keke said with a sharp glare. "I think you've been taking this personally."

Tristan raised a hand. "Mercy, no one has questioned your judgment nor your leadership. The issue is that if Shi Island doesn't unite, then it's only a matter of time until the Defiled threat takes Sorentina and then Badyron."

"Like you have room to talk," Mercy spat. "Besides, what are you saying? That Catania would do any better than we have in this onslaught?"

"It's not a competition," Tristan hissed, but Mercy either didn't hear him or was blatantly ignoring him.

"No," Jazz said, whipping a lock of her hair behind her, "we would die."

"Then why can we not unite here? Together." Mercy's voice fell to a reasonable level. Seemed she was at last growing tired from the constant bickering and yelling.

"If we abandon Catania, then we surrender any hope of restoring it," Ara said. "Much like Anyona."

"You've taken the words right from my mouth." Jazz leaned forward and rested her arms on the table. "I understand your side, Mercy. Sorentina's efforts have been noticed. Even in Catania we still hear of your victories and your losses." A sneer tugged at her features. "And we understand that your losses have begun to outweigh your victories."

Mercy opened her mouth to retort, but one of the girls sitting behind her spoke first. "We've been safe thanks to the hill and the gate. Both let us funnel the roaches and the Defiled into Sorentina."

"Until a hoard of bigger Encroachers sneaks the fuck in," Ravyn spat. "Then you're truly fucked."

Mercy opened her mouth again, but thankfully, I was quicker.

"Like we've said. Repeatedly. Just six girls. Once Catania gets back on their feet, you might have a better chance of cleaning up the rest of the Defiled."

"They 'might'?" Ara repeated. "How, exactly? Speak with conviction, Matt."

I thought it sounded smart. I chewed on my lip. Though, I thought splitting up sounded smart, too.

"There are a number of battle strategies we could attempt and carry out with more numbers and an allied city," Ceres said, saving me from myself. "But that is for future consideration. As of now, even one safe road established from Sorentina to Catania could reopen a modicum of trade. One that our economy desperately needs. More girls well-versed in farming and foraging across the land will stimulate more food for all and more Bells in the pockets of those who need them."

Mercy drew a deep breath. "Fine. You'll have your gatherers and your crafters. And you will personally oversee that not a single hair on their heads is harmed." Mercy pointed her cutlass at Jazz. "You got that?"

The point of the blade was only a few inches away from Jazz's face. And yet, she was entirely unfazed. She used the tip of her finger and guided the sword away from her, lapping at the droplet of blood provided. "You have my word."

Ceres Pro Tip: Mercy means well. Many of the victories in Sorentina are hers to claim. Please have patience.

Chapter 5

The Peacekeeper

It was two more days that we remained in Sorentina while the six girls joining us on the trip back to Catania packed and made arrangements for their homes while they were gone.

Assuming they come back, of course.

My thoughts had turned absurdly pessimistic since our arrival, no matter how hard I pushed them away. Keke made a habit of staying close to my side, and I felt the comfort of her warm hand in mine when that negative voice surfaced. Guess my emotions were on my sleeve after all.

Ceres took the extra opportunity to help Mercy redistribute duties to seasoned veterans who would, in turn, teach their new recruits. Just from chatting with a few of the guards, I learned that their schedules were packed from dawn to dusk. Training, rebuilding, cooking, cleaning, fortifying, more training, and patching the wounds that still remained in the city. I wondered if they ever had time to themselves. Ceres reassured me that they took turns on duty, giving each girl at least two days off per week.

Keke, Cannoli, Ravyn, and I wandered the city proper, visiting many reopened shops and restaurants. Compared to when we'd left right after the mud golem's attack, the place looked brand new. None of the dirt or debris remained in the streets and pathways, and most of the houses and storefronts were immaculately repaired. A few buildings on the outskirts of town were still worse for wear, but it looked like the restoration swapped between the walls protecting the city and the dwellings that remained.

Tristan and Ara vanished on their own, assumedly also patrolling the city and talking with more of its residents. Tristan had done a great job in taking ownership of his role on the island so far. *Wish I could say the same for myself.*

"Hey," Keke whispered. "You have that look again."

We were standing in the back of a tailor's shop while Cannoli and Ravyn perused the array of expensive dresses and cloth combat equipment.

"Yeah, sorry." I rubbed the back of my neck and shook my head. "I was just thinking about Ni Island and how I should be there protecting it. I've been gone for too damn long."

"But what we're working toward is so you can help protect it *better,* remember?" Keke's fingers twined with mine, and she inched closer so our arms touched. "I really believe this is the right thing to do. The other islands need help, and you won't have to face your task all alone."

"I know." I sighed. Saphira came to mind. How long had it been since I'd seen her? Over a month at least. Was it obvious that she was pregnant yet? How was she feeling?

"You're letting your thoughts run away with you again, Matt," Keke cautioned. "You can only take this one step at a time."

I blinked and shook my head. I'd said something eerily similar to Marianne while I was teaching her gardening. *Eat your own advice, Kelmer.* "You're right. I know you're right. I'll try harder to focus."

Cannoli giggled, and I leaned to the right to see where she was standing. She and Ravyn stood in the center of one aisle, with Cannoli holding a frilly pink number up in front of Ravyn's body.

"You don't think you'd look cute in this?" Cannoli laughed.

Ravyn gagged with disgust and pinched the side of the dress, slowly drawing it away from her. "I'd look fucking ridiculous." She squeezed one of the ruffles with her free hand and wrinkled her nose. "I mean, what the hell are these? Why so many *frills?*"

"*No fucking way! Squawk! No fucking way!*"

Buttons crawled from behind Cannoli's hair, then skittered up the length of her arm and hopped on Ravyn's shoulder. He poked his head above the neckline of the pink dress and looked at Cannoli expectantly.

"There. Your blazard can wear it," Ravyn cackled.

"You look wonderful, Buttons!" Cannoli marveled with a gasp.

Ravyn caught us staring. "What do you think, Matt? Me or Buttons?"

"Buttons, for sure." I gestured to the dress. "That doesn't have nearly enough straps or slits for you."

"*Nani?* Why don't you come over here and say that a bit closer where I can *hear you,* boy?"

Keke grinned, then murmured, "See? You're never alone."

All I have to do to keep it this way is everything I can and more.

Back at the tavern, everyone traveling together the following morning met one final time. We wanted to hash out the details and have a battle plan ready on full stomachs and sharp minds. Well, as sharp as they were going to get, at least. Mercy was in attendance, at Ceres's suggestion, to offer advice where she could.

"We should move in two groups," Ceres stated. "Nine in one, ten in the other. The first group can lead with the second behind."

"Keep one at the front within visual range of the second. Make sure you are always able to see one another," Mercy added.

I nodded. "I think the second group should have three capable fighters guarding the six foragers and artisans. The first group should have everyone else."

"Will we not be likely to attract more attention this way?" Jazz asked, her silken voice drifting over the bar. "I thought the point was to stay out of sight."

"It was the first time. But with the obvious threats out there, we should stay closer together," Keke provided. "Six of us per group obviously weren't enough to take down a Defiled if it came to it."

"Oh? So all nineteen of us can be rent to shreds together? An excellent death indeed." Jazz studied her fingernails as if they were the most interesting thing in the world. "Please bury us side by side."

Why did you have blood on your hands, Jazz? I ground my teeth and breathed.

"The nine in the back should not intervene. Not for anything," Cannoli said softly. "We promised to keep these girls safe, and if the ten of us in the front fall, then they can sneak the rest of the way to Catania on their own."

I glanced at Jazz. *What about* my *girls?* I could see it written all over her face. But she had kept a promise to Mercy, who was coincidentally staring at her as if issuing a challenge to speak.

"I agree. If the first group should fail to dispatch any Defiled or Encroacher threat, the second group should hide in wait until it is safe to continue in their travels," Ceres said.

"What if it isn't safe?" a girl in the back raised her hand and asked.

"I'll be there to guide you," Sanaia said proudly. "You can count on me."

"And so will—" Jazz began.

"No. You're with us, Jazz." I had too many reservations to let her go off with these girls alone. I wanted to keep an eye on her.

"I don't really think that's necessary," Tristan whispered over the table. "She's a great fighter."

I glanced at Tristan, and my expression silenced him.

"Jazz is with us," I repeated.

"It's nice to be wanted." Jazz smiled daggers at me and narrowed her eyes. "I won't let all this popularity go to my head, dear Matt."

"Give it a fucking rest," Ravyn sighed. "Back to the plan, please? Some of us want to sleep before the big shitty day."

Thanks, Ravyn.

"I think Ara and I should go with the second party," Tristan announced. "I-I know I'm only a [Mage], but I should be able to do some pretty good damage if it comes to it. And Ara! Well, I don't have to say how good a fighter she is."

Ara blushed and bowed her head. "Young master, you needn't say such things," she murmured.

"Of course I do! I trust Ara with my life. I think all of you should do the same," Tristan continued.

Wow, I didn't know Ara could turn so many shades of red.

Ara muttered an incoherent reply, letting her hair mask her face from the rest of us. Ravyn snickered.

"Then we have Sanaia, Tristan, Ara, and the six from Sorentina in the second party. Then Lord Matt, Keke, Cannoli, myself, Jazz, and the remaining four from Catania. Any final adjustments?" Ceres called.

"*Lord* Matt?" Jazz sputtered. "My, my, what an impression you've made on this island! Not just with Marianne, it seems!"

I hadn't realized I'd moved. I blinked, and Keke's hand was on my forearm. In my white-knuckled grip was my axe.

"*No,*" Keke hissed. "She's doing this on purpose."

Her and Cailu would make a hell of a pair. I relaxed my hand and willed the axe away.

"That sounds perfect, Ceres," Cannoli called over the tension. "I'm so excited to have you back!"

Mercy tilted her head at Ceres with a wry smile. "Got yourself a fan club already, eh?"

Ceres bowed deeply. "They are my comrades, Mercy. I request you remember that."

Cannoli beamed. Ravyn and Keke glanced at me with varying stages of worry. I constantly reminded myself that I only had one more day in Jazz's company before I could quit this place.

Just one more day.

When everyone was in agreement and fed, I climbed the stairs back to my room. Keke slipped inside with me and closed the door behind her.

I chewed my lip and ran a hand through my hair. *I can't do this right now.* "Keke, I—"

"Shh." She pressed a soft finger to my lips and shook her head. "That's not what I want."

I was surprisingly relieved to hear that sentence. Some dumb part of me kept telling me that trying to be intimate with anyone the night before we left assured their death. Yeah, correlation and causation, I know. But damn it, the thought of losing anyone the next day was tearing my insides to shreds.

"Okay," I said when she dropped her hand.

Keke gently smiled. "I just want to be close to you tonight. That's all." She stepped forward and wrapped her arms around my waist, then leaned her head against my chest. "If you don't want me here, it's okay. I'll go."

I kissed the top of her head between her ears and returned her embrace. "I'd like that." She was so warm. Her hair smelled like rain. "Thank you."

"I'm glad," she whispered into my shirt.

My heart sped against my chest, and I inhaled her scent one more time.

Her arms tightened around me, and I felt the first hint of damp tears streak down her cheeks. "We're going to be okay."

I had no idea if that was true or what awaited us. But I wanted it to be. With every damn inch of my being. "Yeah. We'll be okay."

Keke Pro Tip: We'll get back to Catania just fine. Then maybe we can stop by Ni, just for a little while, on our way to Ichi?

Chapter 6

Blood-Soaked Dagger

It was a bit after dawn when we had our supplies and affairs in order. We'd woken up early at Ceres's suggestion—apparently, the more volatile Defiled and Encroachers were more active during the darker hours and into midday. She'd stressed that it didn't mean we wouldn't encounter any, but it would at least reduce the risk.

I made sure that Ceres appeared in my Party on the iPaw, and steeled myself for whatever was to come.

Some of the girls we were guiding back had attached pots, pans, and other assortments of tools dangling from the sides of their hips and packs. I thought about my [Cat Pack]'s inventory restrictions and saw that many of the girls were carrying one in addition to a backpack.

"Too much for the one [Cat Pack]?" I had a feeling I already knew the answer, but I had to ask.

"Yeah," one girl motioned to a couple of the tools on her backpack, "the pack can't carry everything we'll need to get started. So we gotta shoulder a little extra burden if we're to do our jobs right. Kind of a pain to put the big stuff inside a tiny pack, too, so there's that."

"Right. Makes sense." Now that I'd thought about it, I hadn't upgraded my [Cat Pack] even once since I'd arrived in Nyarlea. I thought I remembered Keke or Cannoli had mentioned upgrades were possible, but I struggled to recall the memory. "What does it take to upgrade one?"

The girl's brows raised as if she were pondering the thought. "I think someone needs to have a very high Skill in [Leather-working]." She shrugged. "Pretty sure that's just the first upgrade, though. I'd ask Salt about it if you're curious enough."

Salt? That's unfortunate. "Her *name* is Salt?"

The girl laughed. "Yep! Her mother was a strange one. Name's Fiona, by the way." The scrappy girl stuck her hand out, and I reciprocated with a firm grip. Her brown hair was cut short at the chin, and her orange eyes had dark red rings, like a grapefruit.

"Matt." I gripped her hand.

"So I hear! So you'll be protecting our squad, is that right?" She offered a firm handshake, then returned it to the strap of her pack. Her tail flailed from side to side with excitement.

I gave her a firm nod. "I am. If anyone's going down first, it'll be me. Our goal is to make sure you get back to Catania safely."

"Mhm, mhm," Fiona said, bowing her head forward and looking up at me. "Don't let anything happen to this bodacious bod, okay?" She wriggled her hips and winked.

I think, of all the girls I'd met up to this point, her mannerisms and voice reminded me the most of a cat. Every way her body moved, the lilt in her voice, her ears' constant rotations toward the sounds around her; it all bore the resemblance of a house cat.

I forced a smile. "We'll have your back."

Just as we had discussed, we started the march to Catania in two groups. Our group, the one in the front, moved as quietly as possible in a two-by-five line. Each team of two was ahead of the next by at least a few feet to avoid having more than two people get ambushed at a time. The second squad stayed behind by at least a good ten or fifteen meters so they could have time to assess the situation or flee while we fought for our lives in a worst-case scenario.

Ceres and I led our group through the thickest sections of the forest, weary of staying on the open road for too long. Jazz and one of her chosen guards, Erina, were directly behind us. I couldn't scratch the itchy feeling that I was one inch away from getting shanked by this chick.

If you want a chance to clear your name, Jazz, now's the time.

We snaked through the winding paths, returning to follow the road for short bursts and mostly only doing so to make sure we weren't getting lost. When every little shrub and tree looked the same, it was essential to have something to guide you. I'd learned that the hard way.

Ceres's armor clinked as she motioned for me to stop. I raised my hand and balled it into a fist. I looked over my shoulder to see everyone had stopped, just as we'd practiced.

"What's wrong?" I asked in a whisper.

"There's someone crying. A kitten?"

I frowned. "There shouldn't be anyone else out here. Least of all, a kittengirl."

"Ignore it and move on," Jazz stressed in a hiss. "It's the Defiled I dealt with earlier."

My heart skipped. "You mean the one that—"

Jazz raised a brow. "Yes, Matt. The same one that slaughtered my kin. It must know we're close by. We need to avoid it at all costs."

I could feel my grip tightening, and for a brief moment, I thought I might snap the handle of my axe in two. A voice beckoned me to charge at the source and put every ounce of weight I could into my swing. Vivid images of lodging the blade of my weapon into the Defiled's skull filled my head.

What the hell is wrong with me? No, Matt. You need to protect these girls, not put them in more danger.

I took a deep breath and made a conscious effort to loosen my grip.

"My lord, what will we do?" Ceres turned her head to look at me, a fierce look decorating her features. "If I may be so bold, I agree with Jazz. Avoiding the enemy would be the wiser option."

"Agreed." I nodded my approval. "We can double back to the road, then cross it and head into the other thicket. We can follow that until we get a good distance away."

"My, my. You *did* make the wiser decision," said Jazz, feigning surprise.

"Unless you have something constructive to add, shut up," I replied, fury beginning to boil in my veins.

Jazz lifted her brow. "Well, then. Lead on, boy."

I shot my hand into the air, closed it into a fist, then pointed to my right. Afterward, I rotated my arm around in a circle, and the gentle rustling of leaves accompanied the signal from behind me.

So far, so good.

The entire time we moved, Ceres never took her eyes away from where we heard the crying. Her ears remained tilted to the sound, and her footfalls were silent despite the armor.

The crying grew louder as we put more distance between us and the Defiled. I couldn't care less how loud that monster cried. What did nag at me was that it recognized we were moving away.

There was a brief moment of tension as both groups huddled onto the road. I did a quick headcount and acknowledged that everyone was accounted for. Our groups settled into the woods opposite the road, and our march continued.

My anxiety faded away as the crying grew more and more distant at last. Defiled or not, I couldn't imagine anything in this world legitimately crying for over half an hour. Then again, I'd never had a baby to deal with, so maybe the Defiled had a contender after all.

And aren't you excited to deal with them now? I pushed the thought away.

We stopped when we could no longer hear the crying. I raised my arm back into the air and spread my fingers out, shaking my hand from side to side to motion that it was break time.

I heard an audible sigh from some of the girls. Shortly after, Fiona found her way to my side.

"Want a snack?" she asked.

Jazz met her with a stare that could pierce any heart. Not in a fun way, either. "Get back to your position," she snapped.

Fiona pulled down her lower eyelid with her middle finger and stuck out her tongue. "Back off, lady. I'm talking to Matt, not you." Fiona brought her attention back to me. "Well, Matt? Do you want a snack?"

I blinked. "Uhh, sure. I'll take something."

Jazz shook her head while Fiona reached into one of the pouches on her backpack and pulled out something very familiar from my old world. It looked like beef jerky, and it certainly smelled like it, too. I could feel my mouth watering.

"Got some dried meat if you're feeling the rumblies." The strip of meat wobbled in her hand the same way someone might try and tempt their dog to run out to the backyard, only to have that trust betrayed when the owner shuts the door instead.

Am I that dog right now?

"Might as well beg for it while you're at it," Jazz said with a smirk.

"Please abstain from making such critical remarks of my lord," Ceres said with a frown. "I think you should accept the offering, Lord Matt. It is the gracious thing to do."

Jazz rolled her eyes.

"Then I'll have some. Thanks." I took the strip from Fiona and rotated it in my hand. It looked like the real thing. Question was, did it taste like the real thing?

"It's not going to hurt you. Just take a bite!"

"Well, here goes nothing." I clamped down with my teeth and tugged. The meat resisted, and as it did, I yanked harder. Half of it broke off, and I slid the freed piece into my mouth like a lizard. It was a bit saltier than its modern-day counterpart but not quite as tough. I chewed it without a word for several seconds. My eyes widened, and I looked Fiona dead in the eye. It was a little slice of meaty heaven. "You've done something amazing for me today."

"Nice!" She flashed a toothy grin and rested her hands on her hips. "It was made by yours truly, cured and salted to perfection."

"Almost," I accidentally said aloud. I nearly choked, swallowing the jerky with my realization. "But it's so close! So very close!"

Jazz shook her head. "Commit to your words, Matt. If you're going to say something, just say it."

Ceres giggled and committed a couple of fingers to her lips. "My lord had a moment of brutal honesty."

Fiona's shoulders slumped. "Still not there yet, I see. Well, going to have to keep working on my recipe then." She turned to leave and waved as she did. "Guess we better get back to it. Catch ya later, Matt!"

When she disappeared, I was reminded of the other half of the jerky in my hands. Try as she might, Ceres couldn't hide her desire. I handed it over.

"Here. You can have the rest."

Ceres waved a hand. "No, my lord. I cannot."

"This 'Master' 'Servant' routine is growing dull. We need to keep moving and stop playing make-believe." Jazz stretched her arms high above her head, turning one way and then the other. The bones in her spine cracked, and a relieved sigh escaped her lips. "Ahh. Utter bliss."

"But, Jazz, you prefer we call you mistress—" Erina began.

"Mm? Have I not earned the title?" Jazz flashed her a sharp smile.

Ceres sighed and held out her hand. I put the remainder of the jerky in her palm. As I was about to signal for our groups to start moving again, a rustling came from a few meters ahead.

Jazz motioned everyone to complete silence.

The rustling continued as Ceres, Jazz, and I readied our weapons. I turned my head to see Keke, Cannoli, and Ravyn had done the same a few meters behind us.

And then an arm appeared from within the shrubbery. Small and thin, like a child's. Coughing and hacking followed, and soon, a small kittengirl appeared, bloodied and bruised, her hand clinging to her shoulder.

"Help—"

Before the girl could get more than a single word out, a dagger found itself between her eyes. It'd happened so fast that I hadn't registered Jazz's appearance beside me.

"Get away from her!" Jazz commanded.

Ceres, Jazz, and I backed up, forming a semi-circle between the kittengirl and the rest of our squad.

The kittengirl blinked as a thin line of blood trickled down her forehead, past the bridge of her nose, and dribbled off the edge of her chin. A sinister smile played on her lips.

"You're the one from before." Her voice sounded hollow yet contained. As if she was speaking behind a mask. Her blue hair started to move as if a strong wind carried it. The girl's veins began to enlarge, and the points of her nails grew sharper by the second.

Another dagger found its way into the kittengirl's body, landing in the dip of her throat. The kittengirl ripped it out of her own throat and threw it in the same direction it came from.

"[To Dust]!" Jazz cried.

We braced for the return of the dagger, but just before it could land, it disappeared into a lump of sand and landed in Jazz's hand. Jazz stepped forward and threw the clump of sand into the kittengirl's eyes, eliciting a bloodcurdling scream.

The kittengirl squirmed and roared. "Sister!"

Hanging from the tree above her was a girl who looked identical to her. She dangled from one of the branches above by her tail—like a monkey. She flashed a malevolent smile before swinging down onto the ground beside her other half.

"She's back," said the twin. "That's good. I was just getting hungry again."

Ravyn Pro Tip: *Kuso!* Does EVERY Defiled on this goddess forsaken island have to look like a kitten?!

Chapter 7

You Have My Sword

"Ravyn! The signal!" I screamed without looking back.

"Got it!" Ravyn yelled. "[Fire Ball]!"

I glanced up to see the [Fire Ball] loose into the sky. Soon after, Ball Gag started to fly in figure-eights, the signal warning of impending combat.

The twin girls' smiles continued to grow wider and wider, splitting the skin of their faces like it were a suit stretched too far. Their teeth lengthened and sharpened, glittering in the morning sunlight. Bones cracked and flesh tore apart while clown-like laughs escaped from their mouths.

"What ever are you doing?" one twin asked, bones poking and protruding through her skin as if desperate to escape her body.

I furrowed my brow and readied into a fighting stance. "Who knows?"

"It's them," Erina whispered.

"Things will be different this time," Jazz hissed.

For a moment, I believed her. Then I saw a bead of sweat trickle down her temple, and her face scrunched together in a mix of anger and hesitation.

Shit. You gotta hold it together, Jazz.

Ceres took a step forward. "No harm shall come to this squad."

The twins cackled at a pitch I'd only ever achieved by inhaling a full balloon of helium. The hairs on the back of my arms stood on end. An arrow soared through the air and found its home in the left girl's shoulder. She observed the projectile as if she was mildly curious instead of gravely wounded. Then, she ripped it from her skin, snapped it in the very same hand, and threw it to the ground before lunging at us.

"[Double Image]!" Jazz's immediate copy rushed to my left.

The twin's wounded arm restructured itself mid-flight, molding a half-moon blade between her wrist and her elbow. Jazz's second image took the blow head-on, prompting me to dodge in the opposite direction of the incoming blade.

The sharp, white edge cut through Jazz's replica effortlessly, following through with a slash at my side. I thought I'd moved in time, but the Defiled's response was faster. A searing line of pain sang from my side, and I hissed through my teeth. Without any time to look at the wound, I charged forward and swung my axe overhead into the girl's skull. Bone broke, and blood sprayed, decorating her head and my hands with the sanguine shower.

"*Hee,*" the girl giggled. She raised a brow as she lapped at the dribbles of red down and around her lips.

The fuck?

"[Invoke Frost]!" Ceres appeared out of the corner of my eye, her polearm alit with a frosty gleam. She rushed toward me, glaring at the girl at the end of my axe with a focused fury. Just as she readied her swing, the second twin blindsided her in a terrifying blur. Ceres drove her heels into the dirt, steadying her balance and searching frantically for her attacker. The twin reappeared—both arms converted to blades—and swung mercilessly at the [Magic Knight]. The clashing of metal and skin permeated the area as they dueled.

"*Kee, hee, kee, hee!*" The twin before me laughed, then swung its bladed arm at me once more. The axe was lodged in too deep— I couldn't yank the damn thing free. With no other alternative, I back-hopped away to avoid the edge of its arm.

At least, I thought I did. A gash had opened up across my abs. It stung like hell, but the surprise left me faster than I expected. The Defiled took another step forward.

"[Pinpoint Weakness]!" Keke called out from behind me. "The stomach! Wait! No, the knee! The shoulder!"

Heads? Shoulders? Knees? Toes? I gasped as I managed to evade another swing. *Come on. We need an in!*

"Useless girl," Jazz muttered, then screamed, "[Pinpoint Weakness]! The knee! ...Wait! What the hell?" Jazz launched herself forward to the side of the Defiled I was facing in three steps, then plunged one of her daggers into its temple.

I watched as the monster's body melted and repositioned itself as if it were made of gel or ooze. Jazz's strike missed the mark and nearly sent her to the ground with the momentum.

The Defiled turned to swing at her, but Jazz was quick enough to turn her stumble into a roll, avoiding the attack altogether.

"Slippery bitch's weak point keeps *moving*," Jazz growled.

Three arrows soared through the air and were immediately blocked by the flat edge of the Defiled's arm blade. She let out a screech and darted past us in a sprint.

No!

I turned and watched as she ran toward Keke, her blade arm held at the ready. Keke gritted her teeth, and I gave chase to try and catch the Defiled before it could reach her. When I knew I was no match in speed, I cried out for the only chance at stopping the damn thing, "Erina!"

Erina moved in and clotheslined the Defiled with a mighty swing of her greatsword. The girl was cut clean in two.

As relieved as I was that Keke was temporarily safe, I couldn't believe that would finish it off. Not when my axe couldn't deal a killing blow after nearly splitting its skull in half.

The top half of the Defiled rolled across the grass toward Keke, my weapon falling out of its head and landing beside it in the dirt. To my horror, the top half continued its sprint, 'running' in Keke's direction on its one-and-a-half arms. I snatched up my axe as I barreled toward them, screamed out, "[Adrenaline Rush]," and threw it.

The axe wedged itself into the girl's back, the dull sound of crunching bones like music to my ears. She tumbled once more, never stopping.

"[Provoke]!" I screamed. It was the perfect time to use as far as I saw it. *Even if it's never worked on a Defiled.* Sure enough, the severed body continued its terrifying jaunt toward Keke, not once ever looking in my direction.

"[Provoke]!" Erina yelled.

Suddenly, the Defiled girl stumbled and rolled away from Keke, making its way toward Erina.

The fuck? Why did hers work and not mine?

Keke launched another arrow at the Defiled clawing its way to Erina's position. The Defiled's lower half rolled across the ground and joined back together with the top half. The axe once again fell out of the Defiled's body, and I was quick to grab it.

Not throwing it this time.

I ran in pursuit of the monster, eager to fight beside Erina. A few meters behind Erina, Ceres and Jazz had found themselves preoccupied with the second twin. I was rapidly closing in on my target. Just a few more steps separated me from Erina. I would help her just as she helped Keke.

"[Invigorate]!" Ravyn shouted.

A golden glow enveloped Erina. Moments later, the Defiled's blade met Erina's greatsword. Metal clashed together, and for such a large blade, she sure as hell knew how to handle it. The two swung at each other like wild animals. Multiple cuts appeared on Erina's biceps and forearms, but she kept on going. When some distance was cleared between them, Erina smirked.

"[Onslaught]!" Erina didn't just scream—she roared.

An otherworldly force suddenly battered my limbs—like being blasted by a huge gust of wind. It knocked me off my balance for a brief moment. Even so, I continued my sprint toward Erina and the Defiled.

And then my jaw dropped.

Erina's eyes were consumed by an ominous scarlet glow, and a fierce aura surrounded her body. Her muscles brimmed, and veins covered her from head to toe. "Swing again!" she taunted.

The Defiled girl shrieked at the top of her lungs, and the two began to clash again. I skidded to a stop just short of running into them and backed up, watching in absolute shock as two animals swung chunks of metal at each other in a contest to see who would wither away first.

"[Galvanize]!" Ravyn called out. A bubble formed around Erina's figure just before the Defiled's blade could find purchase in her shoulder. Cracks formed on the bubble's surface, but it was otherwise unaffected. The Defiled's blade was a split-second too late and harmlessly bounced off the bubble.

Erina gained the edge, and, to my surprise, the Defiled jumped backward.

"You're not going anywhere! [Eruption]!" Erina drove the point of her blade into the dirt. A heartbeat later, the ground beneath the Defiled shook, cracked, and broke apart.

The Defiled girl stumbled to one knee. As the ground quaked, grass and dirt started to take on the consistency of sand, burying her legs beneath it.

Erina pointed the edge of her blade at the monster. "You are the ugliest abomination I've seen thus far." She lunged and swung her greatsword with a battle cry, beheading the creature in a single swipe.

The head dropped into the sand, laughing on the way down. Thousands of grains poured into her mouth, and still she laughed. A chill swept over my skin, and I shivered. A clawing pain from my stomach warred with the adrenaline in my ears. The wound was getting worse.

Shit. This is deeper than I thought.

"Matt!" Cannoli cried from behind Keke.

"Don't!" I barked over my shoulder.

A single mistake and all of us would be dead. The vague scenario of what would've happened if Erina hadn't intervened when she did tore at me for a few seconds. Our luck was already being pushed to the limit. As great as her intentions were, I knew Cannoli didn't have the reaction time required to deal with this.

When I looked back to the sand pit, the Defiled's head had vanished. Erina whipped around to where Ceres and Jazz were fighting the twin, and moments later, she disappeared in kind.

"What the hell?" Jazz breathed, her chest rising and falling rapidly.

"Be on the lookout," Ceres said as she turned her head any way she could manage, her polearm splattered with blood.

Then whispers surrounded us.

"Look how they struggle, Sister."

"How very vain and honest," said another.

And then they giggled.

"Show yourself!" Ceres demanded. "Fight us with honor!"

Another giggle. Then she jeered, "Honor! Honor! Honor! Where was the honor in running from your sisters, red woman?"

"Yet here we are, returned to finish the job we began," Jazz snarled.

"Then a joint effort," the other voice said. "To even the match."

A gust of wind blew past us, and for a brief moment, there was absolute silence.

"There." Jazz pointed to our right.

Under cover of a tall tree, a shadowy mist was gathering. It rose higher and higher like a towering flame, and the silhouette of a humanoid figure rested within it. As the fog began to clear, its shape became more distinguishable. The creature that remained had four arms, but one of them was lopsided, like an anatomically confused model assembled by a kindergartener. Sharp edges jutted out of its skin in chaotic patterns, and it walked on four legs—human legs.

At the top of the jumble were the sisters' heads. Their muscles and bones readjusted until their heads rested level with each other between the shoulders. One of the heads had three eyes, all placed on its forehead. The second head had a single eye located where the mouth should've been, shifting its lips instead to the center of its forehead.

I had a hard time believing that this was how they were meant to look.

The two heads smiled, then cheered in unison, "Let's dig in!"

Ai Pro Tip: The Defiled will subvert and test your Skills at every opportunity. Dispatch them with haste.

Chapter 8

And My Axe

There wasn't a moment to spare to call out tactics. The unholy abomination came scuttling toward us like a tarantula, swinging each of its four arms in indiscernible patterns. Jazz took center stage as our vanguard, and just when it appeared that she would be their first target, the beast veered off in Erina's direction.

I reached into my [Cat Pack] and summoned one of the potions I'd created so long ago. Ripping the stopper with my teeth, I cleared it in three gulps. Warmth spread through my veins, and some of the aching in my side subsided. It wasn't a permanent fix, but I didn't have time to get back to Cannoli.

Turning my attention back to Erina, I flexed my fingers around my axe. Metal clanged together, and although Erina was quick, she couldn't manage to land a blow and evade simultaneously. Blood soared through the air when one of their blades met her shoulder, spraying a good deal of it onto me as they made me their next target.

"Matt, look out!" Erina screamed with her hand against her shoulder.

My breath caught when all my brain could define was the whirlwind of blades hurling toward me. Against my better judgment, I crouched, then dove at the Defiled, axe in hand. The blades clipped my hair as I swung my blade at the spot where the legs were stitched together. Blood sprayed on the way through, and although I tumbled on my way out between its legs, I managed to rise to my feet before it had a chance to make a one-eighty and charge me down.

"The one with the axe," jeered one head.

"The one with the axe," whispered the other.

A lump swelled in my throat. I swallowed hard as my fight-or-flight response warred with itself. But when I saw how close the Defiled was to Ravyn, Keke, and Cannoli, fight won. Blades spun and rotated with the deafening stomp of the beast's footsteps. Its charge was slower this time, more deliberate.

I gritted my teeth, unable to follow any of its arms in preparation for what was to come. Erina and Ceres took to my flanks, their weapons extended.

"We're going to get blended together like this!" I screamed. Blood pumped furiously through my veins as the scenario of the girls getting cut up into pieces along with me invaded my mind's eye.

"Not on this day," muttered Ceres. "[Titan of Ice]!" My eyes widened as she screamed out the Skill that I had first associated her with. The icy-blue aura around her polearm disappeared, and a crystalline bubble wrapped around the three of us. Just before the Defiled could strike it, a dozen different scenarios played in my head for how this could go—all of them bad.

The Defiled reared up and struck the barrier with its two front legs. The barrier vibrated and shook, and ice enveloped the Defiled's feet and calves, snaring them in place.

"They will not move, Sister," the left head spoke.

"Why will they not move?" said the other.

One of the four arms struck at the shield again. As the arm moved away to ready another strike, it, too, froze in place. One after another, each arm struck the icy blockade in a vain attempt to shatter our defenses. Each strike formed greater and greater cracks in the barrier, my heart skipping each time one of the Defiled's many strikes clashed against the crystal-like wall.

My breathing turned rapid, and before I knew it, all that was left unfrozen was the Defiled's torso. Save for the back legs, each of its limbs was snared with frost.

"They think they have us," said the right head.

"But they do not," said the left one.

"Remember what I said about this move last time, Matt?" Ceres asked, her lips twisting into a smirk much too wide for such a modest catgirl like her.

"Yeah," I somehow managed to say, "I remember."

"This next one will do it," she whispered.

"We need to run," I said to Erina.

"And abandon her?" she snapped, gaping at me incredulously.

"Now!" I bellowed.

Erina frowned and furrowed her brow but said no more. The two of us darted away from Ceres, running to Jazz's side. Ceres readied the point of her polearm toward the center of the beast's gargantuan mass and waited.

"They left you," said one.

"You'll die now," said the other.

"We shall see," Ceres murmured.

A cavity appeared in the chest of the Defiled, tearing apart what little clothing covered its deformed skin. There wasn't any time to respond. The point of another enormous blade shot out of its cavity with the speed of a crossbow. It struck the barrier like damp tissue, piercing through and slashing Ceres's bicep on its way through. Pieces of her plate armor flew away with the strike as the weapon hurled its way past us and into the forest somewhere. She screamed but held firm.

"Ceres!" I reached out. I wanted to run to her so badly.

"Do *not!*" she commanded. The plate covering her left shoulder had been dismantled and torn to pieces. Blood ran in a gushing river down her arm. I couldn't just leave her there, could I? "You will only get in the way!"

There was nothing left to discuss. The barrier flickered, then shattered outward, like shards of glass blowing in every direction. Glittering ice speckled the Defiled's entire body in a shower of tiny blue fragments. Ceres dug her polearm into the ground and fell to one knee, leaning on the shaft of her weapon for support.

"Trickery!" said one of the heads.

"Foul trickery!" the other said.

Ice overtook the abomination within seconds. It backed away in a useless attempt to fight back, but once the frost had covered it from head to toe, the Defiled fell forward. I'd expected the front legs to snap due to the impact, but they held on as the giant body collapsed.

Ceres panted as she rose to her feet. "To me, my companions!"

As if she needed to ask. Erina took to her right, and I took her left. Jazz situated herself behind us, daggers held between her fingers. Past the Defiled, out of the corner of my eye, Keke's bow was readied, and a palm of fire rested in Ravyn's hand.

There wasn't going to be a better chance to strike it down.

"[Pinpoint Weakness]," Jazz murmured. A moment of pause. "Top arm. Her left shoulder. Can't miss it."

Erina and Ceres struggled to maintain proper posture with their weapons. I was sure both of their [Strength] values were higher than mine—if they could use both of their arms. As it was, we couldn't risk it.

"Let me," I offered. "Both my arms are still okay."

"My apologies, my lord," Ceres breathed through rapid panting.

I shook my head. "You've done enough. It'll be over soon." I moved to stand in front of the group and took my axe into both hands. "[Adrenaline Rush]." Blood coursed through my veins like molten lead. My senses perked up, and my muscles tightened. With one wild swing, I threw everything I had into cleaving the arm off. Flesh tore apart with ease, bits and pieces of frozen muscle shattering apart and falling to the ground.

An enormous insect-like creature crawled from the wound in the Defiled's—like the seed from an avocado—and dropped to the ground, frozen and helpless.

The world's largest and creepiest roly-poly.

"There it is," Jazz growled. She shouldered her way past Ceres and Erina, repositioning one of her daggers into a reverse grip. She wore a dark look as she observed the source of our struggles.

The insect wouldn't receive a painless death. Jazz met its shell with the heel of her boot. Bits of the creature crunched and fell apart. A wicked smile twisted her lips. "Burn in hell." She stomped it again. Then again, and again. I lost count of how many times she'd brought her foot down. The ice was beginning to melt off of the Defiled, as well as the insect. It squealed and screeched at Jazz. Her smile widened as she knelt to stab it repeatedly.

We all watched in silence as Jazz took her aggression out on the insect. As much as I struggled to understand how this thing could've been responsible for the deaths of Marianne and her group, all I could assume was that it had somehow taken control of the kitten's body in some fashion.

Marianne...

Goosebumps covered my arms at the thought of a wriggling roly-poly crawling and scuttling through flesh and blood.

Jazz was clearly over it. When she rose to her feet, she was decorated in an array of red and green fluids, assumedly the blood from both the host and its parasite. I'd expected her to gag or maybe even cry. She didn't. Instead, she laughed.

"Good fucking riddance," she snarled.

My shoulders slumped. My breathing slowed. It was finally over. I looked past the corpse of the Defiled to see Keke, Cannoli, and Ravyn smiling. Even at this distance, I could tell they were just as out of breath as I was.

"Ceres!" I called. She was just ahead of me, already bandaging her wounded arm.

"I am alright!" Ceres replied, her voice trembling as she worked.

I nodded and collapsed backward, sitting in the damp, blood-soaked grass without caring about either. "I'm exhausted." The searing pain across my abs and side reminded me that they were still there and still just as bloody. "Damn, I really pushed it."

Erina laughed. "I think we all did." She dropped her greatsword in front of her, and she knelt down. "A lot of those Skills will take it out of you. I'm glad to see another [Warrior]. Maybe a [Battleguard] in training?"

The idea struck me. "Is that where those abilities came from?"

Erina nodded. "Maybe when you get strong enough, I'll teach you some of what I know."

I smiled. "I think I'd like that."

"Ceres! Matt! Let me heal you!" Cannoli cried, jogging toward us.

"Cannoli, wait!" Keke made to follow her.

"Stop!" Ravyn screamed out. "Keke, Cannoli! Come back! Now!" I shot to my feet and looked to where she was—between a few of the trees in the distance. "It's not dead!" She shivered. "It's coming—"

It was too late. A splatter of blood showered my flank within my peripheral vision, coloring my world red. As I turned to my right, I caught one of Erina's arms flying through the air.

Her scream was deafening. She fell backward, gripping the spot where her left arm used to be. The soil was soaked with the sanguine liquid pouring out of the socket. I couldn't believe what I was seeing. Just moments ago, she was talking to me about [Battleguard].

What the fuck just happened? Hadn't we won?

I sat there in shock while Ceres and Jazz tended to Erina's arm. Ceres shoved the side of her hand into Erina's mouth to quiet her down. All I could hear was ringing.

It felt like I was being watched. I rose to my feet and looked over in the direction where the blade from the Defiled's core had flown. Out of the bushes lurched one of the catgirls in Marianne's group, who had died on our way to Sorentina. I didn't know her name, but I recognized her. Or, at least, what was left of her.

She was mangled and had a poor time walking. Half of her head had been eaten away in some fashion. An eye was missing. Patches of skin had the remnants of teeth marks scratched in. Her left calf was chewed to clumped gore, and—save for the scraps of clothing hanging off of her limbs—she was completely nude.

Someone—or *something* had chewed her apart however they liked, leaving the torso completely intact.

"Blood for blood," the catgirl gurgled.

Keke Pro Tip: Damn it! What is it going to take to bring this thing down?!

Chapter 9
Double-Edged Blade

Erina wouldn't stop screaming. Jazz and Ceres did everything they could to calm her down, their heads twisting around periodically to look at the shambling remains of a catgirl lurching toward us from out of the bushes. I moved to stand between them and the Defiled, my axe held in both hands. My initial shock melted into adrenaline. Unbridled fury and a crazy-mad desire to put this beast to the blade rushed through my veins.

I could hear Cannoli struggling to get free from Keke and Ravyn. I stole one quick glance over my shoulder. Jazz, Ceres, and Erina were behind me and to my left, with Keke, Cannoli, and Ravyn further behind them. There were at least a dozen strides between Jazz and me, which would give me enough room to focus on the monster by myself. What mattered most right now was putting the Defiled down.

"You won't put another hand on them," I growled, stepping forward.

"My sister," the Defiled screeched. "*What have you done to my sisteerrr!*"

"Your 'sister' is nothing more than ooze in the soil," Jazz replied with more emotion in her voice than I'd ever heard out of her. "And soon, you'll look no different!"

Erina was beginning to quiet down due in no small part to Ceres and Jazz's efforts. The muffled screams continued to haunt my ears.

"Cannoli! Come back!" Keke cried.

"No! I'm going to help them!" Cannoli snapped.

Soon enough, I could hear the fast, light footsteps of our one and only [Acolyte].

There was nothing behind me that needed my attention. The only thing that could harm Cannoli and the others right now was the monster in front of me. So I took another few steps forward.

"What are you waiting for?" I asked. "Give me your worst!"

The body shambled toward me. Muscle ripped open at the forearms, revealing a pair of bone-white blades attached to the bones. The very same bones of the girl this monster inhabited, twisted and malformed to suit its evil intents.

I watched carefully and held my ground for a time. No move would be made until I was sure I could get closer. The sisters had been full of surprises up until now, and the last thing I wanted was to be caught flat-footed and gored.

The muscle and tissue re-enveloped the forearm blades at their base. Soon, the sounds of bones and muscles cracking and twisting made their unwelcome return, and, on a gamble, I stepped closer, then stopped. Another step. Stopped again. The Defiled did not approach.

I see. This is starting to make more sense now.

My hands tightened around the grip of my axe. Whenever the bones and muscles moved, the creature adjusted. Maybe I was wrong, but it seemed it couldn't do much while it worked to change things in the body. When the cavity on the conglomerate had opened before, none of the limbs had so much as twitched. That's when it was most vulnerable. Unfortunately, that's also when it was most dangerous.

"Matt, don't!" Keke cried out. "You can't fight it alone! You'll be killed!"

I know that. I know. But I can buy time. Wound it a little, maybe play some tricks on it. Anything I can think of. I just need to buy time.

I thought of turning around to have Jazz distract it, maybe even Ceres. But I couldn't bear the thought of willingly putting them in danger. Not that I could've been of any help anyway, I didn't know a damn thing about bleeding, broken bones—hell, not even basic first aid. I was useless to Erina. To run away now would be to admit how truly useless I was to everyone.

I can do something here. I know how to do this. Mostly.

The remaining sister screeched. Its legs were beginning to mend. It was now or never.

"Come on!" I bellowed. I ran at the Defiled with everything I had. I swung. The phrase, 'How low can you go?' came to mind when the Defiled bent backward to dodge. The bones and muscles cracked. With some momentum left in the attack, I used it to leverage some weight away from the Defiled during the backswing.

I was too slow. Dozens of white spines that were several feet in length shot from the skin of the catgirl like a sea urchin, scraping the front of my chest.

Shit!

The wounds were thin and long, spanning from one armpit to the other. I cupped a hand against my chest and gasped at the sting of my fingers grazing the freshly opened cuts.

Feels like a giant Goddamned cat just scratched me.

I looked down briefly to see that the flesh was swelling at a concerning rate. It might not have been poison, but *something* was lacing those spines.

I drew back, never taking my eyes off the Defiled, and reached for one of the potions left in my [Cat Pack]. White bone flashed before my eyes, and soon after, the bottom half of the bottle and all of the precious fluid within it drained into the soil.

The Defiled had slashed through the air, leaving me with the empty bottleneck and the stopper. I gasped as I realized just how clean the cut had been on the bottle. Not an errant shard of glass to be found.

"*Wee, hee hee hee hee!*" The monster cried, swiping at me with its bladed arms. It moved closer with each slash, forcing me on the defensive.

I continued to step away as it approached, waiting and praying for any opening I could find.

Something, anything!

It was no use. All I could do was continue to evade and parry. I didn't have the reach, the tools, or any utility that could push this monstrosity off of me.

"Matt!" I heard Jazz yell.

Don't look! You look, and you're dead!

And then a dagger found itself lodged into the side of the Defiled's neck. Rapid footsteps approached, and I took the opportunity to swing my axe into the side opposite of Jazz's dagger. I landed just above the beast's collarbone, cutting at least a few inches into its flesh. Blood sprayed upon the blade, Jazz's afterimage following with a swift kick in the ribs.

The blow knocked the Defiled back, and I was suddenly pulled by the momentum of Jazz's attack. The force caught me by surprise and ripped the still-lodged axe from my grip. The monster tumbled a few meters away from us, the axe's handle clinking against the small pebbles and rocks on the way.

The beast lay motionless. I knew there was no way it could be dead. Not until the damn bug inside was ripped out and smashed to pieces. Could I risk retrieving my weapon?

The pain in my chest flared. I grimaced, my fingers clenching at my shoulder. I had to make a conscious effort not to touch the wounds. Something was definitely wrong.

"[Stabilize]!" I heard Cannoli cry. Was that the third time she'd said it so far? The fourth?

When I turned around to see how Erina was holding up, my breath caught. Jazz was in the grass, limp as a ragdoll, Cannoli at her side. Keke was right behind her, her attention on the crumpled Defiled, bow at the ready. Ravyn lifted Jazz's head and fed her a potion that had a similar golden color to the ones I carried.

I turned further still, and there in the grass was Erina, unmoving and unresponsive. Tears poured down Ceres's cheeks. They were very unlike the ones I saw Keke and Cannoli shed. Her teeth were gritted. She wrenched fistfuls of dirt into her hands, then punched at the earth. Her brow furrowed, and soon the polearm was back in her hands, her arm soaked with drying blood.

Not wanting to keep my eyes off of the Defiled for too long, I turned back around. When Ceres was close enough, I held up my arm. "Ceres, you need to stay back."

"Please excuse my insolence, my lord. I humbly request that you allow me passage." Her tone turned my head. That 'request' was anything but. It was a warning that if I didn't do as she said, then it wouldn't be long before she forced me aside and took matters into her own hands.

This wasn't something I could stop her from doing.

"I will exterminate this demon." Ceres swung the polearm to her side, chanting, "[Magic Armor]." A faint white glow enveloped her for a brief moment before disappearing. "[Invoke Frost]." The icy-blue aura returned to her weapon, and as it did, I dropped my arm.

My head snapped back when I heard the Defiled readjust its anatomy once more. Disturbing crunches and snaps made their way to my ears as the creature lurched onto its feet without using its arms. As I observed, I understood why the axe had escaped my grip—tendrils of flesh had wrapped around the head of the blade. It must've done that just before Jazz kicked it. Which left me without a weapon.

Keke pulled her bow back. "[Pinpoint Weakness]!" With an arrow held between each of her fingers, she fired one after another at the Defiled. They landed with a thud in the creature's body, blood dribbling out from the impact points.

The creature smiled wide. "Foolish, foolish, foolish!" Its form contorted, re-aimed the projectiles, then launched them straight back in one smooth motion.

Keke threw herself on top of Cannoli and Jazz, taking three of the arrows into her arm. She screamed, and I felt a wave of furious blood rush through my muscles.

"You can have this back!" The Defiled said, taking hold of the embedded axe and throwing it in my direction.

There was no way I was going to try and catch it. I moved to my side as the axe whizzed by me and soared through the trees. It vanished into the dark, then came the echo of a sickening crunch. A scream followed.

Fuck!

Ceres rushed past me in the confusion, swinging her weapon underhanded. The Defiled evaded her the same way someone performing drunken martial arts might, weaving and moving in such erratic and indiscernible fashions, each dodge appearing to the naked eye that it was just dumb luck.

The [Magic Knight] did not let up. She wielded her polearm with deadly skill, completing each swing in anticipation of a counterattack. It looked more like a dance and less like a hero and monster dueling to the death. Her actions were beginning to slow, and it was only a matter of time until the Defiled would catch her. Ceres's movements were strategic and carried purpose. Not a single attack was without its reason.

And yet...

Ceres's screams penetrated the woods, drawing the attention of all who were near. Seeping red streams traveled the length of her wounded arm. Her hands shook as she struggled to carry her weapon. Exhaustion painted her eyes. She was quickly turning pale, and her stance wavered.

"You will make a good host," the Defiled whispered excitedly. Its ribcage opened wide, ripping the skin and baring another gaping cavity. The front points skewered the [Magic Knight]'s good arm and retracted. Blood dripped from the tips of the spines, a hollow laugh escaping the monstrosity's lips. "My children will eat you from the inside out. Oh, how many children you will make for me."

A chill traveled the length of my spine. What the hell were we supposed to do?

"Do you know [Two-Sided]?" Ravyn screamed out. Ceres nodded faintly. "Then use it!" Ravyn held out her hand and cried, "[Invigorate]!"

A golden glow surrounded Ceres. The Defiled approached, and, as the glow faded, Ceres's eyes widened. "[Two-Sided]." A sensation like a shockwave rippled from Ceres's body and nearly knocked me off my feet. There was nothing fancy, no glow or aura around her outline. And yet, she lifted the polearm without issue.

"What in the hell?" I murmured.

The Defiled was quick. Ceres was quicker.

As the points of the ribcage launched from the Defiled's body once more, Ceres made a long, horizontal sweep across the monster's abdomen with her polearm, severing the torso in half. The beast's motions stopped as if the puppet's strings had been cut. As the blood of the Defiled tainted the soil, Ceres dug the tip of her polearm into the ground between its legs. She turned on her heels and used the strength of her upper body in an upward strike, cleaving the monster in quarters.

There was a pause as Ceres stared her opponent down. Tissue and sinew parted seamlessly, and like a game of Jenga, the Defiled fell to the ground in multiple pieces.

Somewhere among the mess, I could see the pieces of the insect's carapace. Or what was left of it. It squirmed for a few seconds, then lay still.

Ceres whipped her weapon through the air, splattering a nearby tree with the blood of her fallen foe, then pierced what remained of the Defiled with the blade. "It is done."

Now accessing system memory...

Hey, remember when the lule misris bloomed? I remember the roly-poly bugs on the petals. That's what you remember? What? I thought they were cute. Fine. Next time, we'll find more roly-polys for you.

Memory storage successful.

Cannoli Pro Tip: Jazz! Erina! Wake up!

Chapter 10

Excogitation

Ceres fell to her knees with her next breath, the polearm dropping to the ground beside her. She hissed air through her teeth and cradled the more wounded of two arms against her chest.

I rushed to her side. "How did you do that? What was that Skill?"

"[Two-Sided] exchanges...my [Magic] and my [Strength]," she panted. "*Ngh,* it is a— a last resort."

I reached for her, and she responded with one curt shake of her head.

"You have others to worry about. Tend to them first, my lord," she murmured through gasped breaths.

"*Nng-ha!* Damn it!" Keke cried out, and my attention whipped to the group. Cannoli was steadily dislodging the arrows from her arm one by one, waiting in between until she could cast [Stabilize].

Ravyn carefully dripped golden tonics between Erina's lips while Jazz lay motionless a few feet away. Ball hopped nervously around her knees, flapping and muttering anxious chirps to his master. I cringed as another sharp wave of pain echoed across my chest, then jogged toward the group.

I stopped short at Jazz's side. Her spotless skin had been run through by the same rib spikes that had pierced Ceres's arm. Over two dozen gaping holes from her collarbone to her hip revealed muscles, bones, and organs in complete disarray. Blood and gore filled most of the gaps—Cannoli had done what she could, but the wounds were too numerous and too large. If she hadn't died on impact, it wasn't long after. I knelt and touched her forehead.

"She's dead," Ravyn said. Her voice sounded so disconnected and alien compared to the fiery comebacks I'd gotten so used to. "No potion could save her from that."

"*Gah!*" Keke's voice cracked and strained as Cannoli freed the second arrow.

"Only one left. You're doing great. We're almost there," Cannoli soothed quietly, stroking Keke's hair out of her face. "[Stabilize]!"

"She did try to protect her group after all," I murmured.

"So it seems," Ravyn replied.

"Erina's still alive?"

"Mhm." Ravyn looked at her sleeping charge. "She really saved our asses."

"Yeah. I guess I just didn't think—*ah!* Damn it!" The flames in my chest roared, and the pain became impossible to ignore. I stood and tore away my blood-soaked top before examining the rent flesh on my torso.

Keke yelped one last time before Cannoli sealed the final wound.

"There, all done! No more!" Cannoli praised her. "You can rest now."

"Thank the goddess." Keke was covered in sweat, and her hands shook as she repositioned herself in a more comfortable position.

"Oh, fuck." Ravyn's eyes widened, and she left Erina's side in favor of taking a closer look at my lacerations.

"That's always what you want to hear your doctor say," I joked between gritted teeth.

"No, Matt. This is cytotoxic venom." Ravyn delicately brushed the swollen skin at the edge of one of the cuts. To my horror, it fell away with just the touch of her fingertips. "This shit will eat through your skin and feed off of your [Energy] until there's nothing left. If we can't slow it down, it'll fucking kill you. Look." She pointed at Jazz's body.

Upon closer inspection, swollen black circles of skin poked free from the sea of lesions. Ravyn tapped at a few with her shoe, and everywhere it touched came free like ash on a burning torch.

I swallowed hard. *Oh. Great.* "That's good to know," I breathed. Wait. While I'd more or less been scratched up, Ceres had taken the brunt of the blow. "Ceres!"

The color had drained from Ceres's face, and she slumped backward on her calves. "I...I'll be right there," she said with a heavy wave of her hand.

"Cannoli, Ceres needs you!" I called.

"R-right!" Cannoli leaped to her feet, also glistening with exertion, and rushed to Ceres's side without sparing me a glance.

I turned back to Ravyn. "What do we do?"

"I only have one antidote bottle on me. Honestly, I made it just to see if I could. You don't exactly see cytotoxic venom every day," Ravyn explained quickly. "Maybe if you split it with Ceres—"

"No. Give it to her," I interrupted. "We can figure out mine when we reach Catania."

"Were you fucking *listening to me?*" Ravyn's hands balled into fists. "You. Will. Die."

"Then we better get moving," I replied. "Give her the antidote, Ravyn. Please."

There was a scream from the forest.

Shit. That's right. My axe.

"Go. I'll take care of that." I pointed Ravyn to Ceres and took off to the forest before she could say another word.

My breathing was becoming more labored by the second, and the aching burn would not let up, but I would make it back to Catania. I had to. I maneuvered through the trees and foliage, heading toward a group of muffled voices and slews of panicked whispers. I spotted ears bobbing over a line of bushes, and when I cleared them, all eyes turned to me. And mine to the girl with the blade of my axe lodged into the side of her head.

"Jesus Christ," I cursed, stepping toward the corpse.

"Matt! What the heck happened?" Tristan asked, his voice shaking as he gestured wildly from the dead girl, to me, to the direction I'd come from. "We stayed back like we were supposed to. Why did this happen?"

"It's a long story," I replied, kneeling to remove the axe from the face forever frozen in shock. The resulting squelching sound turned my stomach into knots. She was one of the Sorentina girls. Mercy could have it out on me later; I couldn't afford to think about that right now. Too many lives were still on the line. "The Defiled are dead. It's safe for us to move."

"You are hurt," Ara said. "We should tend to our wounded first—"

"No. We can do that in Catania," I replied. "We need to keep moving."

"Where's Jazz?" Sanaia asked, stepping forward. "Is she still with the others?"

Her expression was so carefully composed, but her eyes were tinged with worry. She was the last person I wanted to deliver the news to. "Jazz died fighting the Defiled."

"Oh, no," Tristan whispered, face blanching.

Sanaia flinched, then exhaled. The fingers around her spear tightened to white knuckles, and she straightened her back. "Understood."

"Is it really safe?" I heard one of the surviving Sorentina girls whisper to another.

"Should we go back to Sorentina?"

"This was a mistake."

"Hey!" I barked, the excruciating pain adding weight to the sound. "We're almost to Catania. Come on! Train's leaving!"

"What does that mean?" another girl asked timidly.

I didn't have time for this. I spun on my heel, trying to push away the sight of pulling my axe from a catgirl's head. This day would haunt my nightmares for a long time to come.

When I reached what remained of group one, color had begun to return to Ceres's face. Keke and Cannoli spotted my return and ran to meet me.

"Ravyn told us," Keke said, breathless. "You need an antidote."

Cannoli shuffled through her pack and extracted a small jar. Twisting away the top, she dipped her fingers into the salve and then hovered above my chest wound. "I don't know if you remember what this feels like. It's…unpleasant."

It seemed like years since Cannoli had mended the injury in my shoulder from Keke's arrow. I wiped the sweat from my forehead and nodded. "I remember well enough."

"This won't stop the venom, but it will at least heal the skin in between the cuts," she said.

"Should we keep giving it more to eat?" I wondered. Would my skin continue to mend while I burned alive?

"Better than it running out of food, right?" Keke said. "Ravyn told us the ingredients for the antidote, and Cannoli and I are pretty sure we saw the important pieces while foraging in Catania."

"The important ones, huh? *Shit!*" I cursed unexpectedly as Cannoli's fingers landed between the first cut. "S-sorry. Just. Ouch."

"I know," Cannoli said quietly. She seemed to be going out of her way to not look me in the eye and keep her focus on the task at hand. "I'm sorry, Matt."

"Hey, it's okay," I replied.

Cannoli bit her lower lip but said nothing. Her fingers trembled slightly, and she balled her hand into a fist, then continued her work.

"Potions aren't always exact. You can change some of the ingredients and come out with the same or better," Keke explained. "Between all of us, we should be able to put it together in no time."

"Alright. Let's do it." I nodded, then groaned as Cannoli worked on the next laceration. *Just when I thought it couldn't get worse.*

Warning! Matt's [Energy] is low! Find a safe place to rest!

...Of course it is. It was a notification I hadn't heard in a long time. Shame on me for jinxing it, I guess.

"We need to head there right now. Before I pass out," I managed between hitching breaths. "There's not much [Energy] left to split between me and the venom."

To my relief, the second Party appeared at the edge of the forest, awaiting our signal. Ceres got to her feet and waved them closer, her mouth a strained line with the movement.

"We travel as one group the rest of the way!" Ceres commanded. Stripping her apron away, she handed it to Sanaia before looking over the group. "You and Ara can use this as a sling to carry Erina back."

"What about Jazz?" Sanaia glanced at Jazz's body with a mix of emotions before concentrating her gaze back on Ceres.

"We need to worry about the living right now. I am truly sorry for your loss," Ceres replied. "Erina is alive, and so are we. Our pace must quicken, but our attention must remain sharp. Ravyn and I will continue to lead."

Ravyn nodded. "I'll have Ball keep watch for any other Defiled from above."

"Excellent. We march!"

Leadership fit Ceres like a glove. Sanaia and Ara shifted Erina onto the apron, and both took two edges, lifting the soldier between them. I was impressed that the fabric held, but it seemed there was a lot more to Ceres's armor than the naked eye could discern.

Keke touched my arm, and I stared down into her worried face.

"We have to stop making a habit out of this," I murmured so only Keke could hear.

The ghost of a smile played on her lips, and she shook her head. "You're not allowed to faint now. We're out of girls to carry you."

"Keke—"

"Don't give up. You promised," she said forcefully. "I'll keep watch at the front."

I watched her go between the dark spots clouding my vision. Her place at my side was quickly overtaken by a quivering Tristan hugging Desiree to his chest.

"What happened, Matt? Please, tell me?"

It was going to be a long walk to Catania.

Warning! Matt's [Energy] is low! Find a safe place to rest!

Ceres Pro Tip: It would behoove us to purchase new armor and perform maintenance on our weapons as soon as possible.

Chapter 11

Stalwart Soul

The journey back felt painfully slow. Maybe it was more the wound talking more than anything, but as time dragged on, my shoulders grew heavier. It felt as if someone had put lead in my shoes. I stole a glance at the wound.

Yeah, that still looks nasty. Hang in there, Kelmer. We're almost there.

I'd explained to Tristan as many details from the fight as I could recall, talking myself hoarse with it. Keke left it to him to keep tabs on my consciousness, and there were a few times he clenched and shook my arm with a forceful bark of my name. When I described Jazz's death, all color left his face. I understood what he was feeling, but there was not much I could afford in the comfort department. It was hard enough to stay the hell awake.

Catania was within sight. I'm sure that we would've been able to see it far sooner if not for the smatterings of trees. Keke, Cannoli, and Ravyn picked up the stray herb or weed along the way. And by 'pick it up,' I mean basically clotheslined the bush mid-stride. Ceres had made it very clear that rest periods and stops weren't to be made anymore. We'd already pushed many of our girls to the limit, and it was time that we were back in a [Sanctuary].

The sting returned, then quickly vanished, leaving behind the flickering sensation of fire in my veins. It'd been like this since we'd started walking. It felt like we'd been traveling for days — which obviously wasn't possible. But really, who knew how much time had passed.

When we arrived at Catania, many of the girls collapsed on the floor within Jazz's underground domain. The Sorentina girls abandoned their backpacks on the floor and breathed heavily.

One of the head guards, a limber girl with short red hair and steel-blue eyes, approached Sanaia with a panicked expression. "What in Saoirse's name happened out there?"

Sanaia paused, then motioned to Erina's unmoving body with her chin. "We need to get Erina medical attention. *Now.*"

"This way, then. Please!" The girl gestured Sanaia and Ara past, her stare lingering on Sania's back for a time.

I put a hand on the girl's shoulder. "Hey. Me too, please," I wheezed. And then it was my turn to collapse. My axe made a cacophony of loud clanging noises as it went down with me. I was just glad I could break my fall with one arm in time. As much as they'd stressed staying awake, I was desperate for a nap. Any kind of sleep, really.

"Heh, a cat nap," I mused in a delirious mumble.

The girl turned to look at me and cried out, "Oh, goddess!"

"Matt!" Keke rushed to my side, and her gentle hands rubbed against my arm. "You need to get up! You can't stay down like that. You'll only make it worse."

"You're kidding," I breathed.

"No! Get up! Please!" Cannoli shouted, appearing on my opposite side.

"You fucking die on me, and I'll haunt your sorry ass," Ravyn added. She moved to stand in front of me, then knelt down, offering me a generous view of her undergarments.

At least I get a nice view before I die again.

"Hey! Get the fuck up!" Ravyn turned to glare at the girl who greeted us. "He's been infected with cytotoxic venom. Keep an eye on him. Me and these two need to go find herbs for an antidote." She turned back to me. "Because he was feeling *awfully* charitable today."

The dark shadow beneath her eyes said I'd made a terrible decision by offering the antivenom to Ceres. Despite the look, though, I held no regrets. As awful as the pain was, I'd do it all over again and then some.

I leaned my back against a nearby wall and used Keke and Cannoli's strength to return to my feet. The axe could stay where it landed; it's not like I'd be using it any time soon.

"Allow me to keep watch over my lord." Even if I couldn't see her, I didn't have to know who just raised their hand. "I know little when it comes to the medicinal arts. Pray, allow me to watch over him. He shall not fall asleep under my watch."

"What about your arms?" Cannoli asked.

"She'll be in the same room. We'll tend to both of them," the guard said.

Ravyn rose to her feet and looked to where Ceres was. Ravyn rolled her eyes, but didn't fight back. "Fine. It's your job now. If he dies under your watch, you're next on the shit list." She looked back at me and stared. I don't know what she was waiting for. A joke, maybe?

"The crow caws at midnight." I wasn't sure why I said that. Almost anything sounded funny to me at that point.

Ravyn raised a brow. "Don't know what you mean by that, but it sounded stupid. *Baka.*" She sighed. "Take care of him. Please."

"*What a moron, what a moron, squawwk!*" Ball Gag's painful shrieks were actually a welcomed distraction from the pain, though I can't imagine the girls were too pleased.

"Get that awful thing out of here!" screamed one girl.

"Quiet, Bally!" I heard Ravyn shout.

Then, another person knelt next to me. "I'll be back soon." It was Keke. God, how I missed her touch.

We really need to get a bed together again soon. I'm so tired.

I'd half expected Cannoli to whisper something next, but it never came. I listened as their footsteps grew more and more distant. I caught them leaving through the trapdoor when two more girls replaced them at my sides and leaned my arms over their shoulders.

What a time to be alive.

Under strict orders by Sanaia—and I assume the other girls—I was not to lie down. Sitting upright was my only option. That or standing. I think it goes without saying what option I took.

They'd stripped me down to nothing but my boxers. I was a bit self-conscious about the whole thing, but it's not like I was in any position to fight. By the time I was in bed, the thought had come and gone—much like my fading consciousness.

Ceres sat in an old wooden chair across from me, reading some thick book as I struggled to stay awake. It was unfortunate to see Ceres's arms so badly wounded, but thanks to the combined efforts of the Catania Rescue Squad and the girls we'd borrowed from Sorentina, they were able to get her patched up relatively quickly. While she would heal with time, the armored plates covering her shoulders, biceps, and forearms were irreparably damaged during the fight with the Defiled twins.

Yet, it seemed like I was the only one bothered by the whole thing. I dwelled on the loss of my shield and how I'd almost lost my axe. My armor was torn to shreds, *I* was torn to shreds, and although I was still alive, who could truly say that I'd make it out of this? Keke had taken three arrows to the shoulder and was out there looking for herbs, Cannoli was on the verge of a breakdown, and Ravyn was impossible to read. We'd suffered so many losses, and still…

Why wasn't Ceres bothered?

"What are you reading?" It came out as little more than a squeak, but it seemed Ceres had impeccable hearing.

Ceres's ears flicked in my direction, and she turned the half-finished book around in her hand. "*The Conundrums of Sorcery and Medicine*." She turned it back around and flipped the page. "I admit I have been less than forthright about completing it. Your condition has bolstered my desire to see it to its conclusion."

"Heh. You have a great vocabulary," I spoke a little clearer that time.

Ceres's face grew pink. "Thank you, my lord. It was not without great effort."

I raised a brow. "You weren't always like this?"

Ceres paused. Her concentration was obviously waning. "I was not."

"Sorry if I'm being pushy. I know you're reading, so I'll leave you alone."

A soft giggle escaped her lips. "My lord, it is for your benefit that I read this tome." She turned to the next page.

What incredible reading speed. "For my benefit?" I balked. "Why?"

She raised her brow to look at me. "Does the title not indicate for what purpose it serves?" It took me a minute. Maybe it was the venom kicking in. Maybe I was still an utter moron. Regardless, Ceres was quick to clear it up for me. "Such tonics and remedies are difficult for me to comprehend. Contending with [Alchemy] is something I do to this very day." She frowned. "I must remain steadfast. A moment's hesitation, one incorrect move—" She balled her hand, stretched it, then turned the page. "I cannot afford such mistakes."

I thought about the weight of her words for a moment. "What about what happened to the Defiled twins? To us? To Jazz and Erina?"

Ceres snapped the book shut and rested it on her lap before taking a deep breath. "It is my firm belief that we did all that was available within our power to do so." She clapped a hand to her chest. "There was little we could do to predict the movements of such a dangerous foe. That Jazz lost her life in the battle is proof of that. If not for her knowledge, our lives would have been lost. Of that, I carry no doubt, my lord."

I blinked. "What do you mean?"

Ceres cleared her throat. "With what we knew, we proceeded in the most cautious way we could manage with regard to our abilities. I would not be so bold as to claim that you are ungrateful or petty. You are fortunate that you still breathe. Carry the flame that has been given to you, my lord." She bowed her head. "You would dishonor their sacrifice otherwise."

Yeah, I was definitely delirious. Tears threatened to fall, but I did everything I could to stop them. Despite my attempts, I could feel them glossing over, so I wiped at my face with my forearm. "Yeah. Maybe you're right. Is...that why you're okay?"

She frowned. "I am not 'okay,' my lord. That is not how I would describe my emotions. If I were to have it my way, I would act in ways unacceptable in lieu of our credo—in lieu of what my father wished for me." She let one of her arms dangle, holding it at the elbow with her free hand. "It does no soul good to dwell on what cannot be changed. I learned long ago before I— before I was sent to school by my father, that I stood at a fork. I could continue to let the past weigh me down, binding me to the spot, my memories carried like a ball and chain." Her expression changed. It was fierce, determined. "Or, I could carry it like a torch. To illuminate my path. It would be my guide, my experience. If I could enlighten others, then all the better."

I laughed dryly. "You're a saint." I could feel my eyes growing heavy.

"Though I disagree, that is very flattering. Thank you, my lord." Ceres gave me a curt bow from the neck. "Do your eyes tire?"

"Yeah. I'm not sure I can stay awake much longer," I admitted. The pain was getting dull. There were three copies of Ceres in the room, and I couldn't make heads or tails of any of them. A grin tugged at my lips when I saw the faint images of Keke, Cannoli, and Ravyn behind Ceres.

"Matt! Matt, we got it!" Keke screamed.

The girls arrived beside me as my head lolled from one side to the next.

I hope I wake up.

Ravyn Pro Tip: *Kuso!* Stay awake and drink this or I will never forgive you! *Baka!* Hey! Matt!!

Chapter 12
Hallowed Ground

I stood on Ni Island's beaches beneath the cool shade of its towering palm trees. In the distance, I could make out two dark outlines near the withdrawing tide. One lay motionless on the sand, the second bent over the first while frantically waving its arms. I brought one hand flat against my forehead to cut out the gleam of the sun, then squinted my eyes.

Is that me?

"Hey! Wake up!" Keke's voice rang over the surf as she shook unmoving shoulders. Her long hair trailed over her arms, droplets from the ocean streaming into the sand. "Don't die on me!"

"A memory?" I murmured.

"Of course, [User Matthew]. All of your memories are safely stored," a familiar, monotonous voice intoned beside me. "It is your footprint upon Nyarlea."

"Ai?" I blinked and dropped my arm before looking to my right.

"Yes." Ai was a little taller than Keke, her head reaching just above my chin. Her long, royal-blue hair flowed in the breeze, and deep sapphire eyes stared into the distance. She wore a similar nautically-themed outfit as the other girls from Ni Island, sporting the same white top that I'd seen on the iPaw.

My mouth went dry. "Am I dead?"

"That remains to be seen," she said flatly.

"Some junk from the ocean?" past me asked, now on his feet and inspecting the iPaw. He chucked it with his measly 1 [Strength] and frowned.

"No! You musn't!" Keke squealed.

"Jesus, I was fucking stupid," I groaned, rubbing the back of my neck with one hand.

"All users must begin somewhere," Ai replied.

The scene vanished in a blur of sunshine and glittering water, replaced instead by tall, shifting grasses. Cannoli knelt by a palm civet burrow and sang her siren song.

"Is this the part where I watch my life flash before my eyes?" I asked, drinking in Cannoli's lovely voice with each sweet sound that escaped her lips. "I didn't really get that the first time."

"Not quite." Ai walked with a grace and authority that I'd witnessed in Ceres and Jazz. She stroked Cannoli's hair and watched as the kitten-sized civet appeared in its hole. "You have chosen interesting companions."

"What do you mean?" I was next to sing, and I cringed at the cracking, toneless song.

"Your selections were immediate and based on little more than their proximity to you," she noted, her fingers lingering around one long strand of Cannoli's hair.

I winced. "That's a little harsh."

She tipped her chin to meet my gaze and blinked. "Is it?"

Once again, the backdrop disappeared, warping and reshaping until it landed on its new destination in my memories. Keke, Cannoli, Ravyn, and I stood amongst hundreds of tigers outside of Shulan's gates. Maya was cut to shreds as we helplessly witnessed her death.

"Are you choosing these?" I asked Ai.

"No." One of the tigers padded to Ai's feet and sniffed her hand. She stroked its head, and it purred. "You are in control of this memorial display, [User Matthew]."

Yomi's staff jingled in the distance, and I swore I felt a burning pang in my ear. Or maybe it was the punch to my gut with the memory.

The tiger at Ai's feet dissolved into thin air, followed soon by the other felines, the Defiled, and, finally, the players in the fight. All were quickly replaced by Saphira's quiet kitchen, her arms wrapped around my waist and her lips on mine. Then Saphira's body restructured into Keke's, then Cannoli's, then Myrun's, Yomi's, Marianne's, Ravyn's. Each face flashed by like a strobe light.

"This isn't a memory," I murmured, backing into one of the kitchen counters.

"I believe you would refer to this as a nightmare," Ai said, her tone never wavering.

The room went black. I blinked and suddenly found myself in the [Necromancer]'s pot, my skin burning away from the muscles and bone beneath.

"Ah, my servant at long last!" the kittengirl cackled, stirring the pot with a long wooden stick.

I looked around for Ai, but she was nowhere to be seen. The pain of the brew seeped into every nerve, and I screamed.

"Don't be such a baby! I'm almost done!" the [Necromancer] scolded.

My head sank beneath the bubbling liquid, and the bitter, scalding concoction scored my teeth and tongue. Every orifice in my face was clogged with it, and I couldn't breathe.

"Hey! Hang on!" Keke's voice came from somewhere above.

I looked up and saw sunlight sparkling through clear blue water. I was back in the ocean. Keke dove downward and gripped my arm, pulling with all of her strength to bring us to the surface.

"Matt, wake up!" she yelled, despite us both still being beneath the water.

"You are not dead, [User Matthew]," Ai's voice echoed in my ears. "[Continue?]"

My limbs were so heavy, like sandbags ready to drag the two of us to the ocean floor. My skin continued to sear as if I was still stewing in the necromancer's cauldron. Even so, Keke's face lingered in my vision, her voice still calling my name. I hadn't come this far to quit. *Yes...*

"Matt!" Keke cried again.

Yes! Please! Continue!

My eyelids flew wide, and I gasped for air. My lungs burned, and everything from the neck down tingled with the sudden rush of blood to my limbs.

"He's awake!" Cannoli cried.

"Drink the rest of this. Right fucking now," Ravyn commanded, yanking my chin open and dumping the remnants of a flask straight down my throat.

Keke had one hand on the top of my head and the other on my shoulder. Her face was flooded with tears.

Don't cry, Keke. I haven't done anything to earn that. I swallowed the rest of the antidote and flexed my throbbing fingers, then slowly moved my arm to cup Keke's hand in mine.

"Y-you stopped b-breathing," Keke managed, wiping her nose on the shoulder of her top. She stroked my hair and gritted her teeth. "R-Ravyn thought you were gone."

"You were *dead*," Ravyn snapped. "Cannoli forced you to swallow some of the antidote while I pumped your damn chest back to life. *Baka!* Next time I say, 'Hey, Matt, split the potion,' fucking *listen to me!*" Her voice was wild with rage.

"I..." My tongue felt like heavy sandpaper in my mouth. I swallowed and tried again. "I'm sorry."

"You're sorry?" Ravyn scoffed. "Oh, no. You're not sorry. Not yet. I swear to Saoirse, when you feel better—"

"Ravyn." Cannoli placed a hand on her arm and shook her head. "He needs to rest right now."

Before Ravyn could turn on the [Acolyte], Ceres announ-ced, "My lord, Fiona has prepared a hearty meal with the [Energy] spices from your [Cat Pack]." She stood at the edge of the cot, one bandaged hand resting on my ankle, and offered a knowing smile. "It is good to have you back."

Because I'd waited so long from the time I was envenomed to the time I drank an antidote, the overall damage from the scratches was nearly as severe as Ceres's hole-punched arm. The scars on my chest would likely never go away, leaving behind a sprawling of burn patterns below my collarbone.

Erina came to not long after me, and we shared short, broken conversations between a sporadic sleep schedule. Needless to say, she took the loss of her arm pretty damn rough. Considering her prowess as a fellow warrior, I could only imagine how defeated she felt. I had a very hard time picturing protecting my girls with one arm.

It was pretty damn intriguing to watch Ceres and me heal, though. Both of us would likely have been dead on the spot if we were back where I came from—Ceres from blood loss and me from the venom. The [Hit Points] system seemed to work much like it did in a video game; so long as we didn't hit 0, we were okay. Which had to have meant Jazz was one-shot, or close to, and then bled the rest of hers away. I shuddered at the thought.

Sanaia and a small contingency of guards they could afford to spare retrieved Jazz's body, burying it beneath the house she'd once occupied in Catania. I was told there was little remaining to recover of the girl who'd taken my axe to the head. They buried what they could.

Since we were still underground, it was impossible to say how many days had passed since our return and when I could finally sit up. Each of the girls in my Party would linger at my side at different times, seemingly taking shifts to watch whether my condition improved or worsened. Once I could sit up and eat on my own, their attention shifted to helping the Sorentina clan settle in, showing them the groundwork we'd established so far.

"Appear iPaw," I murmured one day while the girls were occupied and Erina had descended into a fitful sleep. "Hey, Ai."

The blue-haired girl appeared on the screen in all her pixelated glory. It had been so weird to see her in person. Had it really been her? "What can I assist you with, [User Matthew]?"

"So, I know this sounds weird, but, erm, did we meet a few days ago? Like in person?"

Ai blinked and tilted her head. "I do not understand the question."

I winced and tried again. "You and I. Did we meet in person?"

She paused, then shook her head. "That is quite impossible, [User Matthew]. What else may I help you with?"

Guess it really was just a fever dream. "Did I get any Experience from the fight?"

Ai disappeared, replaced by a second window populating the center of the screen.

New Notifications!

Matt has gained: 206 Base XP!
Matt has gained: 206 Class XP!
Matt has gained: 3 Points of Energy!
Matt is now: Base Level 8!
Matt is now: Class Level 8!
Matt has gained: 1 Stat Point!
Matt has gained: 1 Class Point!

Keke has gained: 181 Base XP!
Keke has gained: 181 Class XP!

Cannoli has gained: 165 Base XP!
Cannoli has gained: 165 Class XP!

Ravyn has gained: 185 Base XP!
Ravyn has gained: 185 Class XP!

Ceres has gained: 203 Base XP!
Ceres has gained: 203 Class XP!

I exited the window and navigated to the [Warrior] Class tree, staring at my options and wondering what the hell could have possibly saved Jazz or Erina's arm in that fight.

"I haven't seen one of those since I was a kitten," Erina rasped, pointing at the iPaw in my hands. "Tells you all kinds of nice things, right?"

"Mm. In a way," I nodded. "Just deciding where I should put my Class Point."

Erina chuckled. "Good man, thinking before you choose. I dove ears-first into [Adrenaline Rush]. The thrill of the fight is what keeps me going." She grunted and shook her head. "Well, what *kept* me going anyway."

"Your fight isn't over," I replied, looking up from the screen. "These girls need you. They just lost their leader."

"Me? A one-armed brute leading a city? I don't think so."

"Why not?" I shrugged. "Sure, you may have to downsize your weapon some, but there are plenty of heroes with just one arm." *That I know from video games,* I thought, but I bit my tongue.

"You must come from a mighty interesting place if you know so many heroes." Erina rolled to her back and stared at the ceiling. "Dunno if I'm cut out to rule, friend."

"Just consider it, at least. Sanaia may take Jazz's room, but you're a lot more capable in a fight. You can teach these girls to survive."

Erina hummed a reply; then her breathing steadied into quiet snores.

I threw my Class Point into [Adrenaline Rush] and the Stat Point into [Vitality]. Live longer, hit harder. If it meant cleaving into Defiled like Erina had, I was happy to max that first.

I glanced back at the sleeping Erina. *I hope these girls get to see an ounce of the bravery you showed out there. And, if I keep at this, I hope I can do the same.*

Ai Pro Tip: Raising your Vitality can assist in slowing poisons and venoms in your body.

Chapter 13
Wise to the World

By the time I could walk again, the girls from Sorentina had settled in nicely. Three meals a day became the norm, with Cannoli and Fiona heading the kitchens. Keke and two others formed a daily triad of hunters and foragers capable of taking on the groups of Encroachers that slipped through the cracks. And Sanaia, her group of warriors, Ceres, and one other girl from Sorentina set to work on fixing the gates surrounding the city. While Ceres didn't have the blacksmithing prowess of Espada, she was well-versed in metals and crafting.

That left one final group to attend to the gardens I'd started. I'd insisted on seeing the progress after I was able to walk around without wanting to throw up for a few days. Tristan and Ara accompanied me, along with those assigned to farming.

"Shouldn't you still be resting?" Tristan asked as we made our way up the hill.

Fewer and fewer Encroachers were lurking around the city. The handful that I did see were either harmless—darting from bush to bush and scampering up trees—or quickly dealt with in the way of a well-thrown dagger from Ara. I prayed that dispatching the twin Defiled meant fewer Encroachers as a whole and a faster recovery time for Catania.

"I'm tired of resting," I admitted. "I've been resting for over a week."

Ara pulled one blade from the corpse of a particularly moody roach. "The venom was potent indeed. I should like to know if I could bottle it."

Now, that's a terrifying thought. "I bet Ravyn could tell you."

Ara frowned. "I'm sure."

"Really, though, are you alright, Matt?" Tristan asked again.

"Hey, I'm fine. Really. I promise you won't have to carry me back." I inhaled the fresh air and stretched my arms at my sides. The musky cave environment had become my norm, and I had forgotten how good it felt to have the warm sun on my face. "You can just let me rot where I fall."

Tristan groaned. "That's not funny."

I chuckled. "Alright. Sorry. What about you? Are you hanging in there?"

I knew Tristan had attended Jazz's burial, but we hadn't spoken about her since. He chewed on his lip, and, for a brief moment, his eyes flickered toward the ground. But he recovered with a bright smile and a curt nod. "I'm good. Thanks."

Yeah, I feel that. "Alright."

We arrived at the familiar roofless building, and Kahvi, one of the Sorentina crew, carefully guided me between each crop row and pointed out the minute changes she'd made.

"Some of the vegetables you planted need more sunlight than they were receiving." She pointed to what was left of the overhanging roof. "So I switched them with those that would do better in the shade."

"It seems like each island has its own climate," I noted. "That would change the soil's makeup and your options for plants."

Kahvi nodded. "That's exactly right. I've visited San Island twice in my life. It rains a lot more here than it does over there, but they tend to have cooler temperatures."

I'd have to be careful when I started my own garden on Ni. For some reason I had assumed it would work exactly how Shizen had taught me, but now I realized there were more aspects to [Harvesting] that I had to take into account. *I'm glad I have Saphira to shadow.* "Thanks, Kahvi. We didn't overwater anything, did we?"

"Not enough to do any real damage," she laughed. "Look, plenty of sprouts are coming up. You did just fine."

I knelt for a closer inspection and realized she was right. Many of our crops had already taken root, and long green stems with tiny leaves poked out from the soil. I rubbed one of the leaves between two fingers, picturing Marianne as she dug into the dirt at my side.

I could hear her laughing as I tried to explain the fertilizer situation. I may not have known her very long, but her sudden absence was so damn heavy.

Kahvi placed a hand on my shoulder and squatted beside me. "This world is a harsh one. We wake up every day knowing that it may be our last." She gestured to the plants. "However, our intentions are echoed through those we leave behind."

I pulled my hand away from the plant and ran it through my hair. *I guess I really do wear my emotions on my sleeve.* "Thanks, Kahvi."

A sad smile settled across her lips. "I'll take good care of this place, I promise."

"I'm glad to hear it."

Later that evening, Keke, Cannoli, Ravyn, Ceres, and I joined Tristan and Ara at dinner to discuss our next plans.

"Portia's still waiting outside of Anyona. We need to head back," I began once I'd finished off my bowl of stew.

"You really think she's still there? Personally, I'd have left us by now," Ravyn reasoned.

That was very possible, but we had little choice. It's not like we could just show up in Venicia and ask for Celestia's kind understanding to let us, her kidnapped maid, and the island's man leave.

"What other choice do we have?" I asked. "She waited for us in Venicia, didn't she?"

"Yeah. I guess," Ravyn huffed and crossed her arms over her chest. "All this trust makes me uncomfortable."

"Are you well enough to travel?" Keke asked me.

"The other healers here and I have done everything we can at this point," Cannoli spoke up before I could reply. "He's eating, sleeping, and moving normally, so it should be safe to travel back."

"We'll just have to go through that fucking cave again," Ravyn shivered. "I'd almost rather face off against the head bitch of Venicia than step foot in that shithole."

"The Defiled and her undead minions are no more. It should be an easier journey, provided we don't touch anything," Ara replied. She lifted her mug of tea and daintily sipped from the edge.

"You told me of this creature before. Are we certain it was not a [Lich]?" Ceres asked.

A visible shudder ran from the tip of Ravyn's ears to her tail. "Saoirse's tits. Don't say shit like that."

So that is a possibility. "Assuming the worst-case scenario that she had any phylacteries, we should be cautious all the same."

"I'm sorry, um, phylacteries? [Lich]?" Cannoli blinked. "I'm unfamiliar with these words."

"It's like a Horcrux—wait, no, that's not a good comparison," Tristan began, then quickly cut himself off. Good thing, because I had no idea what a 'Horcrux' was. "A phylactery is an item that a [Lich]—a Class far more evil than a [Necromancer]—can use to save a piece of themselves into. If they die, they can resurrect themselves with that saved piece."

The locket suddenly came to mind. It was obviously cursed, but that may have been there to protect its destruction. *Damn it, the more I think about this, the more it makes sense.*

"So, then, if she were a [Lich], the Defiled wouldn't be dead?" Cannoli's eyes widened. She clutched her hands to her chest, and her face flushed. "S-she nearly killed us all. We can't—"

Ceres placed a hand on Cannoli's shoulder. Cannoli flinched, her ears flicked with her eyes before she turned to look at Ceres.

"We do not have to travel directly north. There is a path around that cuts through Leche, and then we can follow the coastline up to Anyona," Ceres said calmly.

"Leche is where Destiny and Lara were from!" Tristan proclaimed, giving a voice to my thoughts. His excitement quickly vanished, replaced by a furious blush on his cheeks. "S-sorry."

"Is Leche filled with Defiled, though?" I asked. "If it's another situation like the walk to Sorentina, I don't think our group will be enough."

"Seeing as Leche is entirely abandoned, I imagine it was picked clean long ago. Unless a Defiled has taken sanctuary within what remains, the road should be easier to navigate," Ceres explained.

"*Kuso.* Anyona was abandoned, too, and that [Lich] was still there," Ravyn murmured.

I quickly ran through every Defiled we'd encountered so far in my head and the environment where we'd found them. Almost every battle had been close to, if not directly at the gates of, a populated city. "She has a point, though," I said. "The one in the caves was the first Defiled we've faced that chose a place to live miles away from the nearest city."

"An educated guess, then?" Ara asked. "What if another Defiled *has* taken residency in Leche?"

"Then we do our best to move around it," Keke said. "The kitten [Lich] created some kind of connection to Tristan and Cannoli when she marked them for death. Are you really willing to risk that happening to the rest of us?"

Ara bristled, her tail whipping behind her in quick ticks. "No."

"Then we go through Leche," Keke repeated. "Ceres knows the rest of the island better than we do. I trust her to lead us through it."

"Me too! I trust Ceres, too!" Cannoli raised her hand.

"Whatever the hell gets us back to Ni Island," Ravyn sighed. "I need a good bath and a drink."

Amen to that. "Tristan?"

Tristan looked around the group before picking up Desiree and cradling her in his lap. "Through Leche, then."

"Are we good to leave in the morning?" I asked. The faster we could quit this place, the better.

"I don't think we have much to pack," Keke murmured into her tea.

"Some of us less so than we arrived with," Ceres replied good-naturedly, gesturing to her bare arms. "Which reminds me. My lord, what of your combat tunic?"

I grimaced. I hadn't thought of my shredded top since the battle. "I don't know if it's salvageable. They did a number on it."

Ceres exchanged looks with the other girls before returning her stare to me. "Let us take a look at it. Perhaps we can restore it to working order. Or at least enough to help us travel safely to port." She shrugged and tapped one shoulder with a delicate finger.

"Seeing as my armor requires immediate replacement, we must rely on you to stand guard of our Party."

Not to mention, I don't have a shield anymore. "Sounds like we're going to keep Espada busy for a while when we get home."

"Espada?" Tristan asked, leaning over the table. "Like, the Queen's Guard Espada? I read her name in a book!"

"Er, maybe they have the same name?" I tried picturing Espada as a white knight and came up short. "She's a blacksmith on Ni Island."

"Hm. That's interesting." He rolled his fingers along the tabletop in thought. "Maybe you're right."

"Tomorrow's good for me," Keke said, gracefully returning to our previous topic.

"I'll be ready," Cannoli added.

We mutually agreed to turn in early and leave at first light.

Please let us make it back to Portia tomorrow. I'm ready to be home.

Keke Pro Tip: Catania's already changed so much since we arrived. I'm glad we stayed to help them out.

Chapter 14

Essential Dignity

It felt strange to leave Catania and the remaining catgirls of Jazz's army. Though our adventure had initially begun as a way to show Tristan the hard truths of his island, I was proud of the work we'd accomplished on our journey.

Still, a part of me was concerned about what they would do from here. A crestfallen Erina would need to find the courage and the strength to lead the others, and the expats from Sorentina were still discovering their places amongst the Catania crew. By no means did I think them incapable—the Catania girls were nothing short of spectacular. But after having my hands in their lives for so long, I felt like I was saying goodbye to family.

We'd been through a lot together, so many ups and downs. It seemed like I was abandoning them, even if that couldn't be further from the truth.

They'll be okay. There are a lot of experienced catgirls here. One day, Catania will stand again.

I had a feeling that Keke, Cannoli, Ravyn, and Ceres felt similarly. They each did their part to oversee how hunts were going, what meals were cooked, how the [Mage]'s practices and wards were maintained. Ceres was an absolute boon in the areas our group had previously lacked. She looked over their armaments, gave critical advice on approaches to battle, and even debated tactics with some of the more experienced catgirls.

To sum it up, it was a job well done. I would do it all over again if I had to.

Ceres and a few deft hands at tailoring spent the better part of the night piecing back together what remained of my chest armor. To my surprise, it still felt just as strong as before. I could see tiny, meticulous stitching where the Defiled had shredded it. Still, while I was no expert on the crafting and management of armor, it looked almost new again.

By Keke's suggestion, we arose when it was barely dawn. The sun hadn't appeared over the horizon yet, but there was enough light to get by. I couldn't imagine it was any later than five in the morning. Like leaving the site of a camp, we double-checked, triple-checked, and even quadruple-checked to make sure we had everything we needed for the way back.

There weren't very many girls awake by the time we left, save for the handful of guards on the graveyard shift. We'd spent most of the previous night saying our farewells, but it was still nice to wave goodbye to a few girls on our way out.

"I hope they'll be okay," Cannoli said as we reached the hill's peak, turning to look back at the distant Catania.

"They'll be fine," Keke said with a smile.

"They better fucking be. I am *not* coming back here," I heard Ravyn grumble behind me.

I turned to see deep, dark bags hanging under her eyes.

"*Better not, better not! Squaawwwwk!*" Ball Gag screeched from his perch on Ravyn's shoulder.

"*Kuso.* Too fucking early, shh." Ravyn clamped a pair of fingers over the bird's beak, her lips twisted in absolute disgust.

"We have done everything within our power. To remain longer would only weaken them," Ceres said next. "They must learn how to deal with this threat. We can only hope that Shi Island will recover."

"I think Shi Island will," I said as I rolled my shoulders. "They have a lot going for them now. Something bigger than Celestia's rule."

"I'm going to miss them," Tristan said. He stopped to look back at the distant city, a warm smile tugging at the corners of his mouth.

"They're strong," Ara said in a barely audible tone. "This occasion will mark a hard-earned lesson for them."

"What about you?" asked Tristan. "Feel any different?"

Ara paused, clenching her fists. "I don't know." She bowed her head. "I am…unsure what it is I will do from here." She sighed. "I worry for my sister."

Tristan let go of Desiree, and the nimble feline familiar leaped down with a purr. He moved to Ara's side, reaching down and taking her hand. "We'll come back for her. I promise. I'm not going to let this island fall to shambles again." His gaze veered. He seemed to be having trouble finding the words, and as endearing as this was to watch, I couldn't help but feel like I was intruding on something intimate.

Cannoli clasped her hands together, eyes sparkling. Her attention was glued to them like a kid affixed to the TV on a Saturday morning.

Ara's mouth hung open, her cheeks a furious red. "Y-y-young master, that is quite k-kind of you to say." She drew a deep breath and slowly exhaled. "I am in your debt. If you would continue to have me, then I will be your blade."

A soft laugh escaped Tristan's lips. "As if you have to ask. We'll come back for Lynn. You'll see."

Ara's eyes widened. After a moment, they settled, and she returned his smile. "Yes, young master."

The journey back was uneventful, to all of our relief. Ceres's assumptions were correct. The coast was bare, save for the occasional bold Encroacher. The air was salty, and the wind gentle. It was the perfect day to travel.

Leche, like the surrounding cities before it, was a mess. There wasn't much to be had. Splintered wooden planks from quaint stalls were strewn about in what was previously a small market square. Lines of sturdier brick buildings were barely standing, surrounded by the broken rubble that had sheltered their roofs. Occasionally, we would see a stray bone or skull lying around, but the village was quiet save for the coastal winds seeping through the alleyways.

"What was Leche like?" asked Cannoli.

"It was—"

"Leche is—"

Ara and Ceres spoke, interrupting one another.

"My apologies. Please, continue," Ceres said, waving her hand.

Ara paused. "Leche was a small village. Poor, difficult to manage, and often ignored."

"Oh," said a sullen Cannoli.

Ara's breath caught. "Th-that is to say, they struggled. When observing each island and its respective villages and cities, Leche is not only the smallest but is unfortunate enough to be the furthest away from suitable trade."

As we trekked through the hills, Ara opened her mouth, then closed it again. There was something she wasn't telling us, and it seemed to be bothering her.

At last, she continued. "As I've mentioned before, San Island possesses a monopoly on trade. Leche had a poor reputation for harboring thieves and delinquents. It was rare that its citizens were accepted into Venicia's School of Etiquette. To house someone from Leche was simply unheard of, and to put it lightly, the expectations Madame Celestia placed on those from Leche are...unreasonable."

"Well, if we've learned anything from that school, we know it's a total shit show," Ravyn said.

I looked back to see Ara and Ravyn passing glares.

"It was a humble town," Ceres added. "I had the opportunity to visit twice before the attacks began."

"Leche will rise again," Tristan said, his brow furrowed. "I will see to it."

Ara's stare lingered on Tristan. "Of that, I have no doubt."

By the time we made it to the outskirts of Anyona, the sun was setting. I don't think I've ever walked that much in a single day before. Nyarlea was the culprit for a lot of my firsts.

Keke stood by my side the entire time, and I attempted to steal a glance at her any chance I could. I was eager to share a bed with her again. A good bed. Maybe I could help her cook dinner, and she could walk around in a t-shirt for the entire evening.

What would we name our daughter? The thought warmed my face.

Ceres continued to lead as we came to a stop.

"Are you feeling alright, Matt?" Keke asked. We'd fallen behind some.

I guess the red in my cheeks was pretty noticeable. "Y-yeah, I'm fine. Just eager to get back home."

"I know what you mean. I miss the people on Ni Island. The sounds, the smells. All of it."

"Me too."

When the outline of Portia's sloop came into view, I breathed a sigh of relief. To be honest, I had no idea if she would keep waiting. It felt like we were putting far too many expectations on her. I figured it had been almost two weeks since we last saw her.

Portia was reeling something in by the time we were approaching. Gotta say, she wore that black bikini spectacularly. It accentuated her curves and demanded my immediate attention. Her muscles glistened with fresh droplets from the sea glittering on her tattoo. The tan had grown darker since we last left, and the thought of what her tan lines looked like underneath her suit crossed my mind.

"Hey! I thought you guys were dead!" Portia took a hand off the fishing rod to wave to us, then quickly returned to reeling her catch in when the force nearly pulled her into the water. "Sucker's gotta be huge!"

"Portia!" Cannoli squealed. "I missed you!"

"Missed you too! Now hang on!" Portia pulled in her massive fish, knocking it out cold and tying it off to the side of the ship. She quickly maneuvered to raise the anchor and turn the sloop toward land.

Ceres squinted her eyes, her face pinching with the movement. "We are to board this vessel?"

I nodded, suddenly aware that we'd never discussed just how small the ride would be. "Ah, right. Um, yeah. I know it's a tight fit, but—"

"It is beautiful!" Ceres breathed. I moved to wave my hand in front of her. She blinked, but her stare remained on Portia. Something about the boat had bewitched her. "I had no idea we were boarding a sloop!"

"Is that special or something?"

She looked at me so quickly that I worried she'd get whiplash. "If you will pardon my word choice, my lord—but do you not understand the beauty and majesty of such a ship?"

Erm. It's just a boat? "I guess not. It gets us from point A to point B."

Ceres shook her head. "You simply must allow me to educate you on the subject. Please!"

Well, I guess it would be something to talk about on the way. "Sure. Let's eat first, though. Sound good?"

Ceres put one hand over another at her stomach and bowed deep at the waist. "Yes. Of course, my lord. You must be famished."

"Hey! I see how you're lookin' at her! This baby's mine!" Portia cried as Ravyn navigated the shoddy dock toward the boat.

"Who's looking?" Ravyn replied.

"Your new recruit there. Wait, three new recruits?" Portia peered over our group and then roared with laughter. "Goddess above, Matt! Are you trying to fit the whole damn island on my sloop?"

"Just a few pieces of it," I chuckled, carefully stepping over the missing planks to the edge of the dock.

As we all boarded the sloop, my shoulders began to slump, and I couldn't help but relax. At last, we'd made it back to the edge of Shi Island. Our time had been arduous, painful, and a true test of our mettle. While I harbored some regrets, I felt like we'd made an impact. We'd taken what little we had to offer, and we did something with it.

Catania's morale was improving, Celestia's influence waning, and we'd even managed to break a prisoner out of jail in the process.

When we were all situated, I sat down and leaned against the hull, or what I thought was the hull. I was sure Ceres would correct me soon. As the banter between the girls continued, I closed my eyes and listened in. Their casual conversation was the best thing I'd heard in weeks.

Cannoli Pro Tip: I hope one day we'll get to see Catania and Leche restored to how they were before.

Side Quest

Papa's Birthday

Portia dug her toes deep in the sand and looked out over the vast, seemingly unending ocean. She shoved her hands into the pockets of her overalls and hummed in thought.

Papa's birthday was today, and she had nothing to give him.

What could she get him that he didn't already have? She was still too young to hunt Encroachers by herself, and she wasn't allowed to fish on her own, just in case she summoned a Defiled. His sloop was in perfect shape, and he always said that he had everything he needed with her and Mama.

The sweet sound of song drew Portia's ears and her attention.

"*You and me can go fishing in the dark. Lying on our backs while we count the stars...*"

Portia turned to see a golden-haired young woman with a fishing pole over one shoulder and a melody on her lips. She recognized her from a fair few dealings with Papa—Elona was better at [Fishing] than everyone in Junonia. Even Papa.

Elona caught sight of Portia and smiled. "Good morning, Portia. Out here on your own?"

Portia nodded. "Hi, Miss Elona."

Elona knelt forward so their eyes met. The tips of Portia's ears barely came up to the young woman's waist. "You look down. What's wrong?"

"It's…it's Papa's birthday, and I don't have a present for him!" Portia cried, more of her frustration backing the response than she'd intended. She covered her mouth and scrunched her eyes closed. "Sorry. I shouldn't yell."

Elona gasped. "Goodness, this is an emergency indeed. Your yelling is understandable!" She stood up straight and tapped her fishing rod against her free hand.

Portia relaxed her face and clasped her hands behind her back. She poked the tip of her tongue into a gap between two of her front teeth. It had fallen out recently, and she tended to toy with the space when she was thinking. "I want to get him something he'll *really* like."

"Then we'd better think of something very good!" Elona nodded in agreement. "Let's see, we know Emilio likes sailing and fishing."

"Hunting, too!" Portia added excitedly. She was happy to have an adult on her side. Adults knew *everything*.

"Hm." Elona knelt down and set her tackle box in the sand. Lifting the top, she sorted through its contents. "Ah-ha. I have an idea."

Portia leaned over the box in time to see Elona withdraw an intricately wrapped hook. The varied colors of feathers and fur made it look like a beetle jumped through a rainbow. It was beautiful. "Did you make that, Miss Elona?"

"I did. Your papa has bought them from me a few times before."

"But I've never seen them before," Portia murmured, digging at the gap in her teeth with her tongue.

Elona laughed. "They cost quite a few Bells to make and a lot of time." She shaded her eyes and looked over the beach. It was still very early morning—Portia hadn't been able to sleep over her lack of gift—and the sun had just cleared the horizon. "How about you and I make one together?"

"What? *Really?*" Portia's tail whipped back and forth with excitement. *She said that they cost a lot of Bells...* Her ears drooped, and her tail stilled. She shoved her hand back in her pocket and dug out the shiny coin she'd found beneath her pillow in place of her tooth. "But I...I only have five Bells."

"Wouldn't you know it? Five Bells is just what I need for the materials I have." Elona grinned.

Portia's glow returned, and she eagerly passed the coin to Elona.

"Well then, let's get started. We want to make it in time for his birthday." Elona pocketed the Bell coin and sat cross-legged on the sand. She patted the open space in front of her, and Portia mirrored her posture.

She pulled the top shelf of her tackle box out, revealing a bottom filled with hooks, furs, feathers, strands of fabric, and wraps of wire. "Why don't you pick out a few colors?"

Portia stuck her tongue in her cheek and pored over her options. Elona really did have every color of the rainbow in this box. *What are Papa's favorites?* She fingered two teal feathers. *This is the color of Papa and my hair.* Taking the feathers, she set them in her lap and looked again. A long length of honey-colored leather reminded her of her mother's eyes. She set it on top of the feathers. *One more.* The furs felt silky against her fingertips, and a brilliant orange cluster caught her eye. Like the sun at dawn when they took the boat out together. She snagged it and held her choices in her palms. "Okay! These ones!"

"These are wonderful colors, Portia." Elona nodded and took the wire and one long hook from the box. "Now for the fun part."

Despite the hours upon hours of knot practice and sailing the sloop, Portia's fingers felt clumsy and slow. The work was tedious and methodical, and there were many times when they had to unwrap the wires and feathers because they were too far apart or had begun to overlap. But Elona was so patient and nice, helping Portia understand exactly how the thin wire should wrap around the hook and when to add a new feather or some of the fur.

"Did your papa teach you how to do this, Miss Elona?" Portia asked while they worked.

"No. I never met my father. My nyannies taught me how to fish, and my mother taught me how to make lures."

Portia winced. Elona didn't sound sad, but the thought of not knowing her papa certainly *felt* sad. "M-Mama said that most kittens don't know their papas. She didn't either."

"That's true. Emilio is a special case, it seems. Oh, wait, we need to wrap this part a little closer." Elona gently took the lure from Portia's hands and unwound the last bind. "There we are." She returned it and watched Portia nestle back into her work.

"Do you have any kittens, Miss Elona?"

Elona chuckled. "No. Not yet, at least. But, if the time comes, I hope they're as clever and as sweet as you."

Portia blushed and ducked her chin to her chest, her hair falling into her eyes. "Thank you." Another few rounds, another feather. "Oh! You sing really pretty."

"That's nice of you to say. And a little embarrassing," Elona replied. "I thought I'd be the only one out here this early."

Portia shook her head. "I couldn't sleep. I didn't want Papa to be sad on his big day."

"I promise he won't be sad." Elona touched the tip of Portia's nose. "Not with a daughter like you."

They continued to work until the sun rose to the middle of the sky. Portia's stomach growled, and she did her best to ignore it. When she reached the end of the wire, she handed the lure back to Elona for a final inspection.

"Well, my dear, I think we're finished," Elona announced. "This is perfect."

"Really?" Portia beamed.

"Really! You're a fine craftsman, Portia. Now, run this home. I'm sure they're worried about you." Elona returned the lure and stroked Portia between the ears.

"Thank you so much, Miss Elona! You're the best!" Portia scrambled to her feet and broke into a sprint. Puffs of sand kicked up behind her feet, and the salty breeze caressed her hair and cheeks. She was breathless by the time she reached her front door and burst inside.

Papa sat at the kitchen table with a mug in hand while Mama stirred a pot over the fire.

"Portia! Where have you been all day?" Mama glanced over her shoulder, then moved to add a stack of sliced onyans to the pot.

"Well, I…" Portia swallowed hard, then marched to her father's side.

"What've you got there, love?" Papa rested his mug on the table and turned his full attention to her.

"Happy Birthday, Papa!" Portia thrust the lure forward with a giant grin. "It's your day! And I made you a present!"

Papa's eyes went wide, and he accepted the lure. "You made this for me?"

"Yeah! Miss Elona taught me how and helped me, and I even paid for the materials myself! With my Bells from the tooth [Wizard]!" Portia clapped her hands together.

"The tooth fairy." Papa laughed. "This is wonderful, Portia. I love it." He set the lure on the table and swept her up beneath her armpits, placing her in his lap. "You worked for a long time on this, didn't you?"

"You can tell?" Portia asked, surprised. Her sore fingers and rigid knuckles were enough to remind her, but she'd been worried that it wouldn't compare to Miss Elona's wonderful lures.

"I can. This here's a prized piece, sweet." He picked up the lure and turned it over and over. "Good colors, too. They remind me of you and your ma."

Portia relaxed into his embrace, glowing with pride. "I'm so glad you like it."

"I love it." Papa hugged her close and kissed her on the top of the head. "And I love you!"

"I love you, too!" Portia squealed as he tickled her sides. "I want to make all of Papa's days special!"

Papa laughed. "You already do, Portia. Every one."

Portia Pro Tip: I still prefer to make my own fishin' lures if I can. Hard as hell to get all the materials, though.

Chapter 15

Take Me Home Tonight

Stepping foot on Ni Island's dock made me way more emotional than I ever expected it to be. I was choked by the sun's warmth, the soft waves on the sand, and the outline of the town I'd come to call home on the horizon.

Home.

That word felt more true here than it ever had in my last life. The life where my world revolved around a minimum wage job, struggling through school, and wondering what flavor of instant ramen to cook for dinner. When 'leveling up' meant how long I'd played a game that week, and my limited farming knowledge wouldn't kill me.

Yeah, Nyarlea was difficult as hell.

"Come on, Matt," Keke said, twining her fingers with mine. "Let's go home."

And I wouldn't trade it for anything.

On our arrival in Junonia, many of the girls were closing up shop for the day but still took the time to wave. When they saw Tristan with the group, they took a few tentative steps closer.

"Careful. These bitches are ravenous." Ravyn jabbed Tristan with her elbow.

Ara drew her daggers and narrowed her eyes on the incoming catgirls. "I shall not allow them to have their way with you, young master."

"No, you're safe here! They're all sweet once you get to know them!" Cannoli hopped forward and put a hand on Ara's arm. "You don't need to defend him!"

Tristan laughed. "Surely they're more relaxed than Venicia's school, right?" When Ara's face fell, he double backed. "I-I mean, not you, of course! Or your sister, or Destiny, or Lara!"

Ara worked her jaw and blinked. The wheels were definitely turning, but my guess was she couldn't find anything appropriate to say.

Tristan rested his palm on his forehead and shook his head. "I'll just be over here with my foot in my mouth."

"What a darling little cat!" a gentle, familiar voice cried.

I turned to see a very pregnant Saphira gingerly kneeling down to pet Desiree.

I froze. A hurricane of feelings I'd suppressed since we left Sorentina flooded my chest. Relief at seeing Saphira safe and sound. Excitement that we really had made a child together. Fear that I wasn't meeting expectations as an expecting father. *A father.* Jesus Christ.

My mouth went dry, and I rounded the group, taking Saphira's hand and helping her back to her feet.

"Welcome home, Matt. I was—" Saphira began before I embraced her tightly.

I held her head to my chest and breathed in her hair.

"O-oh! Hello!" she squeaked.

I kissed the top of her head and shifted my touch to her shoulders. She drew back to face me, her cheeks a deep red.

"I'm sorry. I'm just… I'm really happy to see you," I said. *Smooth.* But really, it didn't matter. The people I cared about deserved to know it. "How are you feeling?"

"I feel fine. Really!" Saphira grinned and stroked the curve of her belly. "She's very well-behaved so far. I, um, I talk to her while I garden." Her ears flicked nervously, and her gaze lowered. "I hope she can hear me."

"I'm sure she can!" Cannoli replied brightly. "My mom said she used to sing to me like that, and I practically knew every song by heart by the time she taught me."

Thanks, Cannoli.

"Let me know if you need anything at all. Okay?" I said, touching her cheek.

Saphira leaned to the right, glancing at the rest of the group, then steadied her feet. "I'm sure you have a lot to do. But, if you wouldn't mind visiting me while you're here..." Her blush deepened, and she picked at a stray thread on her dress. "Just whenever you have a free moment."

"Of course. I'd like that." I kissed her forehead again. Where even the *thought* of public displays of affection embarrassed me just a few months before, now they felt absolutely necessary.

Saphira slipped from my hands and waved to the others. "It's really lovely to see you all safe and sound!"

"Same for you, Saphira. Don't be a stranger, okay?" Keke replied.

"Please keep your hands to yourself!" Ara barked at the catgirl who'd gone straight for my thigh on my first day in town. Seemed she'd gotten a little too close to Tristan for Ara's liking.

"I like this city. It is most serene," Ceres said, stepping away from the flustered Ara.

"Yeah. This is home," I replied.

"Um, would it be alright if we split up for a while?" Cannoli asked. "There's a few girls I'd like to see now that we're back."

"I don't see why not." I shrugged.

"I can show Tristan, Ara, and Ceres the inn," Keke offered. "Maybe give them a tour of the town if they're up for it."

"That would be wonderful!" Ceres exclaimed, clasping her hands. "Yes, please! Tell me everything of your island."

"Looks like we'll have to save shopping for tomorrow," I remarked. "We'll see about replacing your armor and my shield."

"I can't wait to meet Espada," Tristan mused. "I hope she's the one I read about."

Still seems unlikely. But he's clearly better versed in Nyarlean history than I am. "Could be." I turned to the uncharacteristically quiet Ravyn. Her gaze trailed after Saphira, and her lips twitched downward into a thoughtful frown. "Hey. What are you going to do?"

Ravyn blinked as if I'd awoken her from a trance, then shook her head. "I want to talk to you. Come with me."

Sure! Thanks for asking. But the expression on her face worried me. Her snark levels had drastically decreased since Catania, and her position on my giving Ceres the antidote was made very clear. "Alright."

We divided off into smaller groups, Ara still giving the poor catgirl a verbal lashing. Ravyn whispered something to Ball and sent him high into the air. She then marched forward without bothering to look behind her.

"[Civilian Mode]," she murmured. Her short pleather dress reconstructed into the red, mandarin-collared garb that did just as good of a job accentuating her curves.

I followed suit, feeling a lot more comfortable in my green jacket and jeans. It was a miracle that they'd remained in decent condition for so long. I'd expected the tear in my chest armor to rip my poor jacket to shreds. Thankfully, the damage hadn't transferred. The blood, however, was another story. It'd taken a lot of work to clean it off.

"So, what's up?" I asked Ravyn's back.

"Not here," Ravyn snapped.

Alright. We continued through the market square, past the last stalls and sparse buildings. She led us farther north, and I quickly realized we were heading to her house in the mountain. It seemed like quite a trek just for a walk, but I mean, I couldn't fault her for wanting to check on it. She hadn't been home in a very long time.

When I set foot on the steep path leading to our destination, I expected to feel the same stomach-squeezing terror that I had the first time. Instead, the first thought that came to me was, *Huh. This isn't as bad as the Anyona climb.* I wanted to laugh but feared Ravyn's response if I did.

Instead, we continued our silent traipse up the bewitched steps. The waves thundered against the cliff beneath us, and a cool breeze toyed with Ravyn's long hair.

Ravyn unlocked the door and swung it wide, stepping in and snapping her fingers. The candles lining the walls jumped to life as I crossed the threshold. The wide, cluttered room smelled musty after having been closed for so long. Tiny, glistening webs connected sconce to sconce, and a thin layer of dust had settled on the unmoved books, potion bottles, and shelves. Ravyn snapped once more when I was through, and—much like my first visit—the door slammed shut.

I surveyed the room for somewhere to sit or stand until I found a sturdy-looking desk. There wasn't a readily available chair for me to use, so I leaned against the desk's surface instead. Ravyn paced the length of the room, picking through the toppled book stacks and wooden chests with ease. *I'm betting if we cleaned this place up, she'd never find anything again.*

Ravyn continued to pace in silence. I crossed my arms over my chest and waited. When she finally spoke, I nearly jumped out of my skin.

"When you found me here—the first time you showed up—I wouldn't have been able to tell you the last time I was sober," she said, her heels clicking rhythmically against the floor. "When—" she inhaled deeply, "—when Finn died, I didn't know what to do with myself. I loved him, Matt. I loved him so fucking much."

I could tell this admission was taking everything she had. I wasn't about to underplay it with a dumb reply. I nodded when I caught her eye but stayed quiet.

"We were going to run the hell away from all of this. The Defiled, the Encroachers, the bullshit. He only had eyes for *me!*" Ravyn slammed a hand into one of the still-standing towers of books. Hard leather covers fell to the floor, scattering time-worn pages around her feet. "But you. *You,*" she growled, approaching me. "You're willing to throw your life away for *any* of the girls out there." She pointed toward the door, her eyes wild. "You care about *all of them.*"

"I do," I said.

"I was so goddess-damned angry with you for giving Ceres the antidote. But then, when I saw you with Saphira, it hit me. It could have been anyone who got hit with that venom, and you would have done the same fucking thing. Because that's just you. Just Matt being Matt."

"You're right."

"And you know what the *fuckiest* thing is, Matt?" The toes of her shoes touched mine, and her chest pressed against me.

We were rarely this close to one another. My heart sped, but I did my best to maintain the calm reassurance I imagined she was looking for. "What?"

Ravyn hissed in a breath; her hands balled into fists at her sides. "I want you to look at *me* like that. Like you look at Keke and Saphira and Cannoli." Her voice broke on her words. "I want you to be just as sad if I die as you were with Marianne."

I blinked. All the feeling in my hands vanished. That was not what I'd been expecting. Not in a million years. "Ravyn, I do care about you—"

"Then fucking show me," she snarled.

I cupped her face in both hands and kissed her. Not the peck she'd given me in the hotel room or even the gentle show of affection she probably needed at that moment. I snaked my tongue between her lips and one hand into her hair.

Ravyn immediately reacted with an embrace of her own, reaching beneath my shirt and raking her nails down my back. I groaned with the mixture of pleasure and pain, tightening my grasp around her hair. She broke our kiss, moving instead to nibble my lower lip and drag her nails over my sides.

I snatched the high hem of her dress, tearing it up and away from her body. For a moment of stunned silence, we stared at one another. Ravyn's features were a mixture of defiance and hunger, but I stole the opportunity to memorize exactly as she looked at that moment. Face flush with emotion, her ample chest heaving with rasped breaths, held in place by a black, lace-trimmed bra. The taut line of her stomach and curve of her waist belled into generous hips, where matching black panties strung over her thighs.

"Yeah, like that," Ravyn breathed. "Look at me just like that." She grabbed my jacket and threw it back over my shoulders, barely giving me time to react before she had my shirt pulled up to my armpits. When that joined my discarded jacket, she briefly touched the scars on my chest, her expression unreadable.

"Fuck, you're sexy," I murmured. I reached for another handful of her thick tendrils, yanking backward until her neck was exposed. Cupping her lower back with my free hand, I kissed her throat, then trailed my lips to her shoulder. "Do I have to play nice?"

"No," she chuckled under her breath, fingers searching for the fastening on my belt.

"Good." I bit deep into her sweet skin, living for the gasp that escaped her lips.

Her fingers abandoned their search for my pants, instead encircling my neck as she pressed her body against mine.

I moved inch by inch down the curve of her arm, leaving affectionate marks as I kissed, bit, and sucked at her flesh. Combing my fingers through her thick hair, I followed the slope of her back until I found the fastening of her bra. I prayed that I could actually do it with one hand as I set to work on the hooks with my mouth on her skin.

"Still new at that part, hm?" Ravyn teased. "Can't even unhook a fucking bra. This guy." She reached behind her and helped me unhook the garment, tossing it to the side and baring her chest.

"Jesus Christ. You have the nicest tits." I couldn't stop myself. Dark nipples accented two voluptuous breasts that pooled in my palms. Her flawless skin gleamed in the candlelight, the shadows of her form just as erotic as the highlights.

"Wow. You know just what to say to a lady," she sneered.

I pushed her backward toward a mostly free desk. She swept away the books resting on top with her tail, and they clattered to the floor. I grabbed her thighs and lifted her up until she sat on the edge of the desk with her feet dangling free, then pressed her shoulders so she lay flat on her back. Before she could say another word, I enveloped one nipple with my lips, teething and teasing with my tongue.

"*Ngh!* Fuck!" Ravyn shouted. Her tail wrapped around my back, the soft fur tickling my bare skin.

I hooked my thumb below the string of her panties, pulling them down to her thighs. The heat between her legs bloomed against my palm. Parting her slit with my forefinger and ring finger, I caressed her clit with delicate strokes of my middle finger.

Ravyn gasped. "Holy shit. You tease."

She grabbed my hair with both hands, forcing my lips back to hers and burying her tongue between them. I continued to massage her clit, gradually coaxing more heat and moisture from her body. With a small change in our positioning, I toyed with her breasts while I did so, leaving my lips affixed to hers.

"*Mmm,*" she moaned, her tongue vibrating with the sound. Her breathing quickened, and her cunt dripped with need.

I slid two fingers inside of her, and her hips bore down around my knuckles. Her grip tightened around my scalp, and her back arched against my hand. My erection throbbed painfully against my pants, begging to replace my fingers. *God damn it, it's getting harder to stop myself.*

"More," she breathed into me.

I added another finger. Ravyn was so slick, and her body so readily willing that I added a fourth. Her tail tightly wrapped around my waist, and her hips bucked against my palm. I fit my thumb into the groove of her clit, shifted my mouth to her breast, and my hand to stroke her tail.

Ravyn's thighs quivered, and her audible breathing filled the room. The heels of her shoes clicked against the desk each time she rocked her hips, punctuating the slick sound of my fingers between her legs.

"Fuck, Matt. That's so good," she whimpered.

I committed those five words and the sound of her voice as she spoke them to memory. I'd never seen or heard a more vulnerable Ravyn in all of our travels together. I understood that this was something precious, and I didn't know if I'd see it again.

"I'm coming!" her voice peaked with her apex. Her cries echoed against the walls, and her grip tightened against my scalp as she brought her knees to her chest. She convulsed around my fingers as I shoved them as deep as her body would allow, biting the top of her breast and gripping her tail.

I pushed her climax for as long as I could, waiting for the throbs to slow before drawing my fingers and mouth away from her. She wrapped her arms around my neck and guided her mouth to mine. It was a far more tender embrace than we'd started with, and it took my breath away.

But, when I drew back, there was palpable doubt on her face.

Ravyn sat up and turned her back to me, crossing one arm over her chest to hold the other at the elbow. Her hair fell over her shoulders, and she stared at the floor.

"Matt... I... Look. I'm sorry." She shook her head and stood, yanking her underwear up over her hips. "I need to be alone right now."

She may as well have kicked me in the balls. The pain was pretty damn similar. "Ravyn?"

"I'm sorry." She picked up her bra and refastened it around her chest before fishing her dress from the pile. "I just... I don't know."

I had no idea what to do. What to feel. *Cock-blocked, for starters.* But I couldn't bring myself to be angry with her. The last thing I wanted her to think was that this was a mistake. So, I picked up my shirt and jacket and redressed. "Hey. It's alright." *Holy shit. This feels like death.* "I'll come check on you later, okay?"

"Sure. Thanks." Ravyn disappeared into the depths of her mountain home and closed the bedroom door behind her, leaving me alone in the main hall.

I wiped my hand on my jeans as I left Ravyn's place. My head throbbed as if I had whiplash, which wasn't exactly far from the truth. The sun was just setting over the horizon, and I pondered what to do next.

Ravyn's bliss-filled moans reverberated in my ears with every step I took.

Ceres Pro Tip: Ni Island is like a dream! Everyone here is very kind and welcoming. I cannot wait to see more!

Side Quest

Ravyn's Fairytale

Ravyn flopped on Yomi's couch, stretching her legs and throwing her arms wide with a heavy sigh. "That Defiled was a fuck."

Yomi giggled, shuffling to the kitchen nearby. Her quaint house didn't offer much in the way of wiggle room, but it was more comfortable than Ravyn's two-room cabin down the road. Cleaner, too. Ravyn couldn't remember the last time she'd bothered to pick her place up. They were always so damn busy. Glancing at Yomi's spotless surfaces and polished trinkets, Ravyn wondered where the hell her best friend had found the time to clean.

"It *was* pretty difficult," Yomi agreed. She dug through the cabinet reserved for wine and harder liquor, procuring a bottle she'd been waiting to open for some time. "But Finn really held his weight in that fight."

Ravyn allowed her head to loll to the side, rolling her eyes the rest of the way to see Yomi. "I didn't realize [Chemist]'s bombs did so much fucking damage."

"Imagine that. You were the one trying to convince him to pick another Class," Yomi teased.

"Yeah, well, we can't all be perfect [Acolyte]s," Ravyn quipped in return.

Yomi poured two goblets full and made her way to Ravyn's side. After passing one of the cups, Yomi snatched one of the pillows from beneath Ravyn's legs and set it on the floor.

"*Kuso!* I was using that!" Ravyn snapped.

Yomi gracefully perched on the cushion and wriggled her hips to add insult to injury. "You took the whole couch, and I need somewhere to sit, Princess. This one's mine." Holding up her cup, she grinned. "A toast. To the victories of Nyarela's best trio."

Ravyn carefully balanced her wine as she moved to a sitting position, then tapped her goblet to Yomi's. "Cheers."

They each drank deeply, and Ravyn recalled her conversation with Finn a few weeks before. She fingered the serpent ring around her finger and frowned. "I'm glad it'll be over soon."

Yomi tilted her head, her ears flicking forward with interest. "What do you mean?"

I have to tell her. We can't leave her in the dark. Ravyn inhaled deeply, then squared her shoulders. "Finn promised he'd run away with me. That we'd leave all this roachshit behind."

Just as she lifted her glass to her lips, Yomi froze. Her dual-toned gaze measured Ravyn carefully, and she slowly lowered her goblet. "You can't be serious."

"I couldn't be *more* serious," Ravyn snapped. "I'm tired of this shit, and so is he. Haven't you been listening when he talks about where he used to live? Two people would fall in love, and that was it. No sharing, no fighting, no nothing."

"Of course I've listened. But, Ravyn, that was *his* world, and this is *ours*." Yomi set her goblet to the side and smoothed her skirts over her lap. "Putting my feelings on this aside for a moment, you know the laws of Nyarela prohibit a man from shirking on his duties."

Ravyn drank and rolled her eyes. "Sure, if he gets caught."

"They'll put a bounty on him, Ravyn. And on you. I've read a lot of history books that detail men attempting to abandon their roles. The Queen's Guard has a way of making the girls who help them do so disappear."

"How would they know I'm with him? Would you give me away? After everything we've been through?" Rage bubbled in Ravyn's stomach. Would her closest friend really betray her? Why? Just to have the last laugh?

"I would never. But you'll need food at some point. And somewhere to stay, surely, while you figure out where you're going to go. Anyone could see you and spread the word." Yomi stared at her hands and lowered her voice. "You're being insanely selfish."

"You have no idea how I feel," Ravyn snarled. "About Finn, about you, about anything."

"I love Finn too, you know," Yomi continued. "I know he cares about you more, and it hurts like hell. But stealing him away from what he's meant to do? Hiding away in the hopes that the guard doesn't find you? Are you insane?"

Ravyn drained her still-full glass, then hissed through her teeth. "Maybe I am. Maybe he is, too. It doesn't matter."

"None of us are even Second Classes yet. How do you plan on defeating the Defiled and Encroachers you run into with just the two of you?"

"We'll just avoid them," Ravyn replied curtly. "No reason to fucking fight them anymore."

"Because avoiding them has always worked." Yomi sneered. "If I recall correctly, you nearly got all of us killed trying to 'avoid them' more than once."

"*Baka!* I've gotten better with that!"

"And when you do mess up? What then? You both get beaten to bloody pulps and live happily ever after?"

Ravyn bristled. "That's just it! We shouldn't have to keep doing the same thing over and over again. Take on Defiled, wait for Finn to come home after bedding however many girls, run dumbass errands for the Guild Hall for a pittance. Eat, sleep, rinse, and repeat." The alcohol mingled with the hot anger flowing beneath her skin. "It's not fucking fair!"

Yomi watched and listened with equal intensity.

More emotions than Ravyn could name crossed her features, but what did it matter? She wouldn't have to live beneath the [Acolyte]'s judgment forever.

Yomi finally spoke. "You're living in a fantasy, Ravyn. What you perceive as 'unfair' is based on nothing more than the fairytales that Finn tells us."

"They're not fairytales!" Ravyn sputtered.

"As far as we're concerned, yes, they are!" Yomi snapped. "He could be making them up, and we would have no way to prove it either way. They're stories with rules different from Nyarlea's. Dangerous rules. And you're counting on them working. Like a kitten making wishes on a rabbit."

"Oh, fuck you, Yomi!" Ravyn's rage bubbled over her tongue, and she found herself chucking her empty goblet at Yomi.

Yomi swatted the cup out of the air, and it hit the floor with a loud clang before rolling to a far-off corner. "Look, could you not think of yourself for ten seconds? Think about Finn. Was this his suggestion or yours?"

Ravyn narrowed her eyes and remained silent. *Let her believe it's me.*

"I had a feeling," Yomi said, stealing another drink from her goblet. "And what about the rest of the girls on our island that need protection? If you steal him away, our population could die off with him gone."

"You don't know that."

"What if he lives for thirty more years? Forty? What if he dies tomorrow, and we have to wait ages for another man to appear? You're putting the entire island at stake just to do what you want."

"I don't have to listen to this," Ravyn growled and stood. "I thought if anyone would understand, it'd be you. But I guess I can't even count on my best friend."

Yomi shot to her feet and stepped in Ravyn's path. Despite the top of her head barely reaching Ravyn's nose, she locked her gaze. "Ravyn, please. You can't do this."

"Oh? Can't I?"

"You *shouldn't* do this, then. Just think about it. You know I'm right."

Ravyn shouldered her aside and stormed out of the living room. What the hell did Yomi know, anyway? Even though Ravyn knew that Yomi also had feelings for Finn, she'd never expected her best friend to be so goddess-damned jealous of them leaving. Why couldn't Yomi see that this was the only way to break the cycle?

The only way to actually stay with Finn.

It was late by the time Finn returned home—sometime past three in the morning. He desperately wanted to wash the perfumed scent of the last catgirl he'd shared a bed with from his skin.

More often than not, he'd been sleeping at Ravyn's house in the comfort of her embrace, but he didn't want to wake her tonight.

Ravyn.

Ever since Ravyn had agreed to run away together, it was all he could think about. A quiet life with her at his side was a dream come true. But there were questions that continued to plague him, and there was only one person—well, digital person—he could think to discreetly ask.

After a long, hot shower, he summoned his iPaw and lit an oil lamp. "Hey, Ai, you there?"

The sapphire-haired catgirl appeared, dressed in her usual high-collared dress with her long hair tied back. "I am always here, [User Finnegan]."

Finn flinched. He'd gotten so used to hearing Ravyn and Yomi call him Finn that his full name sounded fake. "A man's duty in Nyarlea is to protect and procreate his assigned island, right?" She'd told him as much before, but it was the first thing he needed to make sure of. He slid into a chair at the small table in his living room and propped the iPaw at an angle to avoid the oil lamp's glare.

Ai blinked. "Yes."

"So, what happens if he were to, say, stop the protecting part? And maybe slow down the procreation?"

"I do not understand what you ask," Ai replied, ever monotone.

Finn scratched his head and sighed. "What if, hypothetically, a man chooses to live with just one girl? And not fight the Defiled or the Encroachers anymore?"

"That is ill-advised, [User Finnegan]. Such a man would be in violation of Nyarlean Law."

"Right. But, like, what would happen?"

Ai frowned. "Should a man be reported missing or abstaining from his duties, the Queen's Guard would be summoned to recall and rehabilitate him."

Rehabilitate? Finn's mouth went dry. He took a deep breath before asking, "What about the girl living with him?"

Ai slowly shook her head. "You have now mentioned a catgirl accomplice twice. I assure you, a Nyarlean citizen would not partake in such an offense."

"And if she did?"

Ai paused, blinking as if trying to comprehend the question.

"The Queen's Guard would apprehend her. She would be judged accordingly."

Ravyn? Arrested? Finn set the iPaw down on the table and leaned back in his chair. What would they do with her? What would they do with *him?*

"Have I answered your questions adequately, [User Finnegan]?"

"Yes. Thanks, Ai," Finn murmured.

"You are welcome." She vanished, and the screen went dark.

Finn watched the lamplight dance on the ceiling and let his hands fall to his sides.

What should I do?

Ravyn...

Yomi Pro Tip: Ravyn, why can't you understand that I just want to help you?

Chapter 16

The Big Chill

Ravyn's words lingered in my ears as a whirlwind of emotions and what-if scenarios clouded my thoughts. I still intended to visit her later, just to make sure she was alright. Even if I did, there wasn't any guarantee she would answer her door. But the last thing I wanted between us was friction.

To be honest, I was at a total loss for what to do.

No matter what I came up with, a nagging voice in the back of my head continued to bombard me with the notion that our relationship would never be the same after this.

That voice grew louder and louder during my walk back to the village, and I was struggling to quiet it. Ravyn had always been so reliable and levelheaded. Snarky, bit of a foul mouth, and a short temper—a little petulant maybe—but reliable. A lot of times, the words she shared with us weren't the best, and the delivery wasn't kind. However, I was quickly learning that there was a big difference between what I needed to hear and what I wanted to hear.

If not for Ravyn, I'm not sure I would've been able to handle what Yomi did. It was thanks to her that I could sleep at night, knowing that it would never happen again. She'd had gone the extra mile whenever possible. When we needed money, it was Ravyn who stepped in. If there was a complicated issue, Ravyn was often the one to provide the solution. Hell, when Cannoli fed her pan to a roach, Ravyn was the first in line to replace it.

I felt for the ring around my ear. My face grew hot as I recollected the day she pierced it. She had a strange way of showing she cared. At times it felt like my mother was scolding me—and I was beginning to wonder if she'd ever depend on me the way we depended on her.

With everything she'd been through, I imagined it wasn't that easy for her. Still, if this encounter had shown me anything, Ravyn was trying to let herself open up again.

Maybe it really just was a matter of time.

My head was starting to hurt, and it wouldn't do me a lot of good to dwell on things I couldn't change at the moment. Plus, anything I could use to escape the feeling of Ravyn's soft skin under my fingers was a boon.

Damn it, man. Concentrate.

I decided to seek out whatever distraction was available.

Make a list.

I wanted to know what had happened on Ni Island since I'd left, and I still had to speak to Espada about getting some new gear. The latter, I'm sure, was close to shutting down for the day, but she always seemed readily available to shoot the shit. Not to mention, Saphira had completely blindsided me in the market square.

I really do need to pay her a visit soon. Maybe she'd enjoy some intimacy? Fuck, Kelmer, you sound as desperate as when you first got here.

Ravyn aside, it was hard to get my head straight. I was frustrated beyond belief, and I found myself teeter-tottering between whether I should just take a girl to bed or continue my trek through the village. I settled on the latter.

"Hey, Matt!" Tristan stood a few feet from Espada's shop and waved me over. Ara was standing a few paces behind him, a rare smile on her face.

"Heya," I said with a casual wave. "Get a good tour of the island?"

"I think so." Tristan beckoned Ara over with a hand. The maid took to her master's side with a curt nod. "I love how friendly everyone is."

"A little too friendly. Many of these girls do not know how to keep their hands to themselves," Ara noted.

"Ah, you've met the welcoming committee," I said with a chuckle. "You won't be stepping on my toes if you'd like to get more acquainted with them."

Ara raised a brow.

"A-ah," Tristan said, suddenly uncomfortable. He blushed and ran a hand through his hair. "Okay, I'll keep that in mind. Thanks. But anyway! The Espada I read about is the very same one! It's her!"

Well, I'll be. Queen's Guard? Who would've thought?

"You're sure?" I asked, slipping my hands into my pockets. The sound of clanging metal rang through my ears. My gaze veered off to the lone blacksmith who seemed to be burning the last drops of daylight hard at work on something. A thin sheen of sweat covered her entire body, her muscles tensing with each swing of her hammer. I couldn't tell what she was working on from where I was standing. "Kinda pictured the guard being a little more, I dunno, eloquently spoken."

The ears atop Espada's head twitched, and I caught her glancing in my direction. She glared before returning to her work.

"Absolutely! The hair, her height, the scar on her face, how she carries herself! She fits the bill! She's the one and only!" Tristan spoke with the fervor of a young boy who'd discovered that his role model was as true as the rumors claimed. There was a sparkle in his eye. He extended his index finger and drew closer as he spoke. Felt like I was back in college with an overtuned professor. "She's so powerful, and she looks so dependable!"

"Wonder why she ended up here," I said, half-interested.

"I have a few working theories, but I didn't want to bother her. She looks really busy."

"And we're about to add to her honey-do list." I shuffled past Tristan and Ara, up to Espada's counter. "Hey, Espada. Long time no see."

The blacksmith glanced our way, then turned back around. "Did you break something again?"

Ow. Just my pride. "You've got to work on your customer service. I'm not feeling very welcome in this establishment." I crossed my arms over my chest and grinned.

Espada sighed, turned around, and then approached the counter, resting her palms on its surface and leaning forward. She was clearly not in a joking mood. "Make it quick. The gear behind me is hot. Start talking before I charge you a hundred Bells a minute."

"Just a few seconds. I'll need to get my armor checked and a new shield made." I pointed toward Ceres. "A new member of my Party also needs to be measured and outfitted for armor. Got time in the next week for me?"

"I do. Your armor's leather, though, yeah?" I nodded. "I got a friend coming into town tomorrow. She's a pro with leather. Let her look over yours, and I'll get your new girl's measurements in the afternoon. You got the ore for a shield?"

I shook my head. "Not yet, but I can get that to you."

"I'll need a couple days to make it once you get it here. But I can sneak you into my schedule."

She's being awfully compliant. My lucky day? "Thanks a ton, Espada. I have the money, so don't worry."

"Of course." Espada put her gloves back on and waved me away. "Don't be a stranger, Matt."

I returned to Tristan and Ara. Keke, Cannoli, and Ceres had joined them now, and the picture of them happily chatting with one another brought a smile to my face.

"Hey. How do you like Ni Island?" I asked Ceres.

Ceres's eyes lit up, and her mouth hung slightly agape. "My lord! This island is breathtaking! Every detail about it, from the crisp scents of the ocean to the luscious forests that take root under our very feet!" Ceres tapped the ground with one foot to emphasize her exuberance. "I had no idea you hailed from such a beautiful land!"

"*Ahaha.* Well, I'm glad you like it. Ni Island is—"

"And the boats!" Ceres huffed. She clapped her hands to her mouth. "I am so sorry, my lord. I cut you off and continued on without consideration for you." She bowed at the waist. "My sincerest apologies."

"It's fine," I said, shaking my head. "It might not have the trade or grandeur of some of the other islands, but it's home. I wouldn't trade it for anything."

Keke and Cannoli flashed toothy grins. I smiled back.

"Oh, that reminds me!" Cannoli exclaimed. "There's a wandering minstrel coming into town later tonight."

"What's she like?"

"A little on the stranger side," Keke said with a shrug. "But what [Wizard] isn't?"

I frowned. "She's not a specific [Bard] Class or anything like that?"

Cannoli giggled. "Of course not." Then her mouth hung open as she thought about it. "That would be so neat! Someone who sings on a battlefield!"

Ara rolled her eyes. "Please. What a ridiculous notion. In what world would music be a proper tool in combat?"

"I've heard some awful, ear-bleeding sounds off of violins," I argued, "so there's always a possibility."

"She does do something pretty unique, though. Her music doesn't sound like most others. There's a rumor going around that she's completely changing how other minstrels perform," Keke said.

"How so?"

"Are you talking about Iggy, the Wandering Bard?" Tristan asked.

A number of confused expressions bore down upon Tristan.

Is there anything this guy doesn't know about? How does a dude who's locked up in a room for years know more about the world than I do?

"Young master has exceptional knowledge of multiple subjects. You would do well to listen." Ara chuckled and rested the fingers of one hand over her lips, her affectionate gaze doting on Tristan like a proud mother.

Keke giggled and folded her arms. "Well, you seem to know all about her. Why don't you tell us then?"

Tristan frowned, and a pink hue decorated his cheeks. "Well, from what I've read about her, you either love her, or you hate her. Her music sounds a lot like, ah—" Tristan looked to me, "like an electric guitar. One of the men from another island wrote an article on her. She's picked up on a lot of rock somehow."

"An electric guitar in Nyarlea?" I wondered aloud. The ice cream shop in Venicia had made sense with magic. But magnifying the sound of an instrument? "How would you even do that without an amp?"

Tristan shrugged. "I don't know. Obviously, I've never seen her myself." He chuckled, then cleared his throat when Ara turned her head. "A-apparently she's a natural [Wizard]. Incredible electrical magic."

"Electrical?" Cannoli asked aloud as if pondering the question herself.

"Lightning, thunder," I explained. "It went by a few other names in our old world."

But damn. If she can put out rock music on a magic guitar? I'd pay to see that.

"Well, she'll be performing here later tonight. Why don't we all go?" Keke suggested.

"I would love to!" Cannoli said.

"I am very curious to see it in action," Tristan agreed.

"Well, I suppose we are deserving of a short vacation." Ara shrugged.

"I welcome the opportunity to learn from fellow spell crafters," Ceres said, clutching her fists to her chest. "I wholeheartedly agree that a respite is in order as well."

"Then it's settled. We'll drink, party, and sing the night away."

Ravyn's potential retorts to the idea, along with her sardonic smile, rushed through my head as soon as the words left my mouth. But the smiles on the others' faces and cheers from Ceres and Cannoli said I'd made the right decision.

Just welcome the distraction for now, Matt. Everything else can come later.

Ara Pro Tip: Have these girls never learned how to properly set a table? Ni is quant, but I find the etiquette lacking.

Chapter 17

Wild Guitar

The sounds emitting from the Junonia Inn were akin to the concerts back in my last world. Cheers, shouts, bottles clinking together, and the unmistakable twangs of a guitar.

Cannoli bounced between her feet, her hands balled at her chin. "Oooh, Iggy sounds so good! Let's go inside! Please?" she begged.

"Of course." I nodded and led the charge through the door.

When Cannoli had mentioned a performer in the city, I'd expected a lot of different things. A lute player in the quiet corner of a bar strumming ballads about love and loss. Maybe a girl who played pipe flutes or drums. Possibly a dancer. Even with Tristan's musings of an electric guitar in Nyarlea, what awaited us inside was a different beast entirely.

It seemed like the whole of Ni Island had gathered to see Iggy perform. All tables and chairs had been removed from the main hall, replaced instead by the twitching, dancing feet of at least a hundred catgirls crammed into one tavern. At the far back was a makeshift stage, and on it jammed the star of the show.

Iggy's flailing, shoulder-length hair swung in a rainbow of strands around her cheeks and chin as she rocked her head back and forth in time with the music. Her ears were decked out with various rings and studs, and when I did catch a glimpse of her face, a sparkle in her nose suggested a nose piercing.

Her outfit was still nautical-themed like the rest of the girls on her island, but the ebony cloth with blood-red accents was a stark contrast to the lighter colors that Keke and Cannoli usually wore. Bracelets clanged and clattered around her fishnet gloves, and ripped fishnet stockings covered her legs and disappeared inside calf-high boots.

In her hands, she gripped a guitar that had a bizarre shape to the body but a similar neck to those where I'd come from. It was definitely influenced by someone from my world; that much was certain. But the slick, red, chaotically curved base was something of a Nyarlean variety.

"*...And then you'll wonder, what, I wonder?*" Iggy sang, her voice harmonizing perfectly to the chords she played. "*When we hear thunder, where do we hide; go under?*"

Tristan had explained it perfectly. Visible threads of electricity flowed from her fingers to the strings, illuminating her guitar and blasting the sound from wall to wall of the inn. Girls in the crowd jumped in time to the music, some with bright magic glowing on the edges of their fingertips—a lot like glowsticks.

It felt loud and familiar, and the tension quickly vanished from my shoulders.

"This is crazy!" I yelled.

"What?" Keke yelled back.

Yeah, should have expected as much. I laughed, then pushed my way through the crowd until I found the bar.

With drinks in hand and smiles all around—even Ara, if you'd believe it—we danced and swayed in time to the sharp, rhythmic beats of Iggy's guitar. At least a handful of girls in the crowd knew her lyrics and sang along. Keke maneuvered her way in front of me, pressing her hips back into mine, and swung them in time to the music.

Keke, this is not helping the mood.

But a wicked glance over her shoulder said she knew.

After we'd enjoyed more drinks than we should have and more music than I'd heard in a long time, Iggy announced her set was over and, if any were able, that she'd be taking donations at center stage.

"I'm gonna give her some Bells," I announced, then handed Keke my cup. "Can you hold that for me?"

"Sure," Keke giggled. "Here, add this to the pool." She passed her own mug to Cannoli and reached into her [Cat Pack], tugging a sack of Bells free and handing it to me.

"Wait! I want to give her some, too!" Cannoli handed her empty cup to Ara.

The cycle continued until Tristan and Ceres were balancing an equal number of wooden tankards in the crooks of their arms and palms of their hands, and I was in a similar situation with the bags of Bells.

"Great. We'll collectively pay her rent for a year," I laughed. "Thanks, guys."

I hauled my dragon's hoard of Bells to the front stage, carefully avoiding the other girls pitching in or passing by. When I finally reached it, Iggy was sitting next to her guitar case, holding a small basket in both hands and looking eagerly from face to face with shining eyes and a slight frown. To my surprise, the basket was pretty damn empty.

She was even cuter up close. Music-themed tattoos peppered her arms, and her bracelets clinked around her wrists when she moved.

"Hey. Great show," I said, fumbling with the multiple bags of Bells to carefully aim them into her basket. "Got a few extra for you."

Iggy's amber eyes lit up at the sight of all of the bags, but she quickly shook her technicolor head and cleared her throat. "Oh, uh, thanks."

I shoveled each bag into her basket and smiled. "I didn't think rock music had made its way to Nyarlea. Where did you learn?"

Her gaze shifted to the left, then the right. "Well, my dad," she replied gruffly.

Is she hiding her real voice? "He has good taste."

"Right?" Iggy's façade broke for a split second, her voice shooting up an octave and a smile breaking on her dark lips. She clapped a hand over her mouth and dodged my gaze, her pierced ears lowering over her hair. "W-what I meant is, yeah, he did have good taste. Before he died, that is."

"Sorry to hear it." *Man, the future's looking pretty damn bleak for me.* I offloaded the last bag and stretched my arms. "Anyway, thanks for the concert. Really. I'm sure everyone here could use a break, and this was a good one."

As I turned to leave, Iggy shot to her hands and knees and grabbed the sleeve of my jacket. "Wait! Y-you're this island's man, right?"

I paused, then slowly turned back to face her. "Yeah, that's me."

"What's your name?"

"Matt." I looked at the hand holding my jacket. "Nice to meet you."

"Iggy." Her pale features turned bright pink, and she released my sleeve. "Matt, could we, um," her voice dropped, and she said something inaudible.

"What?" I had a feeling that I knew what she wanted, but Keke's hips grinding against mine were still at the forefront of my mind. Not to mention Ravyn's sighs still tearing me apart at the seams.

Iggy reset her jaw and locked my gaze. "Spend the night with me," she said, suddenly in control of the situation. "That's your job, right? As the island's man?"

I chuckled. "I guess it is, huh?" Glancing over my shoulder, I tried to spot my group in the crowd without success. "Yeah, we can do that. I'll be right back, alright?"

"Oh! O-okay!" Iggy stammered, clutching the basket close to her chest.

Don't look so surprised, Iggy.

I found my way back to my Party and found an alcohol-flushed Tristan snickering to Ara. Ara clutched Ceres's sleeve and silently pleaded for help.

Keke giggled and placed a hand on my chest. "So, back home?" she asked.

I rubbed the back of my neck and gritted my teeth. "Sorry, duty calls."

Keke's ears fell, and her lower lip jutted forward in a pout. "Really?"

With a quick nod, I ruffled her hair. My heart could only take so much pulling for one night. "Really. I'll find you in the morning, okay?"

"Fiiiiine," she drew out the word as long as possible and rolled her eyes. "You owe me."

"I do. And Cannoli. And probably Ceres. But here we are."

Keke snickered and kissed my cheek. "Be safe, Matt."

"Yeah. Will do."

"My lord, should you need me," Ceres began, bowing deeply. She'd disposed of the empty mugs sometime between my conversation with Iggy and returning.

Does booze do nothing to you? "I'm sure I'll be fine—"

"You need only call," she finished cryptically. "Please."

Is she going to wait outside the window or something? "Of course. Thanks, Ceres."

Before anyone else could utter thinly veiled, stalkerish promises, I found my way back to Iggy. She'd packed up her guitar, and it seemed those who were willing to give her tips had already done so.

"Damn, pack a house and still don't get paid what you're worth, huh?" I asked. *Feel like I should give her more Bells.*

Iggy shrugged. "Some nights are better than others. Your donation will keep me eating for a long while," she laughed under her breath, then caught herself. "I-I mean, I'm fine. My music will carry me where I need to go." She hopped off of the stage and then lowered her voice. "And serving tables will carry me the rest of the way."

I chuckled. "Hey, I get it. I've been there."

"Yeah?" She led the way to the innkeeper.

"For a long time. Working tables sucks."

Iggy glanced over her shoulder. "Glad I'm not alone."

My gaze slid from her hair to her hips. Holy shit, did she have nice hips. Her skirt flared over a voluptuous backside and well-framed thighs. The diamond shapes on the fishnets cast delicious shadows on her skin, and I felt my thoughts drift once more.

It was my turn to blush. Thankfully, my embarrassment was saved when the innkeeper rounded the bar. I promptly paid for a night in their rooms, and we made our way upstairs.

"Do you want me to carry something?" I asked.

Iggy laughed. "No. I'm good."

"So, you don't make enough to live on with your music?" I asked, trying to break the distraction of Iggy's legs.

She shrugged. "Just barely. I wish I could say I was doing this full-time, but I'm not. Have you been to Nautilus?"

I coughed. *Is that on Ni?* "...No."

"Really?" Iggy laughed—a real, unmasked sound that bounced off the walls and rang in my ears. It was adorable. She shifted her guitar case in her hands and the basket beneath her arm. "It's about half a day's walk from here. You must be pretty new to Ni."

"Yeah, I am," I admitted.

"Well, I work the tavern in Nautilus. That's where I really earn my keep right now."

"And you'll be okay with a kid?" The words escaped my mouth before I could think about it. This world wasn't the same—not by a long shot. But I didn't want Iggy to take on more than she could.

"Of course I will be. Why wouldn't I?" Iggy glanced over her shoulder. "There's plenty of nyannies in Nautilus."

Nyannies. That's right. "Right. Sorry."

We arrived at our room, and Iggy shoved the key into the door handle. Reshuffling her things in her arms, she stared at the number on the door and paused.

"Here, let me." I opened the door and held it for her.

"T-thanks," she murmured, hurrying into the room and setting her case down before placing the basket on the small writing desk opposite the bed. "Jeez, I know I shouldn't be so nervous. This is silly."

Lucky for her, I was beyond nerves. After the fiasco with Ravyn and Keke's constant teasing, I was way past the awkward phase of a first meeting. I closed the door and moved behind her at the desk. I slowly wrapped one arm around her waist and the other across her chest.

A small, surprised gasp escaped her lips, but her petite form warmed, and she leaned into me. I nibbled the edge of her ear, just above the piercings, and her fingers dug into my thighs.

"Wait. No one can know that I'm like this," she said in a waterfall of words. "I-I have an image to maintain—"

"Whatever happens here stays here," I reassured her. *Did you just steal that line from Vegas, Kelmer?*

"Promise?" she whimpered as I traced the warm curve of her ear with my tongue.

"Promise."

I held her tighter and moved the hand nearest her chest to her throat. "If you don't like something, just tell me to stop. Okay?" I murmured.

"Okay," she breathed.

I lifted the hem of her shirt and slid my hand over her taut stomach. Her skin was searing hot, and her body twitched with the movement of my fingertips. I tilted her chin and continued to toy with her ears, sucking on the piercings and nibbling the soft skin and fur in between.

Since I hadn't really tried touching a catgirl's ears before, I had to know. "Does this feel good?"

"Yes," she murmured, one arm wrapping around the back of my neck. "That feels *really* good."

"Good." I walked my fingers up her torso, grasping her petite breast and kneading it between my fingers.

A soft moan escaped her lips, and she ground her hips down harder against mine.

I noticed a large, oval-shaped mirror on top of what I had thought was a desk. Realizing the furniture piece was a vanity, I lifted my hand from Iggy's waist in favor of tilting her chin upward.

"Look at me," I murmured.

Iggy blinked, suddenly noticing the same. Her cheeks turned a brilliant red, and she chewed her lower lip. "That's embarrassing," she whispered and slammed her eyes shut.

"Is it?" I asked, kissing the top of her head and nibbling the edge of her other ear. "I think it's pretty damn sexy."

The red deepened, and Iggy gasped. "Really?"

"Absolutely," I replied, switching my hand to her other breast and pulling down her bra. The soft nipple came free, hardening between my fingertips.

Iggy's head lolled back against my shoulder. She hooked her thumbs over the hem of her blood-red skirt and wriggled her hips until it fell to the floor. Lacey crimson panties curved around her generous hips, which caught my gaze in the mirror. She spread her feet apart by a few inches, offering me a better view. Her eyelids parted just enough to catch my stare, and a mischievous smile played at her lips.

"Someone really likes this," I noted.

"Yeah, well," Iggy replied, pulling away from me to slip her top over her head. "It's not like I knew that before." She tossed her shirt to the side and leaned forward on the vanity, resting her elbows on its surface and glancing at me over her shoulder.

More tattoos decorated her shoulders, back, and ribcage. A garnet bra matched her underwear, burning against her ivory skin.

"I'm not the only one who likes this," she mused, watching my eyes wander in the mirror.

"No, you're not," I murmured and kissed her shoulder. Then her spine, then her lower back. I wanted more of her. I *needed* more of her.

I quickly divested my own jacket and top, then added my pants to the pile of discarded clothing. Part of me was terrified that she'd stop us midway. Again. Enough to make me hesitate on the elastic of my boxers despite my throbbing erection.

"Waiting for something?" Iggy teased. Her lips curved into a smile in the mirror.

I smirked. "No." I tossed my boxers to the pile and slid her panties down her thighs. Whether it was the booze talking or my desperation, the truth fell off my tongue without my approval, "Damn, you have a really nice ass."

Iggy covered her mouth with one hand and giggled, her colorful hair falling over her shoulders. "Thanks," she said, the sound muffled behind her fingers.

I wanted to wipe that grin she was hiding from her face. I spanked her right ass cheek with the flat of my hand, watching as her smile reformed into a groan of pleasure. With another strike, her moans grew louder, and her fingernails raked across the surface of the vanity.

"Believe me now?" I growled.

"Yes," Iggy murmured. "Yes!"

I spread her thighs and positioned the head of my shaft at her opening, watching the realization slowly dawn on her face. She repositioned her forearms on the vanity, locking my gaze in the mirror.

"Do it," she whispered.

I slid inside her, gasping at the immediate clench of heat that surrounded me. Her hips kissed mine, and I leaned forward, ensnaring her wrists and holding them down to the surface of the vanity. Her lips parted, and she fought for breath as her eyes rolled back.

"T-that's intense," she groaned. "*Ngh*... Matt, you feel so good."

I rolled my body against hers, and her fingers twitched as if seeking something to take hold of. Her head tipped forward, then resurfaced as her eyes wildly searched out mine in the reflection.

"D-do I feel good?" she asked.

"God, yes," I admitted, chancing another thrust deep inside of her. Just the twitches of her body threatened to bring me over the edge. I was too damn sensitive—it was almost as bad as the first time Keke had touched me. "Too good, honestly."

"Are you close already?" Iggy panted, resting her forehead on top of my left hand.

Did I lie? No, that wasn't fair. "Yes."

She tipped her chin to the side and found my eyes in the mirror. "Can you go again?"

I'd never been able to before. But right now? After everything I'd endured just that evening? "Probably."

"Then come," she encouraged.

I wasn't about to decline that particular invitation. I moved my hands from her wrists to her hips, digging my thumbs into her backside and my fingertips into the dips of her abdomen. Holding her against the vanity, I thrust my frustrations into her like a man possessed. She dug her fingernails into the surface and moaned with me, her body more yielding with every advance.

"I can't hold it," I groaned.

"Come in me, then," Iggy replied, leaning backward and wrapping one arm around the back of my neck.

I sank my teeth into her shoulder and orgasmed, letting the pleasure roll over me like a wave from head to foot. Gasps mixed with moans caught in my throat, and strained, high-pitched squeals sounded from Iggy's lips. Her thighs trembled against mine, and still, she hung on to my neck and reached her free hand around her back.

Resting her hand on her backside, she pried the cheeks open and chewed her lower lip. Her eyes dipped to the vanity's surface, then back to mine. "O-only i-if you want to."

To my surprise, I very, very much did want to. I drew away from her dripping cunt and repositioned my still-stiff shaft against the pucker of her backside. "Yeah?"

"Yes. Please," she gasped.

The slick fluids of our mixed sexes guided me into a depth I'd yet to explore. And her relaxed acceptance of my cock stole the air from my lungs. "You're so fucking tight," I gasped. *And so soft. And Jesus Christ, I can hardly move.*

"*Hah– Hmn...*" The only words to escape Iggy were sounds. She wriggled her hips against mine, then moved one arm down between her legs, her fingers disappearing between her slit. "Matt. Go hard. Please."

My nails still digging into her flesh, I penetrated her over and over again, relentlessly bucking my hips against hers. The desperate noises she made stroked my skin and dragged me closer to another orgasm. I spanked her again and drank in the carnal cry that escaped her while I memorized her face in the mirror.

"I'm gonna come!" Iggy cried at the top of her voice.

"Come," I demanded, finding myself at the peak of another climax.

A handful of desperate gasps filled the space between her warning and her body clenching around mine. A second climax washed over me, and another blissful moan tore from my throat, blending in with hers.

We gasped in tandem and waited for our throbbing to slow. Sweat glistened from every inch of our skin. I kissed Iggy's spine, her shoulder, then nibbled her ear. She shivered. I drew away from her and guided her back to standing.

"So, when are you coming back to Junonia?" I asked, curling her hair around my fingers.

"What, I can't stay here with you?" Iggy teased, then quickly added, "I'm joking. I'm honestly not sure."

"Then I'll have to come to Nautilus," I replied, stroking her bangs away from her face. "I'm going to take care of this island, Iggy. I promise."

"Good. Someone needs to." She turned away from the mirror and buried her face into my shoulder. "For now, though, can we just be close to each other?"

I chuckled. "Of course. We've got all night, after all."
"Thanks, Matt."

Cannoli Pro Tip: That was so much fun! Can we see Iggy again sometime? Or another musician? I love dancing!

Chapter 18
Errand Boy

New Notifications!

Quest Updated!

[A Little of What You Fancy Does You Good] 5/5 Catgirls Successful!

Quest Complete!

Matt has gained: 486 XP!
Matt is now: Base Level 9!
Matt is now: Class Level 9!
Matt has gained: 500 Bells!

Please allow up to one full day to receive your funds.

New Quest!
[The More the Merrier]
Congratulations on mating with 5 catgirls! Nyarlea depends on you for its continued longevity! Successfully mate with 8 catgirls and reap the rewards!

Rewards
- 1 Base Level
- 1 Class Level
- 5,000 Bells

I was seated at the edge of Keke's bed, idly scrolling through the notifications on the iPaw. It fell out of my hands as I read the new rewards to myself in a whisper. It landed on the floor with a loud thud, and my mouth hung open.

"*Ahh!*" Keke shot up and put her hand on my bare shoulder. "Oh, Saoirse, you scared me. What's wrong, Matt?"

I scrambled for the device and quickly turned it off. Not like she could read it, anyway, but why take the chance? "Sorry about that. Butterfingers."

She frowned, obviously confused. "Butter—"

"Clumsy hands," I said with a forced smile. I rose to my feet and dismissed the iPaw. "I got a few things I need to take care of. Espada's given me a to-do list. There's a leatherworker in town today, too." I was quick to put on my shirt and jacket. I don't know what possessed me, but I was suddenly in the mood to get out of the room as soon as possible.

"Oh. Okay." Keke neared the edge of the bed, and a playful smile tugged at her features. "Will I see you later tonight?"

"Yeah. Think so." The comment wiped the smile away in an instant. "Sorry, just a lot to do. I'll be back soon. Gotta meet up with Ceres, too." I paused. "She's staying with Cannoli, right?"

Keke nodded. "Yeah."

"Great. I'll see you later." I shut Keke's door behind me and made my way over to Cannoli's house. I knocked on the door and took a deep breath.

What the hell was wrong with me?

Ceres answered, wearing a long nightgown with complex patterns embroidered into the fabric. It looked mighty expensive and accentuated her curves in that fun sort of way clothes do when fabric cascades over more prominent features.

I swallowed and averted my gaze, the new Quest still fresh in my mind. "Good morning."

"My lord!" Ceres said, delight in her voice. "It's so good to see you! I expect that you require my presence?"

I nodded. "Gotta get your measurements to Espada." When the thought of collecting ore by myself came to mind, a sudden idea accompanied it. "I need to go up to the mountain to get some ore afterward. Do you want to come with me?"

Her eyes widened. "I would be delighted!"

"Ceres, who's at the door?" Cannoli asked as she leaned against Ceres's shoulder, eyes shut, and her hair tangled over her face.

Can't even be bothered to open her eyes? How much did she drink last night?

Ceres smiled warmly and ran a hand through Cannoli's hair. "Lord Matt."

"Tell him I said hi and that I miss him," Cannoli said in a whisper that was barely audible. She spun awkwardly on her heel and stumbled back into the house. My heart skipped a beat.

"I shall do that. My lord, pray, give me but a moment to get dressed."

"Yeah. Take your time."

I couldn't calm down. My brain was all over the place. The promise of what felt like a damn fortune lingered in my mind's eye, taunting me. It's not like it was a difficult Quest, either. Could probably get it done in a week. Hell, Tristan could have finished it in a few days, from what it sounded like. Yet, I felt like my heart was being torn in two different directions. The sooner Ceres came out of that house, the better.

"My lord?" Ceres asked, breaking me out of my daydream. "Are you prepared?"

"Yeah. Let's get going."

Ceres curtsied. "Of course."

The process of getting Ceres's measurements was short and sweet. Espada had clearly done this hundreds, maybe thousands, of times at this point. Ceres's full measurements were scribbled down within minutes with a single elastic band and a pencil. The blacksmith scratched a series of numbers onto a sheet of old, yellowed paper, then set it under her counter.

Espada rolled and played with the pencil between her lips and teeth. I teetered on mentally checking out when she finally spoke. "Alright. Got a few good ideas. Going to need the ore though, Matt." She concluded her remark with a raised brow.

"I know. You'll have it. We're going to go collect it shortly." I turned my head but didn't see anyone different from the usual crowd. "You mentioned a leatherworker?"

"She's sleeping off her hangover from last night. It might be a while." Espada shrugged. "She's an unpredictable type."

Clearly not the business-savvy type either.

"That's fine. We're not leaving the island for a while." I turned my attention to Ceres. "Ready to go grab some ore?"

She wore a confident smile. "Yes, my lord!"

After packing the appropriate gear, Ceres and I took the path up to the mountains that I was familiar with. Occasionally, she would point out the stray Encroacher, pause to admire the view, or comment on the crisp scent of the ocean. I remained as attentive as possible, but couldn't bring myself to say much outside of curt answers.

"Appear, iPaw." The device fell into my hands, and I scrolled through the screen until I had the option to distribute my points.

"Has my lord made more progress?" Ceres asked, her hands resting in front of her.

"Yeah." I realized how short my responses had been coming off, then attempted to put on a better front. "I got a Level from last night."

Ceres tilted her head in thought. "My lord, that is wonderful to hear! Do the options for Skills and Stat Points vex you?"

I shook my head and laughed. "Nah, I feel like my path has been fairly straightforward so far. Hit harder, get tankier."

"'Tankier'?" Ceres asked, tilting her head.

"Tougher. Uh, so I can take more hits. Have more [Health Points]."

Ceres nodded. "Understandably. If I may be so bold to say, though, balance is also of the utmost importance."

I paused. Out of concern that I was suddenly doing something wrong, I pulled up Ceres's Stats and Skills on the iPaw.

Ceres

Base Level 13
Magic Knight Class Level 9
Base Experience: 3962/4275
Class Experience: 2011/2500
Health Points: 98/98
Myana Points: 73/73
Energy: 45/48
Strength: 3 +3
Vitality: 5
Dexterity: 2
Agility: 4
Magic: 3 +3
Resistance: 1 +1

Skills

Two-Handed Mastery 1
Polearm Mastery 1
Two-Sided 1
Invoke Mastery 1
Invoke Frost 1
Icicle Shard 1
Titan of Ice 1
Magic Armor 1

Now that I was looking at it, a lot of things were starting to make more sense. Her Stats and Skills were all over the place. I knew that some of the girls had mentioned that every Stat was important, but her capabilities felt like they were spread thin.

I thought back to the fight with the Defiled and wondered for a moment how [Two-Sided] worked. "Didn't you say your [Magic] Stat was higher?"

"Yes, my lord. I could feel my [Strength] leave me. Thus, there could not be a more appropriate time to use [Two-Sided]."

I wanted to check out the details on [Two-Sided], but I was quickly getting off-track. "Your Stats are all over the place. Why?"

"[Health Points] are useless without armor, my lord. [Strength] has no value if you can't land a hit. Conversely, [Dexterity] and [Agility] are of little use without proper application." Ceres took a deep breath and shut her eyes. She seemed to be thinking hard about something. When she opened them, they remained glued to the dirt path. "Tipping the scale is dangerous. Move forward too far in any direction, and you risk exploitation."

Maybe I was getting a big head, but I couldn't think of a situation where my [Agility] or [Dexterity] would've saved anyone. If anything, keeping the enemies distracted long enough had proven its worth time and time again.

"I think [Strength] and [Vitality] are the way to go." If I had better damage and I wasn't the only tank, then *maybe* I could consider other Stats. Ceres's presence might help to make that possible. But if their Stats remained how they were, then I was obviously the better pick to tank. "[Vitality] saved me from dying."

Ceres frowned. "I may be speaking out of turn. So, for that, I apologize. While I do not deny that your [Vitality] was a strong factor in determining your survival, it was also your decision to pass the entirety of the antidote to me." She drew a deep breath and looked up at me. "I would not have spared a moment to share the antidote with you had I known it was the only dose." Her fingers writhed. "No single entity, no single person is without flaw."

I felt like I was getting schooled again. Wasn't really in the mood for it. "I get it. Thanks."

She opened her mouth to speak, but only a sigh escaped her lips. "I understand, my lord. I apologize for my behavior. Shall we proceed?"

"Yeah. Let's do that. Disappear, iPaw."

Ceres was a quick study in [Mining]. She managed to teach me a few tricks along the way as well. After locating a few healthy helpings of iron, we descended the mountain just in time for the sun to set. Espada was closing up by the time we arrived.

I jogged over to her counter, out of breath. "Glad I caught you!" I opened my [Cat Pack] and put a few ores down on the counter. Ceres did the same.

To my surprise, Espada whistled. "I'm impressed, Matt. The two of you got all of this yourself?"

"We did," I breathed. "Is this enough to suit her up?"

Espada scanned over the helping of ore. Periodically she'd look back up, then reference the sheet on which she'd written Ceres's measurements. After about a minute or two, she smiled and nodded. "When do you need it done?"

I felt a huge weight lift off of my shoulders. "Just in the next week or two. We're going to be here for a while."

"Leave it to me." Espada swooped up the ores and piled them into a basket for safekeeping before departing into a back room. When she returned, she wiped the sweat off her forehead and cleaned her hands on her apron. "You're shapin' up nice, Matt. Keep up the good work."

I was elated to hear those words. Up until now, I was convinced Espada just dealt with me because she had to. I was beginning to see that she appreciated a person who was self-sufficient.

"Thanks, Espada. Really."

Ceres raised her hand. "Espada." Pink decorated her cheeks. "May I please request a design for the armor?"

Espada crossed her arms. "That's not a problem, but it'll be a bit extra."

"That is acceptable," Ceres said with a nod of her head. "I will require the night to design it. May I deliver it to you in the morning?"

Espada stifled a laugh. "Fine, fine. What about you, Matt?"

"Hm?"

"Still need your armor looked at? Quinn's available now." Espada pointed down the road where an extraordinarily petite catgirl with tanned skin and long, white hair was speaking with Saphira.

I tried to line my vision up with where Espada was pointing, convinced she was talking about someone else. "You're not talking about that super short girl, are you?"

"Don't let looks deceive you, Matt," Espada warned. "She's got more fight in her than I do."

That's impossible. "Alright. Guess I'll go talk with her."

Espada's hand caught my shoulder. "Good luck." She let me go with a wry smile, retreating into the back room.

"Do I have my lord's permission to retire?" Ceres asked.

"Yeah. I think I'll pay everyone a visit after I talk to Quinn. Thanks for coming along, Ceres."

Ceres bowed, walking off in the direction of Cannoli's home. I took a deep breath and made my way over to Saphira's stand. Her beautiful blue eyes caught me, and I felt a dopey grin tug at the corners of my mouth. I waved as I approached.

"Heya, Saphira. Excuse me," I said as I repositioned myself to face both her and Quinn. "Are you Quinn?"

"I'm busy here, can't you see that?" Quinn snapped.

Saphira smiled, but even I could tell she was straining. "Quinn, it's quite alright! Matt has a lot to do, so I understand. Please, don't mind me. We can talk later!"

Quinn rolled her eyes. "Okay, let's go."

"Go where?" I asked.

"Away from here. I need a break anyway, and you're not helping."

This isn't going to go over well, is it?

I waved goodbye to Saphira and made a mental note to visit her again soon. It'd been too long, and I was dearly missing her company.

After we got some distance away from Saphira's stall, Quinn stopped abruptly behind one of the houses. She clicked her tongue and pulled a roll of herbs wrapped in paper out of her [Cat Pack], lighting one end with the tip of her index finger. She blew out the flame and breathed in deeply from the substance, then breathed out a puff of smoke. "So what do you want?"

Is that seriously a joint? "You're not what I expected."

"...Choose your next words carefully, shithead."

Ah, there's the attitude Espada was talking about. My voice caught. "I, uh, just needed to get my armor checked out. It was damaged. Just want to make sure it's still in working order."

"You got eyes, don't you? You need me to tell you if some stray spear is going to go through a hole? I refit and build armor. If you can't tell the difference between a working piece of gear versus a piece of trash, then sure, I'll take your damn money and make you something new."

I shook my head. I was letting her lead the conversation, and I needed to reel her back in. "I'd like to avoid that. I'm getting bonuses from my gear."

Quinn took another puff from the rolled herb and blew the smoke into my face. "Fine. Let's see it."

I set the backpack I'd been carrying around to hold the iron down against the wall of the house. "[Combat Mode]." My casual clothes vanished in an instant, replaced by the gear I wore in every fight.

Quinn held on to one end of her, uh, cigarette, and checked me over in silence. I fought the urge to cough. Felt like I was back at my parents' house. I'd never smoked before, but my time away from the old world had saved me from secondhand.

When Quinn was done, she sighed. "Yeah, it could use a touch-up." She clicked her tongue. "What a hassle. Well, whatever. It can be fixed. Whoever made it knew their stuff."

"Great. How much will it cost?"

Quinn's eyes looked me up and down. "Call it one-fifty, and we got a deal."

For a touch-up?! "Uhhh, can we go a little lower than that?"

"Take it or fuck off."

Strange that I remembered hearing something similar when I tried to bargain with Espada so long ago. I sighed and relented. "Fine. Hundred and fifty Bells."

"Cool. Take it off."

I paused and reached for one of the straps. "Sure, give me a second."

"Come on. Strip, boy! Hurry up! I don't have all damn night!" she snapped, clapping her hands together.

Once I got the top off, I handed it to her with a bit of apprehension in my grip. "When can I pick it up?"

"Tomorrow afternoon. Espada's place. Don't be late."

"Sure, thanks." I swapped back to [Civilian Mode] and shouldered the bag. "Payment on pickup?"

Quinn eyed me sourly, the ash at the tip of her smoke glowing red, then nodded. "Sure. But don't you *dare* think of shorting me. I'll rip this thing to fucking shreds."

"Wouldn't dream of it." With another awkward goodbye, I left my gear in her—hopefully—capable hands.

As I left to head back to Keke's house, the catgirl Quest popped

back up in my thoughts.
God. 5,000 Bells. But, still…
I had a lot to think about.

Espada Pro Tip: Quinn's had a rough time of it with her customers. Pay her well and she'll do fine work. Don't underestimate her.

Chapter 19

Irreversible

I didn't sleep well that night. Nightmares of Shi Island tangled all together with strange realities of my previous world. Zombies in elevators. Stacking boxes and taking inventory of Jazz's crated goods while she issued commands, except the stab wounds she'd sustained against the Defiled were present and bleeding. Stuck alone on Portia's sloop in the middle of the ocean, surrounded by half a dozen circling sharks. Searching for Marianne inside a grocery store where the shelves were stocked with pickled body parts.

Flashes of my dreams followed me into the next morning, flickering in a gruesome reel as I poked at my breakfast.

"Matt?" Keke called, gently touching my shoulder. "Are you alright?"

"Mm," I hummed.

"Hey. Talk to me." Her fingers wandered to my cheek.

I flinched, and she pulled back.

"Oh. Um," Keke murmured as she leaned back in her chair. "I'm sorry. I can go. I mean, if you need to be alone."

Tension drained from my shoulders, and I shook my head. The way I was feeling wasn't her fault. "No, I'm sorry. Just a lot on my mind."

"Like what?"

Like these damn Quests. But she'd told me before that this was part of my job and had been nothing but supportive. At this point, I was beating a dead horse. Besides, this was what I wanted, wasn't it? A world filled with catgirls at my fingertips to do with as I pleased? So why did I feel like absolute shit about the prospect of sleeping with eight more? Ni was my island, and it was my job to make sure it stayed populated.

And yet, the fact that members of my Party were off-limits at the moment frustrated the ever-living hell out of me. They were the girls I *really* cared about; the ones I wanted to share that with the most.

Keke carefully placed her spoon back in her bowl. "You've gone quiet again."

I sighed and rubbed the back of my neck. *Pick yourself up, Kelmer. You're bringing the group down.* "It's nothing. Really. Just didn't sleep well, that's all." I forced a smile. "Why don't we grab Ceres and Cannoli and go for a walk? Show Ceres around a little more?"

She tried to return my smile, but worry twisted one corner of her mouth. "Sure. That sounds good."

Abandoning my sad attempt at eating, I washed my face and threw on my shoes. Some fresh air could only do me good by that point. Needed to get these thoughts the hell out of my head.

As it turned out, Cannoli and Ceres were in Cannoli's front yard. Ceres cradled a hunk of wood in one hand while chipping at it with a small knife with the other. Her tongue poked into her cheek, and her eyes were fixed on her project. As we approached, I could make out a long pair of ears and a soft, oval face.

Cannoli's ears twitched, and she looked up at the sound of our footsteps. Waving us over with a grin, she shouted, "Good morning, Matt! Good morning, Keke!"

I raised one hand in reply, and Keke mimicked the greeting.

On closer inspection of Ceres's work, I was able to make out a pair of long ears and a pointed nose. "Oh, hey. Are you carving a rabbit?"

"She is!" Cannoli replied brightly.

"My lord knows of the fabled rabbits, then?" Ceres murmured. "I should have expected as much."

"Fabled, huh?"

Keke nodded. "We have a lot of toys and carvings that resemble rabbits. But they're usually influenced by the men who come here." She shifted from one foot to the other. "I, erm, have a stuffed one."

"His name is Baby!" Cannoli provided cheerfully. "She's had him forever."

Keke blushed. "Yeah. My dad gave him to me."

Well, that's adorable. For the first time that day, a natural smile curled my lips. "You'll have to show him to me sometime." Seeing that Keke very obviously wanted to change the subject, I pressed on. "What do you know about rabbits?"

"They're amazing! They can talk and dance and sing! They harness the power of lightning to run *really* fast. But if you catch one, you can have a wish granted to you!" Cannoli chanted.

"Yeah, I've never caught one myself," I replied. *I will not destroy her dreams on this one.* "Better make it a good wish."

Ceres slowly nodded as she carved out the figure's tiny feet. "There are a few types of Encroacher that look similar to rabbits, but they do not fit Cannoli's apt description otherwise."

Cannoli beamed.

"They come in a lot of different colors. White, brown, black, pink, green. Like a rainbow," Keke added.

I would love to see a green rabbit. "Maybe we'll find one in Nyarlothep," I suggested. "Make sure you have your wish ready."

"Oh, always! Just in case!" Cannoli replied.

"Good. I wouldn't—" I began.

A familiar tinkling carried on the breeze reached my ears, and I froze. I felt the color drain from my face and the feeling vanish from my fingers.

"Matt?" Cannoli asked. Her chin tilted upward, and her ears rotated toward the sound.

Keke's did the same, and her eyes searched the thicket.

The ringing grew louder, and a dark outline appeared between the trees. My hands clenched into fists, and I took a step backward. Pain flared in a ring around the cartilage of my ear, and I blinked it back. *No. She wouldn't.*

"It can't be," Keke whispered, echoing my thoughts.

Ceres finally looked up from her carving and glanced at all of our faces. Pocketing the wood and carving knife in her apron, she murmured, "[Combat Mode]." Her polearm appeared, and she shifted into a defensive stance. "My lord, is it a Defiled?"

A dry laugh escaped me, and I shook my head. "No." *But I'd rather face a dozen Defiled than this.*

Yomi stopped a few meters away, resting her tall staff on the grass and raising one empty hand. "I-I didn't come to fight." Her dark dress pulled tight around her stomach—she was just as far along as Saphira.

My chest tightened, and I struggled to breathe. I'd finally started to feel better. Normal. One look at Yomi and it was like I was back to the starting line.

With a single glance exchanged over the span of a heartbeat, Keke and Cannoli repositioned themselves in front of me, their shoulders touching.

"What are you doing here, Yomi?" Keke demanded.

Yomi slid her hand beneath her distended belly and lowered her eyes to the ground.

Two months it had been. And still, the ringing of the chimes dangling from her staff summoned the memory of the night she'd hypnotized me in perfect clarity. Her hips straddling mine, her face, the runic tattoo circling her navel. I shivered and summoned my axe to my hand. There was no way I could hurt her, not when she was carrying my kid, but I wasn't about to allow her to harm my girls, either.

"I'd like to talk to Matt," Yomi replied, unable to meet the furious gazes of Keke or Cannoli. "Please."

"I know not who you are nor your connection with my lord. However, your presence is clearly disturbing to my comrades. Leave, or else we will be forced to take action," Ceres snarled, lowering her polearm so that the tip pointed at Yomi.

Yomi inhaled a deep, shuddering breath, then peered between the girls' shoulders and locked my gaze. "Matt, I'm sorry."

I didn't know what to say. My feet were rooted to the spot, and my emotions waged a gruesome war for my tongue. *You can't just take it back.*

Yomi chanced a step forward. "Truly, I never should have forced your hand."

"No. You shouldn't have," I murmured.

"My lord?" Ceres glanced over her shoulder. "What are your orders?"

My mouth went dry, and the piercing in my ear throbbed and ached. "Let her through."

Keke gaped, and Cannoli squeaked in surprise. Keke was the first to speak. "Are you sure?"

"Yeah."

"Alright." Taking Cannoli's hand in hers, Keke stepped aside and tugged Cannoli with her.

Yomi's gaze landed on the axe in my hand, and her face blanched. I sighed and willed it to vanish. "Drop the Enchantment, Yomi."

She shook her head. "I don't have one active."

The burning is my imagination? "If you say so." I swallowed hard against the lump in my throat and stepped forward. "How did you find me?"

"I-I took the merchant ship. A girl in town told me where you usually stay, and—"

"What do you want?"

Sweat beaded along her brow, and dark circles framed her eyes. She shuffled forward, and the knuckles around her staff turned white. "I'm scared, Matt. Scared for our kitten, scared that I can't do this alone—"

"We could have talked about these things before you decided to take advantage of me." I couldn't stop the words from flowing free. I heard Ceres make a sound like a hiss behind me. "Before you decided that this was the best outcome."

"I know." Her voice cracked on the words. "I j-just... I don't have anyone else to go to."

A hurricane of emotions held my tongue hostage as I worked through what to say. What to feel. I wanted to scream bloody murder. Protect Yomi and our child. Bury my axe in one of the nearby trees and watch it fall. Hug her and tell her it was fine.

Ceres stepped forward and stood to my immediate right. "If I understand the situation correctly, you forced yourself on Lord Matt."

Yomi flinched, then nodded.

"You are lucky to still walk this plane, Yomi." Ceres's tone was dark and furious. She gripped her polearm with deliberate intent. "It seems my lord did not report you to the Queen's Guard, and for that, you should be thankful. Your isolating yourself from companionship was your own doing."

Keke and Cannoli moved to my left. Keke silently placed an encouraging hand on my shoulder. *This is your choice, Matt.* Her words from so long ago echoed in my ears.

My Party. My girls. I would never have to face this alone. "Make sure our kitten is taken care of, Yomi. I don't ever want to see you again."

Tears slid from the corners of Yomi's eyes, but she nodded. "I'm so sorry, Matt. I—"

"What. The *fuck*. Are you doing here?" a familiar, enraged voice shrieked through the trees. Ravyn stormed across the clearing, snatching the front of Yomi's dress and dragging her forward so their noses were mere inches from each other. "Are you fucking stupid?"

"R-Ravyn. I– I just—" Yomi stammered.

"You just *what?* Thought you could come here and beg for forgiveness?" Ravyn snapped. "Ran away from Cailu before he could put you to *death?*"

"*Cailu the cunt! Cailu the cunt! Squaawk!*" Ball screamed as he orbited above us.

"I didn't have a choice—*ah!*"

Ravyn shoved Yomi backward. The [Dark Priest] stumbled back a few steps, then used her staff to prevent her fall. My first instinct was to help her—it seemed Keke knew as much because she caught my stare and shook her head.

"You *always* have a fucking choice," Ravyn growled. "You chose wrong, Yomi." She gestured to our group, pointing to each one of the girls protecting me. "If you show your disgusting face here ever again, we have plenty of options to make sure that you can't."

"I-I know," Yomi replied more tears soaked her cheeks. "Y-you won't see me again." She drew a wide circle in the air with her fingertip, murmuring an incantation I didn't understand. A dark oval appeared with black and violet tendrils drifting from its edges. "I'll take care of her, Matt." Without another word, she stepped through the portal and vanished.

We all stood in rigid, uncomfortable silence for a few tense moments. As if Yomi would once again appear from thin air and try to take us all on. Of course, nothing like that happened. I stole one deep breath, then another.

"Matt, are you alright?" Cannoli was the first to ask, keeping a careful distance between us.

"I need a minute," I admitted. "Think I can meet you inside?"

"Of course. I'll put on some tea. Keke, Ceres, will you help me?"

"My lord, what—" Ceres began.

Cannoli didn't give her a chance; she hooked her arm with Ceres's and tugged her toward the house. "We can talk about it more inside."

Ceres nodded, and the three made their way to Cannoli's front door.

Ravyn stared at the place where Yomi had drawn her portal, violet eyes still burning with rage while her hands clenched and unclenched. Despite my feet feeling as if they'd fallen asleep, I forced my legs forward and closed the distance between us.

There was so much I wanted to say to her. I wanted to know if she was okay from the other night. If I'd done something to upset her. Instead, I numbly asked, "Ready to tell me how you know Yomi?"

Ravyn looked at me but made no attempt to speak. Her lips pulled into a thin line while her eyes lowered to her shoes.

"Ravyn."

"Yomi was my best friend," Ravyn replied sharply. "There. Happy?"

I wasn't sure if that made me feel better or worse. "What happened? Why'd you split?"

Ravyn crossed her arms over her chest and frowned. "*Mou ii.* A whole load of roachshit. If you'd decided to turn her in and burn her at the stake, there'd be no love lost."

We both glowered at one another in silence, neither knowing what to say. Yomi's sudden appearance had rocked the already turbulent emotions I was trying to get a handle on. Ravyn's unbridled anger was a whole second beast. I couldn't think of a single word I could say to her that I wouldn't want to take back later.

"I'm going inside. You're free to join if you want," I said, turning on my heel. She obviously didn't want to talk about it, and I wasn't in the mood to push.

Ravyn grunted and followed close behind me. Together, we entered Cannoli's house in silence.

Yomi Pro Tip: Matt, I wish I could make it up to you. I'm so sorry.

Chapter 20

Moody Jazz

The tension was suffocating; you could cut it with a knife. For a minute, I thought someone had put a vise around my heart and lungs. Ravyn sat across from me, occasionally aiming a glare in my direction. I wanted to yell, scream, crawl under the damn table.

"I understand that this may be a difficult topic, my lord, but what happened between the two of you?" Ceres asked as she took her seat beside Ravyn.

"Yomi is a [Dark Priest]. We met her on San Island," I began. I felt Keke's hand rest on mine under the table when that was all I said. I took a deep breath and continued. "She was in Cailu's Party, and she believed her only way out was to…conceive a child with me."

This wasn't the way I wanted to tell her. To begin with, it didn't feel like there was much of a reason to involve Ceres when it came to Yomi. I never thought I'd see her again. I was airing my dirty laundry, and I couldn't help but feel ashamed for even admitting it had happened in the first place. The less she knew, the better.

Is this the part where someone revokes my 'man card'?

Ceres's brow furrowed as we detailed the remainder of the tale from San Island. Yomi's hypnosis, the fight with the Enchantress, and the Party's disappearance the next day. The look in Ceres's eyes was fierce, terrifying even. It wasn't the motherly look of concern or worry that I so commonly associated with her. This would be the second time I'd seen that expression, the first being when we fought the Defiled twins.

I'll admit, it put me on edge.

"Yomi should be glad she is no longer present," Ceres said. Her tone was firm, carrying the same air of authority I'd expect to hear from a courtroom judge. Her statement drew looks of concern. Although Ceres's tone and mannerisms didn't change, she did correct herself. "Please, do not be alarmed. No harm would have come to her. I would have apprehended her and thrown her in a gaol myself."

As flattering as that was to hear, I can't say that it made me feel much better.

"This should help us calm down." Cannoli delivered a tray of tea to our table, setting each cup in front of us. The glasses trembled as she set them down. She flashed one of the most forced smiles I'd seen from her. I made no effort to return the gesture.

"I share your ire, Ceres," Keke said. She accepted a saucer from Cannoli, cradled the teacup in both hands, then sipped at the edge. Her gaze locked with mine.

The memory of crying on Keke's shoulder the morning following Yomi's departure returned. My temples flared with a mix of pain and anger. *God damn it, everything about this still feels embarrassing as hell.*

Keke carefully replaced the cup in its saucer, then bowed her head. "If I had known that was going to happen—"

"It is thanks to hindsight that you can make such claims," Ceres reasoned. "Pray, do not fault yourself for matters you can no longer change."

When Cannoli was done passing out the cups of tea, she took the empty seat to my right. She held her teacup between her hands on the table, her thumbs tracing the ornate rim. "What do we want to do about it?"

"There isn't anything to do about it," Ravyn replied flatly.

Ceres turned to look at Ravyn. "A man was forced to conceive a child without their consent. This is not permissible."

"Ceres," Keke said, summoning the [Magic Knight]'s attention. "We're not following Yomi. We have to let it go."

Ceres opened her mouth to retort. After an uncomfortable pause, she sighed and leaned back in her chair. Then she turned to look at me. "My lord. What is your wish? If you would have me pursue this [Dark Priest], then I shall spare no effort. I would depart immediately." When she saw Keke was about to speak, she raised a hand. "However—if it is your desire that I leave this matter alone, then I will trouble you no more."

"They're right. I made this decision after it happened. We let her go." It still felt like shit to say it out loud. But I wanted to do right by my kid, no matter what that meant.

"I've been wondering... What if Cailu finds out?" Cannoli asked. "I-I mean, he just seems like a super-smart person, and I don't think he'd be as nice to her as Matt has been."

"What Yomi did was fucked. But if I have a choice, I won't let Cailu kill her," I hissed. "I refuse."

I expected to get some sort of reaction out of Ravyn, but she was strangely quiet, as was Ball. For being such an irritant, the bird at least seemed to know when to shut its beak.

The clock ticked as the seconds rolled by. Ravyn clicked her tongue. Keke rubbed her hands together uncomfortably. Ceres's brow continued to dip further down.

"I understand," Ceres said at last.

"Will you be able to stand up to him if it comes to that?" Ravyn asked.

Is this the game we're going to play now? "Yes. I can, and I will if I have to. That's the kind of person I am, Ravyn. You should know that by now."

The two of us stared at each other. Ravyn's eye began to twitch, and her chest visibly rose and fell. I could hear the frustrated air exhaling from her nostrils. I was convinced the house could explode at any second. At that moment, I welcomed it.

Say something. Come on; I dare you.

Keke reached for my hand and entwined her fingers between mine. I wrestled them away and rested my arms on the table. "Matt—"

"What's done is done," I said flatly. "Instead of making a spectacle out of this shit, why don't we all move on?" *You can't take it back now, Kelmer.*

Keke stared at me wide-eyed. "Matt, I just—I'm sorry."

"It's fine."

"No, it's not," Ravyn said. "You're right in that there's nothing we can do now. But Cannoli is right, too. Cailu could decide to make a statement out of this when he figures it out. Shithead's full of himself enough to do so."

I drew a deep breath, and my lip trembled. Blood pumped furiously through my veins. In the calmest tone I could manage, I responded. "What does he have to gain by trying to put her to death?"

"String her up as a message to Nyarlea. Take her out quietly and whisper her deeds to the queen. It depends on what Yomi does and what you ask for. If she has half a brain, and—judging from the fact that she showed up here, she clearly fucking doesn't—then she'll lay low and won't say a word. However," Ravyn's voice lowered, "if Cailu *were* to report it to the queen, then there's a strong chance she'd be gutted on the spot."

"Then... I'll..." I clenched my fingers and dropped my gaze. "I'll say I agreed to be with her."

"Yeah? Just as convincingly as you said it now? Then you've signed her death sentence."

"How in the hell is that?" I snarled.

Ravyn threw her arms into the air. "*Kuso!* Are you not paying attention? You aren't stupid enough to bed another man's Party member, Matt. You think he hasn't fucking figured that out? If it's Cailu's word versus hers, whose do you think they're going to believe?"

Ceres raised her hand. "My lord. As much as I am loathe to say it, Ravyn has the right of it. Letting her go free could potentially open the gates for other catgirls to believe that they are allowed to do the same to their island's man. If Cailu were to report Yomi's disobedience to the queen, I can say with a high degree of certainty that she would be put to the guillotine. "

The guillotine?! My mouth hung agape. There had to be another way. There's no way Cailu would go that far, would he? This had nothing to do with him or Naeemah—really, it was none of his damn business. If he was going to do something, he would've done it by now. "Cailu wouldn't—"

"Matt. You don't understand. Cailu is ruthless. He may be biding his time." Ravyn gripped the hem of her dress. "He may wait until the baby is born. He might wait until he can speak with you." She paused. "We need to be ready for that when he approaches you. Because he will."

"I see. If the issue is ignored, the faith in men's power over catgirls would falter," Cannoli said in a whisper.

All eyes were on Cannoli. I'm glad I wasn't the only one who found her statement strange.

"I heard it from my mother," Cannoli continued. "Th-the men are a beacon of hope for all catgirls. They receive power from a magic we don't understand. The iPaw, Matt." She played with a tuft of her hair as she pored over her reflection in the tea. "Their morale, their strength, their courage, their wisdom, all of it is revered. We give thanks to Saoirse every day for their continued presence in Nyarlea."

"Cannoli," Keke murmured.

Cannoli smiled, but it didn't reach her eyes. "Without them, we wouldn't have our way of life. Catgirls would falter and abuse their sign of hope. This is what Saoirse teaches us." And then her tone turned dire. "If Cailu, a [Paladin], were to report this to the leading [Bishop] in Nyarlothep, or to the queen, then Yomi could absolutely be put to death."

"What would Cailu have to gain?" I asked.

"This is larger than Cailu. It would maintain the chain of command in Nyarlea, Matt," Ceres added. "We pledge our loyalty and assistance to men. Some catgirls perform more admirably than others in your absence, but you have an important job in uniting them once more and ensuring our continued existence."

"*Mattaku.* These are all pretty words, but Cailu's pride trumps it all," Ravyn said with a scoff. "Depending on how he and the queen are feeling that day, the fucking cunt could lead an army of [Crusader]s to track Yomi down. Drag her to the town and do it that way. They've made public examples of catgirls before; I'm sure they'd love to do it again."

"Then he destroys his reputation with Tristan and me," I snapped. "Let him."

Cannoli shook her head. "It's not that simple, Matt. I'm sorry."

I was tired of barely understanding this world and its laws. My patience was shot. "Why are you apologizing? Just tell me why it's not that simple." My tone sounded a lot more harsh than I'd intended.

Cannoli squeaked. "R-right."

Keke frowned. "Matt. Stop it."

"Don't, Keke. It's fine. Really." Cannoli continued. "Cailu has been in Nyarlea for a long time. He has immense status. Only a handful on San Island know about you, Matt, but they know nothing of Tristan or Ichi Island's man." Her breath trembled. "The church could favor Cailu, doing whatever he wanted. It would create strife and conflict between the men. Divide catgirls across all islands. It could create rogue factions and lead to war." Tears started to stream from her eyes, and I began to feel like a villain. "I-I don't want to see that h-happen. I'm sorry. Please excuse me."

Before any of us could get a word out, Cannoli darted out the front door. An uncomfortable silence fell over us.

Ravyn pushed her chair back and rose to her feet. "I'm going to go check on her."

When Ravyn was gone, I stood up next. "I need some fresh air."

"Matt." Keke looked at me. I'd seen that expression before—she was beyond worried. I could see it in her eyes. She reached for my hand. "Please talk to me. I'm always here for you." She bowed her head. "Always will be."

Anything I wanted to say would've been taken as cruel, thoughtless, or inconsiderate. I was not about to reassure her or comfort her in a moment that I couldn't. I was one inch from exploding. And so I said nothing.

I left Cannoli's house, unsure of where I was going or what I was doing. I needed to get away before I said something I'd regret.

Ceres Pro Tip: My lord, should you change your mind, I would pursue Yomi with haste. You need only say the word.

Chapter 21

Deadly Queen

'Rest' was a phrase long-evaporated from Cailu's vocabulary. It seemed that mere hours after he and Naeemah had quashed the immediate Defiled threat on San Island, they found themselves once again called back to court.

Their battles across his assigned island had slowed noticeably since Yomi's departure, though neither he nor Naeemah would ever admit it aloud. The Defiled were building in strength and becoming more of a nuisance to the main cities of San, Shulan especially. He hoped Matt's travels were proving successful and that he'd long since moved on to Ichi island.

Though convincing Magni of our meeting could cost him too much precious time.

"You look like you're thinking," Naeemah murmured at his shoulder.

They strolled together through the Capital of Nyarlothep, Ronona. Their destination was the second estate that Cailu was awarded long ago for his heroic deeds to Nyarlea. Despite the casual nature of the errand, both he and Naeemah donned their full combat attire.

He nodded in response to Naeemah's statement, puzzling his thoughts into the right words to say. Catgirls congregating from all islands passed them by, greeting him with warm smiles and afternoon greetings. He returned their grins without a second thought—simply another act he had to perform in his duties to the crown. Should any ear be bent in their direction, he couldn't betray the confidence the citizens of Nyarlea held in him. Showing weakness was never an option.

"You're worried about Matt," Naeemah muttered behind her mask so that only he could hear.

He paused, returning a particularly energetic greeting from a pink-haired catgirl, then offered Naeemah a single curt nod.

"Ichi Island will challenge him, to be sure. However—" she paused, waiting for the next group of girls to pass after greeting Cailu. "If Matt has Shi Island's man in his Party, then that should help convince Magni to meet."

Cailu chuckled—a dry, breathy cough that sounded more like a clearing of the throat. "Assuming Shi Island's man isn't completely worthless."

"Then they die, and we try again with the new men," Naeemah replied. "Isn't that your methodology with your catgirl companions?"

Cailu's smile slipped for the span of a heartbeat, then returned when a blue-haired catgirl touched his shoulder and grinned. Naeemah's comfort with him was both a blessing and a curse. No one else would dare speak to him with such a sharp tongue. At times, he found it refreshing. Other times, he wanted to strangle her shapely throat. "This is a wheel I wish to break, Naeemah. Not perpetuate."

"Mm," she hummed. "That's interesting."

Naeemah's tone dug beneath his skin, serpentine eyes measuring him behind her dark mask. *Do not give me reasons to doubt you, Naeemah.* "Speak your mind."

"Not here. You've taught me better than that."

He sighed. The constant traveling, relentless battles, and lack of a good night's sleep shaped his normally clear perceptions into negative interpretations. Of course he could trust his [Assassin]. Gods knew there was no one else that held such a position.

"Well, well. Lucky me," a new voice purred at Cailu's ear. "I've been looking for you two."

Cailu and Naeemah spun to face whoever had managed to sneak up on both of them so discreetly. The [Assassin] drew her daggers while Cailu's fingers lingered on the hilt of his sword.

The catgirl that grinned at them was unlike any Cailu had ever seen before. Her skin was a deep, rich brown, patterned with ivory stripes on her face, throat, legs, and stomach—like a wildcat. Fiery orange eyes scrutinized the [Paladin] from head to toe. Black hair boasted streaks of brilliant white, and her hairless ears and tail carried the same patterning of her skin. Fabric the color of red wine with dark, geometric shapes wrapped around her chest, arms, and hips, baring her stomach and the tops of her thighs with her short skirt. Teeth of a long-slayed beast bedecked her ears and throat, and in her right hand, she shuffled two smooth, glimmering stones one over the other.

"Who are you?" Naeemah growled.

The woman's grin widened. "I remember you, Naeemah. I expected you wouldn't know me, though." She motioned to herself. "I tend to blend in with the crowd, you see. Nothing distinctive to point out."

"I will only ask one more time. If you wish to keep your tongue, identify yourself," Naeemah commanded.

"Come now. Our tongues were gifts from Saoirse to service men. Isn't that how the scrolls read?" She tilted her head toward Cailu. "Tell me, is that true?"

Her jests were quickly wearing thin. "State your business or take your leave," Cailu snapped.

Other catgirls in the plaza glanced warily at the encounter, giving them a wide berth as they passed. No one wanted to get involved in a conflict. Especially not in Ronona with the queen's right-hand man.

She shifted her weight so that her hips swayed to the right. Her two-toned tail wove back and forth in a hypnotic rhythm behind her back. *Click, click, click.* The stones moving in her hand only added to the effect, and her narrow gaze suggested she enjoyed toying with her audience. "The Guild Hall said you needed a capable healer."

"Capable, yes," Naeemah hissed. "I told them not to send me anyone without proven ability."

"My name is Kirti," she continued, her smile never wavering. "Ichi Island was my home, like yours." She looked pointedly at Naeemah. "We celebrated many peaceful years beneath your guidance, Naeemah. Magni's leadership will bury the cities beneath the sands, and I refused to watch. Clearly, you also fled from beneath his thumb."

"We are not a charity, Kirti," Cailu said. "Are you a healer or not?"

"And here I thought you'd be desperate by now." Kirti laughed. Her voice was warm and rich. "I'm a [Witch Doctor]."

Third Classes were difficult to obtain—even the Royal Guard remained as [Crusader]s for the duration of their service. Cailu felt the first pangs of surprise pepper his features. Had this woman completed such a feat on her own?

"You must know how the court feels about [Witch Doctor]s," Naeemah said, lowering her daggers.

"That we're placed on the same pedestal as [Necromancer]s in the minds of royalty? Of course. Everyone knows that." Kirti shrugged her slender shoulders.

"You truly believe your healing arts are sufficient enough to support the three of us?" Cailu sneered. "Our previous [Dark Priest] struggled to do so."

"A Second Class? Of course she struggled," Kirti replied in a matter-of-fact tone. "She fell behind both of you."

Her nonchalance grated on Cailu's nerves, but he steadied his words. "We will need to test your ability, Kirti."

"I would expect no less from the *Hero of Nyarlea*," Kirti replied.

"Watch your tone," Naeemah warned.

Kirti reached forward and touched Naeemah's cheek. "There was a time when you bowed to no one." The [Assassin] batted her wrist away the moment the woman's fingertips brushed her face.

"We all have a place, witch." Naeemah took a step back. "Touch me again, and you will lose your hand."

"If you say so." Kirti turned toward Cailu. "Shall we head to the gates?"

Kirti's listless tone and irreverence toward him and Naeemah both demanded that he refuse her before putting her to trial. Even so, he could feel a dark magic pulsing beneath her flesh, emanating a dangerous aura that raised the hackles on the back of his neck. This woman was clearly confident in her skill and had the support of forces he dared not speak of, let alone commune.

And, as much as he loathed to admit it, tinges of desperation had crept into his resolve. They needed an adept healer. Neither he nor Naeemah could maintain such a rigorous schedule for much longer.

One mistake on their part, and they'd lose their lives, throwing Nyarlea into even greater disarray. *No, I swore to protect this miserable place.*

For the first time in years, Cailu swallowed his pride. "To the gates, then." He could sense Naeemah's frown behind her mask, but he ignored it.

The forests surrounding the Nyarlothep capital were thick and vast, spanning for miles around. On multiple occasions, Cailu had suggested that the queen create a sizeable clearing to better see any approaching enemies, but Saoirse's adamant followers believed that the spirits of deceased catgirls wandered these woods. To cut them down would remove their shelter and offend Saoirse herself.

So, to Cailu's frustration, the forests stayed.

A group of mid-Level Encroachers had made a nest nearby. Seven four-legged creatures the length of a man covered in deep violet scales patrolled a stream in search of food. Whip-like tails ending in brilliant blue flames moved back and forth as they walked. Canine faces that looked as if they'd been carved from white bone buried their muzzles in the stream, snapping at unsuspecting fish. Blue and pink tendrils flared from the base of their throats, assumedly marking the males from the females.

"Those will do," Cailu said, pointing to the herd. "Your ability to fight is just as important as your healing prowess."

Kirti eyed the Encorachers, a sardonic smile twisting the corners of her lips. "Are you sure? We could find a Defiled to fight instead."

"This is sufficient," Naeemah added, crossing her arms and bearing down on Kirti with an icy stare. "Your test has begun."

"As you wish," Kirti replied, still shuffling the stones in her palm. She sauntered forward without a second glance at those she left behind. "[Shatter Soul]!"

The smooth green stone between her thumb and forefinger shattered, and the tiny shards fell to the grass around her. From each of the broken pieces rose a ghostly image of a skull, surrounded with glittering black mist. Chaotic cackles pierced the forest as the skulls launched forward, striking the unsuspecting beasts on their sides.

Fearful howls joined the skull's laughter. Cailu murmured a prayer beneath his breath before the warm, familiar presence of healing magic slid down his spine. Both he and Naeemah were at full [Health Points], but that wouldn't prevent the same sensation from occurring. He and Naeemah exchanged a quick glance and then turned back to the fight at hand.

The Encroachers scrambled from the stream, leaping and bounding to escape from one another and put distance between themselves and Kirti as quickly as possible.

"[Hand of Regret]!" Kirti cried, casting one open palm toward the beasts.

Blood-red briars of thorns shot from the ground, piercing all seven monsters straight through. Sanguine trails of gore littered the stream, dying the clear water red as it ran further along the forest. Yelps and whimpers of bestial pain penetrated the trees, sending flocks of birds flying from their branches.

Kirti reached into one of her many packs and pulled free another glimmering red stone. "[Haunt Vessel]," she muttered, making her way to the nearest Encroacher. Holding the rock between her forefinger and thumb as if she were looking through its center, she hissed her final spell, "[Soul Trap]."

A spectral outline of the creature was torn from its unmoving body, barking and howling with desperation. It vanished in the blink of an eye, and the stone shimmered with its newly absorbed life. The other six Encroachers stilled; their battered and beaten bodies succumbed to Kirti's magic.

She turned to Cailu and gestured to the stones in her palm. "I can use one to heal you both if you require it?"

"No. That won't be necessary," Cailu said. A cold sweat drenched the skin beneath his armor. Kirti was efficient, dangerous, and terrifying. She was a gamble he was willing to make. "Allow me to extend you a formal welcome to my Party, Kirti."

Naeemah Pro Tip: I will be watching you closely, Kirti. One mistake will mean your life.

Chapter 22

Silver Chariot

I was in the mood to hit things. Maybe break something. Any wall would've done just fine, but I withheld my temper. It wasn't going to be much longer until the appointed hour with Quinn, and even though I had the feeling she might understand my frustration, I wanted to keep up appearances.

To draw my attention away for a bit, I called out the iPaw and scrolled over to check how my [Stats] looked.

```
Matt

Base Level 9
Warrior Class Level 9
Base Experience: 2067/2500
Class Experience: 2067/2500
Health Points: 56/56
Myana Points: 7/7
Energy: 27/28
Strength: 4 +4
Vitality: 4 +2
Dexterity: 1
Agility: 1 +1
Magic: 1
Resistance: 2 +3


1 Stat Point available!
1 Skill Point available!
```

Out of curiosity, I pulled up Ravyn's sheet next. The way I figured it, being a Second Class brought upon a whole slew of boons, so I imagined her [Health Points] were probably higher than mine.

Ravyn

```
Base Level 12
Sorcerer Class Level 8
Base Experience: 3606/3650
Class Experience: 1806/1900
Health Points: 53/53
Myana Points: 122/122
Energy: 35/36
Strength: 1
Vitality: 2 +1
Dexterity: 3
Agility: 1
Magic: 9 +4
Resistance: 1 +3
```

I chuckled. I was only ahead of her by three points. Guess Second Classes weren't to be taken for granted. Ceres's balancing advice rang in my ears, for better or worse. Each of the girls had alluded to how some of the [Stats] can and may work. However, beyond the obvious features of each attribute, I was still unaware of how they were ultimately affecting me. For the first time in a long while, I was paralyzed by indecision.

I recalled the sensation that filled my being when I first leveled [Strength]. I remembered how my muscles felt, how noticeably lighter my axe was in my hand, and how my very skin began to feel more leathery, tougher. It was a difficult experience to describe—felt like I cheated my way out of the gym for some newfound witchcraft—which, I guess, wasn't too far from the truth.

Another thought occurred to me.

What if I were to ask some of the girls where their points were? Did they acknowledge what sort of effect it had on their performance? Would they even notice?

I was sure Keke could answer the latter two questions. Probably Ceres, too. But it wasn't going to do me any good just sitting here and wondering, and it was a long-overdue lesson. Since it was nearly time to speak with Quinn anyway, I made my way over to Espada's shop. If she was even half the person Tristan claimed she was, then there wasn't a better person to ask.

When I approached, Espada was busy lining one of her latest and greatest creations with fur. I waited patiently for her to finish. It dawned on me that she must value the breeze around here. You could catch a salty whiff of the sea from where we were, and the murmurs of the passing catgirls were just quiet enough to offer a peaceful ambiance to a busybody like herself.

A couple of minutes later, she stretched her fingers and approached the counter. "You're awful quiet today. Whatcha need, Matt?" Her tone was friendly—well, friendly for Espada—and I saw the briefest hint of a smile tug at the edge of her mouth.

I couldn't help but smile back. "Do you mind if I ask you some questions?" Her immediate frown put me on the defensive. "Nothing bad, and nothing about your history if that's what you're worried about."

Her frown deepened. "My history? What do you think you know about my history?"

I wondered if I'd dug myself a hole. I had no idea what Tristan's investigation into Espada looked like beyond the limited information he'd shared with me. I was quickly realizing that I should've just cut straight to the point. "Not much, honestly. Sorry, let me try again. I have questions about Stats."

Her expression eased, as did my breathing. "What about them?"

"Do you know how each Stat affects a person? I'm kinda... asking around."

Espada folded her arms. "Mostly. I can only really tell you from the viewpoint of a catgirl, though. I don't know anything about the iPaw or the magic it uses."

My shoulders fell. "That's fine. Nobody seems to really know about Stat Points or what exactly the iPaw does, it seems."

Espada blinked, then laughed dryly.

Why do I feel so stupid right now?

"Ease up, Matt. Look over there." Espada motioned to where Saphira was gleefully doing business with a pair of catgirls that barely stood up to her shoulder—which was saying a lot. I watched for some time, admiring the sparkle in Saphira's eyes, the way she animatedly gestured using her hands. Now that I was paying attention, I never noticed that quirk before. She really did use her hands a lot.

"That's your average catgirl on Ni Island," Espada continued. "Most girls on this island never reach Second Class. Many of them have never distributed a Stat point in their lives. So a lot of them wouldn't be able to help you."

"Right. I mean, yeah, that makes sense."

Espada chuckled. "Oh yeah? Why?"

Uhhh, shit. Um, there could be a couple different points she's making here. I sighed. "Cause the island's quiet. Not a lot happens here."

"You're not wrong. Truth be told, you got lucky when Keke found you. She's the daughter of one of the most well-known catgirls in Nyarlea. A Famed [Sniper]. Few would've been able to help you better than she."

Keke doesn't talk about her much. "I honestly didn't know that."

Espada walked over to a white tarp and pulled it away to reveal a strikingly beautiful silver shield underneath. The glare reflecting off its surface was almost enough to blind me. "Finished this early, by the way. Well… almost. I'll just need another hour on it to tune it up. It's some of my finest work yet."

"Thanks, Espada. I'm at a loss for words. I didn't think you'd put that much work into it." When I realized how that probably sounded, I clapped a hand to my mouth.

Espada laughed. "It's fine, Matt. I didn't think so either." She sighed, then turned back around. "Anyway. What I was trying to say was that these girls couldn't give you much of the information you need. They haven't fought much, haven't come face to face with the Defiled. So go easy on them, will ya? Ask your friends first and be patient with them."

It had been a while, but I recalled a conversation I'd had with Keke about Stats. "I did ask her. She had great information, but I need more details. Her mom may have known them like the back of her hand, but Keke's been limited by the island, I think."

"Hm. Alright." Espada threw the tarp back over the shield and folded her arms. "Let's keep it simple. I'm guessing you threw all your points into [Strength] and [Vitality], yeah?"

I nodded. "That's right. Hit harder, take more hits."

"That's what I did, too. That's going to work for a while. But later on, you won't keep up. You need speed or it'll just be a matter of time before a Defiled catches you." Espada felt for the piece of ear she was missing. "Take it from someone who got caught."

After the encounter we had with the twins, I had trouble imagining *more* things moving so quickly. Even my memories of the fight were blurry—too many details caught between the stances and positioning of both the girls and the Defiled. I didn't have to see Jazz's sheet to know she'd stacked [Agility] like her life depended on it. Ara too.

Now that I think of it, has Ara ever gotten hit?

I struggled to remember if I'd seen Ara take a blow in any of our fights. Even so, she had emerged from every encounter practically unscathed. Her uniform was still in tip-top shape. Not a single scar on her body—at least, as far as I knew. Was that also due to her [Agility]?

"Are you talking about [Agility]?"

Espada nodded. "If you intend to protect these girls, you're going to have to keep up. [Strength] and [Vitality] are going to get you fucked up if you depend on them too much."

It felt counterintuitive to me. For as long as I could remember, distributing points into power and health-related attributes was the way to go whenever I played barbarian or berserking-type characters. I understood that this wasn't a game, and that many of Nyarlea's quirks and penalties applied in different ways. But the concept of throwing [Agility] into my build was not something I'd get used to overnight.

"Are you sure about this?" I asked.

I'd barely gotten the words out when Espada snatched the iPaw out of my hands in a flash. There was no time to react. She held the screen up and shook her head. "Yeah, I'm pretty sure."

My mouth hung agape. I'd never seen Espada move so fast. I called the iPaw back to my side with, "Return, iPaw." The device vanished from her grip and reappeared back in my hands. I paused. "You made your point. What happens when I get it, though?"

"It'll make more sense if you just get it. Don't ignore [Dexterity] or [Resistance] either, Matt." Something caught Espada's gaze. "I'm going to finish up. We can talk more later if you want."

"Oh. You're here," said another voice.

I looked down and over to my side to see Quinn.

She raised a hand. "Yo."

"Y-yo." I raised my hand in response. I don't know why, but Quinn gave me this weird feeling like I was trying to communicate with a long-lost civilization. *Should I be flashing a Vulcan sign?*

"Your hunk o' junk is done. Here." Quinn held out my armor with both hands.

To say that it had been fixed would not do her service. I couldn't tell it had ever been damaged. The leather looked freshly cured, and when I yanked it as a small test run, I couldn't get it to budge an inch.

I was impressed. "Thanks, Quinn. Seriously. You've saved me a huge trip."

Quinn shrugged. "Whatevs." She held out her hand. "Bells, boy."

I reached into my [Cat Pack] and placed a sack of a hundred and fifty Bells in her palm. "Hang on." I reached further into my [Cat Pack] and pulled out an extra ten Bells. "Here's a tip. As a big 'thank you.'"

Quinn seemed less than impressed, then bit one of the coins. "Huh. It's real. You're a weird one."

Takes one to know one.

Espada was already hard at work on her next commission, and as I drew the iPaw close to my face, I pondered the screen for a short while before putting my Stat Point into [Agility] and my Skill Point into [Increase Attack].

I can't afford to get caught off guard. Not now.

Espada Pro Tip: You can't rely on two Stats to carry you, Matt. It's a delicate balance, and every point matters..

Side Quest

Portia Sets Sail

It was a bright, crisp morning in Junonia as Portia and her father, Emilio, trekked down from the house to the sailboat. Portia swung her steps wide, attempting to fit into the footprints left behind by Papa. She hoped one day her feet would be the same size. Just like their hair was the same color. He was so tall and strong and smart. She wanted to be just like her dad.

Once they reached the beach, the task of following his footprints became impossible. The imprints formed, then quickly vanished—filled in by the constantly shifting sand. Frowning, Portia trailed behind for a few steps until she could make out his shadow in the dim light. Filled with new determination, she switched to the challenge of staying inside of his tall silhouette.

"What're you doing back there, love?" Papa chuckled, glancing over his shoulder.

"Catching your shadow!" Portia replied, hopping back into the center of the dark, faint outline. She recalled a fairytale he'd once told her about a little girl who lost her shadow. Stolen by an evil Encroacher. "Careful! I'm gonna catch it!"

Papa readjusted the thick coil of rope over his shoulder. "The sun's barely out yet. You'll have to work hard to take what's there."

"Oh, I'll do it, alright! I can do anything!" Her tail twitched happily behind her as she carefully tiptoed in the center of his shadow.

"That I believe," Papa said with a grin.

They'd stirred before dawn, tiptoeing through the house to avoid waking Mama. He'd packed a few hardboiled eggs, bread, cheese, and fruits to eat once they were out on the boat, but Portia was so excited that she'd forgotten she was even hungry. Each day spent sailing with Papa was the best day ever. And now that she was a big girl—the longest eight summers any girl ever had to wait—he'd started to quiz her on the anatomy of the boat and the basics of sailing. Once, he'd even let her steer.

She *really* hoped she'd get to steer again.

They reached the dock, and Portia's silent steps on the sand transitioned to hollow clicks along the wood. *Second Chance* patiently waited for them in the shallow ocean water, rocking along the humble waves. She struck a noble silhouette against the rising sun, her sails closed against the mast.

"Alright, in you go." Emilio scooped Portia up beneath the arms and placed her carefully on the boat's deck. He followed soon after, setting the rope aside before pulling their breakfast from his [Cat Pack]. "What's a jib?"

Portia knew this one. She beamed as she replied, "That's the sail forward of the mast!"

"Very good." Papa smiled and handed her an egg. "What makes it different from the mainsail?"

"Hm." Portia picked at the shell of the egg, then tossed the pieces overboard. Glistening fins breached the surface before their owners gobbled the floating white pieces. "The…the boom, right?" she asked cautiously. She was half-sure, but there was a lot to remember.

"What about the boom?"

She squinted up at the jib. The memory of Papa standing on the bow while pointing to the long pole extending from the mast resurfaced. "Um, it doesn't have one?"

"That's my girl." Papa ruffled her mop of identical teal hair and passed her a slice of bread coated in a thin layer of nyapple jelly.

Portia grinned and took one bite of bread and one bite of egg. Mama had made the jelly just that week, and the sweetness of the nyapples tickled her tongue.

"Where's the keel?" Papa asked.

That was an easy one. "That's the fin on the bottom of the boat! Like a fishy fin!"

"That's right. Like a fish." He nodded, then took a bite of cheese. Between mouthfuls of breakfast, he asked, "What's a cleat?"

Portia chewed the inside of her cheek and peered around the boat. She always had trouble with this one. For some reason, she mixed it up with the winch. Maybe because they both had to do with ropes. "Is...is that the one that you use to tighten or loosen the tension of a rope?"

"Close, sweet. Try again."

Darn! That's the winch! She huffed a sigh of exasperation. "It's where you tie the boat to the dock. Right there."

"There you are. What's the part you were talking about before?"

Portia rolled her eyes, frustrated with herself. "The winch."

"Hey, you're doing great. I'd gamble that you know more about sailing than any of the other girls on this island."

"Really?" Portia asked, wide-eyed. "That can't be."

Papa lowered his voice and shielded his mouth with one hand. "Well, it helps when you have the best teacher in Nyarlea."

Portia giggled and finished her bread, licking the remnants of the jelly from her fingertips. "I bet you're the best sailor in the whole wide world, Papa."

Papa laughed, a deep, resonant sound that Portia dearly loved. "Now you're just sweet-talking me."

"Nuh-uh! I bet you could sail those big merchant ships we see sometimes! You'd get to the other islands twice as fast as those girls." Portia recalled the gigantic, lacquered schooners that stopped by Ni Island once a month for sale and trade. Papa had purchased her a wonderful set of silver hoop earrings from one of them, both of which went straight into her left ear. He said they brought good luck aboard the ship and would keep her eyesight sharp—much like the single small hoop around his left ear.

"Maybe. But then I wouldn't be around for you and Mom as much."

Portia's ears and tail drooped. "Oh. I wouldn't want that."

"Hey, now. No sad faces on my boat." He moved to sit beside her, wrapping one arm around her shoulders. "I'm not going anywhere, love."

Portia snuggled her head into his chest. He smelled like salt and ink. "Good." Taking another bite from her egg, she looked to the sails, then the deck, silently naming every piece her eyes drifted across. "You were a sailor, right Papa?"

Papa kissed her head between her ears. "All my life. My father before me—your grandad—was a sailor, too."

"Did you see the whole world?"

"Just about. From one edge of the Earth to the other."

Suddenly panicked with this new information, Portia drew back and stared at her father. "The world has edges?"

"No. No, sweet," Papa chuckled. "It's just a saying."

"*Ahaha.* Of course." She blushed furiously and fingered the rings in her ear. "Is that how you found Nyarlea? At the edge of the world?"

"Hm. Something like that." Emilio watched the sunrise and chose his next words carefully. "There was a bad storm. Thunder, lightning, swells as tall as ten men stacked on each other's shoulders."

Portia tried to imagine waves as high as ten Papas. She was about half his size... So, that would be like twenty of her! She shivered. "That sounds scary."

"It was. The crew was all over the place, doing their best to keep the boat from capsizing. We tried every trick in the book—and a few more we'd learned along the way. But, when it was over, I woke up here on the beach."

Her brow furrowed, and she looked up to meet his gaze. Something vital was missing from his story. Had the storm just stopped? What about the boat? If they tried their best, does that mean it did capsize? "What do you mean, 'when it was over'?"

Papa sighed and ran a hand through his hair. "You've a sharp ear like your mother."

"Did the storm stop? What happened to the boat?" Portia gently gave a voice to her questions, hoping she wasn't pushing into something he didn't want to talk about. Papa always got real quiet when she tried to ask about 'sensitive topics,' as Mama called them.

"...The boat went down," Papa admitted after a time. "The water was cold and dark and quiet. Next thing I knew, I was here."

Sensing the tension coursing through his shoulders, Portia snuggled closer to her father. "It was a lucky storm, then."

"You think so?"

"It brought you to Mama. And me."

Papa's muscles eased, and he finished off a second egg. He tightened his grip on Portia's arm and nodded. "A lucky storm, indeed."

They shared a comfortable silence, listening to the breeze play in the nearby pawm trees and along the water's surface. After a time, Papa reached for the length of rope and pulled it into their laps. "Can you tie me a bowline knot?"

Portia grinned. She'd been secretly practicing knots into the early hours of the morning from diagrams she'd sketched based on Papa's example. Whipping the loops into place with dexterous fingers, she completed a bowline knot in mere seconds.

"My stars, you're faster than me," Papa said, eyes wide as he studied the perfect bowline in the rope. "How about two half hitches?"

She untied the bowline and grabbed Papa's hand, guiding his arm to point straight in front of him. "Can I use this, please?"

Papa laughed. "Of course."

She looped the rope around his wrist, then looped the hitches around the dangling cord.

"When've you had time to practice these, love?"

Portia blushed, then carefully loosened the cord from Papa's arm. She didn't want to lie, but admitting the truth may interrupt her late-night studies. "Um, well... When you and Mama are sleeping."

"Portia—"

"Please! I love practicing! I want to be a great sailor just like you!" Portia begged before he could say another word. "I still do my chores and get plenty of sleep. And I work on my reading and writing like Mama wants. Please don't tell me to stop."

Papa hugged her tightly. "I won't tell you to stop. I was asking if you'd like to be the captain of the *Second Chance* today."

Portia's heart soared, and she glowed with pride. "Really?! You don't mind?"

"Not at all. But if you don't remember something, it's important you ask me. Understood?"

"Yes, Papa!" Portia leaped from her seat and rushed to the mast as her father moved to raise the sails. "Mainsail, then jib!" she announced, waiting for his assent once he'd finished pulling the anchor up.

"Ready, love." He saluted and tied the anchor off. "You are your father's daughter."

Porita Pro Tip: I've named my sloop Emilio after my pops. I wish he could've been here to help me christen it.

Chapter 23

Golden Wind

After our brief visit together, Quinn made her exit, and I waved goodbye to Espada before she set back to work. I wasn't sure what to do at this point. All of my necessary tasks and errands had been completed. The day was mine, and our visit back to Ni Island was meant to be a reprieve. At least, that's how I interpreted it when we talked about taking a break.

Starting off our vacation strong.

Each idea that crossed my mind was stamped out by impatience or an overwhelming sense of apathy that came and went. No matter what option surfaced, I found an excuse to run away from it— learning new potion recipes at Nauka's or practicing my swings; getting the Party together to hunt Encroachers, or finding a girl to sleep with. None of it appealed to me, and I was convinced that any dopamine kicks or euphoric feelings would vanish just moments afterward. So what the hell was the point?

Eventually, I stopped wandering the town. The constant suggestive gestures and expressions being thrown my way were losing their luster, and I was quickly losing my patience.

I ground my teeth when I came to a halt in front of Saphira's house. It'd been a few hours since I left Espada and Quinn, but Saphira was still happily chatting up each customer who walked by from behind her fruit and vegetable stall. Her smile was radiant, infectious even.

Saphira saw me out of the corner of her eye. After a short exchange with the catgirl at the counter, she skipped to my side.

"Hello, Matt! Good afternoon!"

"Hey, Saphira," I said through a forced smile. "Business is good, it seems."

"Never better!" She snatched up my hand and intertwined our fingers. "I'm closing up shop now, actually. Would you like some dinner? I'm sure you're famished." Saphira's cheeks turned red, and her smile widened. "There's so much I want to talk to you about!"

How could I say no to a face like that? "Sure. Thank you."

Saphira's cooking filled the air with aromas of fish and what smelled like roasted potatoes. I hadn't said much the entire time she cooked. But she was more than willing to carry the conversation.

"So, how long do you think you're going to stay here?" she yelled from the kitchen.

This time, I smiled for real. We couldn't keep comfortably talking like this, so I walked from the living room into the kitchen and leaned against a nearby wall. "Another week or two, we're thinking."

Saphira giggled, then called, "I would like that! I missed you!"

"I'm right here," I said with a small wave. "Sorry, should've told you."

"*A-ah! Haha!*" Saphira flinched in surprise, then tossed something into the air with her frying pan before stirring it with a wooden spoon. Couldn't tell what it was from here, but it smelled amazing. "How are the girls in your Party doing?"

Wonderful question. "They're okay."

Saphira hummed. "Just okay?"

"Yeah, I guess. I'm convinced one of them might burn me alive, though."

"Did something bad happen with her?"

I shrugged. "I don't know. Can never tell with her."

"I'm really sorry to hear that, Matt. Do you want to talk about it any? That helps me, sometimes. You know, when I have things bothering me."

I thought about it for a few seconds. Felt like I was being torn in opposite directions. Surely, Saphira would also bring to light some other new piece of outrageous Nyarlean law that I hadn't heard of until now. Or offer some sort of unsolicited advice on how to make my problems go away. Or maybe blow up on me for a past I had no hand in.

I sighed. "Thanks, but I did that enough today."

Saphira nodded. "Then I won't pry. Just let me cook for you while you relax. You're well deserving of a good, home-cooked meal."

I frowned. I had to admit I was surprised. I was certain that she would try and get to the bottom of it. Equal parts dreading and preparing for the onslaught of questions that would have come from my Party.

Instead, a few more minutes passed in a silence permeated by Saphira's humming and the sizzle of her frying pan. She took her apron off and placed it over a nearby hook. "Okay! Dinner's ready!"

I took a seat at the table and waited, watching as Saphira carefully sprinkled a number of spices and herbs on top of two heaping plates. When she brought my plate to the table, the smell demanded that I forget all else. Before me was a beautifully cut fish whose name I'm sure I would mispronounce. I made no attempt to guess the name or ask. She'd spent time searing the fish's edges to crisp perfection and served it alongside—well, what looked like—green beans and potatoes.

Saphira took a seat across from me as I cut through a section of the filet with a fork and knife. The meat split apart like butter, and my eyes widened while my mouth salivated. When it hit my tongue, every one of my muscles relaxed, and I breathed a satisfied moan.

"Enjoying it?" Saphira asked while she took a bite from her own plate.

"Understatement of the year." I hadn't noticed how hungry I was until I chewed into that very first morsel. I was quick to slice away another helping and carry it into my mouth. "This is incredible."

"I'm glad to see my cooking is perking you up a bit."

My chewing slowed for a moment. I swallowed and poked at a couple of the greens with my fork. "I've had a lot to think about lately. It's…hard to deal with." I paused. My muscles tensed. "The question that keeps going through my head is 'How does one person deal with it all?'"

Saphira chewed and swallowed. "You're doing a great job, Matt. It sounds to me like you're just under a lot of stress. Probably a lot more than one person can manage." She popped one of the greens into her mouth. "Have you been to the other towns on Ni?"

I shook my head. "Some have made a point of reminding me just how little I know about my own island."

"In their own way, I think they're just trying to help. The reason I'm asking, though," Saphira said as she drained her glass of water, "is that I think you need a couple of days to yourself. Away from the stress, away from your duties."

"That's why I'm here."

"I know," Saphira said with a smile, "but you could take your Party to Abalone. Maybe it'll help you guys relax and sort some things out."

"Abalone?"

"It's a hot spring not far from here. Girls from all over come to Ni to stay there. I think it'll give you all a nice break. Maybe get your spirits up a bit. You deserve it."

"Is it that obvious?"

Saphira gently touched my cheek. "You don't look happy, Matt. Not at all."

I leaned against her hand. "I guess... I guess this isn't what I thought my job would be."

"And what did you think it would be?"

"I don't know. More fun, more laid back. Something like that."

Saphira blinked, then giggled. "Life is what you make it, Matt. If it gives you lemons, you make lemonade. Something my grandma told me. She said it was a popular phrase from a man way back in the day."

Another Earthling, maybe? "My parents used to say the same thing."

Saphira gasped. "Your parents! What were they like? Or is that a bad topic?"

I thought about it for a bit. Military. Strict. That damn parrot. I struggled to come up with any good memories to share. "Maybe another time, if that's okay."

"Another time, then."

The two of us carried on for some time like that. Saphira asking questions, while my answers remained short. No matter how hard I tried, I just couldn't summon up more than ten words in a response. But she was never deterred or impatient. She calmly fit in questions where they seemed appropriate and listened attentively. She asked me where I got some of my new scars and how the battles were going on the other islands. I admitted we hadn't visited Ichi Island yet, but she was impressed enough to know that I'd been to both San and Shi. She marveled at my abbreviated descriptions of the Defiled and the girls of Catania.

We finished dinner and moved to the living room after I did the dishes.

"Oh, I know! What do you think of Quinn?" Saphira asked, seated next to me on her sofa.

"She's, uh, a character. Don't know her well enough, but it seems that for a lot of catgirls, height is cause for a lot of their pent-up anger."

"Oh? If they're shorter, they're angrier?"

"Yeah, something like that," I said with an uncomfortable laugh. Though, Fiona had been an exception in Catania. The image of Quinn tearing my armor to shreds when she'd heard what I said came to mind. "Please don't tell her I said that."

"I don't know," she said with a playful lilt to her voice. "I'll think about it."

Silence surrounded us once more. I listened to the ticking of the clock on the wall, Saphira's warmth next to me. My stresses were gradually washing away, and I had no intention of retrieving them.

"Hey, Matt. Want to feel?" Saphira motioned to her stomach.

My breath caught. "Feel?"

I raised my hand, and Saphira snatched it out of the air. She put my palm on the front of her belly. At first, I didn't feel anything. Who knew? Maybe catgirls were different. Just the idea that a child could be born in three months was nothing short of amazing to me.

But after a while, I felt something. "Was that her kicking?"

Saphira giggled. "That was your daughter, Matt. She's a bit rambunctious. Going to have my hands full with her, I think."

I was entranced. I heard her, and I wanted to respond. Yet, I was so focused on this sensation against my hand. The warmth and life of another person were inside Saphira's stomach. A little girl born from Saphira and me. She'd be her very own person with her own hopes and dreams.

I pulled away slightly and looked at the wall of portraits representing Saphira's family history. All of them were striking in their own right; a lineage carried down for at least fifteen generations.

"You've done something wonderful for me, Matt. I'll never be able to repay you."

I turned back to her to see she had put her hands around her belly, a warm and gentle smile playing on her lips. "You don't owe me anything," I said, returning her smile.

"Still. Thank you."

My walls dropped, and my tension eased. Our conversation flowed easily, and the hours flew by in an instant. Before we knew it, it was far past Saphira's bedtime. As much as I wanted to stay, a part of me understood. Doubt there was a better time than the crack of dawn to get started on a farm. Shizen had burned that into my head.

I opened the front door and breathed in the cool evening air, then turned around to plant a kiss on Saphira's forehead. "You really helped me calm down. Thank you so much, Saphira."

She shook her head. "Think nothing of it. And remember what I said about Abalone. Their hot springs are utter bliss, and you could use the pampering. Just tell them I sent you, and they'll know what to do!"

"I'll do that. Have a great night, Saphira.

"You too, Matt."

Saphira closed the door, and I walked the path back to Keke's house. I'm sure my girls would appreciate a reason to get away, too.

Might as well make this a field trip.

Saphira Pro Tip: Any time you need an ear and a nice meal, Matt, don't be afraid to stop on by.

Chapter 24

The World

When I woke up the next day, Keke's golden eyes greeted me. She was still in her nightgown, body parallel to mine, and her dark hair waterfalled over her shoulder and the blankets. She had her elbow bent, propping the side of her head up at an angle with her hand. Her ears perked as I stirred.

I yawned. "Were you watching me sleep?"

A light blush tinted her cheeks, and she fretted her lip. "Maybe."

I smiled. Through the small window behind her, I noticed the sun was much higher than I'd expected. "What time is it?"

"Nearly midday. I thought you could use the sleep." She moved to touch my face with her hand, then paused. Her gaze said she wanted to ask for permission, but the events of the day before seemed to be holding her back.

I lifted my arm and gently touched her wrist, guiding it the rest of the way to my face. She rested her warm fingers against my cheek, and her shoulders relaxed. "I'm sorry about yesterday," I said.

"No, don't be." Keke shook her head. "I realized that I may have pushed you too hard. To talk, I mean. That's not fair."

"Sometimes I, well, I just don't know what to say," I admitted.

"I think we all have moments like that." She traced my cheekbone with her thumb and searched my face. "I—" she blinked and took a deep breath, "I was like that when my mom died."

The pain that wracked her features drove straight through my heart. She so rarely talked about her mom. Of course I'd wondered about it, but it seemed time and time again like a sore subject. "I can only imagine how hard that was," I replied.

She nodded. "There were full weeks where I didn't say a word. Cannoli and Aurora—oh, that was Cannoli's mom's name—" she explained quickly, "—they took me in and cared for me."

"You were still young, then."

"Yeah. I'd barely turned fourteen. Not quite old enough to live on my own yet." Keke let her hand fall on my pillow, just inches above my hair, then leaned her head against her shoulder. "I guess, when I'm around you, I forget how difficult a time that was. I just… I want to see you smile and take your pain away."

I shifted my arm beneath hers and snaked my hand behind her back. Cupping the side of her face with my other palm, I traced the slope of her jawline with my thumb. I dropped my voice to a whisper—as if anyone else would hear me anyway—but the question I needed an answer for felt so damn raw. "When did it stop hurting so damn bad?"

She snuggled closer to me, tucking her head beneath my cheek and wrapping her arms around my waist. "I don't know. Sometimes it still hurts. But, one morning, I woke up and had breakfast with Cannoli and asked if we could go fishing. By the time we had lunch, I'd talked more than I had in months. Every day after that, it got just a little bit easier." Her ears tickled my cheeks, and she curled her tail around my legs. "I know it's not what you want to hear, but you just need time. And we'll all be waiting for you."

I kissed the top of her head and returned her embrace. "Thanks, Keke."

"Mmhmm," she hummed into my chest, hugging me tighter.

We stayed that way for some time, my thoughts drifting away with each exhale of Keke's warm breath against my skin. For the first time in a long time, I felt completely relaxed.

"So, why were you watching me sleep again?" I chuckled, then tickled her sides. "Hm?"

Keke squeaked and squirmed beneath my touch. "Matt!"

"I'll just keep doing it until you tell me," I teased.

"Aha! Let's get—*ha!*—lunch! Please!" she squealed.

I sighed dramatically. "Fine. Don't tell me." After a few more well-aimed pokes, I kissed her cheeks. "Yeah. Alright. I'm hungry."

She leaped from the bed, her thin nightgown resting on the very tops of her thighs. Her hair was still messy with sleep and our tussle, and her grin rivaled the afternoon sun. "Out of bed, then, sleepyhead!"

After a quick peek at Keke's empty food stores, and when Cannoli didn't answer her door, we decided on Junonia Inn for lunch. Let me go on record to say that checking Cannoli's availability to cook us lunch was Keke's idea, not mine.

Not like I was going to protest, but still.

The inn's restaurant was quiet, and nearly every table was empty. A stray catgirl here or there slurped their stew or enjoyed a cold ale with a friend. I was pleasantly surprised, however, to spot Ceres seated with Tristan and Ara in a corner booth.

"No Cannoli, huh?" I remarked to Keke.

Keke shrugged. "She said she needed some time alone. Generally, when she's upset, she spends a lot of time in prayer. Aurora was very strict on Saoirse's teachings with her."

"I see."

"Ho there, Matt. Keke," Hilda, one of the waitresses that frequently worked the inn, greeted us with a bright smile and a wave of her hand. Her hair was cropped at her chin, and her build suggested she'd pumped way more [Strength] than necessary for a barmaid. Then again, I'd seen her single-handedly carry a barrel of ale over one shoulder before. So there was that.

"Good afternoon, Hilda." Keke returned her smile and wave. "We'll take two bowls of whatever's hot and some tea. I think we'll sit over there." She pointed to where our companions were seated.

"Of course, doll. I'll have that right out," the barmaid replied with a cordial nod, then dismissed herself to the kitchen.

Ceres spied me first, then jumped out of her seat and bowed low. "My lord! I did not know you would join us. I would not have...w-well," she stammered and blushed, then gestured to her dress.

I hadn't realized it from far away since the outfit was still primarily black, but she was wearing an ensemble much more akin to the style of Ni Island. A long-sleeved blouse with a white sash tied around the front paired with a pleated black skirt. White thigh highs topped with black ribbons hugged her sculpted calves, and polished leather ankle boots completed the look.

Holy shit, that's adorable. I rubbed the back of my neck and shifted the weight of my feet. "You look great, Ceres."

"Really?" She beamed. "Oh, thank you! I must confess, the fashions of this island are just so charming! Tristan and Ara were kind enough to help me choose!"

Tristan blushed furiously, hiding his face behind his tankard. "Ara was a lot more help than I was."

"That was nice of you, Ara," I said.

Ara hummed a noncommittal response and spooned another helping of soup into her mouth. Thanks to traveling with her for some time, I understood her embarrassment versus her frustration. This was definitely the former. She was clearly not used to being complimented—not by anyone.

"Mind if we join you?" Keke asked.

"Certainly! We would love nothing more! Please, take a seat!" Ceres gestured to the empty bench behind her.

There was plenty of room on Ceres's side of the table, so Keke scooted in first, then me. Ceres smoothed her skirt beneath her legs and sat back down.

"How are you feeling, Matt?" Tristan asked carefully, avoiding directly meeting my eye.

So, some thread of what happened with Yomi had reached Tristan's ears. I glanced at Keke, then Ceres.

"He was really worried about you. We all were," Keke provided.

"Since we do not know if this heathen [Dark Priest] will dare show her face afresh, we believe it imperative that everyone in our traveling company at least is made aware of the situation," Ceres added.

"After what she's done? She would be a fool to chance such a thing," Ara grumbled.

The anxiety I'd just barely shed began to prickle once more at the back of my neck, creeping down my spine like a thousand-armed beast. Tiny flecks of annoyance, anger, and a burning desire for this whole situation to be over danced along my skin like a hot breeze.

Keke must have caught on, quickly interjecting, "We'll handle her if that day ever comes. There's nothing for it right now."

I took a deep breath and ran a hand through my hair. *Time, Kelmer. Just give it time.* "Yeah. I'm feeling better, thanks," I said, then immediately jumped subjects. "Saphira told me there's a city close to here with some hot springs? Abalone?"

Keke grinned, latching on to the change immediately. "Abalone is great. It's a catgirl's paradise. Hot springs, manicures, massages, and great food! It's only a couple of hours away."

"That sounds divine!" Ceres clapped her hands, eyes glittering with excitement. "Is it a difficult journey?"

Keke shook her head. "Not at all. There's a road that leads straight there, and it's traveled all the time by girls from Junonia. Obviously, there are a few roaches here and there, but nothing we can't handle by now."

Tristan ladled a spoonful of soup, then watched it as he spilled it drop by drop back into the bowl. "Is it really alright? If we go, I mean?"

"Why wouldn't it be?" I asked.

"Every day the young master is away from his island could cause harm to those we've left behind," Ara explained, switching her stare between the three of us.

There were a dozen things I wanted to say in response, the most burning a comment on Celestia's practices of keeping Tristan locked up. Even so, Ara had a point. Throughout my travels from San Island to Shi, I'd felt like I'd neglected my territory. "Well, we need to wait for Espada to finish Ceres's armor before we travel to Ichi since we have no clue what's waiting for us. That'll take a couple of weeks."

"And we've all been through a lot," Keke finished for me. "I think it would be best to take some time off. See more of the island and refresh ourselves before we face Ichi Island."

Tristan repeated the scooping and dribbling of his soup. "What about Lynn?"

Ara's face burned red, and she stared into her lap. "While I dislike being so long apart from my sister, I believe Celestia will have left her alone. Lynn is not aware of what happened. I...I only ask that we return to Venicia before departing to Ichi. She deserves to know my plans."

"Of course, Ara." Tristan nodded.

"Your sister?" Ceres asked.

"Yes. My sister still resides on Shi Island since a certain group of individuals tricked me into thinking the young master was my sister." She shot a glare in my direction.

Keke and I squirmed under her gaze, both of us turning to look at something inconspicuous.

Hilda returned with our bowls of piping hot stew, baked rolls, and a freshly brewed pot of tea that she poured into cups for Keke and me. Ceres took a third teacup from the tray and filled it, watching Tristan and Ara carefully.

"Regardless of my needs, whatever you decide, young master, I will remain by your side," Ara reassured him.

Tristan set the spoon down, drummed his fingers on the table, then looked at Ara. "What do you want to do, Ara?"

Ara paused, her eyes wide and her ears flattening back on her head. "I beg your pardon?"

"I think you've more than earned a vacation. Is it not something you'd like?"

Ara mouthed silent words, then cleared her throat. "I-I believe I would enjoy it, yes—"

"Are you comfortable waiting to return to Shi Island?" Tristan pressed.

She smoothed her apron and readjusted herself in her seat. "So long as we journey there before Ichi, I believe we have time."

Tristan smiled and took her hand. "Then let's take a break."

Ara flushed, Ceres gasped with delight, and Keke laughed beneath her breath.

"It's settled then. Let's spend a few days in Abalone," I said.

Ceres Pro Tip: I hope you do not mind me donning Ni Island's attire, my lord. It is quite comfortable, and I feel right at home!

Chapter 25
Dark and Stormy

When the morning came, Keke was already preparing to leave for Abalone. I rose into a sitting position and ran a hand through my hair, yawning. "What time is it?"

"It's time for you to get up!" Keke called from the room over.

I moved to one edge of the bed, threw my legs over, then leaned my hands on my knees and stretched. It was nice to wake up to her each morning. Her scent lingered among the sheets. You'd get no complaint from me if I could wake up to that every day for the rest of my life.

Assuming my life expectancy is going to be any higher than the average man in Nyarlea.

"Did you talk to Cannoli or Ravyn yet?" I'd tried to find them the day before, but Cannoli refused to come to the door and Ravyn was MIA. On Keke's suggestion, we'd decided to look one last time before we left.

Keke came into the room and handed me a cup of tea with a shake of her head. "I asked everyone in the market about Ravyn, but she's nowhere to be found." She sat beside me on the bed, hesitated with a finger at her lip, then took my hand. "Cannoli wouldn't answer. Ceres says she's still in prayer, locked away in her tiny sanctuary." Something about the look on my face must've seemed grim to her because she immediately changed her tone. "But we're still going to have a great time! I'm going to make sure of it!"

"Ah, thanks, Keke. Really." I didn't want to say anything more out of fear of bringing down the mood, but I made a mental note to visit Cannoli once I had breakfast.

Seeing Cannoli before we left became my prime objective. I had to wonder just how many things she was bottling up. If the timeline of Keke's mom's passing was anything to go by, it would mean Aurora had only died just a few years prior. Which, well, you could've fooled me. Cannoli sure didn't carry herself like someone whose parent had passed away in recent years.

I had to assume some of the more recent events regarding our Party's travels and the gruesome matches with the Defiled had to be weighing heavily upon her as well.

I probably didn't help much in that department.

I approached her door, took a deep breath, and steeled myself before knocking. I tapped my foot while I waited, waving to the occasional passerby. After about ten or fifteen seconds, I knocked again, this time calling out to her. "Hey, Cannoli, are you in there? It's me, Matt. Can we talk for a minute?"

I put my hands into my pockets while I waited. It was a cool morning. White, fluffy clouds paraded through the air, and a gentle breeze blew by. It reminded me a lot of the comfortable Saturday mornings I'd wake up to as a kid. Those were the best. Guess it was a good reminder to live in the now instead of futurizing everything.

Another fifteen seconds passed, and I was beginning to grow concerned. Under any other circumstances on Earth, I would've never tried to jiggle the handle. That was a great way to get the police called on you. The girls had a knack for reminding me just how important men were, though, and what I could get away with was more than slightly alarming. It left a bad taste in my mouth to try and flaunt my powers over the girls.

And yet, I jiggled the handle. Sure enough, it was locked. That wouldn't have been strange to me in the past, but I found that many of the girls on Ni Island didn't worry too much about locking their doors. I assumed that it had something to do with the fact that everyone knew everyone.

Our very own Mister Roger's Neighborhood.

Then I saw it. There was a silhouette behind the shades. With the sun shining so brightly, it was easy to see. Cannoli's shape was undeniable.

"I know you're in there, Cannoli." I watched as the silhouette fled. I sighed and knocked again. "I just wanted to invite you out somewhere. Somewhere fun. Somewhere we can get away from the stress of the daily grind. You interested?"

There was a long pause. Maybe she was mulling it over. I could see it now—she'd be standing in front of the door, twiddling her fingers and biting her lip, afraid to get in anyone's way or disrupt the peace. While I was willing to wait and give her time to come to me—or hell, anyone in her own time—if we were going to visit Abalone today, I needed an answer.

Just as I was about to knock for the last time, I heard a click, and the door slowly squeaked open. It took a lot out of me to hide my shock. Before me stood Cannoli. She was still in her nightgown, her cheeks and eyes pink and puffy.

Has she been crying all this time?

"Hi, Matt," she said in little more than a whisper.

"H-hi." I put my arm down and put on my best smile. "Been lookin' for you."

"Sorry."

One-word responses. Not a great look so far. I tried to keep my head on tight as best as I could. "Is Ceres not here?"

"I guess not," she whimpered and shifted her weight from one foot to the other.

I cleared my throat. "You know, Keke brought up a great point. We've all been stressed out a lot lately. Ni Island is the best place a guy could be, just saying." I was pretty sure my tone came off as sincere and friendly, but Cannoli's expression remained sullen, almost vacant.

She didn't even look up at me. Just crossed one arm across her chest and let her hair fall over her shoulders.

I continued. "Uh, so, what Keke was saying was that maybe we should take a trip to Abalone. She told me it's a great place for manicures and pedicures. A catgirl's dream if she's looking to get away and relax for a while."

"When would we go?"

"Today! As soon as everyone's ready—"

"No, thanks."

Way to shut a guy down. Okay, um, let's dig a bit. "Oh. Uh, okay. Are you sure, though? I'd love your company, and I think you could really—"

She didn't slam the door in my face, but it was rather sudden when she closed it. If I was being honest, a part of me was relieved that she was willing to be this selfish. On the other hand, though, my concern for her worsened.

I raised my hand to knock, then stopped. *No, Kelmer. Just leave her be. If she needs space, then so be it.* I breathed deeply and left.

That just left Ravyn. After everything that'd happened between us, I had no idea how to approach her anymore. Every interaction felt awkward and stiff. It's not like the last conversation we had was anything approaching cordial or friendly, either.

So I wandered. The road was quiet, which was a bit of a weird change from the hustle and bustle I was used to, particularly around Saphira and Espada's workstations. I asked every catgirl I passed about Ravyn. Some of them had seen her shopping occasionally or making the journey to and from her home. A few of them were convinced that Ravyn was up to no good and creating some sort of new witchcraft or other.

Once in a while, I'd catch something out of the corner of my eye, look, and see nothing there. Knowing she had access to [Displace] and a number of other Skills and Spells she hadn't told me about had me convinced that hunting her down was an impossible task.

Is she avoiding me on purpose, then?

I visited her mountainside hideout for the second time in as many days. I knocked on the door a few times, giving her the same courtesy that I gave Cannoli. Unlike Cannoli, however, I had no proof that Ravyn was actually inside. I covered the sides of my face and peered through the small window in her door. Two candles were burned down to their bases, flickering their final breaths in the darkness. Even with the low light, I could tell that the books were strewn about the room more than usual. Some of them were face down on the floor, others had pages torn out. Hell, the ashes of one charred, thick tome blew into the breeze from under the door.

I hoped this wouldn't turn into one of those *Lifetime* original movies my mom used to watch, where the girl ended up parting from the boy forever because 'things just won't ever be the same again.' The very thought gave me anxiety, and as I drew away from the door, a figure descending the stairs to Ravyn's place caught my eye.

"Ara?"

The maid curtsied, her legs trembling as she glanced down the cliff beside us. "Y-yes, Matt. I came here to c-convince Ravyn that she should partake in the," she paused to steady her breathing, "in the festivities at Abalone. But it seems I am no longer necessary." She swallowed and began to ascend the stairs. Very quickly, might I add.

"Wait!" I reached out to her, but she had already left. I was sure she was just waiting at the top where it was safe, so I followed. Sure enough, she was still there when I arrived. "You came to help Ravyn?"

Ara cleared her throat. "I did not come to help that Shulan-birthed travesty of a woman." She puffed out her chest and straightened her back. "It was out of concern for the young master. He understands that there is a rift between you and Ravyn currently. It was his desire to see you both in better spirits—thus, I have come to convince her."

"Well, you're wasting your time. I appreciate the sentiment, but she's not home."

Ara raised a brow. "Are you certain?"

No, I'm not. But, your good intentions aside, I don't think it's a great idea for you two to talk right now.

"Positive. Door locked, lights off. Maybe we should look elsewhere."

"Hmm." Ara didn't seem convinced. The last thing I wanted to see right now was these two go at it. Even if Ara did mean well, she had no idea what was going on between us, so out of respect for our privacy, I tried to wave the idea away. "If that is so. I apologize. I understand that it is not my place to interfere. I simply—"

"Wish for Tristan to be content. Yes, I know."

She frowned. "How presumptuous of you. While it is true that I came here because I wish to see the men get along well, you would be incorrect in assuming that he alone is the reason for my visit."

I couldn't hide it. My mouth hung open, and I could feel a slow grin coming on. "Are we becoming friends?"

Ara's cheeks turned to a hue of red that I'd only seen once before—when Tristan had mentioned the sandwiches she often made for him. She swallowed hard. "I would not go that far, Matt." She turned on her heel and continued back down the road. "Now, please. Let us locate that filthy woman so that we may leave. We have a schedule to adhere to."

"Sure, Ara. Sure."

Keke Pro Tip: I know it's hard, Matt, but Cannoli will come around in her own time. Just let her be.

Chapter 26

Clover Club

We'd all agreed to meet at the tavern as our set-off point. Ara and I returned together, and as we rounded the corner to the door, an agitated Ravyn stormed past us. Her shoulder collided with mine, and she hissed a few choice words under her breath. She smelled of alcohol, and Ball was nowhere to be found. Without another word, she continued on as if she hadn't seen me.

"Hey! Ravyn!" I called after her.

She spared me a single glance from the corner of her eye, her frown deepening, then continued on her way. I moved to follow her, but Ara caught my coat sleeve.

"Let her go," she murmured.

Ceres was next out the door, sighing as she watched Ravyn march quickly from the inn. She folded her arms over her chest and shook her head. "I believe it is clear that Ravyn will not be accompanying us on this excursion."

"Yeah, kinda figured," I replied, rubbing the back of my neck. "She say why?"

"She did not. However, I still believe it is in our best interest to take this time away," Ceres said.

"Is the young master still inside?" Ara asked, changing the subject.

"Yes. Tristan, Keke, and I were awaiting your return." Ceres relaxed and broke into a smile. She was still wearing her new Ni Island garb, and she toyed with the braid over her shoulder. "I am very excited to see more of this breathtaking island."

"Me, too," I admitted. "After you." Gesturing inside the inn, I followed Ceres to where Keke and Tristan were sitting.

"Hey, Matt!" Tristan waved with a smile. "Ready to get on the road?"

"Whenever you guys are. I think some fresh air'll do me good." I stretched my arms over my head and waited for them to finish their drinks.

"Did Ravyn talk to you?" Keke asked me before downing the remainder of her tea.

"No. Cannoli wouldn't either," I sighed.

"Cannoli came out of her room?" Ceres asked, eyes wide. "I have called to her for days. Was she all right?"

That's not an easy question to answer. Cannoli was very clearly not in a great headspace, but she'd made a point to remind me of her desire to be alone. "She doesn't want to come with us, either."

"Cannoli will be okay," Keke added quickly. "She just needs time. That's all."

Thanks, Keke.

"So it will just be us five, then?" Ara asked, meeting each of our stares.

"Looks like it."

"Let's get going, then!" Keke announced, tossing a few Bells onto the table to pay for their drinks.

Even though I was assured that the road to Abalone was safe, I still insisted we travel in our [Combat Mode]s, just in case anything decided to take its frustrations out on our group.

Can't get much worse than Ravyn, though.

I was worried about her and Cannoli. Stuff I said and stuff I should have said assaulted me from every angle, and I found myself picking my own past sentences apart. Not like it would do any good, but the last thing I wanted was to lose either of them.

"Hey." Keke touched my forearm, dragging me out of the quagmire of my thoughts. "They'll be alright. Ravyn's tough as nails. And I know she doesn't look it, but so is Cannoli."

I nodded. "Just wish I knew what to say to fix this, you know?"

"I know. But sometimes, words aren't enough. Enjoy the time away, and we'll try again when we get back. Okay?"

"Yeah. Okay."

The trail was well-loved, paved by thousands of footsteps of frequent travelers going back and forth. We passed a few other small groups returning from Abalone, offering a friendly greeting here and there. Ara's icy stare kept the more boisterous ones at bay, daring them to try and get close to Tristan with her gaze. More of Ni Island's dense forests flanked either side of the road, offering enough shade to keep us out of the heat and a perfect canopy when we paused for a break.

I gauged that we were just coming up on the second hour when the trees cleared, revealing thatched roofs on ivy-coated houses. Floral trellises, framed decorative windows, and gardens in full bloom lined the walls of each modest house. Just from the edge of the town, Abalone reminded me of the miniature fairy villages my aunt would collect. Except this one was filled with catgirls.

As we looped our way around the road and closed in on the town square, I realized that Abalone was more crowded than I'd ever seen Junonia. Benches and outdoor tables were filled with catgirls sharing meals, drinks, or ice cream. The high giggles of kittens pierced the air as they chased one another through gardens and scampered up enormous trees.

"Wait. Kittens?" I asked aloud. "I thought I was the first guy here in a while?"

Keke nodded. "You are. Girls come from the other islands to visit Abalone. Look at their outfits." She pointed to a set of twins braiding each other's hair.

Sure enough, they wore elaborate brocade dresses with high collars and delicate hair ornaments. "Ah. San Island."

"Goodness. I had forgotten how beautiful San Island clothing is," Ceres murmured in wonderment. "It is so flattering!"

I chuckled. "Careful. You'll have to start carrying a wardrobe with you."

"I may need an upgrade to my [Cat Pack], yes," Ceres hummed with thought. "And yet, I am so attached to Ni Island's style. It will be difficult to change once again."

"So, where do we start?" Tristan asked, adjusting the pack around his shoulder.

"This place is filled with inns and taverns. Just pick a direction," Keke replied.

"What do you think, Ara?" Tristan turned to his maid in waiting. "Which way should we go?"

Ara blushed, and her ears flicked at hearing her name. She peered around and tapped her finger to her lips. "I-I would be content with wherever my young master should choose—"

Tristan grinned. "I want you to choose."

The red in her cheeks deepened, and her tail rocked quickly back and forth between her ankles. "Um, t-that one over there looks lovely." Her voice ebbed with every word as she pointed to her right. She bowed her head and let her hair mask part of her face.

A small wooden sign with hand-painted letters proclaimed the inn as 'The Gem of Abalone.' The narrow building stretched nearly three houses wide and two stories high. Vivid purple and blue flowers flourished in the gardens and spilled over clay vases situated on the balconies. Lazy tangles of steam danced high above the rooftop, suggesting the inn had its own hot spring for its guests.

"Oh, I agree! Let us seek rooms!" Ceres clapped her hands.

Keke looked at me with wide eyes, and a tiny smile tugged at the corner of her lips. "I've never been able to stay here before. It's, well," she tapped the toe of her shoe to the ground, "it's expensive."

I still had a decent amount of Bells left over from the quest and our adventures on the other island. And how the hell was I supposed to say no to that face? "Let me go ask." I was six steps away when fast footsteps soon followed.

"I shall accompany you!" Ceres proclaimed, skipping to my side before I could say otherwise. She hooked her arm through mine with a grin, then froze and dropped her hand. "O-oh, my goodness. I have forgotten my place, my lord. Please, forgive my insolence."

"Hey. We're on vacation. You're allowed to be excited." I took her hand and squeezed it. "And you can still call me 'Matt,' you know."

Ceres flushed and looked at our entwined hands while she toyed with her braid, then nodded. "Right. Thank you, M-Matt," she said, barely above a whisper.

My name on her lips made my heart skip. I swallowed the thoughts that followed and led her to the door of the inn.

Inside were polished wooden floors, and elaborate floral paintings hung on the walls. The lobby was set up a lot like the hotels in my last life, with a long marble desk and two catgirls sitting behind it, each poring through their own thick tome. Keys hung on a narrow panel behind them with room numbers carefully inscribed in black above each one. The whole place was spotless—like eat-off-the-floors clean.

The girls caught sight of us and immediately stood, bowing low. "Welcome to The Gem of Abalone!" they greeted warmly in unison.

"Thanks," I said.

They exchanged surprised looks and a silent conversation between themselves before turning back to me. The one on the left lifted her quill and set its tip on a half-filled page. "How many nights will you be staying?"

"Three nights," I said. We'd made a group decision during our walk for the length of our stay. Honestly, I didn't feel comfortable leaving Cannoli alone for any longer than that. "How much is it per night?"

"Twenty Bells," the one on the right replied.

Oh, I was expecting worse. "Per room?"

"Per person," they said in unison.

Shit. Twenty times five…times three… Three hundred Bells, and that's not including food or otherwise.

"Please allow me to add that this fare includes a complimentary breakfast, unlimited use of our private hot spring, and access to our gaming room," the left girl added.

"Gaming room?" My first thought was a LAN cafe. Obviously, that was impossible, but I didn't know what a 'gaming room' looked like in Nyarlea.

"Oh, yes! We offer only the highest quality card games, board games, and more. The tavern serves drinks there at all hours so that you may play to your heart's content," the right girl explained.

"M-my l—" Ceres started, then looked at our still-joined hands. "Matt, please allow me to pay for half of the total cost."

"What? No way. I can get it," I said, still trying to calculate just how much the rest of the trip was going to cost.

Ceres squeezed my hand and smiled. "I insist."

I chewed the inside of my lip, watching her face while I deliberated. She really wanted to do this. And, I had to admit, it would help. If the food was just as expensive, I was going to be in trouble by day two. "Okay. But I'll find a way to pay you back later."

Her smile widened, and she nodded. "I am confident that you will think of something."

Was that an insinuation, Ceres?

We paid for all five people, securing ourselves two large rooms—Keke, Ceres, and I would share one while Tristan and Ara had another. Then we went outside to tell the others. Keke cheered and threw her arms around my neck when I handed her the key to our room.

Something told me that we all were about to get a lot more than we bargained for from Abalone.

Ceres Pro Tip: I have saved my Bells from my work as a [Magic Knight] for just such an occasion! Please, allow me to treat us all!

Side Quest

Dragon's Dream

Ravyn was running out of bars in Shulan. Too many drinks led to a dangerous loss of inhibitions that led to having her name blacklisted from the establishment.

Whatever. Fuck 'em.

She was so sick of the assholes in Shulan. On San Island. None of them remembered Finn or what he'd sacrificed to keep them safe and thriving. Now it was all about Cailu. The blonde elf cunt who expected more out of the girls in his Party than the damn Queen. Yomi could keep him. Seemed she'd forgotten about Finn, too.

Ravyn twisted the serpent band around her finger, and the echo of his hand in hers danced along her skin. She bit back the swelling hurricane of emotions in her chest and let her arm drop. She needed a drink. *Now.*

Turning off the bustling main roads of the illuminated city led to a twisted patch of seedier establishments. The places her mother had always warned her about. Gloomy, winding roads with darkened doorsteps that required passwords for entry. Many of the pick-pocketing kittens shared one-room living spaces in this part of town beneath their thieving elders. There were a few watering holes where a thirsty girl could find a drink, and while Ravyn didn't exactly fit in with the crowd, she certainly wasn't banned from any of them.

Don't have anyone to tell me no anymore, anyway. Not Mom, not Yomi, not Finn.

Just as Ravyn picked a shadowy doorway to enter, there was a tap on her shoulder. She hadn't heard anyone approaching and, as a result, nearly leaped out of her skin. Readying a [Fire Ball], she spun on her heel to face down her opponent.

"Woah, *woah,* there!" Bright green eyes shimmered in the glow of Ravyn's hand. She threw up her hands near her shoulders, palms empty, showing that she wasn't armed. "I come in peace."

Ravyn scowled and sapped the magic away from her hand. "Whatever you're selling, I'm not interested."

The young woman took a step back, and Ravyn suddenly realized how short she was. The tips of her ears barely brushed Ravyn's shoulders. "No holes in your dress, clear eyes, combed hair, white teeth. You don't seem the type craving a trip."

"I'm not here for drugs." Ravyn narrowed her eyes. "I just want a fucking drink."

"Then come with me. Let's get you a drink." Her gaze wandered to the top of the dark building's doorway. "You won't find it in there."

"I can't go to any of the taverns on the main road."

She grinned. "Sure you can. Come on."

Ravyn took one last look at the door, grunted her assent, then followed the stranger back into the glittering heart of Shulan.

"You have a name?" Ravyn asked.

"Sumire. Sumi. Whatever you fancy is fine. You?"

"Ravyn," she replied curtly.

Sumire's hair caught Ravyn's attention in the light—a burnt orange with black and white streaks throughout; a pattern mirrored in her pierced ears and slender tail. One side of her head was shaved, with the remaining hair flipped to the opposite shoulder. A black and red corset hugged her curves, the hips leading into a short tabard draping around tight thigh highs. Twin daggers hung in sheathes on either hip, and the buckles on her boots jingled with each step. Even if she was short, she carried herself with quite the attitude.

Just as she was about to lead them into the warmly lit tavern, Ravyn touched her shoulder. "Hey. They don't want me here."

"Roachshit." Sumire grinned and winked. "Follow me. You'll see."

The tables were packed, and the swell of conversation swallowed them whole as they moved deeper inside. The catgirl proprietress that had thrown Ravyn out just three nights before eyed her over a glass she was polishing with a white cloth.

"What part of 'Don't step foot in my pub again' didn't resonate the first time?" the proprietress growled as they approached the bartop.

"Kayla, sweet. Ravyn here's my guest tonight. Won't you fetch her a drink?" Sumire swiped a leather pouch from her [Cat Pack] and tossed it on the counter. Golden Bells spilled forward, clinking together and glimmering enticingly in the overhead lights. "With a few Bells and your recent delivery, I think we can let her stay. Don't you?"

Kayla scowled, her narrowed eyes flickering from the Bells to Sumire's face. "If she causes a scene, you're both out. Understood?"

Sumire shook her head, her smile widening. "We wouldn't dream of it. Now, two Dragon's Dreams, if you would."

Kayla swept the Bells from the counter into her apron and moved down the bar without another word.

"The hell's a Dragon's Dream?" Ravyn asked.

"An Ichi Island specialty. Had to teach Kayla to mix one a long time ago." Sumire gestured to the stool for Ravyn to sit first before she took the one beside her. "Needs a special liquor made from the desert fruit out there. Just so happens to be an exclusive offering for Kayla's patrons thanks to yours truly."

"You go to Ichi that often?" Ravyn raised an eyebrow.

"Oh yeah. May as well get my own place there at this point," Sumire laughed. "Dry as a fucking bone, and the girls are uh…interesting. But it's good for business."

Ravyn had never been to Ichi. Even in her travels with Finn and limited time spent with Cailu, she'd only visited Nyarlothep, then returned to San Island. Returned home. "Well, good for you."

Kayla returned with two tall glasses filled to the brim with a fiery red mixture, then topped with a pawberry.

"Looks like a fruity bitch drink," Ravyn remarked.

The proprietress opened her mouth to speak, but Sumire raised a hand and offered a slight shake of her head. "Don't let looks deceive you."

"Go easy on them," Kayla hissed and vanished to help a new set of patrons at the end of the bar.

Ravyn shrugged and took a sip. The response was immediate. Warmth trickled through her veins and tickled her fingers, crawling to her toes and then back to her throat. "Fuck," she murmured.

"You don't seem like a 'fruity bitch drink' kind of girl," Sumire said, watching Ravyn take another long pull. "You do seem like you have a lot on your mind."

Ravyn hesitated. "Yeah, well, gonna need more booze to talk about that."

Sumire nodded, watching as she finished her glass. With a wave to a disgruntled Kayla, she ordered Ravyn another.

The Dragon's Dream was probably the strongest thing Ravyn had enjoyed all week. And she was ready to throw back as many of the damn things Sumire was willing to put in front of her.

Visions of Finn flooded her memory with each glass she saw through to the bottom. His laugh, his touch, his voice. His first failed attempts at [Alchemy] and then his numerous successes. Finn protecting her against countless Defiled. Finn confessing his love and suggesting they run from it all.

The pleasant tingling along her skin was intoxicating, and, against her better judgment, the drink worked its magic on her tongue.

"I couldn't protect him," Ravyn whispered. "It's my fault."

Sumire observed quietly, patiently taking sips from her red-tinged glass.

Ravyn looked at her. "The man before Cailu was mine to protect. And I fucked it up."

"Ah. One of Finn's girls," Sumire replied gently. "He was a quiet one. Kept to himself."

Ravyn worked her jaw while the weight of Sumire's words took hold. "You... You remember Finn?"

"Mhm. Didn't get to talk to him, but I'd see him around." She swirled her drink in thought. "I think he had good intentions, but, well, I think you're taking too much credit."

"What do you mean?" Ravyn rubbed at her eyes. Why the hell were they wet?

"This world is a shit show. You have to be able to fend for yourself, or you're fucked." Sumire took another long draw from her glass. "We can't protect everyone, and they can't protect us. Even in a Party, it's every catgirl for themselves."

Ravyn wanted to tell her she was wrong. That it had been Ravyn's fucking job to protect Finn. She'd promised him they could vanish from it all and start their own family. Just the two of them.

And in the end, neither of them was strong enough.

Sumire signaled for Kayla to bring another round. "Besides, aren't the men supposed to protect us?"

"Finn was different," Ravyn snarled.

Lifting her hands at her shoulders as she had earlier, Sumire shook her head. "Hey, no harm intended. You knew him way better than I did."

The creeping thought that Finn just hadn't been good enough for Nyarlea had plagued Ravyn more than once. She'd swallowed it and pushed it away every time, but hearing it out of someone else's mouth had a way of adding a measure of truth to it. Even Yomi had said something of the like a few times.

No. Fuck that. He was everything this world needed.

Another long drink from Ravyn's refreshed tonic. Another long glare from Kayla as she went to tend to other people.

Sumire snagged a hefty pouch of Bells from her [Cat Pack] and set them on the bar. "You can drink as much as you like on me tonight. But let me tell you this while you're still sober." She touched Ravyn's shoulder. "Nyarlea needs strong people like you. But it's impossible to protect everyone you care about. Finn may not be here, but you are. That says something."

Ravyn emptied her glass. "That I fucking failed?"

"Nah. That there's something still driving you to keep going," Sumire replied. "I think you should keep going, Ravyn."

Ravyn shook her head and pushed her empty glass forward. "Thanks for the drinks."

Sumire favored her with a long stare, then replied, "Any time."

Ravyn left the tavern without another word. It didn't matter what some stranger thought. Baka. She looked up at the sky and stared bleary-eyed at the stars.

Keep going...

Ravyn Pro Tip: When did I summon Bally? A long time ago. I just...didn't always keep him around all the time.

Chapter 27

Mint Julep

Our room was on the second floor with a perfect view of the forests beyond. The hot spring itself was masked by tall walls of flat rock, obscuring the water and its visitors but not detracting from the scenery laid out before us.

Keke and Ceres unpacked their things, filling the drawers of our wardrobe with outfits and tiny cosmetic bottles while I stood at the floor-to-ceiling window, letting myself think about nothing for the span of a few heartbeats. It was nice. I'd honestly forgotten what being 'bored' felt like ever since I'd arrived in Nyarlea. Maybe this was my chance at feeling it again.

The steam drifting above the rocks looked incredibly inviting. The last time I'd been in a hot spring was, well, with Marianne. And that pond was a fraction of this one's size. The rocky frame suggested a hot spring the size of an Olympic swimming pool. A separate building stood parallel to the rocks, apparently for guests to change in and out of their clothing while using the facilities, and it ran the length of the hotel itself.

While I let my thoughts wander with the misty haze, I asked aloud, "So, which side is for the guys?"

Keke and Ceres paused in their organization and exchanged curious looks.

"What?" I asked.

Ceres clasped her hands at her waist and bowed, favoring staring at the floor rather than my face. "There…there is not a designated area for men in the hot spring, my lord."

I rubbed the back of my neck. "Am I not allowed inside, then?"

The beginnings of a knowing smile twitched at Keke's lips. *That's not good.* "Of course you are, Matt. We all go together."

I blinked, opened my mouth to say something, then blinked again. "Do we wear swimsuits?"

Ceres shook her head, still not meeting my eyes. "No, my lord."

I chewed on her response, watching Keke's face carefully. She was far more entertained by this prospect than I was. I tried again. "You're saying we all go into the bath together. Naked."

"That's right," Keke said.

"With other catgirls I've never met." *And I have to pretend to feel nothing. Which is real damn obvious if I'm not wearing anything.*

"Yes. Shall that be an issue?" Ceres tugged on the braid over her shoulder, nibbling at her lip. "If it would set you at ease, we can find a less populated area. Perhaps a different town entirely?"

There were a lot of things I wanted to say and do, but wussing out of a public hot spring was last on my list. "N-no. It's fine."

"Are you sure?" Keke stalked to where I stood, trailing one finger from my shoulder to my wrist. "There are other inns in the city."

I vehemently shook my head, reaffirming my stance. "I'm fine. We've already paid for it."

"If you say so." Keke grinned and finished putting her things away.

A knock sounded on the door, and I breathed in relief, happy to drop the subject, even if it was only for a few seconds. Tristan and Ara awaited me, both with smiles on their faces.

"This place is wonderful!" Tristan announced, gesturing to the wide hallways and delicate engravings on the door. "It's like heaven!"

"My young master is quite pleased with my choice," Ara said, practically glowing. "I have never stayed anywhere as lovely."

"I want to go to the hot spring! Can we go?" Tristan asked, looking back and forth between Ara and me as if we were making the executive decisions here.

"Of course, sir. Anything you desire," Ara replied.

Does he know? That we all go together?

"Tristan—" I began.

"Last one there's a rotten egg!" Tristan cried, then raced back to his room.

Keke and Ceres both stared at me with amusement glittering in their eyes. I waved them away and kicked off my shoes. "To the hot spring we go, then."

The building I'd seen from above was sectioned off into small, dressing room-sized areas designated by our room numbers. Each one had four cubbies with towels and empty hangers on metal rods. A single drawn curtain guarded the person changing from others wandering the hallways searching for their room numbers.

"Matt, are you sure you're feeling alright?" Keke asked, touching my shoulder. She leaned forward and dropped her voice to a whisper, "Your cheeks are really red."

"I'm fine," I said, in a pitch much higher than I ever wanted to hear come out of my mouth. I cleared my throat. "I'm good. Really."

"My lord, is there anything I can do to assist in your comfort?" Ceres asked with a bow of her head.

"N-no. I'm perfectly comfortable." I stepped past the curtain and whipped it closed before the girls could follow me. "I'll go first."

As I undressed, the sound of other girls' giggles from many stalls down drifted along the wooden ceiling. Keke and Ceres quietly murmured between one another, harmonizing with the sound of shifting fabrics from either side. I was reminded of when I first changed and showered in the locker rooms during gym in high school. It was the same kind of dread that clenched my stomach—being around a group of people I knew nothing about, all of us stark naked. Like a damn nightmare.

I took a deep breath and shoved my clothes into one of the cubbies, exchanging it for the crisply folded, downy-soft towel that awaited me. Wrapping it around my waist, I ran a hand through my hair and took a deep breath.

What's the big deal, Kelmer? It's just a hot spring. People do this all the damn time.

Tugging the curtain back, I stepped through and gestured inside. "Next?"

Ceres's stare slowly trailed from my eyes to my shoulders, moving over every detail of my chest and stomach before resting at the hem of my towel. "I shall go!" she squeaked. Her cheeks pinked, and she ducked behind the curtain.

Once she disappeared, Keke walked her fingers over the middle of my chest, her mischievous smile still plastered to her face. "Now, there's a sight I missed," she whispered, biting her lower lip in a way that made me shiver.

Think cold thoughts. Ice-cold, frigid, miserable thoughts. "This is going to be torture," I murmured.

"Hm. I think it'll be fun," Keke replied. "Just relax, Matt. Easy, right?"

You know exactly what you're doing. "Sure. Right."

Ceres carefully pushed back the curtain and stepped through, holding a towel just above her chest. The edge danced along her upper thigh, showcasing her long, sculpted legs.

Alaska. Snow cones. Hail in February. Ceres's smooth pale skin. Jesus Christ. I scratched my chin and did my best to keep my eyes on her face. "Alright, Keke. You're up next."

Keke giggled and disappeared behind the curtain. Ara and Tristan approached from our right, both wrapped in fluffy white towels and neither seemingly embarrassed at all.

"I've read of the benefits of a hot spring on skin before," Ara said to Tristan. "They can also promote various kinds of healing."

"I have, too! They used to have these kinds of things back where Matt and I are from, and a lot of people used them to recuperate from injuries." Tristan grinned and tapped my shoulder. "I've been wondering, do you think the ones in this world would cure Status Ailments, too?"

It wasn't something I'd considered when I'd been envenomed. That would have been an interesting test—to have the healers toss me into Jazz's hot spring and pray for my revival. I shrugged. "Guess we lost our chance to test it."

"Hm. Maybe." Tristan tapped his chin in thought. "We'll have to keep it in mind for the future."

Keke stepped out from the dressing room, her towel neatly wrapped around her chest and her hair twined into a low bun at the base of her neck. She smoothed the sides of her towel at her waist and smiled at the group. "Ready?"

Glaciers. Dry ice. Those few strands of hair falling into Keke's eyes are just— no! Wait! Zambonis! "Ready," I croaked.

"You feeling okay, Matt?" Tristan asked.

"Yeah. On vacation. Hot springs. What could be better?" I turned heel and led the charge to the double doors leading to the hot spring. I figured it'd be best just to dive right in. Like when you first jump in a pool.

But this wasn't just a pool.

Six other catgirls were already enjoying the hot spring. Three sat submerged to their necks beneath a steady waterfall while two more reclined on the edge, swirling just their feet and ankles in the steaming water. The last was laid out on a towel, snoozing while the sun tanned her naked back. All eyes shifted to me as I approached the water, and their conversations quieted.

Just don't look at them. Ignore the swaying tails and twitching ears. Don't memorize how their glistening skin shimmers in the sun—

A heat more potent than any hot spring pulsed through my veins, and I took a deep breath. Tristan was soon at my side, ahead of the others in our group.

"Matt, really. Are you alright?" he murmured.

I cupped a hand over my mouth, then ran it through my hair. "Look. I've just… I've never bathed with a bunch of girls before," I hissed. "Shit, I've never skinny-dipped, either."

Tristan leaned forward and looked from side to side. "Here. This way." He tugged on my wrist and led us off to the far corner of the pool. It was a fair distance away from the others, and tall trees shaded the water beneath it. "They won't come over here."

"How can you be sure?" I asked.

Tristan pointed at the trio of our girls making their way toward us.

One of the catgirls beneath the waterfall made a move to swim in our direction, but all three caught her eye. If looks could kill, waterfall girl would have sunk to her early grave.

"They won't allow it," Tristan laughed beneath his breath.

Well, that makes me feel a little better, at least. I sighed. "You're really cool with this?"

Tristan shrugged. "The people in this world are more comfortable being naked than clothed. It's a natural state of being for them. And, well," he hung a hand around his neck, "I spent the majority of my time in the school without clothes. You get pretty used to it."

"Me first!" Keke squealed, tossing her towel to the side and stepping into the clear water. Her tail wriggled with delight, and goosebumps prickled her bare skin as her toes met the heat. She made a point to look over her shoulder and smile. "Coming, Matt?"

"Yeah. Alright." I sighed and tossed away the towel to join her.

Ara Pro Tip: Young master, the water feels wonderful! I'm so glad we came!

Chapter 28
Fuzzy Navel

The way I figured it, the sooner I jumped into the hot spring the better. I'd like to say it went as simply as that. But I found myself paralyzed a few feet away from the water's edge.

It felt as if I was finally getting the catgirl paradise I dreamed of so long ago. Even as I moved forward to join Keke, my eyes and thoughts were pulled in every direction imaginable. Voluptuous curves, suggestive glances, and the giggles. My God, the giggles were the worst part of it all.

Giggling wasn't a great sound to hear when you took your towel off. It had me feeling extra self-aware—like I was one of Michelangelo's sculptures on display in a museum. Doubts clouded my mind. It was only thanks to Tristan that I snapped out of it to join the other girls.

"Come on, Matt." Tristan tugged on the bend of my elbow. "Once you get in, I think you'll feel better."

"Right." The tips of my fingers were trembling. I dipped my toes into the water, and the sensation that wrapped around them was to die for. I let my first leg sink deeper, then the second, breathing a relaxed sigh as I slowly submerged the lower half of my body. "Incredible."

Tristan eased into the hot spring next. "Ahhh, this is nice. I didn't know how much I needed it."

I shut my eyes, letting the steam rise into my nostrils. I could hear the murmurs of girls at the opposite end of the spring. My muscles began to relax. It felt as if my skin was mending on the spot. I could hear the droplets of water falling into the spring.

Wait. Droplets?

I opened my eyes. Before me stood the very definition of beauty. Beads of water trickled down Keke's neck, between her cleavage, then dropped below her thighs to join the pool. With a hand on her hip, Keke flashed a knowing smile before submerging herself and reappearing to sit next to me, her chest laid bare for all to see.

I swallowed hard. Every inch of her was immaculate and entrancing. Her ears twitched as her eye caught something behind me. I had a feeling I already knew what it was.

"My lord?"

I turned around to the voice. Ceres's braided hair hung over her right shoulder, the water barely high enough to hide her chest. She ran a hand over her hair and brushed my shoulder with her fingertips. "Please inform me if there is anything I can do. I do not wish to cause you discomfort," she said.

"Discomfort? Me? Who says I'm uncomfortable?"

Keke came closer. Perhaps it was just my imagination, but it felt as if Ceres was pushing her weight against me.

"Having fun, Matt?" Keke asked, kissing my shoulder.

"Tons." My toes curled.

I looked away, finding Tristan and Ara seated on the other end of the spring. Tristan looked completely unaffected by this moment. Ara seemed to be maintaining her composure for the most part, but I hadn't seen her manage to look at him for longer than half a second.

"If I may, my lord." Ceres was fiddling around her collarbone with a tender finger. "I, um. That is, to say. My goodness, this is embarrassing." The knight took a deep breath, then exhaled. "I find your body very attractive."

"Y-you've seen it before," I stammered.

"Y-yes, I know," Ceres was quick to say. "But in these circumstances, I feel I can speak more freely." She cleared her throat and sat up straight, allowing me a generous view of her ample bosom.

Oh my God. If she said anything else, I didn't hear it. It took active discipline not to stare at her breasts for very long.

I love how the water runs past them. Her skin is so smooth and soft. How does a knight maintain such beautiful skin? How I would love to… frigid cold air. Frostbite. Waterboarding. Flayed alive.

"T-thank you," I managed.

"Hey, Matt," Keke said with a suggestive lilt to her voice. "Why not get out and let me scrub your back? It should help all the dead skin come off."

This tag-teaming thing is a little evil, I'll have you know.

I paused. "I think I'll relax here for now." We were catching the eyes of a few other girls from across the spring. Two more had entered since then, and I could've sworn they were biding their time while slowly making their way over to us.

"Are you sure?" Keke asked.

"Yes. I'm sure."

"How sure?"

I frowned. "Very. I'm uh, enjoying everything this spring has to offer."

"You'll feel much better." One by one, I felt Keke's fingers dance across my thigh. "One last time. Are you sure?"

Now I don't know. "M-maybe we could get out for a second," I said with a hitch in my voice.

Keke bowed her head forward and smiled. "Good." With a splash, she jumped out. Words could not describe how bewitching her thighs and tail were as she exited.

As I stood, Ceres stood with me, catching my arm, my bicep touching her breasts by proxy. "Are you certain, my lord?" she asked. "We only just got in."

I tried to steady my breathing. My stare lingered on her for some time, wandering as it pleased. Beginning with her shoulders, traveling to her cleavage, then snaking its way around the beautiful dip in her abdomen and the curves of her legs. Her grip around me was strong yet gentle—like the longing of a fair princess.

"A-ah. Yes. I'll just be a second."

Ceres released her grip and stood back with her hands clasped beneath her chin. "Yes, my lord."

After Ceres nestled herself back into the water, I made my way over to where Keke stood, beneath a few trees with a sponge in one hand and a bucket of water in the other.

Although her posture said she was as comfortable with this as any other day, the pink hue on her cheeks betrayed that she was probably just as nervous about all of this as I was.

Keke pushed a wooden stool forward and gestured, her golden eyes piercing through me. "Sit."

I couldn't recall if anybody had ever scrubbed my back before. Maybe when I was a kid, and I still took baths with my parents, but nothing like this.

The sensation of the sponge sent chills down my spine. Goosebumps covered my arms.

"Nervous?" Keke whispered into my ear.

"Not at all," I lied.

"Hmmm."

She started at the nape of my neck. Hot water washed down my back, cutting through the cool air and stealing a deep breath from me. The sponge's material was more coarse than anything I'd ever used. My skin felt a bit raw after every passing scrub—my shoulders, my arms, my back. When she was done, she tossed the sponge away.

The soft sensation of Keke's chest pressed against my back. "Do you like what you feel?"

I nodded.

"Great." With that, Keke made her way back into the hot spring, passing one salacious smile over her shoulder.

That's it? Are you serious?

"My lord! Please join us once more!" Ceres waved.

"Right," I sighed. *What a tease.*

None of the catgirls were leaving. It felt like they were waiting for their moment to pounce on Tristan or me at the soonest opportunity. Not that I was particularly worried since we had Keke, Ceres, and Ara around.

I sighed as I re-entered the spring. Keke and Ceres moved to flank me once more.

Ceres's smile felt gentle and shy. She toyed with her hair, maintaining consistent contact with her shoulder and forearm against mine. On the other hand, Keke's grin felt suspicious. Like she had ulterior motives.

I froze when each of the girls took one of my arms for themselves. I cleared my throat. "Are you girls having a good time?" I asked.

"The best," Keke said. "This was a great idea. All of my stress is just floating away."

"I must agree." Ceres put a hand on her chest, and I admired how the water pooled around her breasts. "Ni Island is a resort, as far as I can see."

"Finally calming down a bit, Matt?" Tristan asked from his corner with Ara.

"Yeah, I think I'm finally coming around."

A rare smile crossed Ara's lips. "Perhaps this was a fine idea after all." Her ears twitched as she scooched closer to Tristan. "Your presence alone is worth the island of Shi, young master. But this has its own charm too."

"It feels great to be back in my element," Keke said. She released my arm and moved into the deeper part of the spring, letting her body float upward with her back against the water. She shut her eyes, and I took in every feature of her form that I could—how the sheen of water granted her a glow I rarely saw. How her bosom rose and fell with each draw of her breath. How soft her lips looked. It was enough to drive a man mad.

Time for revenge.

I put a finger to my lips and motioned to the others as I approached her. As stealthily as I could manage, I submerged and swam beneath her. There was just a hiccup of hesitation while I admired her perfect ass and tail from the bottom of the spring.

And then I struck. There was a momentary yelp, but I managed to pull her under. I held her close and let my fingers do their worst on her abdomen. Bubbles erupted from her mouth, and moments later, we both stood up in the spring, pointing and laughing.

I hope things can be more like this from now on.

Ai Pro Tip: Ni Island's hot springs are well known across all of Nyarlea for their healing and restorative properties.

Chapter 29

Sex on the Beach

When the three of us had settled beneath the shade of the trees once more, Keke and I soaked to the skin from me dragging her under, we were approached by a catgirl stalking the pool's perimeter. She was tall—like, legs up to her ears, tall—with deep blue hair that fell around her hips. Her height was exaggerated by a pair of white stilettos that had to be at least four inches high. The suggestion of a silver bikini hugged her tanned skin, strings curving just beneath her hip bones, more strings holding the tiny triangles guarding the center of each breast. She caught my eye and grinned, balancing a silver tray in one hand and her fingers on one hip.

"What will you and your cuties have to drink?" she hummed, coiling her tail around one voluptuous thigh.

Ceres gawked, and Keke snickered behind me. I'll admit, while I let my eyes wander her shape, I kept trying to recall what fighting game I'd seen her in.

"I, uh, don't know what I like, really." I looked at Keke. "You guys usually order for me."

"I-I trust your judgment, my friends," Ceres stammered, sinking beneath the water until her chin and mouth vanished. But not before I caught the dark red hue on her cheeks.

Keke beamed and nodded. "Two nyapple martinis and your best ale," she ordered easily.

"At your service." The waitress bent low at the hips, her chest swaying with the movement. "Should you need me before I return, simply call for Felicia."

That's it! That's the game! "Thanks, Felicia," I replied.

She licked her lips and sauntered away. All three of us watched her hips swing from side to side. Ceres blew bubbles to the surface.

"You alright, Ceres?" Keke leaned forward to better see our flustered knight.

Ceres nodded, her bangs dripping in the water, then seemed to remember herself and straightened her back. Her face was still a brilliant crimson, but her voice regained its noble composure. "The catgirls of Ni are," she cleared her throat, "quite different from those of Shi Island."

"How's that?" I wondered aloud.

"Well, for starters, it seems this island places a high value on tanned flesh." Ceres lifted her ivory arm to the surface as if to demonstrate her point. "Keke, put your arm near mine."

Keke reached across my chest and positioned her arm next to Ceres's. The difference in color was striking when held next to one another.

"Celestia and the other high-ranking officials on Shi believe one of the fundamentals of beauty is skin as pale as moonlight. A girl who has spent her time well in service of her masters and mistresses will maintain an alabaster complexion," Ceres explained.

"Do you think tans are ugly?" Keke asked, her tone more curious than condescending.

"I've never had a basis of comparison before," Ceres murmured, letting her arm slowly fall back into her lap. Her blush deepened, and she chewed her lip. "In truth, I find your skin quite alluring."

I exchanged looks with Keke, who was also beginning to blush.

"Here you are, lovelies," Felicia returned with her tray. She dipped low, passing the martinis to Keke and Ceres before handing the beer to me.

"Wow, didn't even have to ask, huh?" I quipped.

Felicia winked. "Woman's intuition."

"Thank you very much, miss," Ceres squeaked.

"Call me Felicia, sweet," Felicia crooned. "I'll be around."

Ceres hid behind her drink. Keke stifled a giggle in her glass, and I watched the exchange with amusement. Once Felicia was out of earshot, I continued.

"What else is different?" I asked, hoping to ease the building tension. "Between the girls here and on your island, I mean."

To my surprise, Ceres drained half her glass before setting it aside and swallowing hard. "There are so many girls on Ni with large—" she gestured to her chest and waist, not meeting my gaze. "—l-large curves."

Keke sipped her drink, then nodded. "If I had to guess, that's because of Shi Island's food shortage."

Ceres lifted her drink and swirled the bright red liquid in thought. "Could you elaborate?"

"Well, Venicia may eat well, and I imagine Sorentina isn't that bad yet. But all of the other cities are still trying to rebuild and restock. From the looks of Anyona and the limited amount of outside visitors to Venicia, there isn't enough food to go around. Not from other islands or your own." Keke tapped her finger against her chin and took another drink. "Aurora always said it takes good food to grow up strong."

"Aurora?" Ceres tipped her head.

"Cannoli's mom," I provided. "That would make sense, though. Constantly having to run and work on limited stocks would affect the whole island. Not just the smaller towns."

"Ah." Ceres looked across the pool, eyes resting on Tristan's smiling face. "Can one man really fix all of that?"

I rested a hand on Ceres's thigh, and she blinked up at me. It was meant to be reassuring, but I quickly realized it probably came off as me making a move. *Ah, well.* "He doesn't have to do it on his own. Once we find the man on Ichi, we'll meet with Cailu and figure out a plan. We'll fix it together, okay?"

She nodded and drained the rest of her glass. "I will follow you to the end, my lo— M-Matt."

"Let's make sure that's a ways off," I laughed. "For now, we're on vacation. To vacation!"

Keke and I clinked our glasses together, then finished them off. The ale cooled my throat and warmed my blood, adding a hazy glow to the rising steam of the spring. We hailed Felicia and ordered another round. Then a third.

Ceres's gaze steadily lingered between Keke, Felicia, and me. Her and Keke's skin pressed against mine. Fingers mapped my lower back and thighs while mine wandered silken flesh beneath the spring. Breathing came heavier, and air was harder to find.

Having an ever-present waitress and an open bar at a hot spring resort was dangerous. I don't know how many drinks we ordered, nor do I remember how many Bells Ceres fished from her [Cat Pack] to pay Felicia.

Apparently, it was enough money to convince our blue-haired waitress to follow us back to our room.

Ceres, Keke, and I were drunk as hell, bumping against the walls on our way to retrieve our things from the dressing room. I must have been taking too long behind the curtain because Keke stumbled past it and threw it shut behind her. Her chest pressed into mine as we toppled over together until my back was against the wall. Her towel fluttered to the floor, and I caught her at the hips, trying very hard to control my next movements carefully.

"I want you so bad," she leaned forward and whimpered into my ear. "Right now."

I stroked her damp hair and kissed her throat. "There are two other girls waiting for us," I murmured. "You're okay with that?"

She shook her head, strands of her hair leaving droplets of spring water on my skin. "It's fine, Matt. Really," she giggled. "Maybe it'll be fun."

"You sure?"

Keke giggled again, floundering for her clothes in the cubby, then rewrapping the fallen towel around her. "Come on. Just go back in your towel. You're taking *forever.*"

My heart pounded against my chest, and the room spun. Was this really happening? How many drinks had I ordered? "Alright."

We tumbled back to the room, a mess of gropes and wandering hands. Felicia kept a cool smile throughout the journey, steadying tipsy stances and grasping the hands of the unbalanced. When we reached the room and closed the door, I stared at the enormous bed that awaited us, then looked back at the girls.

I had no idea what I was supposed to do.

To my benefit, the three of them seemed to catch on to my confusion. Keke grabbed my wrist, and Ceres cupped my lower back to guide me to the bed while Felicia snagged the towel around my hips and ripped it away.

I didn't have a chance to ask what exactly they'd like to do. I went from standing to lying flat on my back atop the blankets, staring into the three hungry faces above me. It was equally arousing as it was intimidating.

Keke tossed her towel to the floor and grinned. "I'll start here," She hopped onto the bed and swung one leg over my head with her knees resting against the tops of my shoulders. I'd expected her to sit on my chest, but her flank rested on the pillow behind her. She peered down at me between her thighs as she straddled my face. "You don't mind, right?"

"No," I breathed, sliding my hands beneath her thighs and groping just below her immaculate ass. The sweet scent of her heat filled my nostrils, and I kissed the inside of her thigh. "I don't mind at all."

"Come now, don't be shy," Felicia said to Ceres. She pulled the knight's towel free before sliding her own minuscule bikini to the floor, leaving behind fine tan lines where the fabric had rested. "You asked me to join you, after all."

Ceres glanced at me, then offered a resolute nod. They joined us on the bed; Felicia mounted me at the stomach with her back facing me while Ceres positioned herself above my thighs.

Am I dreaming? It felt like I was. Three women straddling me from the face down, three tails undulating above me. The heat in the room was palpable.

I couldn't hold back any longer.

I pulled on Keke's thighs, and she squealed in surprise, then moaned when I buried my tongue between her folds. I brushed my tongue against her clit, drawing back to tease her opening. She was soaked, her taste hot and sweet.

Keke whimpered and leaned forward, snaking her hands around Felicia's back to knead her chest.

"*A-ah.* That's good," Felicia sighed, leaning back into her touch. "Ceres, bring your tail around."

"Like this?"

"Mhm. Now, wrap it around him. Starting here."

Downy-soft fur surrounded the base of my shaft, tightly enveloping my cock and ending just below the head. I gasped against Keke's skin, wanting to arch my back into the sensation but finding it impossible with Felicia's weight.

"I-is that alright, Matt?" Ceres asked.

Can't talk with my mouth full. "Mmmhm."

"He likes it," Felicia chuckled. "Now, move up and down. Not too fast."

Ceres pumped her tail up, then down, maintaining a firm grip that felt like the softest hand on the planet. I plunged my tongue inside of Keke, drinking in her need and living for her moans. Her thighs quivered in my hands, and her back curved.

The slick sound of fingers plying vulnerable flesh permeated my breathing. "*Ngh!* Y-you don't have to—*ah!*" Ceres stammered between whimpers. The fluid gyrations of her tail on my shaft wavered, then her grip tightened.

"You're so tight," Felicia noted, amusement painting her words. "But you're plenty willing."

Ceres gasped, the movements of her tail quick and desperate. Keke's hips bounced with every lap of my tongue. Felicia's mouth met Ceres's. There were so many sounds, so many sensations. So many hands, and breaths, and desires.

"M-Matt, I'm gonna come," Keke murmured.

I doubled my efforts, wrapping one hand around her tail and flattening my tongue against her clit. Ceres's machinations kept me teetering on the most frustrating edge—though I'm sure the alcohol didn't help. The choir of noises coming from the three of them had the world spinning, and I memorized it to the best of my inebriated ability.

"I'm coming!" Keke squealed, her toes curling.

The convulsions took her, and her hands dropped from Felica's chest to mine, nails digging into my skin as she arched her back and cried out in bliss. I plunged my tongue into Keke's depths, teasing out every pulse. Her thighs quivered around my head, and she wriggled her hips hard against my mouth.

"You're close, too. Aren't you sweet?" I heard Felicia murmur as I drank in Keke's pleasure.

"Y-yes!" Ceres murmured. The sound of Felicia's fingers sliding in and out of Ceres grew more intense.

"Give in to it," Felicia encouraged.

I gasped as Ceres's tail squeezed my shaft with her climax. The sensation was intense with how sensitive she'd made me.

"Good girl."

Keke's orgasm had finally slowed just as Ceres's cries filled the room. Keke lifted her thighs and swung to the side before leaning over and kissing me deeply. Her tongue searched my throat, and her hands tangled in my hair.

"I'm close," I whispered into Keke's mouth.

Felicia drew her arm away from a panting Ceres, her smile wide. Keke broke our kiss and moved to the end of the bed. She tugged Ceres's tail free of my cock, then gestured for Ceres to move off of my legs. A dominance I'd never seen in Keke before lit her gaze as she snatched Felicia's shoulders and deliberately turned her to face me. She reached one hand to the underside of each of Felicia's thighs, then she spread them wide and looked at me expectantly.

"This is what you want, right?" Keke asked.

I sat up and stared from Keke to Felicia. I couldn't keep the surprise from my face. Felicia's tan line was even more evident at the juncture of her thighs, where her pink, vulnerable folds welcomed me in. "Keke—"

"Go ahead, Matt," Keke interrupted.

For the first time that night, Felicia blushed and caught Ceres's gaze. Then, she wrapped her arms behind Keke's head, linked her hands behind her neck, and looked at me. "Take me, then."

"Let me watch," Keke murmured. She flashed a devilish grin, and Felicia's blush deepened. I slowly crawled forward, waiting for Keke to change her mind. The command never came.

Ceres repositioned herself behind me, her hands encircling my chest as she kissed my shoulder.

Carefully aligning my hips to Felicia's, I slid inside of her, shuddering with the sweltering fit of her body. Keke captured my kiss over Felicia's shoulder, twining her fingers in my hair. I wrapped my hands around Felicia's waist, letting my fingers sink into Keke's hips. Ceres continued to lay kisses down my spine, on the back of my neck, on my throat.

"I wish it were me," Keke whispered into my mouth, her breath hot on my tongue.

"Me, too."

I pictured Keke in Felicia's place. Thrusting into her without mercy. How her face would look when I bottomed her out and her cries of ecstasy.

"God, I wish it were you," I growled.

The thrusts were fast and deliberate. The time for teasing was over; I needed release, and I needed it now. Felicia's cries were high and desperate, her movements restricted by Keke's grip. But I could feel her excitement dripping between her thighs, coating my shaft with her need.

"That's so good!" Felicia moaned. She sank her teeth into my shoulder. "I—*ah!*" Her body tensed and writhed around me; her convulsions were sharp and sudden.

I didn't have a chance to warn her. My climax pounded in my ears, stole the feeling from my toes, and washed over me and into Felicia before I could say a word. Ceres reached beneath my arm and slid her fingers into Felicia's mouth, crooning sweet nothings against my skin.

Keke nipped my lower lip and drew back. Her expression was hard to read, but she grinned all the same. "That helps my future fantasizing."

You're not the only one. I shivered and pulled out of Felicia, trying to catch my breath. Ceres's hands drifted to my hips, and she traced my spine with the tip of her tongue.

"Matt," Ceres murmured. "I want more. Please allow me to try something else."

I glanced between Keke and Felicia. Both seemed more than willing to continue. Ceres beckoned for Keke to move to all fours. Ceres repositioned herself behind her, a look of starved determination on her face, before sliding three fingers inside Keke's body and grabbing her tail. Keke gasped, and her eyes rolled back.

Holy shit.

Felicia knelt before Keke and grabbed a handful of Keke's hair. "Look at me, girl."

Keke glanced up, chewing on her lip to contain the noises Ceres forced from her throat. Felicia leaned forward and kissed her long and hard, then drew back and spread her legs.

"Now clean up the mess you caused," Felicia commanded, forcing Keke's head down between her thighs. Keke's ass stayed in the air for Ceres's easy access.

Keke's tiny licks quickly turned into long laps of her tongue as Ceres's kneading grew more intense.

"That's a good girl," Felicia purred. "Ceres should reward you with another finger."

Ceres complied. Keke's whole body trembled.

I couldn't believe what I was seeing, and I had no idea when I started touching myself. Felicia glanced at me with a knowing smile.

"Your man likes watching you just as much as you enjoy watching him." Felicia stroked Keke's ears and hair. "You'll work hard for him, won't you?"

"Mhmm...*ngh!*" Keke hummed, then sucked in a moan when Ceres grabbed her tail.

"You're very tight, Keke. Are you close?" Ceres asked as her fingers disappeared inside of Keke once more.

"*Mhm!*" Keke's response was high and desperate.

Even though I'd orgasmed not fifteen minutes prior, I was fully erect and close to another climax. The look on Keke's face as she stole glances at me was breathtaking. She'd submitted to Ceres and Felicia completely, and her eyes begged for my approval. I wanted to be the one in her mouth or the one inside her cunt. Her expression said she felt the same way.

"*Nh...ngh...mhn!*" Keke sank her teeth into Felicia's thigh. A high-pitched squeal escaped between her teeth, and her hips rolled back into Ceres's hand.

"There you go, girl. What a sweet kitten," Felicia crooned, still stroking Keke's hair.

"Oh, fuck!" I tipped over the edge, curling forward and spilling my load onto my hand and the bedsheets.

Still panting, Keke turned away from Felicia and crawled toward me. She slid my fingers into her mouth and licked away my seed.

Ceres carefully withdrew her hand from Keke and looked expectantly at me. "My lord, please allow us to continue."

Felicia laughed. Keke continued her work on my hand. I wondered how long we could keep going and was more than willing to find out.

I don't remember when we fell asleep. But I could hear the early morning birds chirping in the trees, and the sun was low on the horizon.

New Notifications!

Quest Updated!

[The More the Merrier] 1/8 Catgirls Successful!

Ara Pro Tip: Where did our waitress go? The young master and I are in need of more refreshments!

Chapter 30
Tarte Tatin

Felicia had already left by the time I was up and moving later that afternoon. Keke and Ceres still slept soundly in the enormous bed, one on either side of me. After I slipped from their hold to find my pants, Ceres sleepily groaned her displeasure before moving to throw an arm over Keke's waist instead. Keke hummed and wriggled backward until her back was against Ceres's chest.

Events from the night before had crept their way into my dreams, only to follow me in a repetitive reel while awake. So many hands, mouths, and noises. I shivered as I fished my shirt from beneath a communal pile of clothes. What guy doesn't fantasize about multiple girls at once? But, as insanely sexy as it had been, I was worried. Would this change things with Keke or Ceres?

I hadn't seen Keke so dominant *or* submissive before. Had she enjoyed either? Ceres, on the other hand, well, it was clear she'd dropped every filter she'd ever worn. It wasn't a bad thing, not at all. Just…different.

The bedsheets barely covered their hips, and their chests slowly rose and fell with each measured breath. Keke's tail was curled around Ceres's lower back while Ceres's poked free of the blankets, curved just beneath the pillows behind her. It was quiet, picturesque, even. I wondered how they'd feel when they woke up.

Ah, well. Only time will tell.

After getting dressed, I wandered from the room in search of the inn's restaurant. It was probably way too late for complimentary breakfast, but with Ceres splitting the bill and covering what I was sure was a terrifying drink tab the night before, I still had plenty of Bells to spend.

Tristan and Ara were nowhere to be found, so I took a table in a corner and enjoyed a meal on my own. The restaurant was an extension of the hotel, with long windows overlooking the forests surrounding Abalone. It was an empty house outside of me and the waitress, so beyond the idle conversation between her and the cook, it was quiet.

When I thought about it, I couldn't remember the last time I'd been by myself in Nyarlea—maybe right after I'd first arrived. I leaned back in the chair and stared out the window. Letting my thoughts drift was hard. A lot of events and emotions I'd suppressed in the name of moving forward resurfaced, threatening to choke me. The nameless girl who'd taken my axe to the face during the journey to Catania. The deaths of Jazz, Marianne, Maya, and countless others in the battles with the Defiled. The young lich, who was more than likely still alive. Ravyn. Cannoli. Keke. Ceres—

"You doing okay, honey?" the slender waitress reappeared, a worried smile on her kind face.

I rubbed my cheek and jaw, dragging myself back to the present. "Yeah. I'm good, thanks."

"If you're looking for something to do, you should check out the game room," she suggested, holding her silver platter against her lap. "Plenty of folks that stay with us spend most of their time there."

"Not the hot spring?"

Her smile widened. "There's not a lot of competition to be had in a hot spring."

That's an interesting take. "Alright. I'll check it out." It was past free breakfast time, apparently, so I picked my coin purse free and counted the Bells inside.

The waitress held up a hand and shook her head. "This one's on me, honey. Don't you worry yourself over it."

"Are you sure? I can pay for it, really."

"I'm sure. Everyone needs a pick-me-up every so often. It's not much, but I'm happy to do it."

"Jeez. Do I look that bad?" *Shouldn't need a pick-me-up after a night like that. But here we are.*

She shrugged and turned to leave. "Not really. I can just tell, you know?"

I still laid out a handful of Bells as a tip before I left the restaurant. Didn't feel right not leaving her anything.

As I wandered the halls, I saw multiple signs on the walls pointing to the changing house outside of the hot springs, the restaurant, and the gaming room. I followed the carefully painted arrows to the gaming room and heard the playful cries of catgirls as I approached.

"You're a cheat, Mirabel!"

"It's not my fault you're bad at this game."

"Take your Bells and get out."

"Mirabel's buying us all drinks tonight."

I turned the corner to find an expansive hall of round tables. Each one had at least two catgirls playing a game of some sort—cards, dice, board games, ivory tablets that looked suspiciously like dominoes.

I spotted Ara at a packed table, cradling a hand of cards close to her chest while she carefully watched those around her. She'd changed out of her usual maid attire, swapping it instead for a silk robe with painted flowers. The girls I'd heard outside were also at the table, having a good-natured argument about who was responsible for the next round of drinks. Ara sipped from a tall cocktail, a devilish smile piquing the left corner of her mouth.

Well, well. Ara does have hobbies.

Beyond the tables were long sofas arranged in a wide square. A small bookshelf with two shelves of leatherbound tomes stood on one side, and a cabinet packed with more games to play faced its opposite. One far corner held a desk where fresh stationery paper, quills, and ink had been arranged in neat piles.

Tristan perched on the end of one of the sofas, with his head bowed over a coffee table. I excused myself around the girls, catching a few lingering gazes as I made my way to Tristan.

He'd procured a stack of paper, ink, and a quill and was focused on a sketch of Ara meticulously choosing her cards. I'd seen his art on the walls of the caves in Catania, but his work with the quill was another beast entirely. A wide array of line strokes served as the shadows in Ara's soft robe and hair, and the details of her face were immaculate.

"You're really good," I commented, taking a seat on the couch to his left.

Tristan started as if caught in a trance but lifted his pen before he did any real damage to the picture. "Oh, jeez. Sorry, I didn't hear you." He chuckled and dipped the quill in ink. "Thanks, Matt. It's been a while since I could draw like this. It's nice."

"It looks just like her." I glanced between the paper and Ara. Tristan had definitely captured her secretive smile and rigid posture. "I'm glad to see her relaxing."

"Yeah, me too. She deserves it," Tristan agreed, taking the quill and sketching an intricate design on the backs of the cards.

"Excuse me, may I get you anything to drink?" A catgirl wearing a starched black dress and holding the same kind of silver platter from the restaurant bowed at the end of the sofa.

"Just a water for me, thanks." I felt like I was beyond lucky to have escaped a hangover.

To my surprise, Tristan laughed and shook his head. "No way, man. We're on vacation." He looked at the waitress. "Two nyappletinis, please."

C'mon, at least get me a beer. I wanted to object, but I held my tongue.

"Of course. I'll return shortly." The waitress bowed again and vanished.

"You left the hot spring pretty early. Did you have a good night?" Tristan asked, returning his focus to his drawing.

"It was great. Thanks." I felt my face flushing and pivoted the subject. "What about you guys?"

"Ara drank a lot and pledged her life to me. She said she would be more loyal than Ceres." Tristan grinned. "Drunk Ara is hilarious."

I nodded. "Did she feel okay after she slept it off?"

"She was a little flustered, but, I mean, we talked about it some..." Tristan trailed off, his cheeks turning red. He cleared his throat. "We're good now."

Sounds like it wasn't just me who had an exciting night. "That's good to hear."

"Y-yeah." The tips of his ears pinked.

The waitress returned with our drinks—translucent green liquid in crystal glasses. It only took three sips of the fruity stuff to start feeling it. "Damn. That's stronger than it looks."

"These girls can really hold their alcohol," Tristan agreed. "And this place seems to go all out."

It sure does. The right price will even score you a waitress. I hadn't seen Felicia at all. She was probably running another shift down at the hot spring.

"Hey! New girl! What are you trying to pull?" one of the girls at Ara's table cried.

"Hm? I'm not pulling anything," Ara replied mildly.

"You've had three perfect hands in a row!" another whined.

Ara shrugged. "I suppose luck is simply on my side."

"You stole all of our Bells!"

"I stole nothing of the sort." Ara folded her arms. "Will you please deal the next round before I lose my patience?"

The dealer growled but complied.

"Even when she plays cards, she's intimidating," I murmured.

Tristan nodded. "She's got a perfect poker face for sure."

"Hey, why don't we play something?" I suggested, standing and moving to the game cabinet. "I'm sure some of them have the rules included."

"Oh yeah, sure! I'd love that." Tristan replied, putting his finishing touches on the drawing and pushing it to the side.

I picked out a board game as Tristan ordered us more drinks. The pieces included were hand-carved of polished stone, and the board was painted in vivid, brilliant colors. "Reminds me of *Jumanji*," I said as I moved the pieces from the box to the board.

"We were already ripped to another world. Surely it won't happen again," Tristan quipped.

"Who knows? A cursed board game wouldn't be the weirdest thing I've seen so far," I laughed. Shuffling the remaining pieces around, I realized it didn't come with instructions. "Damn. Doesn't look like this is one we can play. No rules."

"U-um," a soft voice hummed from my right. "T-that's a three-player game. I can t-teach you, if you want."

A catgirl with orange hair and large honey-colored eyes shifted her weight between her feet. She was pretty short, but supple curves filled her frame nicely, and she hugged a book to her chest. Her tangerine tail flicked behind her, and she fretted at her lower lip.

I glanced over my shoulder. Ara cackled as she threw down her hand and scraped the stack of Bells to her edge of the table. "Yeah, we could use a third player, I think."

Tristan followed my gaze and nodded. "I think she'll be indisposed for a while. Have a seat." He gestured to the open sofa. "What's your name?"

"Peony," she replied quietly, sitting down before setting her book aside.

Tristan glanced at the cover, and his eyebrows raised. He covered his mouth with one hand, but not before I caught the smile he was trying to hide. *What's going on over there?*

"I'm Matt, and this is Tristan," I volunteered while Tristan subdued his grin. "Teach us how to play."

Ai Pro Tip: Should you require the basic rules of Nyarlean games, I have an extensive database, [User Matthew].

Chapter 31

Tres Leches

The board was triangle-shaped, which probably should have been my first clue that it was a three-player game, but I'll blame the nyappletinis. The board was sectioned off into smaller triangles that formed multiple, different colored spaces. As far as I could tell, there were only five duplicates of each color represented.

"Why are there so many colors?" Tristan echoed my thoughts aloud.

"Each one does something different to your pieces," Peony explained, sipping her freshly procured nyappletini. "For example, the green one here will keep your unit stuck for three turns."

"Why would you want to land on it, then?" I asked.

Peony shook her head. "You don't. But you can force your opponents to land there with some of your unit's Skills."

"That makes sense." Tristan tapped a finger on the tall, crowned piece at the very point of his side of the board. We all had one amongst the additional twelve pieces on the board, and our armies were distinguished by color—white, black, and red. "And you said the point of the game is to capture the other queens, right?"

"Right!" Peony agreed enthusiastically, then turned a furious red beneath her freckles and leaned back on her knees. She'd tucked her legs beneath her, and little by little, her timid nature slipped away when she grew excited.

"I wish we could write down what each piece does," I grumbled. "Oh, hey, wait. Appear, iPaw." The device materialized in my palm, and I enlarged the screen.

"Oh my goodness. A real iPaw!" Peony gasped. "I've never seen one before."

Tristan summoned his and handed it to Peony. She squeaked, drawing her hands away as if she'd touched a hot stove. "Are you certain?"

Tristan chucked. "Of course. Go ahead."

"M-my! The magic is so advanced!"

While Peony picked through the screens and puzzled the impossible language, I turned my attention back to mine. "Hey, Ai."

"Hello, [User Matthew]." Ai appeared, her pixelated form wearing a towel around her chest and her hair drawn back in a bun.

Guess it's Ai's chance for a vacation, too. "Do you happen to have the rules for, er, what's this game called again?"

"The Queen's Gambit," Tristan and Peony replied simultaneously. Peony flushed and buried her face behind the iPaw's screen.

"Yeah. The Queen's Gambit."

"One moment, please." Ai vanished, and a new window appeared, the text scrolling from top to bottom at about a million miles an hour. *Are there really this many games in Nyarlea?* At last, the scrolling came to a stop, and 'The Queen's Gambit' blinked in the center of the screen. Ai reappeared. "I have located the rules for The Queen's Gambit. What would you like to know?"

"A list of what each piece does would be awesome."

"As you wish." Her face blinked away, replaced by a list of the twelve pieces that included their movement ability and Special Skill, as Peony had mentioned. Ai's disembodied voice asked, "Will there be anything else, [User Matthew]?"

"No. That's it. Thanks, Ai." I scrolled through the list. Most of the pieces were pretty easy to identify like the Hunter was the one drawing back a longbow in the center of the board. But some of the others weren't very clear.

"Peony, can you tell us which piece is which?" I drained my drink and waved down the hovering waitress.

"Yes, of course!" She handed the iPaw back to Tristan, who similarly summoned Ai to find rules for the game, then began to list off the units at our disposal. Tapping the heads of each one with the tips of her fingers, she named them out loud. "Hunter, Wizard,

Monk, Myrmidon, Priest, Druid, Paladin, Arbiter, Saboteur, Enchanter, Assassin, Whisper, and then, of course, your Queen."

Yeah, that was gonna take a few rounds to remember all of the pieces. "Great, and the spaces?"

While I'd done the math earlier, twelve different Status Effects and Ailments that could be inflicted on each piece was a shitton to remember. I backed out of the list of unit names and tactics on the iPaw, then pulled up a smaller window explaining each of the colors. *This thing is more intuitive than I gave it credit for.*

"Alright, I think I'm ready," Tristan announced.

"Sure. Let's do it."

With new drinks delivered, we played what must have been the shortest game of The Queen's Gambit in Nyarlean history. Peony had us both out of the game in ten minutes.

"Ouch," I grumbled.

"I have a better grasp on it now, though." Tristan laughed and reset his side of the board. "I like this game. Let's go again."

Tristan gave Peony a good run for her money on the next round, though my performance was still severely lacking. Even so, each round that we played taught me more about the board, the pieces, and their playstyles. Peony even made a few mistakes—though, once again, I'd have to blame the nyappletinis. I couldn't remember the last time I'd played a board game, and it felt great.

Ara was still at the cards table, and her stack of Bells grew to a shockingly large pile before she skidded sections of it into her [Cat Pack] to start again. The other catgirls at the table swapped out when their purses ran low, always offering a new opponent for Ara to render penniless. For the first two rounds of our game, her eyes never left Peony, but she seemed to deem her unthreatening after the third and returned her full attention to the cards.

Keke and Ceres never happened to wander in the direction of the game room. I could only assume they were alright. Even if things were awkward between them, there were plenty of things in Abalone to do solo.

When we were on the sixth or seventh round—I'd lost count — Tristan motioned to the forgotten book on the couch. "Do you usually like romance books?"

The tip of Peony's nose was already red with the flush of alcohol, but the mention of the book took her skin to a deep crimson. "I-I... Wait, you recognize it?"

Tristan smirked. "Yeah. I've read it."

I was beginning to believe that Tristan had read every book in Nyarlea. I guess when your whole day is based around when the next girl comes to your bed, you have to fill the rest of it with *something*.

"Oh no." Peony covered her face with both hands. "That's so embarrassing."

I glanced between them, then at the book. "Come on. It can't be that bad. I mean, what girl *doesn't* like a little romance?"

Tristan's grin widened. "It's erotica."

I'll be damned. It was my turn to chuckle. "Oh, seriously?"

Peony nodded and sank farther away from the table, her hands still covering her face. "I didn't think anyone would recognize it. Not a lot of catgirls like reading."

I reached behind her and picked up the tome. "*Resonance,* huh? And is this Josselyn girl any good at writing?"

Peony sprang to life, snatching the book from my hands and clutching it close to her chest. "Y-you shouldn't read it! It's, um... It's..."

"It's two men and one catgirl," Tristan finished for her.

I hid my laugh behind my hand, adjusting the pieces on the table. "At the same time?"

"Mhm," Tristan hummed.

Peony shoved the book beneath the table, her ears flattening against her head. "I-it's stupid. I know." She drained her nearly full nyappletini and rubbed her cheeks with her palms. "I really didn't think anyone would recognize it. That's all."

I initiated the first move in our new game, and then Tristan made his. We studied Peony and waited. She had her arms crossed on the table with her forehead against them.

"You're really embarrassed for just reading a book," I noted.

"*Mrf,*" she huffed against her arms.

"Could it be," Tristan paused, reaching forward and rubbing the edge of her ear between his pointer finger and thumb, "that it's something you wanted to try?" His voice was low enough that only we could hear.

Well, that's forward as hell. Every dude in the world knows what a devil's threesome is by the time they hit fifteen. Did I ever think I'd be part of one? Fuck no. Then again, I didn't think I'd be naked with three catgirls at once, either. So, there was that.

Peony shivered, then straightened her back and clamped her hands around the edge of the table. "I-I didn't say that!"

Even I didn't know how exactly I felt about it. Tristan's indifference was interesting, to say the least. *What happens in Abalone stays in Abalone?*

"Excuse my assuming, then." Tristan dropped his hand and shifted back to his side of the table. "We can keep playing."

"W-wait!" Peony objected, then winced. She lowered her voice to just above a whisper. "You're right."

I had to admit, having her on the defensive was pretty fun. "What was that?"

"He's right!" Peony squealed, then cleared her throat. She twisted her hands together on the table and bowed her head. Her pumpkin-colored hair fell around her shoulders, covering her face. "I...I mean, the book makes it sound like fun."

Tristan shrugged. "Then why don't we try?" He looked at me. "Matt?"

Great. Now I look like the bad guy if I say no. I ran a hand through my hair. "Yeah. Sure. I'm down."

"We can use my room, then." Tristan stroked the top of Peony's hand and smiled when she shivered. "Come on."

My heart hammered in my chest, and I clumsily got to my feet. The lights were a blurry haze, and the sounds were sharper than normal. *Damn, they really do keep the drinks coming.* Tristan circled the table Ara was at, then bent forward and whispered something in her ear. She blushed profusely, then nodded. We left the game room without her shooting a second glance at Peony.

"What'd you tell Ara?" I asked.

Tristan grinned. "That I'd come back for her later."

"Uh-huh."

Peony skipped between us, then laced her fingers in mine. "A-are you sure this is okay? I mean, goodness, isn't this, um, kind of a waste?"

"What do you mean?" I asked. Her hand was small, warm, and delicate, much like its owner.

"I mean, wouldn't it be better if…well, if each of you was with another catgirl?" she mumbled.

"More efficient, yes. Better? That remains to be seen," Tristan replied, stealing her other hand in his.

Does it hurt? Being so suave? "What he said."

We reached Tristan's room, and he quickly unlocked it. The layout was identical to mine, with an enormous bed and plenty of extra furniture for lounging. Warm orange and purple light from the growing sunset illuminated the furnishings and spotless floors.

Once the door was closed, I exchanged looks with Peony, then deferred to Tristan. I was just as confused as she was about how this should start. *Even after a foursome, you're still this lost, Kelmer?*

Tristan leaned against a nearby dresser and looked at Peony expectantly. "Why don't you tell us what happens in the book?"

"*W-what?* I couldn't!" Peony whimpered, pulling her hand away from mine. "Y-you know what happens!"

Tristan shrugged. "I want to hear it from you. How will we know what to try?"

I wondered how embarrassed this poor girl could feel before she imploded. She desperately looked at me, and I added a shrug of my own. Sounded like a good plan to me. Hearing a girl ask for what she wanted was sexy.

Peony chewed her lip, took a deep breath, then nodded. Moving to Tristan, she took him by the wrist and led him back toward me. She stopped when her chest pressed into my ribs, and she tugged Tristan to stand behind her, sandwiching herself between the two of us. I could feel her heart racing and the short, quick panting breaths escaping her lips.

"S-so, um, in the book, the three of them… Well, they take off their clothes like this," she stuttered.

"Oh? That's it? We take off our clothes?" I teased. Yeah, I could get the hang of this.

Peony squeaked. "N-no! Not just that!" She leaned her forehead against my chest and groaned.

I chuckled, and Tristan ran a hand through her hair. "What else, then?" he asked.

"T-there's a lot of kissing and, erm, nibbling, and stuff."

I slid my fingers beneath the hem of her top. "From who?"

"From everyone," she admitted.

"Better get started, then." I leaned forward and captured her lips in mine. A soft groan vibrated against my mouth as Tristan slipped his hand under her top. Her tail wrapped around his thigh, and I tore her shirt over her head.

She shivered beneath our dual touch, reaching for my neck to pull me back into her embrace. I parted her lips with my tongue and drank the resulting moans from her throat. Tristan tossed his clothing aside, circling her waist to find the fastenings of her pants. His teeth sank into her shoulder as I moved one hand to knead her breast.

Peony gasped, her head tilting backward to rest on Tristan's shoulder. I maintained our embrace, lifting her hips so Tristan could pull her pants free. She was easy to lift, and her skin responded to every provocation we offered. Her panties and bra came next; the freckles from her face carried over to her arms and chest. Her ivory skin held the warm glow of the sunset, and her orange hair and tail shimmered as if they were in their element.

I left her to Tristan's grasp to divest my own clothes, adding them to the growing pile. She wrapped her arms around his neck and arched her back, hissing air between her teeth as Tristan's teeth met her throat.

"What's next?" I asked, taking a moment to admire the view.

Her breathing rasped, and Tristan kept a firm hold around her waist as she brought her eyes back forward. "B-Bed. Go." She pointed at me, then to the bed.

I shrugged, then hopped on the bed. Tristan released his hold, and Peony stumbled forward.

"Farther back," she murmured. "Move farther back."

I did as she asked, and she crawled onto the surface. "Tristan, get behind me."

Peony leaned on all fours and straddled my calves, stretching her spine flat. Tristan joined us on the bed and knelt behind her.

"Yeah. Then, like this." She reached between her legs and grabbed Tristan's shaft, guiding his cock between her legs.

"Like this?" Tristan rocked his hips upward.

She grabbed the blanket on either side of me with both hands, her body tensing and her knuckles turning white. "Yes!" she moaned. "H-hold on!"

Tristan stopped moving and waited. After a few long seconds, one of Peony's fists on the sheets relaxed. She lifted her hand, then gingerly wrapped her fingers around my shaft before sliding the head inside her mouth.

I moaned, relishing the trickles of hot saliva that escaped the corners of her lips.

"Now can I move?" Tristan teased.

She hummed in agreement, letting her hips roll back as her tongue snaked its way from base to tip. It felt amazing, and I had to wonder if there was a catgirls 101 class on blow jobs somewhere. Or, hell, maybe there *was* something to be said about the book.

Tristan bucked against her, and a strained cry tore from her throat.

Peony came up for a split second to mutter one word. "Harder."

"Gladly." Tristan complied, and Peony set back to work.

I tangled my fingers in her hair and pressed against her scalp, encouraging her to keep her mouth lower and let me in just a little deeper with every bob of her head. Her tongue was blazing hot, and she sucked all the excess air from her cheeks. It seemed the harder that Tristan thrust into her, the longer she was willing to keep her lips at my base without coming up for air.

"Fuck, that's good," I growled, rocking my hips against her chin.

"Yeah, it is," Tristan added, scraping his fingernails down Peony's back.

She moaned, the sound reverberating into her tongue and dragging a shiver down my spine. Her darting tongue and desperate groans edged me like nothing else. Her nails dug into my thighs, holding her steady while Tristan fucked her.

Whether it was the alcohol or the night before, I was just glad that I could last longer than ten seconds. But if she kept on like this, she was going to drag me over. "Do you want me to come like this?"

Peony slowed, then lifted herself on quivering arms to stare me in the face. Bestial need had replaced the cautious bookworm, and she licked her lips. "Actually... Can we try another position?"

"Yeah. Sure," I murmured. Tristan nodded his assent.

She lifted her hips away from Tristan, then crawled up my chest and straddled me at the hips. She held on to my shoulders and studied my face before stealing another deep breath. "Okay, hold still." She lowered her hips, fitting her dripping cunt around my cock.

I sighed with pleasure, withholding the urge to grab her hips and relentlessly buck inside of her. She trembled as she slowly accepted every inch of me, and her breathing hitched in her throat. I bit into her shoulder and had to constantly remind myself to wait for her instruction. *God, just let me move.*

Peony finally settled around me and tilted her head to rest against mine. I could feel every tiny spasm of her body, and her heart hammered against her chest. At last, she lifted her head, reached behind her to part the supple cheeks of her flank, and caught Tristan's gaze. "In here."

"You sure?" Tristan asked.

"Yes. Please."

Tristan slid inside of her, and the effect was immediate. Her whole body tensed, and I felt Tristan's added girth separated only by a thin layer of skin. Each twitch and pulse from either of them rocketed through me, adding a whole different sensation to anything I was used to. I couldn't hold back anymore. I grabbed her thighs and lunged as deep as her body would allow.

"*Ngh!* G-goddess!" She cried out and squirmed between us.

"How do you feel?" I breathed.

"Crazy. Full." She craned her neck back, and I groped her breasts. Tristan stroked her tail and combed a hand through her hair. A new string of moans slipped from her lips. "It feels amazing."

"Was the book right?" Tristan teased.

"I... I don't think so," Peony breathed and stammered. "This is so much *better*."

"I have to agree." Tristan grazed her throat with his lips, then bit into her shoulder.

Peony whimpered. She held the back of my neck with one hand and buried the other in Tristan's hair.

I wanted more. Deeper. I sat up, then shifted Peony to my lap before wrapping her ankles around my back. Tristan read the movement, adjusting with the momentum until we had her between us again. The new position allowed me to bottom her out while Tristan's advances forced her into convulsions that I experienced on the other side.

Peony's head lolled back, resting on Tristan's shoulder as we plied and manipulated her body to our whims. Tristan massaged her breasts and pinched her hardened nipples. I toyed with her tail and nibbled her throat, adoring the noises that escaped her throat.

Her sucking me off had already brought me close. I wasn't sure how much longer I could keep going.

To my relief, her body tensed, and she cried, "I-I'm coming!"

"Come," Tristan and I replied in tandem, our fingers bearing down on her skin.

Her desperate cries were music to my ears. I rode through the convulsions, letting my climax take hold in response to hers. It seemed Tristan did the same—his groans soon joined ours. It was a tangle of sweat and skin, and I memorized the press of her body against mine.

We gasped for air, our arms wrapped around one another. I rested my forehead on Peony's chest and traced the lines of her waist. Tristan kissed the back of her neck and her shoulder. As the high faded and we both withdrew, I chuckled.

"Better than the erotica, huh?" I asked.

Peony smiled and nodded. "I'm, um, probably the only girl in Nyarlea who's actually experienced it." She shrugged. "I don't think Josselyn actually knows how good that feels."

Tristan laughed. "Maybe she'll get lucky."

"Maybe." Peony paused, licking her lips and finding her words. "So, um, can we try another position?"

I chuckled. Wasn't sure exactly how long I could keep going, but hey, vacation, right? "Sure."

New Notifications!

Quest Updated!

[The More the Merrier] 2/8 Catgirls Successful!

Ara Pro Tip: Young master, I've procured enough to sustain us for a long while. How? Entirely by fair play! ...Why do you ask?

Side Quest

Ara's School of Etiquette

The Venicia School of Etiquette was a time-honored tradition of Shi Island. Girls from every city worked hard to memorize their letters and mannerisms well enough to be accepted. The school's students learned proper behaviors, maths, sciences, and art within its opulent halls. Special studies were offered for the rare cases of magical aptitude as well as those who would eventually transfer to Sorentina's knightly curriculum.

Though the alumni were considered the elite of Shi Island's catgirls, the school's atmosphere was warm and supportive. All were welcomed with open arms. Every girl understood what to do should they be chosen for a man's Party when the time came.

That was the school Ara remembered. Before Celestia became its headmistress.

Ara and Lynn were in their final term when the previous headmistress stepped down. The reasons surrounding her retirement were veiled with suspicion, but it wasn't the students' place to question her.

Almost overnight, the Venicia School of Etiquette was completely changed. Derogatory whispers aimed at the catgirls hailing from other cities were passed behind backs. Competition replaced camaraderie. Service, Grace, and Urgency were prioritized above all else. And for any that dared go against this new normal? Well, there was the Room.

Ara was never sentenced to the Room. The relationships she kept outside of her sister were few and far between, and her studious nature helped her stay at the top of her class. Lynn, however…

It was a sunny afternoon, barely a month before Ara and Lynn would graduate. Earlier in the week, the sisters were moved from the school's dorms to a home of their own—one that would be open to visitors from other islands and cities. It was far more space than either of them needed, but years of training had taught them to maintain it well. When their studies concluded for the day, they went home together instead of the dormitories.

Ara waited at the entrance for Lynn, their usual meeting spot. She watched a few other girls trickle down the steps while others made their way back to their rooms. Felsi, a pink-haired catgirl the same year as Ara and Lynn, swerved between the others with quick, panicked steps.

"Ara!" Felsi called.

Ara's ears perked, and she turned to face the flush-faced young woman. "What is it?"

"Lynn is— She's—"

"Calm down. You're attracting attention," Ara hissed, taking note of the glares from the others. Any 'Ungraceful' showing could net them detention or a meeting with Celestia herself.

Felsi rubbed her cheeks and shook her head. "Lynn's in the Room," she whispered.

Ara blinked. "What?"

Felsi's tail whipped back and forth behind her, and she smoothed her skirts. "One of the girls a few years behind us—Notch, I think?—was put on the spot because she's not from Venicia. Even the teacher joined in."

Ara grimaced. She knew what happened next. "And Lynn stood up for her?" The recent discord between students loomed over Lynn like a raincloud. She was the champion of all, no matter their background.

"Mhm. Next thing we know, Celestia's at the door calling for her. She—"

"Thank you, Felsi." Ignoring whatever else Felsi was about to say, Ara excused herself and marched back inside.

While she'd never seen the exact location of the Room, Ara had seen plenty of red-eyed girls with dark circles stumbling from one particular direction of the school. It would take a bit of guesswork, but she would find it eventually.

A tug on her shirt sleeve tore her away from her thoughts. Felsi once again stood at her side, face still blanched and gray eyes wide. "I... I know—" She paused and swallowed hard. "I know where it is. I can show you."

"I can find it on my own," Ara muttered.

"No. This is faster. Come on." Felsi took the lead without asking, and Ara followed close behind.

By now, many of the girls had returned to their rooms, left for home, or spent their leisure in the small shops around the school. Their travels went mostly unnoticed, drawing a curious glance here or there, but primarily accompanied by silent hallways and lavish tapestries. The further they went, the fewer catgirls they saw.

"This way." More twists and turns. Ara counted two rights and three lefts, silently grateful for Felsi's guidance. She'd never imagined it would be so deeply hidden past the classrooms and dorms.

The quick sound of approaching footsteps caught Ara's ear. There wasn't time to think. "In here." She snagged Felsi's sleeve and pulled her inside a darkened classroom. It seemed the teacher had forgotten to lock the door on her way out.

Nudging Felsi to the side, Ara let the door remain open a crack and peered out. The pair that headed in their direction forced Ara to cover her own mouth, masking a gasp.

Ara had never seen a man in person before. There were art pieces and books here and there and the occasional sketch by a daydreaming catgirl, but this was entirely different. This one had a head of tousled blonde hair and a smooth, clean face. Bright blue eyes glimmered as he looked in every direction, taking in the features of the school.

"This place is so big! And clean!"

His head barely reached Madame Celestia's shoulder, and his limbs were far thinner and more lithe than the muscled depictions Ara had seen in the past.

"We can supply you with anything you desire for the duration of your stay, master," Celestia replied evenly.

Ara couldn't help but think that 'young master' would better suit him. If men aged similarly to catgirls, this one had barely reached adulthood.

His cheeks turned a brilliant red, and he rubbed the back of his neck. "You can just call me Tristan. Really."

"I could never *dream* of being so impolite." Celestia shook her head. "You are the most important person on this island, master. Your title should reflect it."

"She doesn't believe that for a minute," Felsi hissed in Ara's ear.

Ara curled her fingers into a fist, keeping one to her lips to shush her companion.

"Are you sure you just want me to stay here?" Tristan murmured a word, and a square device appeared in his palm. "I fought a few monsters outside. I'm sure I could get better at it with practice. But the iPaw—"

"My goodness! You shall never have to lift a finger, master! Protecting *your* life is our humble reason for living. Come, allow me to show you to your quarters."

Tristan hummed his assent, following Celestia down the length of the hallway. When they vanished behind a giant lacquered door at the end, Ara released the breath she was holding.

"A man? *Here?*" Felsi whispered.

Ara considered the circumstances. "I'm loath to admit it, but Celestia may be doing what's best for the island." As far as she'd known, the previous men on Shi Island had died of unusual circumstances. It had been a long time since the last one's unfortunate departure, creating an undercurrent of worry throughout the city. How would their population continue if the men arriving continued to die so quickly?

"What do you mean?" Felsi's voice pitched. "Could we really take care of him?"

"Well, keeping him here ensures he's safe from danger. It'll also be easier to produce kittens this way." Ara shook her head. "Perhaps Celestia knows what she's doing."

"That would be a first," Felsi murmured.

Celestia reappeared without Tristan, moving down the hallway with a new spring in her step. Her twin braids bounced on either shoulder, and she held her hands together behind her back. The thin smile on her face sent a chill down Ara's spine. She shivered.

They watched her disappear around the corner and waited until they could no longer hear her footsteps on the soft carpet. Ara carefully opened the door, then crept around the wall to confirm the headmistress had, in fact, left.

"We are safe for now," Ara called to Felsi.

Felsi still tiptoed onto the carpet, then pointed to an enormous door to their immediate right. "The Room's right here."

Ara dashed to the minuscule window carved high into the Room's door. Lynn was silently sobbing inside, rubbing warmth back into her arms while dancing from one foot to the other.

"Lynn! Hang on!" Ara called.

Lynn's eyes snapped open, and she locked Ara's gaze.

"Are you alright?" Ara asked.

Lynn vehemently shook her head, fingers trembling.

Ara slid a pair of slim twin rods from a hidden pocket in her apron. "Why isn't she saying anything?"

"You can't speak in there. It's Enchanted to stop you," Felsi explained.

"I see." She knelt before the door's lock and set to work. "You would think with an Enchantment like that, the headmistress would utilize better locks."

"What are you doing?" Felsi squeaked.

"Getting my sister out of there," Ara growled.

"Celestia will return for her in the morning! Are you mad?"

"Then we will spend the night in the classroom. Lynn can return to the Room at dawn."

"But—"

Ara sighed. It was impossible to search for the lock's pins with Felsi fretting over her. "Thank you for your assistance, Felsi. If you do not wish to serve as an accomplice to this infraction, you may leave."

Felsi chewed her lip, looked back at the door, then nodded. "N-no. I'll stay."

"Then I require your silence."

Ara had expected more of a challenge. Maybe an additional lock. But the pins gave way with a satisfying click, and she used the second rod to act as the 'key.' The door gave way, and Lynn fell into her arms.

"Not here. This way," Ara whispered.

Lynn nodded. Felsi closed the Room's door, and they returned to the darkened classroom. They settled into a far corner where Lynn sunk to her knees and cried into Ara's shoulder.

"I'm sorry, Ara. I should never have—*hic!*—said anything! I just— I can't—" Lynn sobbed.

"Shh. It's alright. I'm certain you did the right thing." Ara coaxed, stroking her sister's hair.

"Why don't I find us something to eat?" Felsi suggested. "Maybe a warm bowl of soup would cheer you up?"

"Be sure to hide it in your [Cat Pack]," Ara instructed. "But Felsi, if Celestia sees you, do *not* return here. Understand?"

"Of course. I'll be back as soon as I can." Felsi bowed, then skipped from the room.

Ara quietly consoled Lynn until her crying slowed.

"C-Celestia is so— she's so *mean*," Lynn replied. "Why has she turned the girls against one another?"

"I've wondered that myself. However, it's impossible to tell if her choices are ill-intended."

Lynn hummed a noncommittal reply, then changed the subject. "Thank you, Ara. You didn't have to do this."

"No reason to thank me." Ara embraced her tightly. "I will always protect you, Lynn."

Lynn Pro Tip: Every Shi Island girl deserves a chance at the school. It shouldn't matter what city they're from.

Chapter 32
Rabanadas

By the time Peony was satiated, it was close to midnight. She returned to her room in giggling fits while Tristan went to hunt down Ara. His night wasn't over, it seemed. *Who did you trade your soul to for that kind of stamina, man?*

I didn't feel right calling it a night without finding Ceres and Keke first. I couldn't imagine they'd be too pleased with me disappearing the full day. Guess I'd been caught up in the moment with Peony. Well, a lot of moments.

My room was empty, and a quick peek into the gaming hall revealed an Ara with more Bells than I could count and a circle of furious catgirls. But no Keke and Ceres. No luck in the restaurant, either.

Well, only one other place that'll be open this time of night.

I went to the dressing room outside the hot spring and stripped for the second time that day. Even if they weren't there, I could still wash myself off.

Wrapping a towel around my hips, I walked barefoot to the steaming hot springs. The Gem of Abalone really outdid themselves at night. Dark green circles shaped like lily pads floated along the water's surface with tiny candles at their center, twinkling brightly in the darkness. Beyond a few dozen of those, there were two torches in the far corners of the area and the dim light that escaped the dressing room. I had to let my eyes adjust to the sudden shift. I stood next to the spring and blinked away the black frames around my vision.

Two pairs of familiar cat ears on familiar heads bobbed near the waterfall. Keke's soft laughter bounced across the spring to my ears, followed by a few hushed words from Ceres. No one else was taking advantage of the waters so late. That worked out.

I tossed the towel to the side before sliding into the water. After that afternoon's exertions, the heat in my muscles and joints felt amazing. Scratches from Peony's desperate grasps tingled and faded while the tension in my shoulders evaporated.

"Oh? Matt? Have you finally come to join us?" Keke called.

Oh. Right. [Low-Light Vision]. "Hey."

"It is impolite to keep your ladies waiting, Matt," Ceres added. There was no stutter or trace of a hidden 'my lord.'

Ouch. "I know. I'm sorry." I paddled closer to them, finally able to make out their faces. Soft candlelight cradled their captivating features, flickering in pools of gold and blue. Ceres's hair was out of its usual braid, the flowing tendrils cascading over her shoulders. "I should have left a note."

"Or woken us up." Keke's fingers poked free from the surface before she splashed me with a wave of hot water. "Don't you think we would've liked to eat together?"

I brushed the streams of her attack away from my face. "Yeah. That would make sense."

Ceres pulled her knees to her chest. "Keke and I… Well, it was odd to wake up on our own."

"You're very soft to cuddle. If that's what Matt would rather, it's fine," Keke said, touching Ceres's shoulder.

Are you trying to get a rise out of me? It was working. This wasn't like her. "Keke."

Keke huffed, and a long piece of her bangs floated in the air before falling back over her nose. "Last night was strange. I didn't hate it, but it felt strange."

Ceres blushed, then murmured, "I quite liked it."

"We didn't have to do it. If you wanted to stop, you could have said so," I argued.

"And ruin your and Ceres's fun? No." Keke shook her head, then blew the strand of hair away from her nose again. "I guess I thought if we all woke up together and went to breakfast together, I'd feel fine. Like, yeah, it felt weird, but at the end of the day, you're still min—" She covered her mouth, then dropped her eyes.

"Speak your mind, Keke," Ceres encouraged.

Slowly lowering her hand, she raised her gaze to mine. "Instead, it was just us, and Ara said you'd vanished with another girl. Which I know is what you're supposed to do, and that's *fine*. Because we're not allowed to lay claim to you. Or be possessive. I know this is irrational behavior, and still I... I..."

"You what?" I asked.

Ceres rested her hand on Keke's shoulder and gave her a reassuring nod. "As soon as kittens are considered grown, we are taught that bearing children becomes our highest priority if we ever encounter a man," Ceres supplied. "We must put his needs first, and our emotions are irrelevant. We must stand aside and allow him to perform his duties. However, the reality is," she paused and squeezed Keke's hand, "it is not so easy."

Before I'd arrived in Nyarlea, that would have sounded like heaven. Now, each time I heard about the 'role' of catgirls, it twisted knots in my stomach. "I won't ever ask you not to feel what you're feeling," I said.

"Perhaps not. But we stand in violation of numerous laws for such desires," Ceres replied. "I have heard there are...establishments—in Nyarlothep—that rehabilitate catgirls who've become too attached to the men on their islands."

Keke shuddered. "I couldn't... I can't—"

I felt nauseous. "Hey, no one's getting put behind bars for that. I would never let it happen." I pushed the loose hair still tickling Keke's nose away from her face. "I'm sorry. I should have waited for you two."

"Mm." Keke nodded, her expression solemn.

I touched their arms, searching out both of their gazes. "You'll always be my girls. My Party. There's no one who can replace you." *Maybe mushy, but it's the damn truth.* "Really. I'm sorry. I won't leave you like that again."

They nodded, but even Ceres still looked pretty put out. I pushed their arms to the sides, sandwiching myself in between them before wrapping an arm around each of their shoulders and pulling them tightly against me.

"Matt!" Keke laughed with surprise.

"It's our last night of vacation. I won't have sad girls just because I was a dumbass. Now, tell me you didn't waste the day waiting for me?"

"Heavens no. We had a wonderful day together. You think us so painfully dependent that we can't entertain ourselves?" Ceres chided.

"Wow. Guess I'm not off the hook yet, huh?"

"Not for the night, at least." Keke leaned her head against the curve between my neck and shoulder. She lifted her hands from the water and held them forward for me to see. "Here, look. We had our fingernails and toenails filed and painted!"

Ceres copied the movement, tipping her fingers toward Keke's so I could see both. Keke had picked a forest green that reminded me of her combat attire, while Ceres's nails were a vivid pink.

"They look great," I complimented.

"I've never had them done before," Ceres marveled. "Venicia does not believe in colored nails—it goes against the efficiency virtue. And, well, the rest of Shi Island does not have the time nor luxury."

"That makes sense."

"I remember Aurora painting Cannoli's and my nails when we were little. My mom never liked the idea." Keke chuckled and let her arms fall beneath the water. "I've never bothered to try since then."

"Well, I've never bothered with my nails either. So we're even." I shrugged.

"Do the men where you're from perform such maintenance?" Ceres asked. "I am trying to imagine your nails in a similar pink and—" she snorted, "—it is funny."

"Some of them do. Just wasn't really my thing. I was bad enough about getting my hair cut. Forget trying to remember anything else." It was probably due for a trim again, now that I thought about it. "What do you want to do with our last day tomorrow?"

"I'd like to shop for gifts. For Cannoli and Ravyn," Keke said. "Maybe we can find something that would cheer them up."

"That is a spectacular idea!" Ceres exclaimed. "I spotted a tea shop during our walk earlier. Perhaps something there for Ravyn?"

"I think she'd really like that. And some sweets and new hair ribbons for Cannoli," Keke replied.

"That sounds great. We'll all go together after breakfast," I agreed.

Ceres relaxed her head against my shoulder, and the three of us sat in silence, watching the starlight sparkle through the waterfall.

"Hey, Matt," Keke said.

"Hm?"

"Thanks for coming to find us."

I kissed the top of her head. "Of course."

Keke Pro Tip: I think I saw a stuffed rabbit in the window of one of the shops. I'm sure Cannoli would love it!

Chapter 33

Fleischsalat

My joints had never felt better. Sure, my mind was all over the place lately, but considering our circumstances, that was par for the course. Hot springs time had been exactly what I needed, and the conversation with Keke and Ceres had gone over much better than I'd expected. The last thing I wanted to do was hurt them.

With that out of the way, we talked about what to do with the remainder of our day. We checked out of our hotel rooms and settled on visiting the local shops and eateries to see if anything caught our eye. I would've felt like a heel if we didn't return with some sort of souvenir, especially considering the available merchandise.

To me, Abalone felt like what would happen if you mixed hospitality and nature together. The dirt roads were well-kept but not extravagantly designed. Shop stalls lined the streets, with each of the shopkeeps casually calling for any to come and take a look at their wares. Unlike San Island, these girls didn't practice the cut-throat business model of getting in your face with a questionable rock of dubious value.

Too bad it felt like a ruse.

Whispers would pass from stall to stall whenever Tristan and I passed by. Wide-eyed stares would follow us from one stretch of the road to the next, sometimes accompanied by the sudden crash of some object and a catgirl's panicked attempt to clean up whatever mess she just made.

Keke, Ceres, and Ara did their best to stay alert. Ara's pointed stare was enough to send most of them reeling. A few girls were particularly courageous, though Ceres and Keke were quick to snatch their wrists before any of them could sneak a touch.

"This is kinda stressful," I admitted.

"Maybe we should go back into the hotel and just shop around in there," Keke suggested as she released the wrist of a dainty, green-haired catgirl. The culprit hissed and stuck out her tongue, and Keke responded by smacking the back of one hand into her open palm.

Is that a catgirl warning sign? Or did Keke really just threaten to smack her?

Ara drew a dagger from under her sleeve as her eye caught the stare of someone who'd locked eyes with Tristan. The girl turned on her heel and skittered away, drawing small dust clouds in her wake.

"That seemed a little much," I grumbled.

"Please do not misunderstand. I do not find protecting the young master to be a chore. However," and then Ara turned to look at me, "for the sake of your own enjoyment, I must agree with Keke. Shopping at The Gem of Abalone may be the most beneficial option."

"As must I, my dear Matt," Ceres said.

We changed pet names? No more 'my lord'?

"I'm not bothered," Tristan said easily. "This is just the culture." Then he turned to look at me. "Unless you are, Matt."

I had to be honest. "Yeah, actually I'm a little uncomfortable. I'm cool shopping at the hotel if you are."

Tristan and the girls shrugged.

What a relief.

I could feel the stress leaving as soon as we walked through the doors. One of the attendants frowned, then approached.

"Have we done something to upset you, sirs?"

I see we have our priorities set. I shook my head.

"Not at all," Tristan said with a smile. "We remembered a few of the gift shops here and simply had to take a look."

The attendant put a hand to her chest and breathed a sigh of relief. "Oh goodness, I'm glad to hear that." She stepped to her side and gestured down the hall. "If you follow this hall, it'll lead you to the strip of shops. Please take your time. We'll even offer a discount for your continued patronage."

"Thanks!" Tristan offered a wave and led the way.

While there weren't very many of them, every shop carried exceptional quality products. One that caught my eye was a shop that specialized in kitten toys. Each of us wandered around the store, and for a rare moment, I was on my own as I perused one of the aisles. There was something I was looking for in particular.

Then I saw it. Two shelf-like extensions boxed in a corner protecting a tall table. And, to put it lightly, the table was bizarre. Like someone had rolled a tree stump into the store and glued four legs to it. Around the stump were lightning bolts painted in haphazard sizes and shapes in an array of colors. It looked like it'd been thrown together by a child.

Maybe it was, Kelmer. Don't underestimate the imagination of a child.

Atop the table were stuffed rabbits of every shape and size you could imagine. Fluffy ones, tiny ones, fat ones, some with…eight legs. That last one I had to assume was meant to illustrate the speed of the animal, and not necessarily an accurate depiction of rabbit legs. At least, I hoped so.

I picked up one of the stuffed rabbits, who was a bit of a middle grounder among the lot. The little dude was a pale green with bright red eyes. He had his arms held out to his sides like he was expecting a hug. He seemed like the sorta thing Cannoli would buy for herself.

Is any color rarer than the next?

I'd set my sights on seeing a green rabbit if such a rumor was true—there was a hint of truth to every myth, after all. But if I had to pick a color for Cannoli, I imagined tried-and-true white was the way to go for a rabbit. Or maybe a pink one.

Maybe those are just the colors I associate with her?

It was time to get Keke's advice. With the green rabbit in hand, I made my way out of the corner and snaked my way around several shelves and brightly colored tables on the way. "Keke, where are you?"

"Over here!"

A voice to my right called to me. The area I found her in was very bright and filled with small wooden toys and objects that I'd expect to see a toddler playing with. Keke seemed to be pretty enamored with a set of tiny chimes. She ran her finger across the hollow pipes and shut her eyes to listen.

"That's really pretty," I said as I moved to stand in front of her.

"I think I might buy it," she admitted. She opened her eyes, but only halfway. "It's nostalgic."

"Did you have chimes as a kitten?"

Keke nodded, her attention glued to the object. "I was a troublemaker."

"Not sure what kid isn't. I wasn't the best kid myself."

Keke turned her head to me. "What were you like as a kid?"

I blinked. I couldn't recall if anyone had asked me that before. "I got a lot of scrapes and bruises climbing trees, digging in the dirt, looking for dinosaur bones."

She frowned. "What are dinosaur bones?"

I had to think for a second. "So imagine Buttons, but with horns and large, pointy teeth. And far bigger than us." I emphasized this by stretching my arms out to my sides.

"Sounds like a Defiled."

"Defiled got nothing on the dinosaurs. They're every kid's favorite creature."

Keke cupped her elbow between her index and middle fingers. "Sounds a lot like how I was as a kitten."

"We probably would've made good friends."

"I have no doubt."

"So then, why the chimes?" I asked, pointing to them.

Keke laid the chimes flat in her hand. "They helped me calm down. I'd always get my hands on something I wasn't supposed to. Whether it was bottles or weird-smelling herbs from Granny Nauka, getting nyapples with Cannoli, finding some strange bug from the dirt, you name it." Keke breathed a sigh. "I couldn't sleep. So, Mom got me these."

"Sounds like you had a great mom."

"She was the best." Keke pinched the bridge of her nose, then raised her head before I could ask anything more about the subject. "So, what did you need? Is it about that rabbit?"

"Oh, yeah!" To be honest, I'd nearly forgotten. "I was thinking of a green rabbit as a gift for Cannoli, but I don't know what colors she likes. Can you help a guy out?"

A smile tugged at one end of Keke's mouth. "She likes bright colors. That would work, but if it were me? I'd get her a light blue or pink. Those are safer choices." Keke shrugged and half-laughed. "But she'll love any of the rabbits that you give her. I promise."

"Thanks, Keke." I gave her a quick peck on the cheek, and as I turned to leave, she caught me by the hem of my shirt, turning me back around.

"Hey." She pulled me close, and her lips met mine.

I shut my eyes and returned her embrace, wrapping one arm around her waist. It was slow, warm, and comforting.

Keke drew away, and her mouth opened as if she was about to say something. A pink hue decorated her cheeks, and she twirled a lock of hair around her finger. "Well, off you go." She cleared her throat. "I'll be here if you need anything else."

I smiled. "Thanks, Keke."

After much deliberation, I settled on a pastel-pink rabbit, just as Keke had suggested. Whether Cannoli liked it or not, I just couldn't see another color matching her as well. Sure, it was the easy route, but I'd gotten advice from Keke.

We checked out and left the store. Keke was a bit on the quiet side after that, but I knew we all had a lot on our minds. I was glad she bought the chimes, though.

I wonder what her mom was like.

Ceres Pro Tip: I very much enjoyed my time here. Please let us return ere long? With Cannoli and Ravyn, too?

Chapter 34

Neua Pad Prik

Leaving Abalone was an incredibly bittersweet experience. On the one hand, I was upset that we couldn't stay longer. It'd been a while since we'd been able to kick back and enjoy ourselves. We'd spent our time relaxing, partying, playing games, shopping around, all the things one would expect to do when they were taking time off. It was time we all needed—that much was certain.

On the other side of the coin, I felt like if I'd spent any more time here, one thing would lead to another, and I would end up spoiled and penniless. I was eager to get back anyway. I'd enjoyed my time living like a frat boy for a few days, but Cannoli and Ravyn were still back home, and no matter what I did to try, I couldn't get my mind off of them.

"Got everything you need?" asked Keke.

I held up my [Cat Pack] and shook it for effect. "All set."

It was back to business as usual. It wouldn't be long until we'd set sail once more. We still had another island to visit, another man to convince. Tristan and Shi Island had been its own can of worms, and there was still the matter of Ara's sister. I didn't know whether they were tight as nails or not, but they sure seemed that way. Ara's questions about returning were starting to resurface, and we had a long road ahead of us.

If Ara's concern was even a pinch of concern I felt for Ravyn and Cannoli at this moment, then she did a great job at putting on a face.

"Alright, let's get going!" Keke said.

It was going to be a couple of hours before we arrived. The five of us sat in a wagon and watched the scenery whisk by. I did everything in my power to keep my attention on the scenery, the sights, the smells, and the sensations. Mindfulness was a trick I'd been meaning to practice more. I was never very good at it, but with no internet or social media or really any high-tech means of distraction, I had to let myself be bored. And that meant my mind drifted into places I really didn't want it to. It was all I could do to stop my heart from racing at the thought of meeting Cannoli and Ravyn again.

Our recent interactions reminded me of a crush I had when I was about fourteen. I'd fallen hard for this girl at a mutual friend's party. We didn't do anything special or romantic—I couldn't even get up the courage to hold her hand. We'd just danced and laughed together. Like any guy at that age, I was enamored, and I asked for her phone number. She was a little taken aback, and I was convinced she'd just rattle off a number beginning with 5-5-5. It did have a five, but only one. We parted ways, and I was on top of the world.

Thinking I could invite her out to a movie, I gave her a call. To my surprise, someone picked up. A man. I asked to speak with Amber. There was a bit of a pause, but he got her on the phone. Long story short, she was interested, but she found it 'inappropriate' to go to a movie together at that age. Even though it was a sentence probably parroted straight from her dad, at that age, any semblance of rejection from a girl is heartbreaking. I was devastated.

Afterward, he wouldn't give Amber the phone when I called anymore. A few times, my friend called on his phone, then passed it to me so she and I could talk together. But, eventually, she stopped picking up, and as the weeks passed, I couldn't bring myself to call her anymore. It was just too awkward, and I felt like I was forcing myself into the situation. My nerves got the best of me. I never called her again.

That same sensation was coming back. The latent dread that I was forcing my nose where it shouldn't be. That awkward anxiety that no matter how many times I knocked, Cannoli wouldn't answer.

Mindfulness, Kelmer. Mindfulness. What do you see? What do you hear?

I watched the landscape pass by like one of those old movie reels—the ones where a painted background gave the illusion of the main character running away from some baddie. I'd catch the stray Encroacher here or there dodging between the tall grass or roosting in the trees. Most of them never got close enough to become an issue, and a few cute furry ones displayed mild curiosity at the cart's appearance.

"So, what's next on the order of business, Matt?" asked Tristan.

I hummed in thought, pulling my thoughts back together. "I'm thinking we should make Ichi Island our next stop." I rested my chin over the wagon's edge and scratched my elbow. "I'm gonna pick up my shield, see if I can get some better potions made, maybe see if Quinn knows how to upgrade [Cat Pack]s." And then I remembered something Keke and Cannoli had said when I first arrived. I turned my head to Keke. "Where did you and Cannoli upgrade your packs?"

Keke blinked. "My mom upgraded our packs. She'd learned from some of the catgirls she'd fought with over the years." She shrugged. "Cannoli and I were set before we started adventuring."

Well, there goes that idea.

"I can ask Quinn. Worst-case scenario, maybe she or Espada know someone who can upgrade them."

"I see," Tristan said. "Well, I have another idea."

I twisted around and leaned my head against Keke's shoulder. "What's the other idea?"

Keke chuckled and stroked my hair.

Tristan looked to his left at Ara. "Ara?"

Ara glanced at him with a furrowed brow and wrung her hands. "Young master, it is…impolite and selfish. I cannot."

Tristan's smile vanished. "You need to stop that. Your needs are important too, Ara."

"Y-young master, please. It is fine." She shook her head. "I understand we have a task at hand."

"No, it's not fine. We want to hear your thoughts as well. You're as much a part of this group as me, Matt, Keke, or Ceres." His smile returned. "I'm sure Cannoli, and, to some extent, Ravyn would also agree." Then he looked at me. "What do you think, Matt?"

How do you so easily say these kinds of things? I sat up straight, returned his smile, then looked at Ara. "I have to agree." I crossed my arms. "Speak your mind."

Keke frowned. "Is this about your sister, Ara?"

Ara sighed and twirled a lock of hair around her pointer finger. "It seems the young master enjoys placing me in difficult positions."

Tristan averted his gaze and sucked in his lips. "I just want you to be honest and forthright. I understand we're on a mission here, but it's not fair that your voice goes unheard. Besides, we found that you work best in difficult situations, right?"

Ara's face turned beet red. "I-I, uh."

Did I miss some innuendo there?

Ara cleared her throat and straightened her posture as she laid her hands on her lap. "If you would have me speak my mind, then be prepared for the consequences." She let out a sigh, and Tristan nodded. "I understand I have mentioned this before; however, I would still very much like to see Lynn before we continue on."

"My l— *ahem*, Sir Matt." *Oh no, now we've upgraded to Sir Matt? What happened to just calling me Matt? You said it with such ease just hours ago.* "We did previously agree that a visit to Shi Island was in order."

Oh, that's right.

Ara turned to Tristan and took his hand in hers. "I want my sister back. It is not fair that I left Venicia while she remains." She lowered her voice. "Lynn knows how to take care of herself. Even so, under the watch and tutelage of Madame Celestia, I fear she will not flourish without my assistance."

"I fear for anyone beneath that woman," I murmured.

"I must agree," Ceres whispered in reply.

"Young master," Ara continued, "Lynn cannot face the Venicia School of Etiquette alone. It is only a matter of time before she makes a mistake beneath the madame's watchful eye. Some nights, I lie awake at night, praying to Saoirse that she is still happy and healthy." She shook her head, and her grip around Tristan's hand tightened. It was clear that she was fighting back tears. "Please. The longer I'm away, the worse my anxiety becomes. We must go back for her. I cannot proceed to Ichi Island with this on my conscience."

"Then we go back," I said. "I'm sorry, I should have remembered."

"T-thank you," Ara murmured.

A silence swept over us. Rocks and imperfections in the road staggered the stability of the cart.

Ara's chest rose and fell, and it seemed she was unable to look Tristan—or any of us for that matter—in the eye. Her devotion to Tristan was clear as day, and I couldn't imagine how hard it was to ask for anything for herself. The habits she'd picked up from Nyarlea's teachings and Celestia's indoctrinations wouldn't go down easily.

Tristan put one hand over Ara's. "Thank you for being honest. Do you think you can do this more often?"

Ara let out a half-laugh. "Let us see where the future takes us."

"We can consider it repentance for all the poor catgirls you robbed at cards," Tristan teased.

The blush extended to the tips of Ara's ears. "I-I did not rob them!" She slipped her hands out of Tristan's grasp and resumed her prior stature. "I played the game. They were slow on the uptake."

Keke giggled. "Back to Shi Island, then?"

I admit, I wasn't looking forward to it. Going back to Shi sounded like suicide. The image of a few dozen catgirls hiding on rooftops with their sniper rifles primed came to mind. If Celestia had the opportunity, I wouldn't put it past her. But, after a while, I nodded. "Yeah. Let's do it. Let's get Lynn out of there."

"We can always count on you," Ceres said.

Don't put me too high on that pedestal, please. I don't deserve it.

"We'll get Ravyn and Cannoli to come along, too," Keke said. "I doubt Ravyn would object."

That was a good point. The entire island had pissed Ravyn off to no end. This might've been just the occasion we needed to get her back to normalcy.

All we could do was hope Cannoli and Ravyn were up to it.

Guess time will tell.

"But, Sir Matt, you never did tell me." Ceres touched her chin and cocked her head. "How did you trick Ara into thinking Tristan was her sister?"

This was going to be a very long cart ride.

Keke Pro Tip: I'm not looking forward to going toe-to-toe with Celestia again, but Ara's done so much for us.

Chapter 35

Disappearing Cookie

We returned to Junonia with a red-faced Ara and stunned Ceres. I realized that I hadn't regaled the entire tale of Tristan's kidnapping—er, rescuing—to anyone. Ravyn was really the only one who knew most of it since she'd gone in with me. She was also the only person who understood the insane transitions the [Impersonate Soul] scrolls had when you swapped to a member of the opposite sex.

And this is probably obvious, but Ara was *not* happy to hear how I'd, uh, fed Tristan the potion. To be honest, I'd tried not to think about it too much since it happened. It didn't seem to bother him much, but Ara didn't take it well. Keke kept her silence, though I swore she hid her snicker beneath a well-timed coughing fit.

In summary, there weren't a lot of words exchanged when we got back. As I hopped out of the wagon, the nervous tension in my stomach returned, and it had nothing to do with Ara or Ceres. The longer I waited to talk to Ravyn and Cannoli, the worse it was going to get.

On our way back to Keke's house, I paused at the edge of Cannoli's walkway and stared at her door. Ceres stalled next to me, looking between me and the house.

"Sir Matt?" she asked.

Keke caught on and touched Ceres's shoulder. "Let's wash up at my house. I'll make us some tea."

"But, Matt—" Ceres began, then caught Keke's stare. "R-right. Of course."

I waited until they disappeared inside Keke's house, then approached Cannoli's door. *Will she answer?* I swallowed. *You're not fourteen anymore, Matt. Don't mess this up.* With one more deep breath, I knocked.

The seconds ticked by in silence. I reached in my [Cat Pack] and tugged the rabbit free. Its fur was soft like Cannoli's skin, pink like her hair. *God, please answer.*

At last, the door creaked open. But it wasn't Cannoli's face that greeted me.

"*Mou ii.* About time," Ravyn hissed. "We wondered if you'd ever come back."

I stuffed the rabbit back into my pack. "Ravyn—"

"Get in here." She stepped back and jerked her chin to the side.

Cannoli sat at the table, the dark circles beneath her eyes gone, and the cheerful sheen I'd grown to adore had returned. A plate of baked cookies shaped and frosted like Ball Gag sat at the table's center with a tea kettle beside them. The parrot himself and Buttons were nowhere to be seen.

"W-welcome back, Matt." She smiled, tracing the rim of her cup with her fingertip. Her shoulders slouched, and her ears were lowered against her head.

Is she afraid I'm mad? "It's really good to see you. Both of you." I couldn't kick the nerves yet; this could be the calm before the storm.

"Sit," Ravyn commanded, pulling a third chair back from the table before retaking her seat.

I did as I was told, terrified to say the wrong thing. Felt like if I moved too fast, I would startle Cannoli into a panicked sprint. Instead, she poured me a cup of tea and added two sugar cubes before passing it my way. I accepted it and chanced a sip before setting it back on the table. *Should I say something?* I didn't know what was expected of me in this situation.

"So, I—" Ravyn began.

"I think—" Cannoli murmured.

They paused and looked at each other, then broke into awkward smiles. Cannoli shifted in her chair, and Ravyn grabbed one of the parrot-shaped cookies and bit off its head.

"I'm sorry, Ravyn. You go first," Cannoli squeaked.

"Alright," Ravyn said, bits of cookie spraying from her lips. She chased it with a drink of tea and cleared her throat. "I'm sorry, Matt."

I couldn't feel my toes. Ravyn? Apologizing? "Why?" I couldn't stop myself. I'd spent almost a week wondering how best to grovel at her feet to regain her trust, and here she was, apologizing first.

"*Baka!* Because I—!" Ravyn stopped herself. She ran a hand through her hair and flicked her ears. After one long exhale, she started again with a softer tone. "Because I misplaced my feelings and pushed you too far. And I got pissed at *you* for it. That wasn't how it was supposed to go."

I wonder what it was you wanted to happen? "Thanks, Ravyn. Really, though. I'm sorry, too. I should have stopped it."

She laughed under her breath. "Yeah, right. We all know how easy you can be."

My cheeks and ears burned. But if she was making jokes like that again, that was a good sign. "You're probably right."

"*Kuso.* I'm always right." She bit down to the wing of her cookie, then said while chewing, "Your turn, Cannoli."

"O-okay." Cannoli laid her hands in her lap and stared into her teacup. "I'm scared, Matt." Her words quivered on her tongue.

"Why?"

"A lot of things. I'm afraid of blood. I'm afraid of losing my friends. I'm afraid that I'm not good enough to be in your Party, but if I'm not there to help, one of you may die." Cannoli toyed with her tail. Her hair fell over her shoulder. "I'm afraid if I can't get control of my feelings, I'll… I'll—" She sucked in a shaking breath. "I'll be taken away from you."

"Cannoli, I would never let anyone—" I began.

Ravyn held up her hand and shook her head. "You wouldn't have a choice, Matt. This is a promise you can't keep."

"It happened to m-my mom." Cannoli's voice broke. "She loved my dad, and they took her away."

Holy shit. "Who took her?"

"The Queen's Guard. There's a reward for turning in criminals," Ravyn explained. "That's how they're seen. As *criminals.*"

Tears escaped the corners of Cannoli's eyes. "I've been praying *so much.* And *so* hard. Why won't Saoirse listen to me?"

I ran a hand through my hair. What could I say? Don't travel with your friends anymore, Cannoli? Just shut out your feelings? "Cannoli, I want to help. How can I help?"

"I don't know." She sniffled and rubbed her nose against the back of her wrist.

"Hey. We talked about this." Ravyn popped the rest of her cookie in her mouth and laid her arm across Cannoli's shoulders. "Someone has to find out. No one in this Party is going to tell on you, alright?"

"That's what Mom thought, too," Cannoli squeaked.

Ravyn shook her head. "Those bitches would have to get through all of us. Matt may not be able to stop them on his own, but we're an unstoppable Party, remember?"

I blinked. This was a side of Ravyn I didn't remember. Apologizing? Consoling Cannoli? *Should I put her through a Voight-Kampff test?* "You still want to be a Party, then, Ravyn?"

Ravyn scoffed, opened her mouth for another biting reply, then closed it. She looked at Cannoli, then nodded. Her voice dropped, and I barely caught her next words, "This Party was the best thing that could have happened to me."

I burned her words and the scene before me into my memory. Ravyn's moments of vulnerability were few and far between, and I wanted to cling to it. They were like precious stones in the abrasive desert of her personality.

Cannoli dabbed her eyes with a napkin, and I took another drink of my tea, searching the hurricane of potential things I could say to her for the right ones. I was scared, too. That if I didn't know how to properly console her now, we were going to lose her.

"Cannoli, I can't stop all of your fears." I set my cup back on the table and brushed my damp palms against my jeans. "But I *can* stand by your side with you while you face them. And I know you can face them. I've seen you do it over and over again."

Her ruby eyes widened, and she fretted her lower lip.

"Ravyn's right. There are going to be circumstances where I can't protect you. Those are the times I need all of you most. That's how it's supposed to work—we're a team. No one can *ever* fault you for caring for your Party."

"If they do, we'll give them hell," Ravyn added.

I nodded. "It's your choice what you want to do now. No one's going to force you either way. What do you want to do?"

Cannoli sniffed, looked at Ravyn, then back to me. A smile quirked the sides of her mouth, and her ears perked. "I want to stay with you. All of you. You guys are the best thing to happen to me, too."

I finally breathed a sigh of relief and relaxed in the chair. My girls. All of them back together. *Thank Christ.*

"Hey. What was in your hands when I answered the door?" Ravyn asked.

"Oh, right!" I snatched the rabbit from my [Cat Pack] and passed it to Cannoli. "Straight from Abalone."

Cannoli squealed with delight and accepted the stuffed rabbit. She squeezed it between her arms and rocked it back and forth. "A bunny! I love it!"

"Don't forget to make a wish," I reminded her.

"You remembered!" Cannoli laughed, and the sound warmed the room. "I'll make it a *really* good one!"

I hadn't realized how heavy my heart had felt until I heard her laugh again. Like the weight of the world had been lifted.

"What'd you get for me?" Ravyn snickered.

I leaned forward and crossed my arms on the table. "How does payback on Celestia sound?"

Ravyn gasped, then mimicked my posture on the table. Her eyes narrowed, and she wore a wicked smile. "I'm listening."

Cannoli Pro Tip: My new bunny is SO CUTE, Matt! I think I'll name her Bubbles! My wish? Oh! That's a secret!

Side Quest

We Need to Talk About Ball Gag

Ravyn stared at the floor of Yomi's living room, chewing her lower lip while mentally sifting through hundreds of Encroachers.

"Remember, if you don't like it, we'll have to ask someone to help send it back," Finn cautioned.

"I know," Ravyn murmured.

Yomi giggled. "You say that like a familiar is as easy to return as a letter at the wrong address."

Finn blushed. "I know it's not! You know what I mean."

"Hm," Ravyn grumbled beneath their exchange. *Not a wolf. We've had too many bad run-ins with wolves. I don't really want a cat, either. Catgirls are bad enough as it is.* "I wonder if they can talk," she mused aloud.

Yomi and Finn exchanged glances, then shrugged.

"I've never asked another [Mage]," Yomi said.

"Well, let's see. Summon iPaw," Finn declared, the device appearing in his hand. "Hey, Ai—" he continued to speak, swapping to the strange language he only ever used with the iPaw. It was weird, and Finn himself couldn't explain it. After a while, Ravyn got used to it.

"Remember the Encroachers on Nyarlothep?" Yomi asked quietly while Finn bantered with the iPaw. "They were so pretty!"

The outlying forested areas of Nyralothep's capital were filled with roaches unlike any Ravyn had ever seen. Brilliantly colored birds, bugs, and critters scampering across the forest floor. She'd heard stories of beasts like that when she was a kitten, but she hadn't believed they existed when she got older. "Yeah. The birds especially were nice."

"*Mou ii.*" Finn sighed, and the iPaw disappeared. "Alright, Ai says that certain familiars *can* talk. But, as usual, she's really vague on the details."

"We'll just have to hope, then." Ravyn ran her fingers through her hair, then clapped her hands together. "Let's see what we can do."

She recalled their first afternoon traveling through Nyarlothep. Finn had barked a laugh at one of her silly jokes, and a flock of bright blue birds took flight from a nearby tree. She'd never seen anything like them.

Yeah, one of those would work. Who cared if it could talk? So long as the thing could fight and help protect them, what else could she ask for?

"[Summon Familiar]," Ravyn cast the spell while holding both hands forward.

Finn and Yomi watched in silence as the familiar glowing red circle appeared on the living room floor. Magic sigils danced around its perimeter, speeding to a blurred haze as she focused her magic. She cleared her thoughts and pictured the Encroacher.

"Oh, here it comes!" Yomi exclaimed. "This is so exciting."

"Shh," Finn gently hushed her.

Ravyn's magic molded and shaped the dark figure at the center of her circle. Sweat prickled the back of her neck as the creature pulled more and more of her Myana pool from her fingertips. At last, the circle faded, and the drain on her Myana ceased, leaving behind a black-beaked, royal blue bird.

"*Squaaawk!*" the Familiar screamed. He beat his powerful wings and flapped furiously around the room. "*Squaawk! Squaaaawk! Squawk!*"

Finn and Yomi clapped their hands over their ears.

"*Squawk! Squawk! Squawwwk!*"

"It's so *loud!*" Yomi shrieked, ducking as it swooped in toward her head.

Ravyn snickered. The bird was equally as loud as a shrieking kitten, and if this thing could squawk, maybe he *could* talk.

Flinching, Finn took a step back and whipped his head to try and catch sight of the unleashed bird. "Get that parrot a ball gag!"

"Ball Gag, huh?" Ravyn tapped one finger to her chin. It was a term from Finn's world that he'd explained once before after a failed attempt at crafting one. A little sexy, a little obscene. It would certainly turn a few heads as a name. "I like it."

The roach towered over the three of them, drool dripping from its sharp, narrow teeth. A dozen eyes peered over its tiny nose, taking in the whole Party at once.

"*Kuso!* How is this thing still alive?" Finn cried. "I used my last bomb, but we're gonna need more firepower!"

"I already used the fire scrolls I brought!" Yomi yelled back. "You're up, Ravyn!"

Well, let's give Bally a go. "[Summon Familiar]!" Ravyn shouted, holding out one hand. Ball Gag appeared in midair, eagerly flapping his wings as he glanced between the roach and Ravyn. Ball hadn't seemed to grasp the concept of carrying her magic outside of battle. Maybe he'd understand in a more serious situation. "[Fire Ball]!"

A sphere of flames erupted from her hand, launching toward the parrot. His tiny eyes widened, and he narrowly dodged the fire.

"No! Ball Gag! You're supposed to fucking *catch it! Baka!*" Ravyn screamed.

The fireball exploded in the roach's face. It uttered a guttural cry before sinking to its knees. Every eye on its ugly head closed before it crashed to the ground.

"You got it, Ravyn!" Finn cheered.

"No thanks to *my familiar!*" Ravyn bellowed at Ball.

"*Fuck you! Squawk!*" Ball Gag shrieked, flying higher into the sky.

Ravyn froze, her anger pivoting to delight. "You…you can talk!"

"*Squawk! Fuck you! Squawk!*" Ball circled the Party, repeating the phrase at the top of his lungs.

Finn laughed and moved to carve what he could salvage from the roach. Yomi moved beside Ravyn and stared up at the sky with her. "Maybe he doesn't like his name."

"Oh. He'll learn to like it." Ravyn sneered up at her familiar. "And he'll learn to say it."

After weeks of one-on-one training, Ball Gag began to understand that magic wouldn't actually hurt him. That Ravyn's [Fire Ball]s were intended to make him stronger—not fry him for dinner.

Guiding him to the target was a whole different story.

Twice he'd set Ravyn's thatch roof on fire—thankfully, San Island was filled with catgirls with elemental affinities, including water. On one occasion, his flaming wingtip caught the hem of Yomi's dress, an issue quickly solved by Finn gracefully stamping it out with his foot. However, the worst of it was an incident where he'd nearly collided with Finn's [Alchemy] storage.

Finn started storing his bombs in a more secure location after that one.

Oh well. Another day. Another chance. Another scene of Ball Gag veering into her roof—

"Bally!" Ravyn shrieked. "Damn it! The target is *right here!*" She gestured wildly to a hastily built scarecrow. "Set *this* asshole on fire! Not my roof!"

"*Squaawk! Master's a bitch! Squawk!*"

"Master's going to serve you for dinner if you *set her roof on fire again!*" Ravyn stamped her foot and balled her fists. "I mean it! Yomi *loves* fried chicken!"

"*Be nice! Be nice! Squawk!*" Ball banked his flight path, missing the roof by a hair's breadth.

Ravyn growled, then took a deep breath. "Bally. *Please* attack the scarecrow?"

Ball evened out his wings, then soared directly into the scarecrow's midsection. The straw ignited into a brilliant burst of flame as the parrot changed direction to fly straight into the sky.

Relief and frustration washed over her in equal measure. *Really? The bird has feelings?*

Ball Gag descended from the sky, the last licks of flame sizzling harmlessly from his feathers. He alighted on Ravyn's shoulder, then nuzzled his head against her cheek. "*Good master,*" he squawked.

Ravyn cackled, then stroked his back. Maybe they weren't so different after all.

The third bottle of wine didn't make her feel better. Neither did the fourth. How many would it take to just feel numb?

Finn was gone. Finn was gone, and Yomi blamed Ravyn. Had she ever been so fucking alone?

Her chest felt impossibly tight, and her eyes burned with the thousands of tears that had escaped them. The whole world had turned against her. Her house felt so empty and quiet.

Another drink. Another memory.

"[Summon Familiar]," she slurred, waving her hand above the small dining table. The table Finn had sat across so many times.

"*Squawk! Master?*" Ball Gag appeared, standing stationary on the table's surface instead of his usual feather-filled entrance. He hopped forward, then preened one of his wings.

"Bally, I...I can't..." Ravyn's voice broke, her forehead slumped against her arm, and another wave of sobs stole her words.

"*Ravyn.*" Ball moved his beak from his wing to Ravyn's hair, cleaning it as if she were a fellow bird.

"Don't...don't ever leave my side," Ravyn pleaded quietly.

Ball finished his attention on her hair, then brushed his cheek to her ear. "*Good master.*"

Ravyn chuckled between her gasps. "Good Bally."

Ravyn Pro Tip: You've learned so much since then, huh Bally? Such a good boy.

Chapter 36

Fishing Net

While part of me wanted to get on the boat and head back to Shi right away just to get the confrontation over with, we didn't really have the option. Espada still needed a few more days on Ceres's armor, and none of us were comfortable facing off against the school without it.

I imagined the meeting going one of two ways. In the first scenario, Celestia gave in without a fight. That would make the most sense since going toe-to-toe against two men in Nyarlea seemed tantamount to suicide. Still, knowing her, the second outcome was just as likely. That we'd arrive and have to fight Celestia and whoever she'd convinced to stand with her. The latter of the two gained more traction every time I heard something new about how Tristan and the girls were treated at the school.

Keke, Ravyn, and I were moving through the market square, puzzling out Celestia's intentions while we gathered items for the journey. The sun was setting, and most of the shops were closing up for the day, but plenty of merchants were willing to make last-minute transactions and add a few extra Bells to their pockets.

"Why do you think Celestia took his [Cat Pack]?" Keke asked. "She should have her own, and it would have made sense for him to keep one just in case. I mean, I get that it's better served if you *go outside*, but still."

"My guess is the bitch spent all his Bells," Ravyn snarled.

Keke raised an eyebrow. "Bells from where? He never left the school."

Thanks to the addition of the newest Chain Quest to bed catgirls, Ravyn's words struck a truth I hadn't realized before. "The sex Quests," I murmured.

"*Kehehe.* Finally caught up, have you?" Ravyn sneered.

"What do you mean?" Keke tilted her head, studying Ravyn, then me.

I ran a hand through my hair. Ravyn had made mention of the Quest once before, so she obviously knew about them. But Keke wouldn't really have a reason unless her mom had said something. *How do I explain this?* "Men receive a series of Quests for, er, procreating with catgirls."

"Wait. Seriously?" Keke crossed her arms over her chest.

"That's right, sweet cheeks. Matt gets Levels and Bells for doing his job," Ravyn supplied.

Keke's eyes widened, and she studied me intently. It was impossible to tell what she was thinking.

"I'm only on the second Quest." I cleared my throat. "Look, that's not the point. What I was getting at is it seems like the Bells increase with each Quest you finish. That money gets deposited straight into your [Cat Pack]. And, well, knowing Tristan's Level, we can guess how many times he's completed them."

Keke trailed, realization dawning on her face. "How much money are we talking?"

I grimaced. "Hundreds of thousands of Bells."

Keke gasped. "And if Celestia took his [Cat Pack]—"

"—Then Venicia would have plenty of funds to build, expand, and offer free services to a visiting man and his Party," Ravyn finished for her. "Sound familiar?"

"How could she do that? That's not her money!" Keke growled. "My feelings on the Quest aside, that isn't for her to decide."

"Well, she decided to keep Tristan locked in a room, too. So." I shrugged. "She's pretty unhinged."

Keke bristled. "Can we get his money back for him? He needs Equipment and Potions. We can get him the basic stuff, but—"

Ravyn shook her head. "No way. Unless you're willing to steal it from the girls living on that island, those Bells are lost."

"Yeah, I think we should—*wah!*" One moment, I was standing, then the next, I was surrounded by a cage of ropes cradling me from the branches. "What the hell?"

"Matt! Are you okay?" Keke asked, desperately searching around her for the source of my capture. I hadn't been paying incredibly close attention to where I was walking, and we'd wandered beneath a cluster of tall trees at the edge of the merchant stalls. That wouldn't have been a problem unless, of course, someone had set a trap.

"Yeah, just…confused," I admitted, shoving one arm through a hole and reaching for the knot at the top. It was a futile effort; there were far more ridges and bends than I'd expected. There was no way I could get myself out of it.

"*Kuso!* What the fuck is this?" Ravyn growled, storming over to my net. "Is there a visiting group of Kitten Scouts?"

I noticed another length of rope trailing from a nearby tree trunk too late. "Ravyn, wait—"

"*Iyaah!*" The rope snapped around Ravyn's ankle, stealing her foot from the ground and dragging her upward. "What the fuck!" she screamed.

Ravyn dangled by the ankle next to me, her dress sliding over her thighs and baring the inches of flesh she usually reserved for the imagination. She grabbed at the hem and tugged it down, her body swinging from side to side like a slow pendulum.

Ball descended from his vantage point high in the sky, landing on the branch the rope was tied to. He futilely pecked at the knot with equally as much luck as I'd had with mine.

I had to admit the whole thing was pretty damn funny.

"Just hang on. I'll get you down," Keke said between a sputter of laughter. She took two steps toward Ravyn from the opposite direction before the ground gave way. With a high-pitched squeal, she sank into the ground, a loud *squish* sounding with her fall. "Oh, no. *Gross!*" A barrel awaited her beneath a thick overlay of leaves. One that was full of…some seriously smelly contents.

"Yeah. Ha *ha*. Who's laughing now, bitch?" Ravyn cackled. The back of her dress rolled to her hips. "*Mou ii!* This is fucking stupid!"

Reminds me of Home Alone, *but neither of you would get that joke.*

"Nah, you know what's stupid? A man who doesn't do his job." A new voice joined the choir of shrieks. A short catgirl with shoulder-length brown hair and a striped tunic rounded one of the trees. Silver bangles dangled from one wrist, and silver earrings pierced her ears to match. The left side of her scalp was shaved, giving her a scrappy undercut. She rested one hand on her hip and aimed a gun-shaped hand at me, pulling it back with a click of her tongue. "Gotcha."

"Nixie, right?" Keke asked.

"Oh? You've heard of me?" Nixie turned to Keke and grinned.

"Everyone knows who you are, Nixie. We know of your schemes. Though it's my first time falling victim." Keke squirmed in the barrel, her skirt and top dampened by whatever was inside. "What's *in* here, anyway?"

Nixie shrugged. "Roach bait. How else am I supposed to fish?"

"*Mattaku!* I'm too old for this shit. [Fire Ball]!" Ravyn cried. Without her usual verbal wind-up on the Spell, a ball of flame bloomed from her palm and loosed into the rope. Ball squawked and narrowly dodged the explosion. She fell to the ground with an '*Oomph!*' and then scrambled to her feet. "We have more important things to do, *Nixie.*" She smoothed out her dress and held her arms out to Keke. "Come on, get out of there."

Keke accepted, and together, they eased her out of the barrel.

"You're the witch that lives in the mountain, aren't you?" Nixie asked Ravyn. "I've heard things about you."

"Seems we're both popular then, bitch," Ravyn spat. Once Keke was free, she shook her head and called for Ball. "Come find me when you're done playing games." She turned and left without another word.

"What is it you want, Nixie?" I asked. The net wasn't exactly comfortable, and we had shit to do.

"You know what happens when Portia leaves the island?" Nixie asked, walking around the net, then Keke's barrel. "*I* have to do all of the transportation. *I* pick up the slack. Sailing, trading, whatever these girls need."

"You're overexaggerating," Keke said. "There aren't that many girls here, and there's another boat on the other side of the island."

"Am I? Were you here for it?" Nixie challenged.

"Look, if you want an apology, you have it. We're sorry," I sighed. "We have a lot to do. Would you please let me go?"

"Oh, that's not the only thing I want. You have a job on this island. Don't you, *Matt?*"

"So that's how it is." I sighed.

"That's right."

I was losing my patience. Fast. "If you want a kitten, just say it. Don't put us through all of this."

"You're a hard man to find, Matt. And these girls keep you *very* preoccupied." Nixie slapped Keke on the backside.

Keke swatted her arm away and rolled her eyes.

Now I was mad. "You want a kitten? Fine. But hands off my girls."

Nixie clasped her hands behind her back and danced back and forth between her feet. "Hey, I was just having a little fun. Don't you like fun?"

"This isn't the way to do it."

"But I saw you *smiling*," she pointed out. "Come on. You owe me. Let me have this one."

I looked at Keke.

Keke shook her head and shrugged. "Up to you. You're the one in the net. I just...need a bath."

I sighed. "Alright. Sure. Let me down, then?"

Nixie went to the tree, holding my net, and slowly lowered me down. Once I was sitting on the ground, she slipped a knife from her boot and cut the net free. I stood and brushed myself off.

"You okay?" Keke touched my shoulder and gave me a once-over.

"I'm fine. Thanks Keke. I'll catch up with you later."

"*Tch.* Gross," Nixie spat.

Keke smirked. "Good luck."

I waited until Keke was out of earshot before I turned back to Nixie. "So, then. Let's be clear here. You set this all up so you can have a kitten?"

"*And* to tell you what a *pain* it is when you just *disappear* for weeks at a time!" Nixie replied in a huff. "You've made so much extra work for me!"

"We have to leave again soon. I have a lot to do. What can I do to help?" Somehow, I couldn't imagine there was *that* much extra work. Portia seemed pretty bored most days, and, as Keke had said, there was a boat on the other side of Ni for those in the cities farther off. "Is there someone else we should ask to be in charge when Portia leaves?"

Nixie crossed her arms and pouted. "No! Of course not! I can handle it!" She kicked a rock at her feet, the bangles around her wrist clanking together. "Just...a daughter would be nice."

Way to dance around the topic. "Let's go, then." Not the most romantic thing I could have said, but I was running out of ideas.

"C-can we go to my house?" she asked.

Oh? A crack in the armor? "Sure."

She smiled, and even I had to admit, it was really cute. As she skipped away from her traps, my eyes drifted from her face to her body. Her tight pants framed her generous backside perfectly. *Definitely some good booty on this pirate.*

As Junonia was a smaller city, we made it to her house in good time. It was a small, rectangular building, much like Keke's and Cannoli's dwellings, with colored windows and white foundations. She ushered me inside and closed the door behind us.

"I bet you're *really* experienced by now, huh?" Nixie teased, sneaking behind me to pinch me on the backside.

"Damn it!" I hissed, batting at her hand. "You don't know when to quit it, do you?"

"Maybe." Nixie skipped into her bedroom. "Coming?"

I mumbled a string of profanities under my breath and followed her back. She had nets strung around her walls decorated with seashells and smooth, glassy articles she must have recovered from the ocean. A small bed, nightstand, and dresser served as her only furniture. But if you're living alone, you don't really need much more.

Nixie put her hands on my chest and led me backward. My thighs hit a solid surface, and I glanced behind me before sitting on the bed. She dropped to her knees, spreading my legs wide before staring up into my face.

Oh. Getting right to it, then?

She giggled, running her hands over my legs and kissing the inside of my thighs. Even through my jeans, I could feel how soft her lips were. I rested a hand on her head, stroking her hair and enjoying the heat of her breath so close to my skin.

"You like that?" she murmured.

"Yeah. I do," I replied.

"Wouldn't it suck if I stopped?"

I couldn't help but chuckle. Staying mad at her wasn't getting me anywhere. "I wouldn't be surprised."

"No fun." She walked her hands beneath my shirt and tore it over my head.

Her fingers were already at my belt when I shuffled my feet to kick off my shoes. I didn't want to be the only one sitting there naked, so I reached over her shoulders and tugged at her striped shirt. She slid my belt from the loops and let go of me just long enough to slide her shirt over her head. But as soon as it hit the ground, she was back at my pants.

"Eager, are you?" I murmured.

"I'm a lot of things," she replied, unzipping my fly. I went for her pants and she swatted my arms away. "Me, first."

"Jeez. Alright." I stopped and let her pull down my jeans.

Once my shoes, socks, and pants were free, Nixie divested her own, leaving her standing in just a black bra and a lacy thong. The panties traced the curves of her ass and held my stare.

"Don't stare for too long!" She shrieked a giggle and pounced, tackling me to the bed.

We laughed and wrestled back and forth, but she grabbed something from beneath her pillow. I didn't realize that she bound my wrists until she pinned me at the hips and held them above my head.

I'd never been tied up before. Had never thought about it, really. But as I relaxed into it, I grew to like the idea of letting her lead.

"You just had that ready?" I laughed. "Were you expecting me, or do you always sleep with a rope under your pillow?"

"Wouldn't you like to know?" she teased. Then her mouth met mine.

I was suddenly very aware of her calves around my waist and the warmth of her hips straddling mine. Her hair brushed my cheek, and her tail tickled my thighs, then stroked the top of my underwear. She tasted like the sea and moved like a riptide.

Her grip on me relaxed. I wrapped my arms around her back, using the bond to pull her tighter and trace the length of her spine.

She shivered beneath my touch, and I let it wander, groping her ass when I reached the end of the curve.

Nixie moaned, then ground her crotch against mine. Two thin layers of fabric were all that separated me from her, and that knowledge stole my breath.

"Who's the eager one now?" she whispered against my lips.

I searched for the clasp of her bra and unhooked it. With my wrists bound, I yanked at one of the straps with my teeth, loosening it from her body enough to free one breast. Couldn't help but notice her gorgeous tan lines before I latched my teeth around her nipple and reveled in the sound of her gasp.

"N-not fair!" she moaned, her back arching in response.

I hummed against her skin and held her trembling form. She'd effectively locked us both together by binding my hands. *Yeah. I could get used to this.*

Following the curve of her back, I hooked my thumbs in the strings of her thong and pulled it down around her thighs. I couldn't exactly get to my underwear, so I had to hope she got the hint. She reciprocated, working to keep her chest at my mouth as she stripped my underwear away.

With how tightly I had her pinned against me, I barely had to move to slide inside of her. She hissed and buried her hands in my hair. "*A-ah!*"

I gasped with her soaking heat, and she pushed my arms above my head once more, drawing her shoulders away to sit up. Her thighs quivered, and she moaned with the movement.

"That's so deep," she whimpered.

"Yeah. It is," I breathed. I wanted to grab her legs and thrust into her. Throw her on her back and let loose. But I couldn't. And somehow, that made the situation that much more interesting.

"Can I move?" she asked, then shook her head. "I'm gonna move."

You don't want to ask permission for anything, do you? "Then move."

While pinning my arms with one hand, she held my shoulder with the other and rocked her hips. The sensation had both of us gasping for air, and my hands balled into fists. *Faster. Harder. This is torture.* And yet, I wanted her to decide.

Nixie's pace was slow and deliberate. Her wicked grin was replaced by an open mouth and drooping lids. Goosebumps seeped from her throat to her navel, and her tail wound tightly around my ankle.

"You can go faster than that," I groaned.

"I'm sure I can." Her smile returned, and she looked down at me with incredible authority. It sent a chill down my spine. "I can do what I want."

Before I could protest, she leaned in to kiss me again, thrusting her tongue between my lips and exploring my mouth. Her tantalizing rhythm continued, and my heart slammed against my chest. She was edging me, and she knew it. It was a very thin line between pleasure and frustration, and trying to move my hips in response wasn't helping.

She drew away from me and whispered in my ear, "Is that all you've got?"

Something snapped. Any submissive thought in my head vanished. I bucked my hips and pulled my arm free from her grasp. In one swift movement, I had her on her back with her arms above her head.

Nixie wrapped her legs around my lower back and giggled. "I thought so."

That was enough for me. I gripped her arms and thrust hard into her yielding body. She cried out with pleasure and clenched her legs.

"Better?" I growled, plunging into her depths again.

"Y-yes!" Nixie whined.

I nibbled on her ear, and she moaned, responding by sinking her teeth into my chest. I let her arms go, tangling my hands into her hair. She spanked me, and I hissed.

"I'm gonna come," she whispered, wrapping her hands around my neck. "M-Matt, *ngh,* I can't hold it!"

"Then come." I was teetering on the edge, but I'd be damned if I went first.

Her moans rang in my ears as she convulsed around me, her whole body writhing with release. I was close behind, the climax washing over me until my toes went numb and my lips turned cold.

Nixie panted for breath, and we stared at one another as we descended from the high. Being caught in her net wasn't as bad as I'd feared.

Half-giggling, she reached above her head to untie the knot at my wrists. "Well, that was fun."

I swallowed against my parched throat. "Yeah? Worth working a few more solo shifts while we're gone?"

"Hm. I guess so." She smiled. "I can always trap you when you're back if I need you."

"Hey. Once was plenty." I touched my forehead to hers. "Just call for me if you need me, okay? That's what I'm here for."

"Mmm." She tossed the rope aside and kissed the tip of my nose. "Okay."

New Notifications!

Quest Updated!

[The More the Merrier] 3/8 Catgirls Successful!

Ravyn Pro Tip: We still need food, potions, gear... Can't that girl see that we're BUSY? *Mattaku...*

Chapter 37

Jumping Peanut

It was late in the evening when I left Nixie's house, and I wondered who to track down first. I was starving, so the girls would be hungry by now, too. Lucky for me, I found everyone sitting at a long table in the Junonia Inn.

"Matt! We saved you a seat!" Tristan waved when he spotted me.

Keke and Cannoli tapped the empty space on the bench between them. It reminded me of the picnic tables you'd see in parks but carved from wood instead of molded plastic. I took a seat, and Ravyn slid me a mug of ale.

"It's a little warm. Figured you'd need a drink after that bullshit," Ravyn grumbled.

"Thanks. Warm is fine." I gulped down half the mug before I continued. "You guys eat yet?"

Ceres and Ara shook their heads.

"We were waiting for you, Sir Matt," Ceres said.

"That was nice of you."

Frida approached the table, balancing three bowls and five more mugs on a large tray. The bowls were stocked with peanuts, and she exchanged them for the three empty ones on the table. *Wonder how many of those they've gone through already.*

Buttons jumped from Cannoli's shoulder to the table, then sprang head-first into one of the bowls. His blue body vanished beneath the shells, sending a few peanuts flying from the bowl. Ball took to the one closest to Ravyn, snapping one between his powerful beak.

"Looks like everyone's hungry," Frida chuckled. "Portia lugged in a helluva catch today. Plenty of fish for searing."

There was a resounding "Yes, please!" from the girls at the table. Tristan and I exchanged glances and shrugged. I couldn't imagine anyone could cook up a fish like Cannoli, but the tavern hadn't failed us yet.

"Sounds good to me. And can I get another one of these, please?" I downed the rest of the ale and passed it to Frida.

Frida added the mug to the tray next to the empty bowls. "Coming right up, Matt. Anyone else need anything?"

"Just fish!" Cannoli cried happily.

"Fish it is. Be back soon." Frida excused herself, and Cannoli hummed in bliss.

It was impossible to describe how relieved I was to see Cannoli smiling again. She probably still had a lot on her mind, but I hoped she'd let us help out as much as we could. Even Ravyn had dedicated herself to the cause. Something I never thought I'd witness for myself.

"So, how do we think the trip to Venicia is going to go?" Tristan asked.

"Not well. We all get along like a house on fire," I admitted.

"That's putting it lightly," Ravyn added. She grabbed a peanut and tossed it to Ball. The parrot squawked and caught it, cracking into the shell with a happy chirp.

Ara entwined her hands and set them on the table. "I believe Celestia's intentions are...sound."

That's a reach.

"How could that be?" Ceres asked, giving a voice to what I'm sure we were all thinking.

Ara cleared her throat and inspected her fingers. "She wishes to see all of Shi Island prosper. Her restoration efforts are genuine."

"But you had no idea how bad things were in the other cities," Keke pointed out. "Catania was living *underground.*"

"I understand that. However, Celestia informed me that the island had begun to diminish long before she took the role of Head Mistress. And things must get worse before they get better," Ara replied calmly.

Cannoli stroked the top of Buttons' head when it appeared between the peanuts. "How could locking Tristan in a room help the island get better, though? Wouldn't that only make things worse?"

"That would depend on what she's using his money for," Ravyn said dryly.

Tristan tilted his head and pursed his lips. "What money?"

I felt Keke tense next to me. So, he didn't know about the Quests either. It would make sense—he'd never distributed his Skill or Stat points before we'd met. He had no reason to use the iPaw once Celestia got her claws into him. I debated letting Ravyn tell him, but she'd handled it less than tactfully so far.

"The men in this world get a series of Chain Quests," I explained carefully. "For successfully impregnating catgirls."

Tristan blinked. "Is that why my Level is so high?"

Keke and I nodded.

Ravyn snickered. "This is *gold*."

"The Quest also gives you Bells each time you complete it. I've only completed it once, but from what I can tell, the Bells increase every time." I ran a hand through my hair. "There might be a cap, but you'd have to check your iPaw to know for sure."

Tristan flushed, then summoned his iPaw. Ara laid one palm on the screen and caught Tristan's attention.

"Young master, are you certain you want to know?" she murmured.

"I..." Tristan paused, toying with the point of one of the cat ears on the device. "Is it all gone?"

Ravyn opened her mouth to say something, but I caught her eye and shook my head. *You've said enough.*

"More than likely. Celestia shared with a few of her closer confidants that she was using it to enrich the economy across the cities." Ara released the screen in favor of Tristan's arm, then continued earnestly, "Venicia flourishes thanks to your efforts."

Tristan exhaled a huge breath and shook his head. "I mean, it's not like I needed the Bells before. Knowing that it exists doesn't change the current situation. I don't have good equipment or weapons like you guys. I'm dragging the Party down."

Ara's eyes lit up. "That is not a lost cause, young master. I earned plenty in Abalone to purchase you a fine set of equipment. Please allow me to?"

"That's your money, Ara. I don't want to—" Tristan began.

To my surprise, Ceres interrupted him. "You should let her, Tristan. It would bring her much satisfaction." She looked at me. "The ability to serve the ones we care about is the highest honor for the members of Shi Island."

Tristan blushed, then nodded. "Alright. I would appreciate the help."

Ara smiled and shrugged her shoulders like a well-groomed cat. "We will find you the best equipment that money can buy!"

"That's nice and all, but can we get back to Celestia?" Ravyn stretched, then threw another peanut to Ball.

Frida returned with seven plates heaped with fish, vegetables, and fresh bread. The conversation paused as we tucked in, each of us managing to clear half of our meals before our talks continued.

Ceres dabbed her lips with a napkin and spoke first. "Celestia took her current position after I graduated. I remember hearing the news. However, the Defiled situation was already problematic by that time. So, what Ara says concerning Celestia's restoration efforts may hold some weight."

"Then let's say that she *is* trying to help," Cannoli mused. "What if she's just not sending *enough* of the money to the other cities? Or if it's not being received by the right people?"

It wasn't too much of a stretch of the imagination. Any person in a difficult situation would do whatever it took to survive—whether that meant Venicia girls were pocketing the Bells for themselves or were robbed during their travels. Jazz's band had been ready to strip us down and string us up if it came to it.

"In that scenario, we would need to devise a different distribution method for Tristan's hard-earned Bells. Something more secure that ensures goods like food and potions make it into the hands of those who need them," Ceres said.

"Our first priority is Lynn, but it sounds like we have to sit down and talk to Celestia. Figure out what her plans really are," I said. "There are a lot of 'what if' scenarios here."

"Yeah. Like what if she has a bunch of girls waiting to sink Portia's ship as soon as we're in sight of the dock?" Ravyn proposed.

"Would she really do that?" Keke asked.

Ravyn shrugged. "If she thinks that we kidnapped Tristan, and he's the only thing keeping Venicia running, how do you think she'll react?"

"I've been wondering about that myself," I admitted. "Part of me says she won't try to hurt Tristan or me, but I worry about what she'd do with the rest of you."

"We won't let that happen. *I* won't let that happen," Tristan said, his expression suddenly serious. "I want to help Ara and Lynn. I want to save my island. It should never have reached this point."

"You don't have to do it alone, Tristan. We'll help you," Cannoli said with a smile.

"Yeah. We're in this together, remember?" I added.

"But I call dibs on roasting Celestia if it comes to it," Ravyn said, stabbing her fork into the fish. "Her ass is mine."

"*Roast the bitch! Roast the bitch! Squaawk!*"

For the first time in weeks, I felt like everyone was back to their usual selves. Even if it wasn't entirely set in stone, we had a plan. One that we'd see through together.

Ravyn Pro Tip: Give me five minutes with Celestia, Matt. Just five minutes. I'll show her what it means to be from San Island.

Chapter 38

Whistling Armor

I wanted to do something nice for the group before we got back on the boat. Most of us had the vacation in Abalone, but since Ravyn and Cannoli had stayed behind, it didn't really feel like they got much of a break. Or maybe it was just me wanting to see everyone have a good time together.

Regardless, I teamed up with Cannoli, and we came up with a plan. We spent two full days foraging, fishing, and cooking together. By 'fishing,' I mean I wound up buying a good chunk of Portia's daily catch because, let's face it, neither of us was Keke. And by cooking, I played sous-chef to Cannoli's Gordon Ramsey, chopping, rolling, and mixing at her every command. We had an enormous basket of food, drinks, and baked goods by day three.

I did have to let Tristan in on the plan so he could help keep Keke, Ceres, Ravyn, and Ara away from Cannoli's house. Ara and Keke were definitely suspicious of something going on, but Tristan did a great job keeping them distracted with questions and requests for more tours of Junonia.

The day Cannoli and I were ready to unveil our plan was the same day Espada had finished Ceres's armor and my shield. We went as a group to pick up both. I had hoped to line it up pretty close to the surprise, so it worked out.

Espada was waiting at her shop, leaning against a post with her well-defined arms crossed over her chest. She waved when she saw us, then momentarily disappeared into the forge. She emerged with multiple sections of polished, glimmering golden metal grouped in her arms.

"Some of my finest work yet, if I do say so myself." Espada grinned. "Go ahead and get into [Combat Mode], Ceres."

A high-pitched hum sang between Ceres's lips as she swapped into her combat equipment. The black and white maid dress looked so bare without her armor. Espada made quick work of rectifying it.

"Come on around. We'll get you sorted." Espada gestured behind the counter.

"Of course!" Ceres all but skipped around the booth, presenting herself with a straight-backed salute when she reached Espada. "This is such an honor."

"Save that for after we're sure it fits." Espada chuckled. "Arms out."

Espada carefully slid and fastened each golden pauldron to Ceres's shoulders. They were wider than her previous silver pair, covering more of her upper body and her neck if she raised them a few inches.

"How do those feel so far? Good?" Espada asked, picking up the elbow pieces next.

"They feel impeccable!" Ceres gasped. "I know it is redundant to say, but they feel made for me."

"Because they were." Espada laughed.

Ceres blushed. "I know. This is just…You are wonderful. Thank you."

"Gonna make me blush." She fitted the armor to Ceres's elbow while we watched. "We got more to go."

"What's that part called?" I asked. I'd always liked finding the biggest, shiniest armor sets in video games, but I had no clue what each individual piece was called.

"Couters," Espada replied. "Good ones'll give you excellent mobility."

Ceres bent her arm. "This is so light! How is it so light?"

"Short answer is the metal I used and the forging method." Espada shrugged. "Your armor should help you, not hinder you. Vambraces next."

The fitting continued with gauntlets, greaves, and a chest piece that hooked around her top like a corset. After a few test thrusts and twists of her polearm and adjustments to the ties, Ceres was fully mobile and suited for battle.

"This is perfect. Better than perfect. Goodness, my Lady, how can I thank you?" Ceres was glowing with glee. Her armor looked great, and, knowing Espada's craftsmanship, a truck could hit Ceres, and she'd feel nothing.

Espada chuckled. "Just the payment. And don't die out there."

Ceres drew an enormous sack of Bells from her [Cat Pack] and handed them over. "There's a tip in there as well. Saoirse be praised; I've never felt better."

"Good. That's what I want to hear." Espada turned to me. "And now you. One second." She disappeared again.

"Ceres, you look amazing!" Cannoli marveled, brushing one of the pauldrons with her fingertips. "You have to be the best-geared knight in Nyarlea!"

Ravyn scoffed. "I wouldn't go that far." She glanced over her shoulder, checking for Espada. "But it does look nice."

"Wow. A compliment. How rare," Keke noted.

"*Kuso!* Why do I bother?" Ravyn spat.

Espada reappeared, holding the gleaming shield in her hands. "Don't lose this one, alright? It's a lot more expensive."

I accepted the silver buckler with an appreciative nod. It was lighter than my last one, the leather strap on the back taut and secure around my arm. "I'll take good care of it, Espada. Thanks."

I paid her with a tip as Ceres had. It was a huge chunk of my Bells, but better protected than dead. We wished Espada well and moved to stand in the middle of the marketplace.

"So, what else do we need before we depart for Shi Island?" Ara asked.

"Nothing. We're all set," I replied, studying the intricate engravings on the shield's surface. Espada had carved a pouncing tiger into the metal with a surprisingly delicate hand. *Damn, even matching the aesthetic. Thanks, Espada.*

"Spill it, then. What have you and Cannoli been up to for the last two days?" Keke asked.

I grinned. "Everyone has swimsuits now, right?"

"Yup! I made sure Ceres, Ara, and I all had them ready." Tristan shot me a thumbs-up.

"We're going to have a beach picnic!" Cannoli cried with a clap of her hands.

I nodded. "We spent the last two days cooking and gathering so we can spend the whole day out there. Figured we could use it."

Keke's eyes widened. "Really?"

"Really. Who knows what the heck awaits us, so let's take one more day and relax," I said.

Ceres's eyes glistened, and she clasped her hands at her chest. "What a blessed day this is! Thank you, Cannoli and Sir Matt! And Tristan for getting us ready."

"Yeah, it's okay, I guess," Ravyn said, studying her nails.

Ball chewed her hair and squawked.

"Hey! What the fuck?" Ravyn snapped. "Whatever. It was nice of you. Thanks."

"Race you there!" Cannoli cried, then broke out into a run.

"Oh, no, you don't!" Keke giggled and ran after her.

I turned to the rest of our group. "Meet you guys down there?"

They nodded, and I chased after Cannoli.

Cannoli and I spread two giant blankets across the sand, placing the basket at the back center to anchor them from the breeze. As we spread the plates and glasses across the surface, Ceres and Keke jogged across the sand with Ara, Tristan, and Ravyn close behind.

Ceres and Ara had both picked out black and white one-piece swimsuits. Ceres's had two tiny silver chains crossed over her waist, and her curves filled the rest nicely. Ara's had pinched white ruffles across the bust, giving the illusion of a larger chest. She blushed when she saw me looking.

"This is so much food!" Ceres exclaimed. "Fish, cakes, appetizers, nyapple cider—you thought of everything!"

"We wanted to make enough for two meals!" Cannoli explained. "That way, we don't have to leave."

Buttons jumped down from her shoulder and wriggled his way to a bowl of peanuts we'd brought for him and Ball. It seemed to be one of the blazard's favorite foods, and the tavern was happy to supply us with a bag.

"I don't see any booz—" Ravyn began, adjusting the brim of her giant hat.

I snatched a dark bottle from the basket and held it toward her. "You were saying?"

Ravyn accepted the bottle, looking from it to me. "...*Baka.*" But her bushy tail swayed excitedly behind her.

I knew it was one of her favorites, but I didn't need to rub it in. Just seeing her at ease was worth it.

"Is that violet ryba?" Keke gasped and licked her lips. "Did you catch more?"

"Portia did," I admitted with a sheepish grin. "Cost a pretty penny, but we couldn't have a picnic without it, right?"

Keke kissed my cheek, then dove for the fish. She ate it straight from the tray, not bothering to move it to a plate.

Tristan grabbed Ara's hand and smiled. "C'mon. Let's go in the water!"

Ara's face flushed, and she stammered, "O-of course, young master!"

"Oh! Me too!" Cannoli popped a cookie in her mouth, then ran across the sand to join them, the ruffles on her swimsuit bouncing just above her tail.

Bursts of sand kicked up from their feet, and Tristan tackled Ara as soon as they reached the water. Ara shrieked, and a flurry of giggles ensued.

I fished out a piece of cake and sat down on the edge of the blanket before digging in. The frosting coated my lips and nose, and I chuckled at myself. *Slow down, Matt. It's not going anywhere.*

Ceres moved to my side and knelt. Without warning, she leaned in and licked the frosting from the tip of my nose. She grinned and touched her braid. "Thank you, Matt."

Before I could respond, she joined the others at the water.

"Keke! Keke, come play!" Cannoli cried.

Keke waved, her mouth still stuffed with violet ryba. She swallowed and licked her fingers, then left the blanket.

Ravyn took a seat next to me on the blanket. She broke a cookie in half, offering one half to Ball and nibbling the other between straight sips from her bottle. We watched the others in a comfortable silence while I finished my cake. When I turned to find a napkin, Ravyn laughed.

"Saoirse's tits, Matt. You're supposed to eat the cake, not wear it."

"I didn't remember it being this messy," I argued.

She reached over and dragged some of the icing away from my cheek with one finger. I froze. She never dropped her gaze as she sucked away the frosting.

"That's pretty damn good," she murmured.

I couldn't breathe. "Thanks."

She took another swig of wine, then screwed the bottle into the sand to keep it from falling. "Let's get in the water. You can wash your damn face off, and I'll get Cannoli back for last time."

I wiped the rest of the icing off with the back of my hand. "After you, then."

She sneered. "Why? Want to watch my tail as I leave?"

"Maybe."

"*Baka.*"

Ceres Pro Tip: Oh? A splashing war? I shall conquer you all single-handedly! Cannoli! You are formidable indeed!

Chapter 39
Hoisting Anchor

As day turned to dusk, we all lay across the blankets and watched the sunset. There were only crumbs left from the food haul that Cannoli and I had prepared, and we all earned a healthy tan and sore bellies from laughing as we were pulled beneath the waves.

"Thank you, Matt," Keke said, reaching over to take my hand in hers. "And Cannoli, for preparing all of this."

"I wish we could stay like this forever," Cannoli admitted, sliding her fingers through my other hand.

"Yeah. Me, too," I murmured.

"Eventually, we will settle into Ni Island, correct?" Ceres asked, the top of her head touching mine. "Once we've convened with the final two men?"

"Mm. That's the plan, anyway," I replied. There was no way of knowing if Cailu would hit us with another expedition in the name of Nyarlea. Or how long we'd be on Ichi Island. Honestly, I was doing my best to take things one step at a time. Lynn first, Ichi next, then worry about whatever Cailu wanted.

"Then we will do this again soon," Ceres said confidently.

Tristan and Ara sat behind me at the edge of the blanket, their shoulders and legs touching.

"Lynn would love this island," Ara said idly.

"Then we can bring her here. Things are going to change, Ara. I'll make sure of it," Tristan replied.

Ara laughed beneath her breath, something close to a giggle but not quite. To my surprise, she leaned her head on Tristan's shoulder. "I know you will, young master."

Ravyn perched farther down the sand's slope, nursing her second bottle of wine and watching the tide ebb and flow. Her knees were pulled up to her chest and she adjusted her hat before resting her chin on her arms. Ball circled overhead, occasionally diving to the water and snagging a small fish or two from the surface.

Wish I knew what you were thinking, Ravyn.

Ceres sat up and stretched. "Shall we head back before it is too late?"

"Yeah. Let's not get caught out here in the dark." I squeezed Keke and Cannoli's hands, then pushed myself to standing.

While the others folded the blankets and collected plates, I quietly padded my way through the sand to where Ravyn was sitting. Her tail and hair were still damp, errant strands clinging to her face and back. The last rays of light flickered against her pale face, illuminating the pink circles on her cheeks from a day of sunshine. I sat next to her and took the bottle of wine from the sand, killing the few droplets remaining. I positioned myself similarly, knees drawn up and arms resting on them, letting the bottle hang freely between them.

The ocean waves lapped at the shore, rolling in a soothing rhythm that harmonized with the soft breeze through the nearby pawm trees. The warm sand seeped between my toes and partially covered the tops of my feet, the dimming sunlight reflecting against the grains like a thousand tiny diamonds. I inhaled the salty air, memorizing the orange and purple lights dancing across the water's surface.

"Can I tell you something?" Ravyn asked, breaking the silence between us.

"Sure."

She lifted a pinch of sand and rubbed it between her finger and thumb. "As much as I want to burn Celestia to a crisp, I'm more worried about Lynn."

Ravyn? Sentimental? That was new. "Yeah?"

"Mm." She grunted a sound somewhere between a growl and a sigh. "I'd feel like it was my fault if anything bad happened to her."

I shook my head. "We needed someone to swap with to get Tristan out of there. She was the closest to his room."

"Yeah. In the fucking jail cell that Ara's since described to us." Ravyn shuddered. "If Celestia's kept her in there since we left, well... I don't know many girls who could withstand something like that."

"I don't think it's that bad. We'll get her out of there."

She stared at me for a few long seconds, then shook her head. "*Mou ii.* You've got to stop making promises you can't keep."

I shifted uncomfortably. "What do you mean?"

"You have no idea if she's okay or even if she's still alive. None of us do. Don't set us up for disappointment should the worst come to pass." Ravyn slipped off her hat and ran a hand through her hair. "Nyarlea can be a shit show. Expecting the best will get you killed."

I wanted to ask if that was what happened to Finn. But not now. Not when we'd finally circled back to decent terms. She'd tell me when she was ready. "I'm sorry. I'll try to be better about it."

She snickered. "*Baka.* I don't hate that part of you. Just don't want to see anyone get upset."

"Matt! Ravyn! We're losing daylight!" Keke called.

I stood and brushed the sand from my trunks before offering her my hand. "Ready to head back?"

She glanced back at the ocean, then up at my hand. "Yeah. I am." She nodded. After a brief hesitation, she took it, allowing me to help her to her feet.

I don't want to see anyone upset, either.

Her hand lingered in mine as we returned to the group. She let go when Ball descended to land on her shoulder, then nibbled at her hat.

"Tomorrow's the big day," I said, collecting the basket beneath one arm. "Let's get some rest."

With one final look at the sunset against the ocean, I followed Keke back to her house.

I didn't sleep well that night. I had vivid nightmares that I kept falling back into every time one woke me. Being trapped in the Venicia School of Etiquette, but the halls twisted and turned into an impossible maze. Celestia taking Tristan and Ara hostage. All thirty-two flavors of Felsi's ice cream shop turned to poison. In one particularly terrible dream, Celestia had a team of archers waiting at the docks with flaming arrows at the ready, sinking Portia's ship before it could make land and leaving us all at the mercy of a Defiled with a thousand sharp teeth.

"Matt. *Matt!*" My arm shook, and a very concerned Keke came into view. "Are you okay?"

Sweat soaked my back and hair, and my breathing rasped. My vision cleared, and I sat up, pushing aside the image of Keke being gnawed in half by the creature from the Black Lagoon. She was standing next to me, perfectly intact, dressed for the day with her bow strung across her back.

I leaned forward, letting my head rest against her stomach. She ran her hand through my hair. "Bad night?"

"Yeah." I circled my arms around her waist and sighed. "Time to go, huh?"

"It is. I tried to let you sleep as long as I could. You were tossing and turning all night."

What an angel. "Thanks."

"You sure you're alright?"

The feel of her embrace and her delicate fingers in my hair cleared the last of the nightmare's immediate terror. I breathed in her scent, then let her go. "I'll be fine. Let's head down to the docks. I don't want to keep Portia and the others waiting."

I changed and made sure I had the last of my supplies before we left together for the dock. The others had arrived shortly before us, and Portia appeared the most hale and hearty of them all, her bright eyes and sharp smile flashing as we approached.

"Back to the weird island again, huh?" Portia hooked her thumbs through her belt loops and rocked on her boots. "Not gonna make me wait on the shitty end for another two weeks, are ya?"

I frowned, feeling the first waves of embarrassment hit my face. "No. This should be *a lot* quicker."

"Goodness, I did not realize you waited for the entirety of Sir Matt's journey," Ceres blustered, bowing low at the hips. "Please, forgive me. It is surely my responsibility for your inconvenience."

Portia guffawed and patted Ceres on the back. "You're a fine piece of work, Ceres. Just teasing Matt is all."

"Excuse me, but why do you find Shi Island weird?" Ara asked, tilting her head.

"Erm. Well, you see," Portia backpedaled, stretching her words between hems and haws.

My turn. I crossed my arms. "Yeah, Portia. Why are they weird?"

"Shut up." Ravyn elbowed me in the side, and I hissed.

"Jeez. Fine." I rubbed the area she'd struck. That was gonna leave a bruise.

"Just different, I guess. All prim and proper." Portia shrugged. "Not bad. Just not what I'm used to."

"Then, there really are no other schools of etiquette outside of Shi Island?" Ara asked, meeting each of our gazes in turn.

"I think there's one in Nyarlothep, but that's it," Ravyn replied. "Shi *is* pretty weird for that."

Oh? Do I get to elbow you *in the ribs now?*

"Not weird! Just different!" Cannoli chanted. "We all have different backgrounds, and it's wonderful. It's what lets us work together!"

"Cannoli's right. It's good that we all bring different perspectives to the Party," Tristan added. "We can learn a lot from one another."

Cannoli blushed, then twirled a long strand of hair around her finger. "T-thank you, Tristan."

I shouldn't have felt jealous. Okay, maybe I was a little jealous.

"Everyone ready to head out?" I asked, hoping to shift Cannoli's attention.

There was a circle of nods.

"Oh, Tristan. Change into your [Combat Mode]," Keke said.

"Oh, yeah! Sorry! [Combat Mode]!" Tristan cried.

His jeans and top vanished, quickly replaced by multiple layers of flowing fabrics. He had a pair of black pants tucked into leather boots, covered by a dark blue tabard with gold edging. A white tunic with draping sleeves and a high collar poked out of the top of the tabard. A red cloak wrapped around his chest then flared out behind him, topping off the ensemble alongside a brown belt with a freshly purchased [Cat Pack].

Shit. I forgot to ask about upgrading my [Cat Pack]. Guess that'll have to wait.

"How do I look?" Tristan grinned, grabbing the edge of his cloak and giving it a flourish.

Cannoli clapped her hands and squealed with delight. "You look wonderful! Did Ara get this for you?"

Ara blushed, then nodded. "I did. Quinn helped us put it together."

Tristan summoned a thick tome covered with runic symbols and a brilliant gold star. He murmured a quick spell, and Desiree leaped from its pages. The cat familiar wove between his legs, brushing against his calves and purring in delight.

"I should be able to help now! I refuse to be dead weight anymore." Tristan knelt and scratched Desiree between the ears. "Oh, I've been meaning to ask. Ravyn, wouldn't it be easier if you called Ball when you needed him? Familiars can come at your command, right?"

Ravyn's eyes went wide, and she glanced at the blue parrot on her shoulder. "I mean, I guess so, but…" Her fingers clenched air at her sides, and she shook her head. "It's not important. Get on the damn boat."

Keke coughed into her hand, masking a laugh. Tristan shrugged and boarded Portia's sloop, looking far more ready for adventure than he had since we'd picked him up.

"I'm glad I never have to dismiss Buttons. I love him too much," Cannoli crooned, touching her nose to the blazard's face.

"Never a dull moment with you all, is there?" Portia chuckled.

I took a seat near Portia in case she needed help manning the sloop, and Keke sat nearby.

Once we were all settled, Portia raised the anchor and steered us away from the harbor. "Hold on to your hats, friends. Next stop: Shi Island."

Portia Pro Tip: Never been able to play a proper hand of cards with the girls on Shi, either. I think I'll just fish.

Chapter 40
Tae Kwon Do

I readjusted my grasp around one of the many ropes of Portia's sloop. My heart was pounding. The thought of seeing Celestia and not knowing what would happen next made me more anxious than I wanted to admit.

Keke, Cannoli, and Ravyn had taken to playing some cards on deck, occasionally glancing toward the ever-looming island ahead. Tristan, Ara, and Ceres stood at the end facing Shi Island—the starboard side. Barely a word had come out of any of their mouths.

Can't say I blamed them. A lot was going on and trying to focus on anything else felt impossible. Tristan occasionally bowed his head, mumbling something that only Ara and Ceres caught. They'd say something back, and, as curious as I was to hear it, I shook my head and allowed them their privacy. It was none of my business, nor was it my place to poke my nose. If it was something important, then they'd let me know.

All I could do for the time being was offer support when asked.

"We're gettin' close. Keep your wits about you!" cried Portia. She kept a weather eye on the horizon the entire time she manned the ship. We'd warned her of a potential ambush, just in case. She bore the same fierce look of attention that I'd seen from soldiers in war movies. It helped bring me some ease. I wondered if she'd ever experienced something similar.

Cannoli collected the cards as Keke, Ravyn, and I stood behind Tristan and the others.

"Do you think we should stay in [Combat Mode]?" I was glad that Keke asked. I'm sure it was on everyone's minds.

"No," Tristan said quickly. "I refuse to let this come to blows. I want to handle this amicably."

Ara furrowed her brow. "You are certain, young master?"

Tristan turned to Ara. "Yes. Hostility builds mistrust. We need to start this peacefully."

Ravyn folded her arms, apparently unconvinced. "And if the bitch attacks us?"

"She won't." Tristan didn't look back at any of us. His voice was firm and confident.

"You weren't so sure about that before," Ravyn growled.

"I've had time to think about it. We have the edge here. By attacking any of us, she declares war on two men." He glanced in Ara's direction. "If what you said is true, Ara, and if she truly desires the best for Shi Island, then she wouldn't dare harm a hair on any of our heads. Her goal will be to return to the status quo. For better or for worse."

"That would mean you're locked up in the school again, wouldn't it?" Keke tilted her head in thought.

"That won't be part of the bargain. We'll find another way," Tristan replied.

I didn't know if I should offer my input. We'd talked this over a few times, but I'm sure the same questions continued to plague all of us.

I'd played plenty of games and read…a fair share of stories. I'd started to understand how easy it was to make these decisions and play them out from the comfort of a couch. With a dozen save files at the ready and a cold soda next to you as NPCs and fictional characters acted out their roles. When there was no risk, there was no fear of defeat, death, ruining relationships, no irreparable mistakes that could change the course of those lives forever.

I swallowed hard and took a deep breath. Sweat was collecting around my forehead, and it had nothing to do with the sun overhead. No matter what I did, I couldn't shake the wild imagination of this going terribly wrong. The price of a mistake this far into the game could have dire consequences. I pictured dozens of arrows striking the sloop, poisoned food, and an [Assassin] like Naeemah showing up to shank us one by one.

We're going to be fine, right?

I caught Ravyn's eye, and she held my stare. I wanted to know what this woman was made of that made her so strong and dauntless in these kinds of situations. I wish I knew what was going to happen so we could just get this over with. The anticipation was killing me.

A disturbing silence welcomed us when Portia pulled the sloop near the dock. While she worked to anchor the sloop, dark clouds moved in, blanketing the entire town in an eerie daytime darkness. A single catgirl stood about a dozen meters away. Right where the planks met the road. The maid kept her eyes glued to me the entire time.

"Watch her," Portia muttered to Keke.

"Right."

Surely no catgirl would ever attempt to kill a man. Right?

"You gonna keep hanging out there, or are you going to welcome us?" Ravyn snapped. Ball had taken to the air, keeping a watchful eye over us—well, probably just Ravyn. But a guy could hope. "What happened to your sense of Service, Grace, and Urgency? We are left wanting of these luxuries."

The catgirl remained expressionless. Her blonde hair was cropped evenly just above her shoulders, and I felt as if at any moment she could fire laser beams from those deadly ruby eyes.

Ravyn clicked her tongue. "Creepy bitch."

"Please. Allow me." Ara gestured with her hand, offering a gentle smile when Tristan caught her shoulder. "I will be fine, young master."

Of that, I have no doubt.

If anyone could match the cold gaze of the catgirl that was staring at us, it was Ara. Without a hint of hesitation, Ara strode the length of the dock, ascended the small series of stairs, and stood a few feet before the catgirl.

"Hey, are you almost done?" I asked without looking back. For the first time since we'd traveled together, we'd requested Portia to come on land with us. If a fight did break out, we wanted every able body at our side.

"Workin' on it, Matt. Just a sec," Portia stressed.

Just calm down. If everyone else catches on to your uneasiness, you're just going to drag them down with you.

I drew a deep breath, then watched as Ara beckoned the other catgirl to follow. Before I knew it, both of them stood before me.

Ara stood to one side and gestured. "This is Misery. She and I were often on cleaning duty together."

Why doesn't that make me feel better? "Oh. So you know her?"

Ara nodded. "Yes."

Misery curtsied and bowed her head. "Madame Celestia awaits."

Each of us passed looks between one another.

"She's expecting us?" Tristan asked.

For the first time since our arrival, Misery looked away from me, finding a new target in Tristan. Misery's lips curled into a sadistic smile. "She is."

Tristan frowned. "Are these under peaceful pretenses?"

Misery smoothed out her apron. "Possibly."

Each word Misery spoke came out like the hissing of some character out of a horror story. Every bone in my body was giving me the cue to get the hell off of this island. Instead, I steeled myself, balling my hands and waiting for a sign to act. Hopefully, it wouldn't come.

Tristan stepped forward and took Misery's hands. They shared a moment of locked eyes. "I wish for peace. Misery, please take us to where Celestia is. I want to speak with her. Candidly."

A gentle hue of pink colored Misery's cheeks as she looked away, her face as emotionless as before. "Understood."

Damn, dude. I'm impressed.

Misery guided us around the outskirts of Venicia, and, as it had been the first time, we were surrounded by silence. But, somehow, it was heavier. The town was devoid of the slight movements in shop windows or girls peeking behind curtains. No ice cream day at Felsi's. Notch's shop had its blinds drawn. Not a single person was wandering the streets. The trees were missing the familiar chirps of birds, and there wasn't a hint of civilization.

It was as if the town's residents were plucked out of existence.

"Where is everyone?" I asked while we walked.

Misery stopped and turned around, her hands clasped one over the other in front of her. Tristan, Ara, and Ceres stopped ahead of me. "Hiding."

"From what?" Keke asked from behind me.

"Defiled."

My heart skipped a beat.

Tristan glanced behind him at us. "A Defiled has appeared?"

Misery shook her head. "No."

Was this girl capable of more than single-word sentences? Felt like I was talking to a machine. *At least Ai gives me complete sentences.* Well, most of the time.

Tristan cocked his head. "Then why?"

"Madame Celestia," said Misery.

Ara sighed. "Misery, you need to be more clear. They aren't going to understand you if you don't explain."

Misery paused and stared at Ara. If looks could kill, we'd all be dead. "They are not aware of Tristan's absence."

I opened my mouth to speak, but Ceres beat me to the punch. "You cannot be serious. The townspeople were not informed? Pray tell, how have you convinced them of his inability to perform?"

"Sickness," Misery said simply. "Ill."

"I see," Ara said.

"Finished?" asked Misery.

I had a hundred questions I wanted to ask but reminded myself that this was Tristan's task. I kept my mouth shut, shaking my head at Ravyn when she opened her mouth to speak next.

Misery scanned her eyes over us, then turned on her heel. "Onward."

After a few more minutes of exploring the alleyways and thickets, we came upon a small house situated at the edge of a cliff. The paint was chipping away at the corners, and the wood looked like it hadn't been treated in a long time. A small swing set was anchored to the ground about a dozen meters away from the house. It was old as dirt, barely clinging onto one of the ropes while spinning in slow circles.

The image of jumping off the swing and landing in the ocean crossed my mind for a brief moment. I was snapped out of the thought by Misery's monotone voice.

"Here." She gestured to the entrance.

Before us was a raised patio made of wood; it reminded me of those old Victorian homes.

"Thank you," Tristan said.

As he led the way, we followed close behind. I brought up the rear. I wasn't about to have any of the girls' lives held hostage if the worst were to come. The floorboards creaked as we ascended the steps. Tristan drew a deep breath and knocked on the door.

"Come in," came a cold voice. Even after all the time that'd passed, I could never forget Celestia's unnerving tone.

Tristan pushed the door open and let himself in. The apprehension I felt was beginning to dissipate. The door shut behind me when I was the last to enter. Misery walked past us to take her position beside Celestia.

Celestia stood at the far end of an ornate dining table, her clasped hands resting on the decorated wood. The white curtains behind her had been left open. Red carpet embroidered with complex golden threads rested beneath our feet. A flash of lightning washed the room in white as if the storm itself was on her side.

Cannoli yelped and grasped my arm. When the lightning passed, she muttered, "I'm sorry."

I didn't look at her. I felt for her hand and squeezed it. "It's okay."

Two unfamiliar catgirls flanked Celestia's sides while Misery and Felsi stood at opposite ends of the curtains.

"Celestia," Tristan said.

At first, Celestia said nothing. Then she motioned for the chair on the opposite end of where she sat. "Please. Sit."

Tristan took his seat while Ceres and Ara took the two nearest chairs, each of them sitting on opposite sides.

Celestia raised a brow to the rest of us. "Your seats, please?"

I shook my head. "We'll stand. Thanks."

I was glad to see Ravyn, and I had the same thought when she took to my side with Keke and Cannoli. Portia leaned against the wall next to the front door, her arms crossed.

"Have it your way." Celestia straightened her back and puffed out her chest. Her eyes narrowed, and her words struck like the lashes of a whip. "You may have the floor. Now, before I have you arrested for treason, explain yourselves."

Keke Pro Tip: Treason?! If Celestia thinks she's forcing Tristan back into the school, she has another thing coming.

Chapter 41

Capoeira

"That's a big word for your pretty little mouth," Ravyn snarled.

Tristan held up a hand with a placid glance over his shoulder. "Treason?" he repeated.

A sharp smile quirked at the corners of Celestia's lips. "Holding an island's man hostage. Forcing him from his duties." She gestured to Ara and Ceres. "The same may be said for these two young women."

Tristan shook his head. "They weren't holding me hostage, Celestia. I went with them on my own."

"Oh? Is that so?" The smile widened. "I have it on good authority that both you and Ara were taken against your will." Celestia withdrew a bundle of papers from a nearby stack of items and spread them along the table's surface. "A young woman named Esmerelda confirmed for me that these particular scrolls contained a magic that would allow you to cast [Impersonate Soul]. I say 'contained,' as the insignia required for the cast is missing—a sign that they have been used."

Shit. I hadn't thought that leaving the spent scrolls behind would mean anything. Ravyn's harsh glare in my direction said otherwise.

"Two were found in Destiny and Lara's residence, and two more in Tristan's room. Also in Tristan's room was this empty bottle." Celestia shifted the glass bottle from the pile to the middle of the papers. "Esmerelda was kind enough to test the remaining contents. A [Trance] potion, it would seem."

Ravyn's searing glare on me intensified.

I swallowed against the building lump in my throat. I must have left the empty bottle on the bookshelf and didn't consider it. I'd been too focused on getting the damn stuff into Tristan.

"Now, tell me, if you left of your own accord, why were such items necessary?" Celestia withdrew her hands and folded them against her apron.

Tristan took a deep breath. Another flash of lightning and crack of thunder sounded behind the Head Mistress, and Cannoli's fingers wound into mine. Keke's scowl never left the girls flanking Celestia. Ravyn's never left mine.

"They didn't have a choice. They had to make it look like a kidnapping," Tristan said slowly. "Matt was sent to find me by San Island's man."

"Who has deep connections with the queen, might I add," Ravyn growled, finally turning her attention away from me.

"Ah, yes. The San Island girl. I should have expected you'd be behind this," Celestia growled.

"Listen here, bitch—"

I touched Ravyn's wrist and shook my head. *We won't be the ones to force this fight.*

She snatched it away from me, her frown deepening.

"The young master continued to do his secondary duty of protecting Shi Island, Madame Celestia. Your negligence to relay the current state of disarray in the other cities speaks volumes," Ara said evenly.

Celestia clicked her tongue. "Ara, I am most disappointed in you, young lady. A fine example of Venicia's values and an immediate informant of mine. Aiding and abetting this filthy group of traitors—"

"Enough, Celestia," Tristan snapped. "Ara has done nothing *but* argue for Venicia and your methodology. You have no right to speak to her—or any of my companions—this way."

"Young master—" Celestia began.

"No, you said we have the floor. Let's talk about *your* transgressions for a minute." Tristan stood from his chair. He leaned against the table with one hand and ticked off Celestia's sins with the other. "Hiding me away inside of the school and deciding who was 'good enough' to bear children. Stealing my [Cat Pack] and using the Bells from the resolved quests as you saw fit. Masking my presence to Matt and his party when he arrived.

Ignoring the needs of the other cities on Shi Island, like Sorentina, Catania, and Anyona."

Celestia's jaw worked, and when Tristan finished, she quietly asked, "May I?"

Tristan opened his hand and gestured for her to speak.

"Three other men arrived on this island before you and died before they could even *begin* their duties. Keeping you safe and out of the clutches of Defiled, Encroachers, and those who would wish you harm was my top priority." The ice in her words slid down my back. I shivered. "Your 'stolen' Bells went to the other cities to repair the damages of the growing Defiled threat. Anyona had already fallen by the time I took over as Headmistress, and Catania was close behind."

"It is as she says," the girl to her right added. "Catania was my home."

"Then why the blatant discrimination between cities, Madame Celestia? You reap and sow competition between those from Venicia and girls from outside," Ara asked.

Celestia's nose rose into the air. "Competition breeds perfection, Ara. Do we not strive to be the *crème de la crème* of the island? Those who offer perfect Service, Grace, and Urgency?"

Wonder where she picked up that saying.

The headmistress sneered. "You have seen the state of the island. Are those the girls you want to see coupled with the young master?"

"That is not for you to choose," Ceres said as Ara flushed with rage.

"We are all equal in Saoirse's eyes," Cannoli whispered quietly beside me.

Ceres continued, "With all due respect, Headmistress, you act as if Tristan is incapable of thinking for himself. I was a graduate of the school before I moved on to train as a [Magic Knight] in Sorentina. While what I learned here was invaluable, to say that others are undeserving of his time is incorrect."

"Tristan is well-read, articulate, clever, and artistic," Ara snapped when Ceres had finished. "You've treated him like a kitten. I am absolutely certain that he's perfectly capable of distributing *his* Bells accordingly to the other cities. He has done more work to bring this island together in a month than you have in *years*."

Tristan dropped his head, but not fast enough that I didn't catch the red blooming on his cheeks.

"And yet, you wish to take him from his home," Celestia replied. "Pray tell, how will he help his island if he is absent?"

My turn to speak up. "No one said we're taking him permanently. It's a temporary thing. All four men are going to meet and come up with a plan for our islands. This way, we can help each other out."

"Then what shall we do in the meantime, hm?" Celestia's fingers balled into her palms. "Cause panic amongst the girls when I announce that you are gone? Your Bells have sustained Venicia and Shi Island's cities for three years now. Your defection will cause a collapse."

"*Nani?* You should have pulled hundreds of thousands of Bells from this boy, and you're saying there's not a single one left?" Ravyn snarled.

Celestia's lips pulled into a thin line. "I am neither incompetent nor a spendthrift."

"Then how much is left?" Tristan asked.

Celestia hesitated, then admitted, "Enough to maintain the current status quo for a year."

"This won't take a year, Celestia," I replied.

"Besides, if you open better lines of communication with the neighboring cities and allow Venicia girls to help begin rebuilding, you can re-establish trade with the other islands to bring in more money," Tristan suggested.

Celestia's eyes darted to Ravyn. "And allow her like to stand on our hallowed ground?"

It was Ara's turn to stand. She slammed her hands on the table and barked, "And allow *all* girls from *all* islands to stand on your *hallowed ground.*"

Their eyes locked, and the room went still. Another lightning strike crossed the window, and Cannoli squeaked, stepping closer to me. The rain pattered against the roof while everyone focused on Celestia.

"What are your thoughts, young master?" Celestia asked Tristan, venom dripping from her tongue.

"I agree with Ara. Use the able hands here to help rebuild other cities. Send more apt fighters to Sorentina to help fight back the Defiled threat. Open up the island for trade again. To *everyone*," Tristan punctuated every word. "And bring us Lynn."

The last request seemed to catch Celestia off guard. She blinked, touched one braid in thought, then regained her composure. "My apologies. You wish to take more of Venicia's citizens away from the island?"

"You understand that she's my *sister*. Where is she?" Ara growled.

"I am very well aware," Celestia countered, then looked to the girls at the door. "However, before I do, in what timeframe can I expect Tristan's return?"

As long as it takes. I wanted to say, but it didn't seem like the best option.

"No more than three months," Keke said, speaking for the first time in the meeting. "It took us a month to navigate Shi, and we don't know what awaits us on Ichi. You have to give us time."

"Oh? Do I?"

Honestly, I never want to make Tristan come back here. I hadn't wanted to play the threat card, but shit, she was being difficult. I imagined a few words to Cailu, and she'd be done. "Yes. You do. Or I can return with an order from the queen and let her decide what to do with you after you're summoned to Nyarlothep."

Celestia's confidence deflated, and her shoulders fell. She didn't stand a chance against three men and a summons from the queen. "That will not be necessary."

"Then three months. Maybe sooner. For now, we need to see Lynn," Tristan said.

"As you wish." Celestia bowed and strolled from the end of the table to an incredibly detailed oil painting of the Venicia School of Etiquette.

With a quick hand signal, Felsi and Misery removed the large frame from the wall, and Celestia slid her hand down the peeling wallpaper. She paused about halfway down where the painting had been, then dug her nails into the paper and pulled open a slim door that could barely fit one person between its frame. It was impossible to see when closed, especially with the artwork hanging over it.

This can't be good.

Misery disappeared into the dark room, and Ara followed on her heels. Keke went for one of the candles on the table, but Cannoli put a hand on her arm.

"Let me help," Cannoli whispered. She padded across the room and summoned her staff. "[Illuminate]," she murmured, then passed the scepter to Ara.

Ara gasped, and the sound of sharp metal exiting its sheath rang above the rain.

"Ara, wait!" Tristan called.

I pushed past Celestia's other lackeys and peered through the door. There were no windows, no light sources. Three slender forms lay on their backs on the floor, each wearing short, thin gowns that looked like prison attire. The color had drained from their skin, and bruises pocked their arms, legs, and faces.

Destiny, Lara, and Lynn were barely recognizable. They were wounded and emaciated.

Not one of them moved as Ara screamed her sister's name.

Ara Pro Tip: Lynn! LYNN!

Chapter 42

Hapkido

My breath caught when I recognized the forms of Destiny, Lara, and Lynn. Ara's voice rang through the house as she shouted her sister's name. For a moment, I'd nearly forgotten where I was.

Ara's daggers gleamed in the flashes of lightning. Her desperate cries demanded vengeance. In an instant, I threw my arms beneath Ara's arms and curled them inward. Tears streamed down her face as she fought against me.

"Unhand me!"

"Breathe!" I toyed around with the notion of trying to disarm her, but it was a miracle I'd managed to subdue her without losing a finger. Any further movement, and I was sure Ara would outmaneuver me to make an attempt on Celestia's life. Not that I could blame her, but... "Check on them first!"

Celestia crossed her arms. "I must agree. Contain yourself." She motioned with a flick of her head. "Tend to your sister."

"She...she's alive?" Ara's struggles began to slow, the tension in her muscles relaxing. Somewhat, anyway.

"Of course they're alive. They are of no use to me dead."

I shot Celestia a glare before turning Ara back around to the hidden room. The air was so uncomfortable, so stilted, so unnatural. I loosened my grip and slowly uncoiled my arms.

Ara said nothing as she fell to her knees before the bodies of the three maids.

"What have you done to them?" Tristan growled.

Celestia's eyes moved in his direction like a predator observing its meal. "I was rehabilitating them. Certain measures had to be taken to ensure they didn't act out of line. They caused enough trouble as it is." She motioned to the three still bodies with a sigh.

"However, I had little success carving the truth of your disappearance. Fear not; they will wake. Felsi?"

The ice cream shop owner stepped forward.

"Wake them," Celestia said with a wave of her hand.

"Stop!" Ceres and Ravyn cried in unison. They looked at each other, and then Ceres closed the distance between her and Felsi.

"Do not wake them," Ceres said to Felsi. Ceres tilted her head and shot Celestia a glare. "Their waking would only cause panic and thus aggravate their wounds. It is a mercy to keep them asleep."

The string of events that went down after we disappeared began to click into place.

"What did you do?" I asked, looking at Felsi.

The girl's eyes widened briefly before her gaze drifted to a cracked pot in the corner. Whatever had been growing inside of it had wilted a long time ago.

"[Slumber]," Ravyn said simply. "Powerful magic. You have to touch someone for it to take effect, but it puts them to sleep for a while. A *long* while."

"How long are we talking?"

The hint of a smile tugged at Celestia's lips. When Ravyn didn't say anything, I asked again, only to be met with more silence.

"Matt, maybe we should get them somewhere where they can relax," Cannoli said, her hands bunched at her sides.

"Sir Matt, I must agree," Ceres said barely audibly. "They need help."

"How will any of us wake them if she's under a Spell?" I asked.

"There's more than one way to break a Spell," Ravyn snarled, her glare turned to Celestia. "And more than one way to kill a rat."

Portia opened the front door and gestured outside. "Come on, let's go. We can talk later."

Tristan stood before Celestia, looking her in the eye as he spoke. "We've said everything we need to. There won't be any more room for discussion. If there's anything more to talk about, it'll be on our time. Is this understood?"

Celestia paused before delivering a curt nod.

"And if you harm another hair on *anyone's* head, you will never see this school again," he growled.

"Understood, young master." Celestia shifted uncomfortably, her eyes glittering with hate.

I wanted to let Ravyn set her aflame. Let Ara carve her like a Thanksgiving turkey. But this was Tristan's island, and we had to let him handle it. Discussions about what would ultimately happen to Celestia and the entirety of Shi Island would be up to him.

As far as I saw it, there was no forgiving a person for what Celestia did.

"Good." Tristan approached Destiny and motioned for me. "Matt, help me get her on my back."

"Sure."

I couldn't imagine what nightmares Celestia had put them through. Judging from how they looked and the amount of venom seeping out of the headmistress' mouth, I wouldn't have been surprised if they'd been there for days—hell, even weeks.

I helped Destiny onto Tristan's back, and Ara insisted on carrying Lynn. Once Lynn was situated, that just left Lara.

With help from Ceres, we positioned Lara on my back so that her arms dangled over my shoulders while I held her securely by the legs. I winced each time I looked at the wounds. Part of me wondered if the pain was enough to knock them unconscious.

I buried the thought. Taking care of the girls was the best thing we could do now and trusting that Tristan would keep his word should Celestia pull the same stunt with any of the other girls.

"Into the pouring rain, then?" asked Celestia. She gestured to a catgirl on her left, one of the girls I didn't recognize from my first time here, and I watched as she ascended a staircase to the right of the front door. "She is retrieving umbrellas."

"Thanks," Tristan said.

The girl reappeared moments later, her arms filled with numerous multi-colored umbrellas. She approached us, and one by one, we each took one from her arms.

We shared no further words with Celestia. Portia was kind enough to shut the door behind us. We all stood on the porch and unfolded our umbrellas. Keke, Cannoli, and Ravyn had each taken two umbrellas—one for themselves and another for those tasked with carrying duties.

To my surprise, Keke had taken to Ara's side—the two were discussing something quietly. Cannoli walked beside Tristan. Admittedly, she was probably the best person he could talk to. She had a gentle way of bringing calm to a storm.

That left me with Ravyn. She pinched the bridge of her nose, then moved the umbrella close enough to shield me from the pelting rain.

"How considerate. What is it going to cost me?" I teased.

"Oh, shut the fuck up." She gritted her teeth, but it didn't hide the red on her cheeks. "Focus on walking. These girls need our help."

"Yeah. I can't believe what Celestia did to them."

"I can. She's fucking insane." A growl rumbled in her throat. "Should have let me torch the bitch."

"I wanted to," I admitted. "But we have to let Tristan take the lead on this."

She grunted.

"Hey, everyone!" Keke waved her arm through the air. "We're going to follow Ara since she knows a place we can recuperate!"

"Was it where we stayed before?" I called back.

Keke shook her head. "We want to avoid Celestia's enchantments as much as possible."

"Got it. Lead the way!"

Ravyn released Ball into the air to scout while Ara led us down the hill, straight into the middle of the town. The rain had a way of making every step feel like it took twice as long, but it was a short walk, all things considered. We approached the front door of one of the many uniform homes. A white picket fence surrounded the building, and a beautiful garden with flowers of all shapes, sizes, and colors flanked the pathway leading up to the door.

Keke reached into Ara's skirt pocket and pulled out a small, silver key. She unlocked the door and held it open for the rest of us. I drew in a deep breath before entering.

The home was extremely well-kept. A red carpet spread before me, lining the hallway ahead. Beneath it was some of the most immaculately maintained wood flooring I'd ever laid my eyes on. A sweet fragrance for which I had no name filled the air and brought a sense of calm to my nerves.

"This way." Ara gestured to the second floor and began to ascend the stairs, Tristan close behind.

"I'll be right back," I said to the other girls folding up their umbrellas. The floorboards creaked beneath my passenger and me with each step I took. As I rose, I noticed a thin film of dust had covered the wooden railing, and a few cobwebs dangled between the supports.

"Over here. In this room," Ara said when I reached the second floor. She continued onward, opening another door with the end of her foot and motioning Tristan inside.

The light cast upon us by the storm was just enough to let me see through the house. Unlike the floor below, the entire second floor was covered in violet carpeting. Thick gold ropes drew a pair of lush curtains aside a window at the hall's end. Ornate lanterns hung beside the doorframe of each bedroom—I counted five.

I brought Lara to the room Ara had appointed for her and laid her gently on the bed. The longer I looked at her marks, the worse I felt. My blood boiled again, and I took a deep breath to quell the anger I was feeling.

When I exited, I shut the door behind me to see Ravyn coming up the stairs.

"Hey," I said.

"Hey, you." She closed the distance between us and opened the door to Lara's room.

I put a hand on her shoulder. "Wait, you're not going to let her rest?"

Ravyn paused. "I need to find out how long we have until the [Slumber] Spell breaks." She turned her head toward me.

"Can't that wait? She needs her rest. You saw how she looked."

"She's not sleeping, Matt. Magical sleep isn't like normal sleep. It's stasis."

I frowned. "Stasis? What do you mean?"

"It's like being thrown into a fucking well and drowning." Her hand clenched tighter around the doorknob. "It's like every time you gasp for air, more water pours into your mouth. Like someone just froze you on the spot, and all you can do is watch." She showed off one canine fang, hissing under her breath. "It can kill a person."

"Then why didn't we wake them if it's so dangerous? I understand the pain will be awful, but—"

"They've suffered enough. Like Ceres said, we need to keep them from panicking as much as possible. Once I know how long we have, I'll talk with Ceres and Cannoli, and we'll make sure they come out of it alive."

I looked down the hall, where I saw Ara take Lynn. "Does Ara know?"

"Probably." A moment of silence passed, and Ravyn batted my hand away. "I'll just need a few minutes."

After Ravyn shut the door, I weighed up my options. Did I visit Tristan and Ara to check up on them? Or did I give them some space? I put my hand on the railing as I took a step down, glancing in Ara's direction before descending.

Just when I'd thought we'd saved Lara, Destiny, and Lynn, their lives were back on the line.

Ceres Pro Tip: Those with years of magical practice can sense the duration and potency of many powerful Spells.

Chapter 43

Tai Chi

I was in the dining room for only a few minutes before returning to Ravyn's side, curious about the next steps. Ceres, Ara, and I watched in silence as Ravyn swept her hand over Lynn's body. She started at her feet and then worked her way up as if scanning her body for abnormalities. It reminded me a lot of getting a CT scan.

Ara looked beside herself. She rested beside Lynn, tightly clinging to her sister's limp hand. Her face was deathly pale, and her eyes were bloodshot. She must have been crying on the walk home. I didn't know what to say that would help her feel more at ease.

After a while, Ravyn exhaled and rested on her knees.

I put a hand on her shoulder. "Hey, are you okay?"

"I'm fine." Ravyn put her hand on top of mine. "Just takes a lot out of me."

"Rest if you need to."

Ravyn shook her head, then rose to her feet while she removed my hand from her shoulder. "Part of why these girls are like this is my fault. I don't have the luxury of rest."

"Dear Ravyn, please listen to Matt," Ceres said. "I understand your concern. Truly, I do. But we mustn't exhaust ourselves in our efforts."

"I know that," Ravyn said. "I'm fine." Then she clicked her tongue, delivering her next words in a hiss. "What fucking monster would do this to these girls?"

Ara's head hung low. She'd spoken choice few words since Ravyn began checking Lynn. Seeing her sister beaten and bruised, I couldn't imagine how she felt right now. I grimaced as I tried to picture myself in Lynn's shoes while we were gone. I realized that

I had no idea what she was actually like. The last time we were here, I was on the defensive the entire time—I couldn't trust a word out of hers or Ara's mouths.

And now look where we are. How the hell do we fix this?

I had to admit that I felt responsible for Lynn, Destiny, and Lara's current situation. In our efforts to accomplish the goal that Cailu had given me, we'd put Shi Island in a compromised position. From Celestia's immediate treason accusation, she'd assumed the worst for a long time—believing Tristan had been kidnapped or killed. It was no small wonder that Lynn, Destiny, and Lara weren't executed for their 'assistance' in our plan.

"I'm sorry, Ara." The words flowed out of my mouth so effortlessly. There was no getting around it. Despite Tristan's circumstances, no one could deny that this was ultimately our doing. Even if we were right, by all accounts, the island and its issues were none of our business to begin with. This was not my island. These were not my girls. It was *not* my responsibility.

Ravyn drew her hand away from Lynn's body. "The Spell is still strong. It's not showing any signs of weakening. We should have a few days. We're going to need some strong potions before we wake them up."

"But we can wake them, right?" I asked.

Ravyn nodded. "Yeah. Waking them up is the easy part. We need to get them out of pain first. Ara. Felsi is a [Wizard], right?"

"Yes," Ara said.

Ravyn sighed. "*Mattaku*. What a pain." She stepped away from the bed, and Ara buried her face against Lynn's shoulder.

I frowned. "Beyond the obvious, what does this Spell do, exactly?"

"[Slumber] is a magical sleep," Ceres explained. "Very potent, but very simple. Many [Wizard]s learn the Spell for self-defense in close quarters. Like Ravyn said earlier, you have to be touching the person in order to deliver it."

"We used it a few times to incapacitate enemies," Ara said. "But I never thought it would be used like this."

Ravyn folded her arms. "We need to get them in better health as soon as possible."

I could understand getting the person out of pain before they woke, but I still wasn't following why this could be such a big deal beyond the fact that while they slept, they also couldn't eat, exercise, or anything else for that matter. I assumed they weren't getting the normal sort of rest that a person would typically get from falling asleep naturally, but I couldn't help but feel there was still a hidden message behind this Spell that I wasn't getting.

"What makes this Spell so dangerous?" I hesitated and ran a hand through my hair when no one immediately replied. "I'm sorry. I really wanna know every single issue about this Spell. Magic has been a driving force for most of the issues we suffer from." I scratched the back of my head. "I feel like I could learn a lot from you and Ceres."

The faintest hint of pink colored Ravyn's cheeks. She cleared her throat. "Well, boy, if I must. First off, to understand [Slumber], you need to understand magical sleep. Like I said earlier, it puts you in a kind of stasis. As if someone froze you in time. You can't feel, think, dream—you can't do anything. All you can do is watch."

I blinked, taking another glance at Lynn. Her eyes were still closed. "Then... they can see us?"

Ravyn seemed hesitant but answered, "Yeah, if their eyes were open. We're doing them a favor by keeping them closed. Don't force them open."

"I wasn't going to."

"I know, I just—" Ravyn grunted. "With that in mind, since your mind and body are frozen in stasis, you can't sense or experience much. She could see us, but she wouldn't be able to comprehend anything. Following so far?"

I crossed my arms and thought about it. "I think so. Carry on."

"It does *not* mean that those things are not still happening to you." Ravyn turned around so that she faced me. "So, what do you think happens when a person who can't feel or experience anything at that moment is suddenly woken up?"

I tilted my head to look up at the ceiling while thinking about it. It didn't take long for an idea to come to mind. My eyes went wide, and when I met Ravyn's gaze, I suddenly realized why this could be so dangerous. "Do...they feel everything all at once?"

Ravyn nodded slowly. "That's right. Anything their bodies suffered from while they were in that stasis happens all at once. Any slight budge, any damage, any hunger pangs, sleep deprivation, all of it. Like a waterfall. It can get real fucked up real fast."

I was no medical expert back in my old world. Not by a long shot. Even so, I recalled reading stories and articles about people dying from shock. A lot of times, bites, explosions, stabs, gunshots, and other severe wounds wouldn't actually kill the person. It was the shock. Too much of it, and the person could die right on the spot.

"What the hell do we do?" I asked.

"A numbing agent is the best treatment for a situation like this," Ceres offered without a hint of doubt. "When I attended the academy, we were taught the importance of tinctures and agents that could remedy, boost, or weaken the effects of certain Spells."

Ravyn pointed at Ceres. "That's exactly it. We get the agent. We feed it to the girls, and then we wake them up. If the numbing is strong enough, it should dull most of the residual pain. Then we can get them a good meal and let them heal."

"Then let's get to it." I turned around and opened the door out into the hallway. "I don't want to waste a second when we could be out there helping these girls."

"Of course, Sir Matt. Please, lead the way," Ceres said.

I gestured for Ceres to leave first. After she exited, I stood by the side and waited for Ravyn to pass through next. When it was just Ara and me, I spoke. "I mean it. I'm sorry, Ara. I promise I'm going to do everything I can for your sister."

Ara nodded without looking at me. I shut the door behind me as I left.

As Ravyn and Ceres descended the staircase, I stopped with my hand on the railing. "You two go on ahead. I'll catch up in a few."

Ravyn frowned, but Ceres nodded, ushering Ravyn downstairs.

I made my way to the room where Ara had escorted Tristan. I put my hand on the knob, drew a deep breath, and opened the door.

The room was dark beyond a single candle glowing from the bedside dresser. A thick blanket was pulled up to Destiny's torso. Tristan was on his knees, Destiny's hand clasped between his palms. When he turned to look at me, it was with puffy cheeks and red eyes.

"Can I come in?" I asked quietly.

Tristan nodded slowly, then rasped, "Sure."

I shut the door behind me. "How are you holding up?"

Tristan hesitated. "Could be better."

I stood next to him and took in Destiny's features. Strands of her short, blue hair clung to her cheeks, and her shallow, rhythmic breathing whistled from her nose. Destiny appeared no different from Lynn—the casual onlooker would assume she was sleeping peacefully. Even if I'd only met Destiny once or twice, I still remembered the day she welcomed us at the docks with her twin sister, Lara.

"We're going to help them." I wanted to be as reassuring as possible, but to be honest, I was trying to push down the building guilt and rage. There was nothing we could do about the past. It was too late to think about do-overs. It's not like I could just load a save file and try a different route. However, I'd be lying if I said I didn't want to see Celestia burned at the stake. "I promise."

"I know. I just wish I could've prevented this," Tristan said. He rubbed his thumb against the indent between her thumb and index finger. "I drew her more often than any of the other girls."

That one scene from *Titanic* came to mind. *Draw me like one of your Shi Island girls.* I shook it away. Now wasn't the time. "I'm sure she finds that flattering."

"She doesn't know. I was going to tell her. I was supposed to meet her later that night—the day you ki— rescued me. She'd sneak into my room and visit me from time to time. We'd share a drink, and she'd tell me about her day." Tristan touched his forehead to her hands. "I let her down. I let everyone down."

"You're not to blame, though. Look at the hellhole Celestia created. Look at how she orders and barks like some mad woman on a mission. She's like Miss Trunchbull."

The slightest hint of a smile quirked Tristan's lips. "Now that's a reference I can agree with."

"But seriously. We're going to get them taken care of. Ravyn's given me the lowdown on what we need to do. We just gotta numb them up and slowly wake them all." I knew it wasn't so simple, but

I had to pull Tristan out of this slump somehow. "I'll do everything I can to help."

"Thanks, Matt. I think I'll be calling on your aid a lot from now on."

I shook my head. "Don't mention it. We need to work together. This whole one-man-per-island thing is stressful enough. You saw Ni Island. Let's be real. I've got an easy job. I could drop off the face of Nyarlea, and no one would be the wiser."

"I wouldn't be okay with that," Tristan said. "And I know that Keke, Cannoli, Ceres, and even Ravyn wouldn't be okay with that. I can tell how they feel about you, Matt. They lean on and depend upon you. They'd be a wreck if you left this world."

I was at a loss for words. No matter what I came up with, it was short of what I thought was appropriate or necessary. I let the silence speak for a time. When I thought about what would happen to these girls afterward, I spoke.

"I doubt there's going to be room for three more people on the boat. What do we want to do?"

Tristan swallowed. "I don't trust Celestia. I'm afraid she'll hurt them while I'm gone."

"She can't. She knows she fucked up big time."

"Even so, she might. I don't know enough about her. Who is the real Celestia? Is she just an inch away from snapping and hacking their heads off? She was capable of feeding me information and keeping me complacent in my day-to-day. Of torturing her students for information, which is unforgivable." He gritted his teeth. "Even if she intended to heal the island, her actions don't warrant her continued position as headmistress."

"I'm surprised you let her walk," I admitted.

"Just until we figure this out. I didn't want it to come to blows. More innocent girls shouldn't be punished for what she's done." He shook his head. "The school and this city need a different leader. Especially while I'm gone."

"Anyone in mind?"

"I admit, my relationships with the girls in the school, well… Didn't go much farther than the bed."

I had to be honest. "There might be room for one more person, but even then, I think Portia might disagree. I don't know for sure.

But there's no way Ara's going to leave without Lynn. Not if Celestia remains in charge."

"And I can't leave Destiny and Lara here knowing what Celestia did to them. I just can't. I meant every word I said. This island needs me." A knock came at the door. "Come in."

The door opened to reveal Ara. Tristan let go of Destiny's hand and shot to his feet. "Ara, what did—"

"I'm sorry, young master. Please forgive me; I was eavesdropping on your conversation." Ara kept her hands clasped in front of her. Tristan gestured for her to enter, but she refused. "This will only take a moment." Ara averted her gaze.

"What's wrong?" Tristan asked.

Ara's fingers writhed, and she shifted from one foot to the other. "If I may be so bold, I…I have a proposition for you."

Cannoli Pro Tip: Esmerelda's shop should have what we need to make the elixirs Ravyn suggested. We can go tomorrow!

Chapter 44

Muay Thai

I exchanged looks with Tristan, then turned to Ara. "Should I leave?"

"No. I believe you should hear this too," Ara murmured.

Tristan gently set Destiny's hand on the bed and stood, setting his shoulders and shifting his attention. "What is it?"

"There is no easy way to suggest this, so I will be brief." Ara pulled her arms behind her and straightened her spine. "Please allow me to take Celestia's place."

I'd expected her to request an exit from the Party for her sister, but the sudden suggestion of her taking over the school? That about knocked the wind out of me. "Seriously?"

Tristan held up a hand. "I couldn't put that kind of pressure on you, Ara."

Ara's lips quirked into a sad smile, and she gave a small shake of her head. "You wouldn't be. I am the one making the request. Not to sound immodest, but I believe I am the most qualified of the girls in the Venicia School of Etiquette—or in Venicia, for that matter—to become acting headmistress."

"How do you figure?" I asked.

"After my formal education, I was one of the select few girls Celestia often called on to manage her books and records, as well as take deliveries and messages around the town. She would call on me first to resolve conflicts and seek my opinion on changes." Her tail flicked behind her ankles, and she took a deep breath before continuing. "Thanks to my travels with the two of you, I have a greater understanding of the current situations across Shi Island. While...while you're..." She paused, chewing on her lip as her eyes dropped to the floor.

"Ara, you don't have to—" Tristan began.

She raised her voice, speaking over him. "While you are away, I can simultaneously initiate immediate restoration efforts while moving the school in a more positive direction."

Tristan waited until she was finished before asking, "And what about Celestia?"

"That, of course, is ultimately your decision." Ara cleared her throat. "However, if it were up to me, I would consider keeping her confined to a room. Perhaps the one of her own design for some time."

I thought Celestia deserved far worse than that. Let Ravyn sear every nerve on her body, then throw her in a pitch-black cell. Ara's frustrated stare and tense shoulders implied that she felt similarly but held back what she really wanted to say.

Tristan's fingers balled into fists, his knuckles white. "While I agree that Celestia needs to be punished, I don't know if torture is the way to do it."

"Torture?" Ara's smile turned wry. "But, young master, the Room was always seen as a disciplinary measure. A place to 'reassess your actions.' There is no *torture* involved."

I watched the warring emotions take their time with Tristan's features. He didn't hide his feelings very well—Ara would be wise to teach him her poker face sometime. I could see how badly he wanted to be the good guy in all of this, and none of the options presented were great.

"What about our Party?" he asked after a few heartbeats of silence. His voice broke halfway through the sentence.

Ara flinched. As if we'd already covered that part. "I-I know. However, Destiny is a capable [Alchemist] and Lara a [Conjurer]. They should be the ones to go with you."

"But I want *you* with me. You and Lynn." His plea was thin and desperate. Gut-wrenching coming from a guy who'd suffered the full wrath of his island. I couldn't imagine what he was feeling. It'd be like if any of my Party suddenly left. "We started this together."

"And I will be here when you return. So will Lynn," Ara reassured him gently.

I set a hand on Tristan's shoulder. Wanted to remind him that he wasn't alone. "Ara, is this really what *you* want? Not just for the good of the island or your sister?"

She slowly nodded her head. "It would be irresponsible to believe otherwise."

"Maybe, but I'm sure we can find someone else to lead. We can all see this through. You've earned your spot a hundred times over," I replied.

"That is kind of you to say, Matt. But I am certain that this is the best course of action." Ara bowed. "Young master, please let me know your decision as swiftly as possible so I may make the necessary arrangements."

Tristan nodded, running a hand through his hair. When Ara left the room, he looked at me with bloodshot eyes. "I… I need some time alone."

"Yeah, no problem." I patted him on the back and moved to the door. "We'll be downstairs if you need anything."

"Mm," he hummed, kneeling next to Destiny once more.

I closed the door behind me. It seemed Ara had already vanished into Lynn's room, so I made my way down the stairs to find Ceres, Ravyn, and Cannoli at the large dining room table. Multiple candles and two oil lamps flickered from nearly every surface, illuminating Ravyn's perfect penmanship across the parchment.

Ball Gag perched on the mantle of a fireplace with more dust and cobwebs than kindling inside. Ceres and Cannoli were seated on either side of her, leaning forward with focused concentration on Ravyn's list. Keke stood, leaning against a nearby corner with her arms crossed over her chest, tail listlessly whipping back and forth behind her. Her gaze was miles away from anything in the room, and I wondered what she was thinking about.

Only a few soft words were exchanged between the girls when I entered the room, and all four pairs of eyes snapped to me as my footsteps echoed against the wood flooring.

"Sir Matt, is aught amiss?" Ceres asked, immediately standing from her seat and offering a curt bow.

"Sorry, I didn't mean to interrupt. Please, you don't have to stand up like that." I gestured for Ceres to sit back down. "I don't know about amiss, but I do have some news."

Ravyn set her quill to the side, carefully balancing the nib on the bottle of black ink. Buttons was curled around the circular glass, dozing with his head resting on his tail. "What the hell did we miss in the ten minutes you were gone?"

I pulled a chair across the table away and slumped into the cushioned seat. "Well…"

Keke took a seat beside me, and they attentively listened as I explained Ara's proposition to take over Celestia's role and offer Destiny and Lara as Party replacements.

"Oh, no. Tristan must be devastated," Cannoli murmured, touching a hand to her lips.

"He's not taking it great, no. Can't really blame him," I agreed.

"Yeah, but, like you said, this isn't forever. Tristan will come back here eventually." Ravyn shrugged.

Keke nodded. "Ravyn's right. All of us traveling together will end once the men meet. I think Ara could really make a difference here."

"It would let her keep an eye on Lynn, too," Cannoli noted. "But still. Poor Tristan."

Keke's comment about our travels ending set off a pang in my gut. I guess I hadn't really realized how attached to our caravan I'd become. Having Tristan and Ara with us felt so normal that the idea of splitting up with them was strange as hell.

"Matt? Are you alright?" Keke asked, touching my shoulder.

"Yeah. Yeah, I'm good." Whether I was reassuring her or myself, I couldn't tell you. "Has this ever happened before? The four men in Nyarlea trying to meet up?"

All of us looked at Ravyn. Her eyebrows raised, and she bared her sharp white teeth. "*Nani?* What the fuck are all of you looking at *me* for?"

"You're the, um, most experienced, Ravyn," Cannoli replied carefully.

Good job not calling her old.

"Wow. Smooth. *Kuso,*" Ravyn cursed quietly. "No. I don't think it's ever been attempted before. Or if it has been, I've never heard of it in my *advanced experience.*"

"Perhaps you could ask Tristan as well? He is well-read, it seems," Ceres suggested.

"Why do you ask?" Keke wondered.

I shook my head. "Just thinking out loud, really. Without Cailu sending us, we wouldn't have met so many great people or traveled so far. It's crazy to think about."

"Gross. Don't give him compliments," Ravyn hissed.

"Nah, not really a compliment. Just something I noticed." I shrugged. "So, yeah. Ara wants to take over. Destiny and Lara may be joining in her place. You're all caught up, and now it's my turn. What's on the list?"

"Cannoli's helping me come up with ingredients we can use for the potion we need. Since not everything from San Island or Ni Island grows on Shi Island, Ceres gave us some options for herbs and materials that would act the same way," Ravyn explained.

"And I'm Keke," Keke grumbled.

I squeezed her thigh beneath the table, and she snickered.

"That reminds me." I let my hand rest on Keke's leg, and her fingers snaked through mine. "I didn't know that [Alchemist] was a Class."

"Wait, really?" Ravyn sneered. "Did you even *look* at your options before you chose [Warrior]?"

"I...no," I admitted. "I wanted something tanky that could do a good amount of damage. So here we are."

"*Baka.* You should seriously read your iPaw once in a while. For Saoirse's sake."

"[Alchemist] is one of the options for second Class after [Chemist]," Cannoli explained cheerily. "I tried [Chemist] out for a little while, but it's, uh, really expensive."

"Why become an [Alchemist] Class instead of just practicing [Alchemy]?" I asked.

"[Chemist]s and [Alchemist]s have the ability to add additional effects and options to everything they craft. Whether it is offensive or defensive. As Cannoli said, however, the materials and ingredients required are exceedingly rare and expensive," Ceres explained. "For most, it is better to simply practice [Alchemy] and have the option while using a more powerful Class to Level."

"Offensive [Alchemy]? And that isn't your Class, Ravyn?" I teased.

"No," Ravyn replied in a tone suggesting that the conversation was over. She picked up the quill again. "Let's get back to work. I want to leave as soon as the sun's up."

What did I screw up now? I sighed and stood. "Is there anything I can do to help you right now?"

"I believe we are sufficient. Thank you, Sir Matt." Ceres stood again.

How do I tell her not to do that without hurting her feelings? "I'm gonna get some sleep, then."

"I'll come with you," Keke said and got to her feet. "I'm not helping much here anyway."

"We'll need your foraging tomorrow, Keke! You're the best of all of us!" Cannoli cheered.

Keke cracked a smile. We gave them one last wave and a good night before heading upstairs.

There were two rooms still unoccupied upstairs and two more I spotted downstairs. I figured everyone else could figure out their sleeping situations and picked the empty bedroom farthest down the hall. Keke followed me inside and had her arms around my neck by the time I shut the door. She pulled me down and captured my kiss, and I circled her waist to draw her close.

Nyarlea was a crazy world. There were still so many things that didn't make sense and subjects that completely evaded me. Yet, in Keke's embrace, I felt safe and sure. For just a few moments, the rest of the world melted away.

Please don't ever melt away.

Ravyn Pro Tip: Let's find a catgirl with an [Alchemy] set up, too. I'd bet 1,000 Bells that Felsi has one.

Chapter 45

Hip-Hopping to a Store Near You

When I awoke, the tiniest hint of sun peeked through the blinds ahead. Sleepy brain wondered if we'd been moved to one of Celestia's cells. I smiled when I discovered I was in the same bed from the night before. Keke was still sound asleep beside me. I turned my head to the right to admire the curve of her bare backside. Her body rose and fell with every breath she took. It mesmerized me.

With reluctance in my motion, I reached over and gently shook her shoulder. "Hey, Keke." Mumbles and groans escaped her lips. She yanked away what remained of my covers, wrapping herself in a cocoon of blankets. The cold air nipped at my skin, and I rubbed my hands against my biceps for a bit of warmth. I shook her again, this time with a little more force. "Come on. It's time to get up."

"Just a couple more minutes," Keke whispered.

I made several disapproving expressions. I wanted to let Keke rest, but Ravyn was right. We needed to get this done as soon as possible. Every minute we spent resting or lazing about was another minute our [Slumber] victims were suffering.

"Keke, get up. We need to get going."

She turned toward me in her sleepy trance, and the morning chill completely evaporated with the sight of her breasts. This was still taking some getting used to. I averted my gaze, then scratched the back of my neck and got out of bed before the more bestial side of me could take control.

Where are my clothes? Oh, over there.

Halfway to the pile of garments, a fierce knock came at the door. Keke shot up into a sitting position. Dark circles hung under her eyes. A gnarly growl emanated from the deepest part of her throat while she squinted at the door.

"Time to get up! Get dressed! We're burning daylight!" Ravyn's voice boomed from behind the door. The doorknob rattled, and soon after, another knock came.

"Get up, dumbasses, get up dumbasses, squawwwwwk!"

Did she really have to bring the demon bird?

Keke continued to growl, then swooped up the covers and wrapped them around her until she became a ball of sheets and blankets. After I got my undergarments and pants on, I unlocked the door and swung it open, a finger to my lips.

"Can you be a little more gentle?" I asked.

Ravyn was already dressed. Ball Gag sat atop her shoulder, munching on a cracker. She folded her arms and raised a brow. "*Baka*. We don't have *time* to be gentle. Got shit to do. Cannoli's already prepared your breakfast, so hurry up before it gets cold."

"Did you already eat?" As eager as she was to get started, I had a hard time believing she'd leave without at least getting a bite.

"No, of course not. I offered to wake you up. You and Keke are the only ones who aren't eating, so hurry the fuck up before I eat all your food."

"Hurry the fuck up, squawwwwk!"

I didn't fight back. It wasn't worth it. Besides, she was right. We'd already agreed on getting out by the time the sun was up, so any lost time would be on Keke and me.

"Alright, just need a few minutes. We'll be right down."

"Chop chop!" Ravyn exclaimed, clapping her hands together.

I shut the door in her face and locked it. Curses spouted from Ravyn's mouth, and I ignored them. Then I turned around to face the bed. I got down on all fours and crawled across the mattress, putting both of my hands on the blankets. With a sigh, I started to remove them one by one.

"Noooo," came a voice from within the ball of comfort. "Just five more minutes. Pleeeease."

"No, Keke. Come on, get up. We got shit to do, just like Ravyn said." I tugged harder at the fabric. It was coming loose, and for a moment I wondered if this was how my parents felt every day before school.

The idea of waking up one of my own kittens crossed my mind, and I quickly shook it away.

"Breakfast is downstairs," I continued. "I bet Cannoli and Ara made it. It's gotta be delicious."

There was a pause, but I could feel her wriggling inside. At last, she relented. "Fine. I'll get up."

Despite how tired we both were, we were quick to get our clothes on, taunted by the enticing aroma of Cannoli's, and presumably Ara's, cooking. Afterward, we soared down the stairs. Even if I was pretty quick, Keke was the faster of us. She'd managed to reach the bottom before me.

"Winner!" She threw her arms into the air for a quick victory stance, then took an empty seat next to Ceres.

"Good morning, Keke," Ceres said with a slight bow of her head.

I lazily walked the remainder of the stairs and caught Ravyn's glare. "Loser," she said, pointing at me with her fork. She directed the utensil to an empty seat across from her. "Sit, boy."

I rolled my eyes. "Yes, ma'am."

"Good boy."

"Good morning, Sir Matt," Ceres said with a warm smile.

"Morning." I took the other spot next to Ceres, avoiding Ravyn's gaze.

Right after, Cannoli and Ara approached with a nice spread of food I was familiar with by now. Potatoes were mashed, some of the local fish was fried in a pan, and a few bowls of cleaned fruit sat at the center of the table.

"Did you make this too, Ara?" I asked.

A rare smile, probably one of the most honest I'd seen on her, tugged at her lips. "I did. With Cannoli's help, of course. No catgirl would go to Venicia's School of Etiquette without learning the essentials of cooking."

"I'm impressed. Really, this looks amazing. Thank you."

Ara offered a curt nod before placing a plate of potatoes and fish in front of me.

"Try the fruit, Matt. We picked it this morning," Cannoli said as she put a plate of food down in front of Ravyn next. "It's really fresh!"

"Oh, this looks so good." Keke's eyes went wide as she plucked a smaller nyapple from the bowl in front of her.

"Why are they so small?" I asked.

"The smaller, the sweeter," Keke said.

I frowned. "I never saw you rip down a nyapple that small before."

"Bigger is better." Cannoli was wearing a beautiful pink apron with frills on the ends. Come to think of it, so was Ara. The two were a cute cooking duo, and it put a smile on my face to see them passing by each other to put food on the table for us. "Typically, catgirls want more food. Ni Island isn't very particular about taste, so much as quantity."

I guess I can see that.

"Typically, anyway," Keke said as she tossed the nyapple around in her hand and took a big bite out of it. Her face scrunched, and her lips puckered. "Oh, Saoirse, that's sweet."

"How are the sleeping girls doing?"

Ravyn shrugged. "About as well as they can be. We still have two days on the Spell, but we need to get them food and water as soon as possible."

Ara and Cannoli set down two more plates of food, then took two of the seats on Ravyn's right. Now that I was getting a good look at everyone at the table, I had to ask. "So, where's Tristan?"

"The young master is attending to business in the town," Ara said with stony indifference.

"I see. Did he take off to go talk to Celestia?"

"I would presume so."

You would presume so? How unusual for you.

This was kind of strange. I struggled to think of a world where Ara wasn't at Tristan's heel, available at a moment's notice. Their circumstances weren't something they would get over in just a night's rest, but I felt that an argument might've occurred.

I picked up a fork next to my plate and used the flat end to cut off a piece of the fish on my dish. "Is he going to be back soon? There were a few things I wanted to ask him about," I lied.

"I do not know. Let us take care of the matters at hand first. We can return to your queries later," Ara said.

"Yeah, stick to the plan. We finished the list last night," Ravyn said as she procured a rolled-up scroll from beneath the table. "Simple stuff, but potent. Even if the bitch ratted us out, Esmerelda had some good wares. I think we should visit and pick up what we need from there. Maybe we can save ourselves a trip to an [Alchemy] lab while we're at it. Esmerelda would have to have one."

Cannoli chewed her lip. "I don't think she intentionally hurt us, Ravyn. Celestia may have just asked her her opinion on the empty bottles and scrolls."

"Yeah, not like she's been telling anyone here the full story." Keke rolled her eyes, taking another bite of her nyapple.

"That's reasonable," I said. I shoveled a hunk of fish into my mouth, chewed, and swallowed. "Who's going to stay and watch our sleeping beauties?"

"Ara, Ceres, and Tristan will stick around to keep an eye on them. The rest of us are going to Badyron," Ravyn said.

I did a quick count with my fingers. "You, me, Keke, and Cannoli?"

Ravyn nodded, spooning a helping of potatoes and delivering them to her mouth. "Cannoli seems pretty well-versed in [Alchemy]," she said between fits of chewing. She swallowed and lifted another helping to her mouth. "She came up with a few herbs that I didn't think of."

I sliced free another helping of fish. "That's right. She helped me make my first potions."

"That was such a wonderful day. You caught on to it really quick too, Matt!" Cannoli noted. She was hard at work on her own breakfast and was managing to pass most of us by. I reckoned she had a busy morning. Was probably eager to get outside too.

Up long before dawn, were we?

"Well, sounds good to me." I shrugged. "I don't see what you need me for, though."

Ravyn pointed the spoon at me and formed a flat line with her lips. "You know [Alchemy]. Novice or not, we'll work faster if we have more people to throw at it. Simple addition, Matt."

"Right, right."

Most of breakfast passed by without interruption. Tristan never showed up. As much as I wanted to ask about him and Ara, I decided against it. I already had a knack for putting my nose in places it didn't belong, and I didn't want to be responsible for any more mishaps. This was, of course, coming from the guy going to Ichi Island to take yet another man away from his duties.

I hope Cailu's plan works.

As much of a cuntbag as he was, I couldn't fault the reasoning behind the task. If the four men could meet and build a council, or at the very least, just manage our resources together, then maybe we could fight the Defiled threat and return these girls to a life of normalcy.

I helped clean up, then moved outside. I stood on the front porch, my hands in my pockets, pondering over Tristan and Cailu. Both of them had unique circumstances, and I'd been fortunate as hell to end up on Ni. Considering what we'd encountered up until now, I'm not sure I would've survived if I'd found myself in Tristan's or Cailu's position.

A sensation on my shoulder broke me from my thoughts. "Hey. It's time to go," Ravyn said.

I turned to face her. "Oh. Yeah. Are Keke and Cannoli ready?"

Ravyn nodded. "They will be in a moment. I'm going to get us a ride while we're waiting."

"Wait." I grabbed her by the bicep. She turned her head and looked at me. Part of me hoped there might be an angry hue of pink on her cheeks or that she'd snap at me. Something Ravyn-like. There was nothing of the sort. The last thing I wanted from her right now was for her to let the guilt of the slumbering girls drag her down. I wanted to ask if she was okay. But I didn't. "How will I find you?"

Ravyn paused, then shook away my grip. "Same place we did last time, boy. Remember where the horses were stationed?"

"Yeah, I do."

Ravyn smirked. "Good. At least you have a good memory for geography." Nothing else came out of her mouth. Ravyn continued on her way with Ball Gag perched on her shoulder. I watched for as long as I could see her.

"Hey, Matt?" I flinched at the sound of Cannoli's voice. "Are you okay?" Concerned ruby eyes stared into me, analyzing me. Keke stood just behind her.

I drew a deep breath. "I'm fine." I forced a smile. "Come on, let's catch up with Ravyn."

Cannoli nodded. "Yes, let's! The sooner we get these girls back to full health, the better! Lead the way, Matt!"

Cannoli Pro Tip: Cooking with Ara was so much fun! She's so fast! I would love to make more meals with her.

Chapter 46

Trapped in a Box Step

Tristan walked to the center of Venicia, circling the fountain and listening to the birds sing their first morning melodies. He lapped the perfect stone once, twice, then a third time, not sure what he was hoping to accomplish. No one came outside. Every window was closed with curtains and blinds drawn. The city was still hiding from a nonexistent Defiled threat.

He abandoned the fountain in favor of weaving between closed shops and abandoned buildings. Thoughts and memories bombarded his head and heart, colliding in a chaotic cluster. Like an abstract painting that lacked any kind of control or balance. Ara taking Celestia's position and leaving the party. Jazz dead and bleeding on the field. Drawing pictures for the kittengirls in Catania. The [Necromancer] of Anyona. Destiny's late-night visits and addictive laugh. The slumbering girls beaten and bruised, emaciated, and freezing cold.

How do I even begin to fix this?

Without realizing it, his feet had taken him to the shoddily kept house that served as Celestia's temporary establishment. Was she still here? Had she returned to the school? *What the hell do I even say?* He straightened his shoulders and knocked.

There was a short pause, then Celestia answered. That surprised him—he'd assumed one of her followers would bring him in as they had the day before. Misery, maybe.

"I'm surprised to see you again so soon, young master," Celestia said with a bow, gesturing him inside.

The feeling is mutual. "Good morning, Celestia." The sun had just crested the horizon when Tristan crossed the threshold. "Are Felsi and Annabelle here?"

Celestia tilted her head quizzically. "They are upstairs asleep."

"Wake them up." Any patience he'd had with the headmistress was sapped. He hadn't slept a wink the night before, choosing to stay at Destiny's side. How many welts and bruises had he counted? At least two dozen.

"...Yes, sir," she assented after a brief hesitation. She padded up the stairs, her brown tail swishing back and forth behind her.

Every time he'd felt the first nags of cabin fever at the school, there was something new to catch his interest within the hour. Paints, pictures, another girl to bed. Books. They'd given him so many books to read that he hadn't realized how rare they were until his travels with Matt. Fiction, fantasy, Nyarlean history, romance. Celestia made a point to replace the ones he said he wouldn't read again with something new. What she hadn't realized, however, was the wealth of knowledge she'd handed to him on a silver platter.

There was no denying that he still wasn't the best [Mage] or offensive fighter. He'd known so little about the current state of Shi Island, only shreds of what it had looked like in its prime.

But if he were the gambling type, he'd bet every Bell stolen from his [Cat Pack] that he was better versed in Nyarlean law than Celestia. There were a dozen things she could have called Matt rescuing him from the school; 'Treason' was the wrong one.

"Here they are, young master," Celestia announced as she descended the stairs.

Felsi and Annabelle followed close behind, averting Tristan's gaze in favor of the wooden banisters and slick flooring. They moved to the center of the room, Felsi and Annabelle flanking Celestia on either side and clasping their hands against their aprons.

"There are going to be some changes to Venicia effective immediately," Tristan said, working to keep his voice still. *How many of you helped torture Lynn, Destiny, and Lara?* "Felsi, Annabelle, I would like to believe that I have your confidence and trust?"

"Of course," they murmured in unison.

"Good. First, tell me, how did you force information from Destiny, Lara, and Lynn? What happened to them?" He could corroborate their story with the girls once they woke up.

Felsi and Annabelle shifted uncomfortably. Celestia's icy glare slid to the corners of her glasses, but her face stayed forward.

"We brought them here on Celestia's orders," Annabelle began. "Felsi kept them asleep between...between questionings."

Celestia reset her jaw and blinked. She smoothed her apron and retook her strict posture.

"Misery, Katrin, and Celestia would interrogate them in the room you saw. Annabelle and I stood watch," Felsi supplied.

"Is that true, Celestia? Felsi and Annabelle cast the Spell and stood watch?" Tristan asked.

"They are just as guilty as accomplices—" Celestia began.

"That isn't what I asked!" Tristan snapped. He wouldn't let her worm her way out of this. This woman who'd taken him in when he was reborn on Shi Island. Convinced him that his job was to stay safe and populate the island. There were many days he saw her like a mother. Not anymore.

Celestia's ears flattened against her head, and she narrowed her eyes. "Yes, young master, that is correct."

"Felsi, where's Solonie?" Tristan asked.

She winced as if surprised to hear her daughter's name. Or maybe that he'd remembered. But he'd committed all of them to memory. It gave him a sense of purpose. "S-she's with a nyanny, sir."

"And Kiora?" he asked Annabelle.

Annabelle shifted her weight from one foot to the other. "The s-same nyanny, sir."

"Am I correct in my assumption that you both were coerced into this?" Neither Felsi nor Annabelle had the same sadistic disposition as Misery or Celestia. Never had Tristan believed them capable of torture or standing by while it happened.

Felsi flushed a sickly shade of white while Annabelle's neck and face flared bright red. *There it is.*

"I-I would never!" Celestia's cool façade faltered, and she looked between Felsi and Annabelle. "Tell him. Both of you."

Felsi rolled her shoulders back and glanced at the ceiling. Annabelle blinked tears away from her eyes.

"I haven't seen my kitten since you left," Annabelle whimpered. "I don't want her hurt."

Felsi nodded her agreement, her pink hair bobbing around her chin, but her lips remained in a tight thin line.

A new wave of rage rolled through Tristan's blood. His fists balled at his sides, and he took a deep breath before continuing. "Celestia of Shi Island, you are hereby removed from your position as Headmistress of the Venicia School of Etiquette. You, Misery, and Katrin will be held in isolation until escorted to Nyarlothep by the next trade vessel that comes to this island."

"Young master, wait—" Celestia held up a hand. That same hand had consoled him through a slew of nightmares and passed him small gifts here and there whenever he missed home.

Tristan swallowed and continued. "Felsi and Annabelle will accompany you, carrying a writ of your transgressions penned by myself. There, you will be tried by the Royal Guard and handed the Queen's Justice. Do you understand?"

"Tristan—" She hadn't called him by name in ages. Her voice through his door, holding a plate of milk and cookies. Or waiting to introduce him to his next catgirl companion.

"*Do you understand?*" Tristan barked. All three women flinched with surprise. His knuckles were white. Celestia had held him in a cell for three years, hiding him from the world. And now she *dared* harm the very girls he'd sworn to protect.

Celestia slid her hands down her twin braids, squinting through her glasses as if taking her first real look at Tristan. "I understand."

He looked to Felsi and Annabelle. Their eyes were wide, and neither looked as if they were breathing. "From this day forward, Ara will take Celestia's position as Headmistress of the Venicia School of Etiquette. While I'm away, her word is my word. Any rules or decisions put forward by her are to be treated as my own. You both stand witness to my demands, do you accept?"

The most essential piece of Nyarlean verbal contracts was the presence and agreement of two witnesses who hailed from the island. Even if a man made the claims, they wouldn't be carried through without the sign-off of at least two island natives. A ruling that had been placed into effect nearly a hundred years before when a man began carelessly overhauling an island's culture with dangerous and self-serving laws.

"I, Felsi of Shi Island, accept your terms," Felsi said with a small bow of her head.

Annabelle looked at the seething Celestia, then at Tristan. "I-I, Annabelle of Shi Island, accept your terms."

"Traitors to your island, the lot of you," Celestia growled. "You do not understand the effort and experience needed to lead Venicia. Ara is doomed to fail—"

"[Slumber]," Felsi whispered, touching Celestia's shoulder.

Celestia froze in place. Her eyes and lips slowly closed, and her arms fell to her sides. Felsi and Annabelle caught her before she could fall.

"I've wanted to do that for *years*," Felsi admitted sourly.

Annabelle giggled nervously. "Me, too."

Tristan ran a hand through his hair. "I'm so sorry that I wasn't here. To both of you. Are Solonie and Kiora safe?"

Felsi nodded. "A quick word from you should do it. I don't think the nyanny wants to be on that boat to Nyarlothep."

"Then I'll do it. Are there empty rooms in the school where we can keep Celestia, Misery, and Katrin until the next ship arrives?" Tristan asked.

"Plenty," Annabelle replied. "We'll be able to move them in easily, and I can lock them from the outside."

"Great. I know I'm putting a lot on you both. Will you be comfortable traveling with her?"

Felsi shrugged. "Wouldn't have agreed if I weren't. I think Annabelle feels the same way."

Annabelle nodded.

"Thank you. Sincerely." He glanced up the stairs to the second floor. "And now we have to tell the other two. I hope they don't run."

Felsi swirled her free hand in the air and grinned. Tiny crystalized particles circled her palm and wrist like a miniature snowstorm. "It'll be impossible to run with their feet frozen to the ground."

Tristan wanted to smile with her but found that he couldn't. It was impossible not to stare at Celestia. Three years beneath her 'care' and tutelage. Three years she'd spent manipulating Venicia to her every whim.

He sighed. That was officially the past. Today, everything changed.

Ai Pro Tip: Men have the power and authority to make dynamic changes for the islands. However, law dictates the presence of two island natives for verbal mandates.

Side Quest

Ceres's School Of Etiquette

Ceres hid behind the sweet shop, knees deep in the mud, while she carefully shaped another ball in her hands. The girls were still there, just in front of Mindy's Tailor Shop, pining over the newest fashions in Sorentina. Expensive silks and skirts from San Island, opulent hats from Nyarlothep. Who cared about that stuff? Not Ceres, that was for sure.

And it's none of their business whether I care or not.

After a long day of schooling from Nyanny Leona, they'd been released to head straight home. And Ceres would. Just…right after she showed them that it didn't matter if there was dirt on her knees or cheeks. Who cared if the hem of her skirt was coming loose? They giggled and poked fun without mercy. Ceres stayed silent the whole time, biting her tongue raw. When the sky had opened, and the rain poured during luncheon, she knew she'd get her chance.

While most of Sorentina was well-paved with bricks and stepping stones, a few of the shops hadn't bothered to maintain their alleyways well. Which made for the perfect mud puddles after a downpour.

The drops had weakened to a gray mist from the dark clouds, but Ceres still had *plenty* to work with. She grinned at the final ball of mud in her coated hands, then collected all four in her apron. She stood, the brown muck clinging to her shins like a coat of muddy armor and held tight to the edges of her white pinafore. Her shoes squished through the swamp she made until she reached the edge of the brick road.

"You would look *so* cute in that dress, Viola," Winter crooned. "Stripes suit you."

Viola cupped one dainty hand over her lips and blushed. "Oh! I couldn't!"

Brianne twirled her umbrella in her hands and spun. "Can you just imagine those shoes with this parasol? Absolutely divine."

"Too true! Too true!" Titania added.

They sound like tittering old bats. Ceres gritted her teeth and kept her back against the wall, creeping closer and closer on the balls of her feet.

When she'd reached the edge of the shop, she curled her fingers around the first mud ball. The scent of sweet fruit and sugar wafted from the open door to her right, perking her nose and ears. *No! Focus!* Narrowing her eyes, she wound her arm back…held her breath…then…

Smack!

The first mud ball struck Viola square in the back, exploding all over her blue velvet dress.

"What in the world?" Viola squealed.

Before they could register what had happened, Ceres snatched another ball and hurled it at Brianne. It found home against the puffed red shoulder of her top, plastering the underside of her umbrella and her hair in brown. She sucked in air with her surprise, abruptly spitting out the mud that came with it.

Titania's landed squarely against her chest, spreading mud to her face and arms. As for Winter, Ceres poured every prayer for aim into her arm. Winter was the instigator, the heckler, the one who *always* commented on the state of Ceres's disarray. For Winter, her ball of mud slammed into her nose, erupting against her face.

Ceres's adrenaline melted in laughter as she fell to her knees with her hands wrapped around her abdomen. Tears threatened the corners of her eyes while the four girls futilely wiped the mud away from their bodies.

"You should *see* yourselves!" Ceres cackled, pointing at each of them in turn. "You look *ridiculous!*"

Brianne shook her parasol, then slowly closed it and turned to face Ceres. "Classless, commoner Ceres," she hissed. "You'll *never* be a lady."

"Not if I have to look like *you*," Ceres retorted, falling into another fit of giggles.

Winter ran the back of her forearm over her eyes, clearing the mud enough so she could see. Flecks of dirt marred her sky-blue hair and ears, and her silver eyes turned to steel. "I will *ruin* you, Ceres," she growled. "Come on, ladies!"

She led the charge with a scream. Ceres scrambled to her feet, the adrenaline returning to her veins with the thrill of the chase. She turned heel and fled, clearing the bricks in one wide leap and then landing in the mud. Puddled rain splashed on her skirts, and she laughed as she navigated the mud with ease.

Titania was the first to abandon the chase as soon as she noticed the muddy lake. "S-sorry. Mother would be displeased," she stammered to her friends.

The other three sped toward Ceres full bore, ignoring the splashing sludge against their knee socks and expensive skirts. But it would take more than going through a little bit of mud to get to Ceres. No one knew the alleys and roads like she did. They'd never catch her. *No one* could catch her.

Ceres squeezed through narrow openings between shops, dodging across the road and weaving between ladies who offered her a curt word and sour expression. But she didn't care. She was breathless with excitement, reveling in the shrieks of the three girls behind her. Viola was lost to the crowds, leaving only Winter and Brianne in pursuit.

The rain was beginning to pick up again, heavy droplets splashing against Ceres's cheeks and forehead. She welcomed it with open arms, hoping that it may clean at least some of the mud away from her dress and shins. As it was, Mother would be furious. But she could worry about that later. Right now, she needed to get away from Winter and Brianne.

Ceres whipped around the corner of the armor shop, jumping the fence, skidding across the anvil, then skipping through the forge. "Good luck, *ladies,*" she called over her shoulder.

Brianne stopped at the edge of the anvil and looked dejectedly at Winter. "I may tear my skirts. I'm sorry, Winter."

"Ceres! You— You bitch!" Winter snarled and hurled herself over the anvil.

"That's not very lady-like, Winter!" Ceres shouted over her shoulder. Her house wasn't far now. Mother's anger would be a lot easier to handle than Winter's rage. "Better go back to Nyanny Leona!"

A loud growl and a scream erupted from Winter's throat. "[Freeze]!"

The Spell was immediate, binding Ceres's shoes to the cobblestone. She pitched forward, feet sliding free from her strapped sandals, coming to a skidding stop on her hands and knees. Coarse granite ripped at the soft skin of her shins and calves, the sudden scrapes loud and painful. "You're not allowed to cast magic, stupid Winter!"

"Don't you lecture me on rules, you filthy degenerate!" Winter was quickly gaining ground.

Ceres was sure she wouldn't be so lucky with Winter's next cast. She scrambled to her feet, ignoring the searing pain in her hands and legs, and made a break for home. The dark green roof was just there in the distance. Just a little longer…

"[Freeze]!" Winter howled.

"[Myana Wall]!" a deep voice bellowed.

Ceres dug her heels into the ground just as her father appeared from behind the baker's shop. An iridescent shell formed behind her, blocking Winter's attack with ease.

"What is the meaning of this?" Father barked, looking between Ceres and Winter. "Casting offensive Spells in town, Winter? At a civilian?"

"She started it!" Winter squealed, pointing at Ceres. Just as the words escaped her lips, her etiquette teachings struck her like lightning, and she straightened her back. "I-I mean, apologies, Master Janusz, sir. I meant no harm."

Father looked Ceres over from head to toe, taking in the mud on her arms, legs, and apron. His identical blue eyes narrowed to slits, and his mouth drew into a long, thin line. "Go home, Winter," he growled.

"Y-yes, sir. Thank you, sir." Winter bowed over and over again as she vanished from sight.

"Get your shoes, Ceres," he snapped.

Ceres hummed her reply, all feeling disappearing from her fingers and toes. She jogged to where her shoes had frozen in place, plucking them from an overgrown weed patch. The town's

[Alchemist] was really letting her property go, Ceres thought idly. Her feet were too covered in dirt and grime to slide them comfortably back into her shoes, so she padded across the road in her socks back to her father.

Janusz scowled. "*Kurwa mać!* Can you not put all of this…this energy into your studies?"

Ceres flinched. He saved that phrase for when he was especially angry. "I'm not *learning* anything. What does it matter how we hem our dresses or which fork goes where? I want to learn something real. Like how to fight!" She whined. "Like what *you* just did! Then stupid Winter would never think to cast at me again."

"Enough!" he roared.

Ceres shrank, her ears drooping to the top of her head and her tail tucking between her legs.

"I thought Nyanny Leona would teach you some manners, and you'd behave better. Clearly, I was wrong." His hands balled into fists, and he looked to the dark sky. "There's a school of etiquette in Venicia. I hear their program works miracles."

"Father!" Ceres squeaked. She didn't want to go to *Venicia*. Everyone she'd ever met from that city was so…so stuck up! "Please! Let me stay here!"

"No. You're seven now and grow wilder by the year. I cannot, in good faith, release you to the world like this. That's final."

Ceres's chin dropped to her chest. She studied the stones beneath her stockings. It didn't matter how much kicking or screaming she did. Father's word was as good as law. She was sure he'd be taking her to Venicia within the week.

But I will never *be like* them, she thought defiantly. *Never.*

Ceres Pro Tip: Sir Matt, I beg you do not judge me too harshly based upon my actions as a kitten. I did not know better…

Chapter 47
Takes Two to Tango

The ride proved to be a short one. When we arrived in Badyron, I was welcomed by a flood of memories, both good and bad. At a distance, I could see the shack where we spent time experimenting with the [Impersonate Soul] scrolls. Esmerelda's shop was within view, and before anything could occur, I put my hand on Ravyn's shoulder after she jumped off the cart.

"Remember, we want to smile and not put any blame on her," I said with a toothy grin.

Ravyn batted my hand away. "I know that, dumbass. We got along just fine last time. What do you think I'm going to do, just light the whole place on fire?"

The idea did cross my mind, yes. I put my hands up. "No, just saying."

She rolled her eyes and started her march toward Esmerelda's shop. I helped Keke and Cannoli down from the cart, and we followed a few paces behind Ravyn.

A chime rang throughout the shop when Ravyn pushed the door open.

"Welcome to Esmerelda's Eclectics, where all—" Esmerelda was leaning on one elbow and thumbing through a book when we entered. Even at this distance, I could tell her eyes locked with Ravyn's. Both women shared a glare, and Esmerelda stood up, crossing her arms. "Oh. It's you."

Ravyn raised a brow. "What a warm welcome. Do you greet everyone this way?"

"No, I reserve this one for my favorites," Esmerelda replied with a half-smile.

Coming on a little strong. Good start.

For the second time, I put my hand on Ravyn's shoulder and whispered into her ear. "Ravyn, pull it back."

"Saoirse, are you my nyanny?" she whispered back, grabbing my hand like it was some dirty rag and moving it away. "Stop that."

"I'm surprised to see you back here." Esmerelda's stare landed on me next. "I take it then that my wares were sufficient?"

"Yes, thank you so much for last time," Keke said.

We marched up to Esmerelda's counter, the floorboards squeaking underfoot with each step. I scanned the shop as we made our way over, noticing that the shop looked a lot cleaner than before. The boxes appeared freshly dusted, and the empty jars were replaced. Not a single cobweb stuck out to me, and a glance at the floor said that it was recently swept.

When we reached the counter, Ravyn opened her mouth only to be interrupted by Cannoli. "I love what you did with your hair! How do you keep it so shiny?"

I admit the question caught me by surprise.

It seemed to catch Esmerelda off guard, too. She blinked twice, then whipped her long, curly green hair behind her, her expression unchanged. "Trade secret."

Maybe she's born with it.

Cannoli crossed her fingers. "It's lovely!"

A faint smile tugged at Esmerelda's lips. "Thank you, sweet." Her attention came back to Ravyn. "You brought your lovely familiar back as well." She put her arm out, and Ball flew from Ravyn's shoulder to Esmerelda's forearm. She used the middle knuckle of one finger to play with the underside of his beak, her smile widening. "He is such a beauty. When did he answer your summon?"

Maybe it was my imagination, but I could've sworn I saw Ravyn's eye twitch. "Long time ago," Ravyn growled.

A moment later, a scaly creature slithered its way around Esmerelda's waist, past her bust, and relaxed comfortably around the top half of her torso and neck. Numerous shades of red speckled an emerald body. "Mine came to me as a child." Esmerelda caressed the top of the viper's head, and the snake responded by flicking out its black forked tongue.

Ball is strangely complacent right now for being around a snake.

I had to know. "No offense, but should a snake be hanging around a bird?" I didn't have any particular opinion on snakes, but I knew enough that one that big could eat a bird if given a chance.

"It's fine. They won't hurt each other," Ravyn said.

Esmerelda nodded, and for a moment, I was distracted by how the snake looked coiled around her lithe body. "It's as she said. They are not Encroachers. They are familiars."

"Desiree didn't have any urge to eat Bally either. They all come from the same place," Ravyn explained. "There's no reason for them to fight or eat each other."

"I see." The longer I looked at Esmerelda's familiar, the more features I noticed. Its fiery-red eyes, its black underbelly, and a strange, feathery bulge about a quarter of the way down its body. They looked like tucked wings from where I stood. Somehow it felt like the longer I looked at the familiar, the more it entranced me. As if it was luring me in. The snake turned to look at me, then flicked its tongue.

I've had enough Enchantments for a lifetime. My ear wasn't burning, but better off safe than sorry. I shook my head. "Sorry, Esmerelda. This is fascinating stuff, but we need to get a few things from you."

"My apologies. What brings you to my shop today?" Esmerelda lowered the arm that Ball was sitting on, and the viper turned to look at him. I wondered if the familiars were sharing a telepathic conversation.

Ravyn leaned on her forearm and narrowed her eyes like she was about to do business with the local mafia. "We got three girls caught under a [Slumber] Spell. They're in bad shape, and we need some potent materials to make sure they don't wake up screaming." With her spare hand, Ravyn procured the list from her [Cat Pack] and put it on the counter. "Do you have any of this stuff?"

Esmerelda set Ball down next to the parchment, unfurled the scroll, and began reading off the components in a mumble. After a minute, she put it aside and nodded. "Yes. I have everything you need."

"That's great," Ravyn replied.

"Guess I didn't need to come after all," Keke said with a frown.

"Never hurts to be cautious," Cannoli said with a consoling smile. "We had no idea if they were going to be in stock!"

Keke let out a nervous laugh. "Thanks."

"Will you need an [Alchemy] lab as well?" asked Esmerelda.

"Yeah. How much is that going to cost me?" asked Ravyn.

Esmerelda put a finger to her violet lips. "It's two hundred Bells an hour." Ravyn opened her mouth, and Esmerelda put her hand out. "I'm not done. In addition, if you are using materials from my shop, there will be an additional charge per hour equal to fifty percent of the total cost of materials."

Ravyn gritted her teeth. "That's robbery."

"That's business." Esmerelda drew a deep breath.

Sighing, Ravyn put her [Cat Pack] down on the counter and pulled out a handful of Bells, counting them in a whisper.

I untied the [Cat Pack] around my waist and threw it onto the counter. "I'm pitching in, too. It's not fair that you have to cover the entire cost."

"You have a nice man there," said Esmerelda.

"Y-yeah," Ravyn murmured.

By the time we estimated the price of materials and how long we'd need, the total came out to six hundred Bells. Assuming we finished in two hours like we claimed we could, that meant Ravyn and I would be paying three hundred Bells each.

After we got everything sorted out, Esmerelda led us to a room at the back of the shop where an impressive [Alchemy] lab was stationed. Bottles of varying shapes and sizes, tools I'd never seen before, and shelves after shelves of herbs, spices, and who knew what else lay in jars, bags, and bins.

"Damn, this is nice," I expressed out loud.

"It's pretty good," Ravyn said with a hint of irritation in her voice.

Cannoli looped elbows with Ravyn. "I think it's a beautiful lab. It's got so much more than the one on Ni Island!"

Ravyn scratched one cheek. "Yeah, I guess so."

"Please clean up when you're done." Esmerelda had a scroll and quill in her hands. I assumed she was taking note of her inventory. Her viper continued to hang around her neck, its head perched between her cleavage. "I don't want any herbs lying around, or else there will be an additional charge."

Ravyn rolled her eyes. "You and your additional charges."

"You can go somewhere else if you like." Esmerelda paused for a reaction, then bent one of the bins on the shelf forward, scribbling something down on her quill. "I will leave now. You have the lab for two hours. Let me know if you need more time." She rolled up the parchment, brushing shoulders with me on the way out.

That's a nice scent.

Esmerelda shut the door behind her, and Keke breathed a sigh of relief. "I'm glad she didn't ask about Celestia."

"Yeah, you and me both," I admitted, scratching the back of my head.

"But hey, it all worked out, right?" Cannoli said.

"Thankfully. Well," I said, cracking my knuckles, "shall we get started?"

Keke wore a wry smile. "Been a while since I did this."

Cannoli used her spare arm and hooked it around Keke's elbow next. "Do you need a refresher? Teacher Cannoli would love to assist."

Keke's cheeks reddened. "I think I still remember most of it, but I wouldn't mind a crash course."

"Of course!"

After a bit of discussion, we figured making the potions in pairs was best since there were enough tools for two brews at any time. Considering I had the least experience, I paired up with Ravyn. At first, the experience was miserable. I wondered if this was how people who entered Boot Camp felt whenever their instructor yelled at them for every tiny thing.

Eventually, though, I found a rhythm, and even she admitted I was doing a decent job. Never did she use the words 'good' or 'yes.' No, instead, I got 'acceptable' and 'sure.' It was usually a matter of being off by a point or shaking instead of stirring or forgetting that I let something boil for too long.

An hour passed. Ravyn and I worked in silence. I would periodically confirm with her if I was doing something right. Short discussion would follow, and soon the silence would return. Ravyn taught me that some chemicals and herbs made certain sounds when they were ready, so I ensured that I never spoke much higher than necessary. But the long silence bothered me a bit, so I decided to start a conversation.

"So, did you ever become an [Alchemist]?" Knowing that the catgirls could switch Classes, I wondered if Ravyn ever dabbled in something else. I never took my attention off of my work as I spoke. I'd learned that Ravyn had no tolerance for a driver who didn't watch the road while they talked.

"No. Never considered it."

Another short reply. Like the one last night. "So, uh, can you sum up what an [Alchemist] can do? If Destiny's going to be coming with us, I'd like to know what I should expect."

For a while, Ravyn didn't answer. I could hear Cannoli and Keke giggling in the background. If I listened closely, I could hear some of the details, but for the most part, it was all whispers.

"A bit of everything," she said flatly at last.

When she didn't elaborate, I pushed. "Like what?"

A deep sigh escaped through her nose. "Bombs, poisons, tinctures, things like that."

I nodded, and although I'm sure she knew what questions were coming next, I asked them anyway. "But that's what we're doing now, right? Creating tinctures? Hell, we could make some poisons and bombs right now, I'm sure. Why don't I make some of those?"

"You can, but they won't be as effective. [Alchemist]s use a special type of magic."

Finally, an answer. "Ohh, okay." I poured the violet-colored contents of a vial into another filled with a clear solution. Carefully, I shook it around nice and slow until the concoction turned to a pastel version of its previous appearance. "How does the [Alchemist] use magic?"

Ravyn set down the mortar and pestle and turned to look at me. I noticed out of the corner of my eye but maintained my focus. At least until I was done with this step of the concoction. After a few more seconds, I corked the vial and put it on the rack with the others. That was one dose down. Ravyn could tell me later if I did it right.

"Depends on the Skill they're using. [Alchemist]s use a combination of magic to call out the more potent versions of their concoctions." She looked down at the rack of vials I made and pointed at one. "Imagine if I could cast that tincture from the bottle on another person instead of drinking it. It still uses the contents, but the effects hit someone else. That's how [Alchemist] works. Loosely."

"Can they double as good healers?"

Ravyn smirked. "Some of the best."

The entire time we spoke, Ravyn seemed distant. Her answers detached. As much as I wanted to know more about the [Alchemist] Class, I decided against probing any further.

Time passed, and with a bit of luck, we managed to finish ten minutes earlier than we intended. I wiped a sheen of sweat from my forehead and exhaled.

"That's a lot tougher than it looks," I said.

"You'll get used to it," Ravyn said. "You did good, Matt. No mistakes."

"Yay! Great job, Matt!" Cannoli squealed. "My protégé has come so far!"

"You're a quick learner. How many times have you done this?" Keke winked.

I struggled to remember but leaned into the only time that came to mind. "Only once, I think. Maybe twice?" I looked at Cannoli for confirmation, thinking back to when Keke waited outside the lab. "Right?"

"Unless you've been sneaking out to make potions with Granny Nauka, I think so!"

Ravyn didn't take much time to examine Keke and Cannoli's work. The way we'd done it was split into two groups—one working on a salve and the other a tincture. The salve was meant to act as an external numbing and healing agent, while the tincture would be for any internal damage suffered. The second one was the iffy part. That would have to be ingested. All we could do was hope that the salve would be strong enough to allow the girls a moment to swallow the tincture.

"The salves are perfect," muttered Ravyn. "Perfect. Let's get the hell out of here. Sooner we're off this island, the better."

"Maybe she'll give us a discount," I quipped.

Ravyn sneered. "Don't hold your breath."

New Notifications!

Matt has gained: Two Levels of [Alchemy]!

Keke Pro Tip: It felt good to do [Alchemy] again. It's been a really long time. Thanks for inviting me, Cannoli....

Chapter 48

Bolero

The house smelled like freshly baked bread when Tristan returned. A cheerful fire lapped at fresh logs in the hearth, and Ceres descended the stairs with an empty tea tray.

"Welcome back, Tristan," she greeted warmly. "May I cook you something to eat? Procure another pot of tea, perhaps?"

Tristan shook his head. "I ate before I left. Where's Ara?"

"She is in with Lynn at the moment." Ceres closed the distance between them and lowered her voice. "I apologize if this is beyond my rank. However, is aught amiss, young master? You both seem…out of sorts."

He blinked, surprised that someone else had noticed. Ara's conversation and demeanor became short and snappy when he'd given her his reservations about her staying behind. But, in every light he cast on the situation, he realized that his reasons were selfish. Venicia— no, Shi Island needed Ara as much as they needed him.

After a brief pause, he hummed and nodded. "We'll be alright, I think."

Ceres adjusted the tray in her hands and offered him a small bow. "Forgive my asking, sir. However, please allow me to offer my services if you need someone to speak with." She smiled, a slight blush pinking her cheeks. "You do not have to face this world alone."

"I… Thank you, Ceres." Tristan felt his chest tighten. When was the last time he'd had a group of friends? *Not since kindergarten, I think.* Always the last to be picked for a team and the first one to be picked on. "Really, that means a lot."

"Of course. I will continue my cleaning duties for now. Simply call if you should need me." Ceres bowed once more.

Even though we're not going to be here much longer? He considered saying it, but the gleaming banisters and dusted hearth *were* really nice to return to. "Don't overwork yourself."

"I would not dream of such a thing." Ceres winked before returning to the kitchen.

Tristan slipped off his shoes and padded up the stairs. He counted the doors until he reached Lynn's room and entered after a gentle knock.

Ara closed the book in her lap, set it to the side, then stood straight-backed as soon as he entered the room. Like a soldier moving to attention.

"Young master," she greeted curtly.

"Ara, please. You can relax." He ran a hand through his hair. "I went to see Celestia."

Her posture tensed—she leveled her chin parallel to the floor and straightened her shoulders. The corners of her lips twitched into a frown, but she stayed silent.

"I had Felsi and Annabelle arrest her."

Ara blinked, then furrowed her brow. Her lips pursed, and her tongue poked behind her cheek. It was clear she hadn't prepared for this. "You... What?"

"They'll accompany her on the next boat to Nyarlothep. I'll draft a writ of arrest for them to bring with them. Misery and Katrin, too. The Venicia School of Etiquette is yours, Ara." Tristan crossed his arms over his chest and took a deep breath. *Don't cry. Do* not *cry.* "I'm sorry for what I said before."

Ara's features softened, and she crossed the room. With a hesitant hand, she brushed his cheek with the tip of her fingers. "Tristan. I'm sorry, too."

He swallowed against the building lump in his throat. "You were right. This is the best place for you and Lynn. Even if I—" A tear slipped from the corner of his eye, and he hurried to brush it away. *Damn it!* "Even if I'll miss you. Dearly."

"I know," she whispered.

He cupped her hand with his, memorizing her touch. The nights in Abalone seemed so far away and short-lived. Their travels together over Shi Island like a distant memory.

Stop it. This isn't forever.

But it felt like it was. Even when he returned, Ara would have to stay at the school and keep things running in Venicia. She wouldn't be able to join him on Defiled hunts, and traveling together would be limited. "Damn it," he murmured.

She slid her other hand behind his neck, gently pulling him down until their lips met.

She pressed her chest into his, eliminating the space between them. How was it possible that after hundreds of partners, her kiss still sent electric shocks through his skin? That her touch made his heart race?

"Ara," he muttered against her lips.

"Come with me." Ara twined her fingers through his, then led him out of the room. They moved down the hall to the bedroom Tristan was using as his, where she guided him inside, then closed and locked it behind her. She stroked his hand with one thumb as she stared at the handle. "There are…many things I wish to say to you that are forbidden."

Tristan waited. To press her to say them was cruel—he'd read countless tomes of Nyarlean law detailing the actions and repercussions of falling in love with a man. No matter how desperately he wanted to hear her tell him, it was just one more selfish desire in a long list of keeping Ara by his side.

She let her hand fall from the handle. "I guess the easiest way to convey it is… You aren't alone in your feelings, Tristan." Turning to face him, she rested one hand on his chest. "And if I cannot say them, then let me show you."

Before he could reply, she was tugging his shirt over his head. Tossing it aside, she gently pushed him back toward the bed. He sat down, and her mouth claimed his as she climbed into his lap, wrapping her legs around his back.

Tristan slid his hands beneath her skirt, circling his arms around her thighs and groping the taut muscles of her backside. He traced her lower lip with his tongue, and when she let him in further, he curled her tail around one hand, caressing it gently between his fingers.

Ara gasped, then moaned. She tangled one hand in his hair and used the other to draw pleasurable patterns on his bare back with her nails. Tristan shivered beneath her touch, committing every sound, taste, and sensation to memory. Even her scent was distinct—like lavender on a spring breeze.

With every twist of his wrist, her hips rocked against his hand, then forward in his lap. Even with the layers of his jeans and her panties, he could still feel the growing heat between her legs; his need for her was growing with it.

She drew away from him for the span of a few heartbeats, pulling her dress over her head and tossing it to the side. The sight of lacy black lingerie against her pale skin was enough to make him dizzy.

You've seen this a million times. And yet, the voice was silenced by his pounding heart. This was different. Ara was different.

Ara unwrapped her legs, straddling him at the thighs. "Move back," she instructed breathlessly.

Tristan nodded and shifted his weight backward so that everything but his feet was on the bed. She worked at the button of his jeans, unfastening and divesting them in seconds, following suit with his boxers. She shifted her weight to his calves, then reached behind her back and pulled her short blonde hair to the side so it fell over one shoulder. The gesture itself was simple but elegant. Just as he'd thought to comment on how stunning she looked, she leaned forward and enveloped his shaft in her mouth.

"*Ngh!*" Tristan groaned, and his thighs tensed.

She glanced up at him, eyes locking his, glittering with satisfaction while she teased him with her tongue. He'd learned during their first encounters together that she was a fast, attentive learner. Every noise that escaped him encouraged her, and if silence drew on for too long, she adjusted her machinations. His breath caught in his throat, and goosebumps peppered his legs. He rested a hand in her hair, tracing the soft outline of her ear. She leaned into his palm, humming as she descended the length of him.

Ara's mouth reached his base, and he gasped. Her throat was searing hot, tight, and soft. Her tongue danced along the base of his shaft and lapped at the veins beneath the head as if she knew every

spot that would drive him wild. His heart pounded against his chest and his eyes fought between staying on her face and rolling backward.

"That feels so good, Ara," he moaned. "God, please don't stop."

Ara chuckled, her laugh vibrating through him. She slowly raised and lowered her head, dragging her tongue along every inch that forced a gasp with each rotation. Every thought that plagued him vanished, replaced by a desperate need for release. The sight of her bent over him, her clear blue eyes flickering to his, her hair draped over her shoulder...

"I'm gonna come." It was a sudden sensory overload, and there was no way he could hold back.

Ara sped her movements, keeping a delicious pressure against his base and forcing him over the edge. Tristan's back arched, and his toes curled. She lapped and sucked at him until she'd swallowed every drop. His lips and fingers felt numb.

She sat up and licked her lips with a teasing half-smile. Sliding her underwear free, she positioned her hips over his and reached for his still-erect shaft. The soft, vulnerable skin between her thighs parted around the head of his cock, sending a new, desperate desire through his veins.

Just as she lowered her hips, the gravity of what she was about to do hit him. "W-wait. Are you sure?"

"I wouldn't want a kitten with anyone else, Tristan. I'll have plenty of help." She bent forward and nibbled his lower lip, her voice dropping to a purr. "And if you don't take me right now, I'm going to scream."

Tristan grabbed her hips and thrust into her. Their cries harmonized, ringing in Tristan's ears and echoing against the walls.

"You're really deep," Ara whimpered, her thighs trembling around his. Her head rested on his shoulder, and she giggled nervously. "I don't know if I can move."

"Then just relax," he replied.

"N-no. Let me." She slowly sat up, moaning with the new position. "*Mnnh.* I feel so full."

"You feel amazing, Ara," Tristan breathed. Every twitch and shift of her body resonated into his.

"So do you." She slowly rocked her hips, drawing as far away as she could before advancing once more. Her breathing skipped, and her face flushed.

"Take this off," Tristan said, tugging on one of the cups of her bra.

Ara paused her rhythm, reaching behind her to unhook the clasp before tossing it to the side. Tristan rested one hand on her thigh, using the other to knead her breast. She bit her lower lip, curling her tail around her lower back and resting it against his fingers on her thigh.

He smiled and took her tail into his palm, running his hand along the plush fur while teasing her hardened nipple. Her eyelids grew heavy as she resumed the deliberate thrusts of her hips.

Watching Ara's face gave Tristan more pleasure than he could say. The way she clenched and relaxed her eyes with every rotation of her hips. How she'd switch between biting her lip and gasping for breath. The thin sheen of sweat across her brow. He captured every instance like a photograph, hoping he could scrape together enough materials to draw her later.

"I'm close," Ara murmured, leaning heavier into his touch and thrusting faster against him.

"Then come," Tristan encouraged, massaging her breast and tail, trying to hold back his own quickly building climax.

"I...I'm coming!" Ara squealed between rasped breaths. Her maddening pace and the sudden clenching of her body pushed him over the edge once more, stealing his orgasm with hers. She melted forward, pressing her chest to his and wrapping her arms around his back.

Holding her thighs, he thrust through his climax. For a few perfect seconds, their heartbeats aligned. He reveled in her cries and groaned when her teeth sank into his shoulder.

When her jaw relaxed, he slowed to a halt before moving his arms to her lower back. She lifted her hips away from his, then straightened her petite form against his body. She tucked her head beneath his chin and traced the lines of his bicep with one finger.

"Tristan," Ara whispered.

"Hm?"

"You…" she paused, swallowed, then began again. "You will return for me, won't you?"

Tristan kissed the top of her head and tightened his embrace. "I'll always come back for you."

"Good." She nodded and sighed, snuggling against his chest. "Good."

Ara Pro Tip: I will do my best to return this school to its former ideals. And…I'll be waiting for your return, Tristan.

Side Quest

Yomi's Nightmare

Yomi's symptoms were growing worse in intensity and frequency. Splitting headaches that made even soft candlelight awful to look at. Back and leg pain rendered her immobile. And every time she ate, no matter how small the meal, she felt as if she'd throw it up—oftentimes, she did.

I can't do this alone.

She was well aware of the nurseries set in place for pregnant catgirls. [Priest]s and nyannies worked side by side to care for expecting women. Then, once the kitten was born, they trained mothers who decided to personally raise their offspring on best practices for newborns. Otherwise, they found a communal house accepting new tenants to tend to the child.

Do I deserve that kind of care?

But every day that passed grew worse. Each morning it was harder to get out of bed. The overwhelming pain and nausea paralyzed her in place. She knew if she didn't seek help, it wouldn't just be her life she'd compromised. Ruyah deserved better.

Another sunrise dragged into purple dusk. Yomi forced herself from the bed, sweat coating her skin and weighing heavily in her thin nightgown. With one trembling finger, she drew a violet oval in the air, closing the warp with her intent. She remembered visiting a nursery in Nyarlothep with Finn and Ravyn many years before. Her spell would deliver her straight to it as long it was still there. She rasped a shaking breath and stepped through.

To her relief, the portal gave way to a well-lit doorway. Aromas of fresh bread and hot soup wafted through the windows, accompanied by cordial conversation and heartfelt laughter. Yomi knocked, teetering on quaking knees.

A [Priest] in pink and white garb answered the door with a kind smile. Gentle laugh lines creased the corners of her eyes and lips. A mane of silver hair was swept back into a braid trailing down her back, and her warm brown eyes peered into the night. When she spotted Yomi, her smile evaporated, replaced by deep, furrowed brows of concern.

"Oh, goodness. My poor, sweet girl. Come in," the [Priest] crooned, stepping forward to take Yomi's arm and steady her. "Jesna, prepare an emergency bed and call for the [Hermetic] immediately."

"Y-yes! Right away, Miss Miral!" A young nyanny in a modest brown dress stood from her meal and vanished from the room.

"What is your name, love?" Miral asked gently, slowly guiding Yomi through a long hallway.

They passed multiple curtained-off rooms on either side. Through the tiny gaps, Yomi noted catgirls sleeping peacefully or resting comfortably with a book. Some rooms had bassinets near the beds with a nyanny attendant standing close by. "It's Yomi, ma'am."

"Please, call me Miral." Miral touched her hand to Yomi's forehead, her eyes widening. "What symptoms are you experiencing, child?"

"Everything...Everything hurts," Yomi admitted, tears leaking from the corners of her eyes. "My back, my legs, my arms. It's hard to breathe and—" she paused for another shallow breath. "I can't eat without throwing it back up."

"How long have you felt this way?" Miral led them into an identical room to the others. She stepped away from Yomi momentarily to light the oil lamp on the wall, then returned to help her toward the bed.

The blankets on the bed were freshly cleaned and pressed, and a bouquet of yellow flowers bloomed from the side table. A short wooden table with multiple drawers was positioned opposite the bed. An empty bowl, folded cloth, and metal tools that Yomi didn't recognize were neatly lined along the top.

"I-I don't know. At least a week." Yomi let the tears fall free. *I'm so stupid.* "I lost track of time."

"Oh, sweet. Everything will be alright. We will take care of you." Miral ensured Yomi was situated in bed before drawing the curtain at the door. "You've come to the right place."

"Will my...my kitten make it?" Yomi asked between sobs.

Miral returned to Yomi's side, pulling the blankets up to her chest and tucking them around her sides. "I'm certain you and your daughter will be fine. For now, we shall make you as comfortable as possible until—"

There was a knock on the outer wall before a young woman with pale violet hair poked her head around the curtain. Large white feathers dangled from tiny hoops on each of her ears. "Miss Miral? You called for me?"

"Latali! Praise Saoirse for your excellent timing. Come in. Please." Miral brushed the damp strands of Yomi's hair away from her face. "Yomi urgently requires your assistance."

"I was on my way here to check on the others." Latali entered the room with a grin, making sure to readjust the curtain to offer them privacy. Her hair hung all the way down to her hips, and her attire was unlike any Yomi had ever seen before. She wore a deep green top that cut just beneath the bust and an ankle-length skirt that appeared hand woven, bedecked with geometric shapes and angled lines. Strappy sandals wrapped around her calves and feet, offering little protection from the elements. A tattoo of a flowering vine that began at her cheek curved around her throat and shoulder, lining her waist until it vanished beneath her skirt. "It's nice to meet you, Yomi. I'm Latali, a [Hermetic]."

"Hello," Yomi said meekly.

"It's my job to keep you out of pain and help Miss Miral get you on the mend." Latali crossed the room and set her sizeable [Cat Pack] on the floor next to Yomi's bed. After touching her forehead and a brief physical inspection, Latali folded her hands against her skirt and asked, "Can you tell me what symptoms you've experienced the last few days?"

Yomi relayed every ailment and symptom she'd felt for the previous week while Latali listened intently and slowly nodded. Miral stood at the foot of the bed, watching the exchange with more worry in her eyes than Yomi wanted to see. *Am I really going to be okay?*

"Alright. I'll be blunt. You're not in a good way, Miss Yomi. But I think you got here in time," Latali said once Yomi had finished. "I'm going to give you two tinctures tonight. One will ease the pain and help you rest. The other will begin to fight the infection. The latter of the two can have powerful side effects. Nightmares, hallucinations, sudden shifts in mood. We'll have Jesna stay in your room, and Miss Miral will be close by. We've had great success with this combination of tinctures before, so you should sleep soundly."

A new wave of chills crept up beneath Yomi's fever. She shivered. "Okay."

Miral gently patted Yomi's feet beneath the blanket. "We will take excellent care of you, sweet. You have nothing to worry about."

Latali knelt and opened her pack, procuring two glass bottles. One contained a foggy blue liquid as if she'd bottled the sky, and the other was a brilliant silver. She chuckled as she stood. "They don't taste great, but I need you to drink all of them."

Yomi nodded and accepted the first bottle from Latali—the sky blue one. She pinched her nose—a trick Finn had taught her—and drained it in four gulps. Despite looking pleasant enough, the potion burned her tongue and throat like a bottle of fire. Violent coughs racked her chest when she was through, and Latali swapped the empty container for the silver bottle.

"This one's easier. Promise," she assured, uncorking it for her. "It'll stop the burning."

The flames were quenched by cool, bitter liquid as soon as the silver tincture reached her tongue. It was thick and difficult to swallow, but Yomi was eager to stop the pain.

"There you go. You should be feeling that one pretty quick." Latali took the bottle from Yomi and placed both in her pack. "I'll be crafting custom tinctures for you over the next few days based on your progress. Depending on how tonight goes, we'll see what strength of potion you need." She snapped her bag shut and swung the strap over her shoulder. "I'm sorry to pour and run, but there are a few more patients expecting me tonight, and I have one more nursery to drop by."

"Thank you, Latali," Yomi whispered. The draught was already taking effect, slowing her tongue, and numbing the pain in her joints. For the first time in weeks, the aching in her back and legs eased. The soft blankets caressed her skin and promised a full night's sleep.

"Yes, thank you so much, Miss Latali. We shall expect you in the morning?" Miral asked. Her voice sounded more distant with every word she spoke.

"Bright and early!" Latali smiled, her tail twitching happily behind her. "Hang in there, Yomi. We'll do everything we can."

"Just...just save Ruyah," Yomi muttered, not sure if she'd enunciated any part of her words. "Please."

"Of course, Yomi. Get some sleep. I'll send Jesna here at once."

Before the lamp was extinguished, Yomi had fallen asleep.

"This is amazing!" Finn's green eyes glittered with excitement as they moved through the nursery. "It's just like a hospital. Better than a hospital. Why don't none of the nurseries on San look like this?"

Ravyn shrugged. "The economy went to shit a long time ago, and trying to get help from Nyarlothep is a joke."

"The island should be able to fund itself," Yomi argued. "That's part of our job as its protectors."

"*Our* job, huh?" Finn grinned, and Yomi's heart skipped.

"I-I don't want you to feel like you're in this alone." She blushed and fingered the silver pendant at her throat. "You'll always have us."

"Then we should work together to fix the nurseries on San," Finn proclaimed. "I don't think they have a designated [Hermetic] there. I could work on that! I just hit [Alchemist], after all."

Finn's excitement was contagious. "I'd love for my kitten to grow up in a place like this," Yomi agreed.

His expression suddenly darkened. The sweet smile he reserved for Ravyn and Yomi disappeared, replaced by a malicious sneer.

The excited gaze turned to ice, and venom dripped from his words. "You? A kitten? After what you did?"

Ravyn laughed beneath her breath, crossing her arms over her chest and sharing the same disgusted aspect. "*No one* wants a kitten with a rapist."

A cold sweat broke over her skin. Blood seeped from the nursery walls, and flames licked at the edges of the curtains. "N-no, I didn't mean to—"

"Didn't mean to? You hypnotized him, you stupid bitch," Ravyn cackled. "It wasn't an accident."

Yomi fell to her knees. Heavy shackles bound her wrists and ankles while the chimes of bells rang in her ears. "Please, I just—"

Finn stepped forward and snatched her chin, forcing her to look up at him. Pure, unbridled hatred burned in his gaze. He spat in her face. "When will you stop making excuses, Yomi?"

Tears streaked her cheeks. The shackles grew heavier. The blood on the wall thicker. "I'm so sorry. I'm so, so sorry."

"You're pathetic," Finn snarled, throwing her face to the side and stepping backward.

"Worry not, young ones. There is still a place suited for her." Belial's deep baritone voice sounded from behind her. "An eternity where she can never harm another person."

A hundred blood-soaked arms shot from the walls, wielding swords, daggers, and scythes. All manner of sharp implements were aimed at Yomi.

Finn held up a hand, and the arms paused. "But first, we should carve her kitten free."

Yomi screamed.

"**Yomi! Yomi, it's Jesna!** Please wake up!" Jesna held Yomi's shoulder down with one hand and a cool cloth to her forehead with the other. "You're safe. I promise you're safe."

Yomi forced her eyes open, the dim oil lamp light seeping through her heavy lids. She was trembling uncontrollably with her knees curled up beneath her stomach. Her throat was hoarse as if she'd screamed it dry, and the blankets were drenched.

"I'm sorry," Yomi whimpered through tears. "Matt, I'm so sorry."

Jesna threw the covers back, her eyes widening. She grabbed a small bell from behind the flower vase and rang it vigorously. "Miss Miral! Miss Miral, come quickly. Her water broke!"

Yomi Pro Tip: Finn...how do I fix this?

Chapter 49
Le Ballet du Guérisseur

I was starving by the time we'd finished up the potions, but I understood that we were pretty strapped for time. It was getting close to lunch, and one of the market stalls had fruit and cheese for purchase. So we loaded up on nyapples, a loaf of bread, and a white block that looked like swiss cheese before we went to find our horses. It'd be weird to cut chunks off during the ride, but I could manage. Or I could just eat the whole damn thing, whatever was easier.

Since we'd left so early, we were back just as the sun reached the middle of the sky. It was a quiet trip, punctuated by awkwardly trading around the bread and cheese without running into one another. At one point, I thought Ravyn was going to fall off her horse trying to hand Cannoli her utility knife, and I laughed until she chucked her nyapple core at my head.

Regardless, the journey had lightened all of our spirits, I think. We were one step closer to reviving the girls and getting the hell off of Shi Island.

A grinning Ceres met us at the door, and she curtsied before gesturing for us to come inside.

"What's so funny?" Ravyn asked.

"Oh, it is not amusement I feel," Ceres replied softly. "You shall see."

When we entered the common room, Cannoli's ears perked, and she covered her mouth. I followed where she was staring and found Tristan lounging on the sofa, Ara sound asleep with her head in his lap. He was reading a book with one hand while stroking her hair with the other. When he looked up, he smiled sheepishly and set the book aside.

"She dozed off while I was reading to her," Tristan murmured.

"Must have been a boring book," Ravyn quipped.

Keke nudged Ravyn with her elbow, but I caught the mischievous grin tugging at the corner of Keke's lips.

"That's so sweet," Cannoli squeaked beneath her hand. "I don't think she slept a wink last night."

"She definitely deserves some rest. There's... there's a rough road waiting for her." Tristan sighed.

"Does that mean you've made a decision?" Keke asked.

Tristan nodded. "Ara will stay here and lead Venicia."

"It is a wise decision, if I may add," Ceres said, moving to stand beside Cannoli. "Ara is a capable leader and knows well the plight of our land."

"Yeah," Tristan murmured, glancing down at Ara's steadily breathing form.

"What happens to Celestia?" I asked.

"She'll be escorted and tried in Nyarlothep. Likely they'll execute her," Tristan replied carefully. "I don't want this island to see me as its executioner."

I nodded. "You'll have to tell me how that works."

"Sure thing. We'll have plenty of time for it." He chewed his lip and shook his head. "Anyway. How was your trip?"

"It went great. We have everything ready to go," I said. We could talk more about Ara's staying back later. I couldn't imagine how difficult it had been for Tristan to agree.

"We can start waking them up as soon as you're ready." Cannoli toyed at a section of her hair. "Assuming you wish to be present, anyway."

"Is there anything I can really do to help?" Tristan asked.

"Honestly, just talk to them while they wake up. Familiar faces and pretty words can go a long way in reducing shock," Ravyn explained. "Matt and I should probably stay out of sight when they start waking up."

I frowned. "Why's that?"

"Who were the last two people Destiny, Lara, and Lynn saw before we used the scrolls, hm?" Ravyn scoffed. "They've been tortured for weeks because of what we've done."

"You can't blame yourselves for this—" Tristan began.

Ravyn held up a hand. "Blame has nothing to do with this. We'll have time to explain *after* these girls are awake. Got it?"

My stomach sank. She was right. "Yeah. Got it."

"Should we wake them up one at a time or all at once?" Keke asked.

"I believe one at a time would be best. This way, we have all hands available should we need them," Ceres answered.

Cannoli nodded. "Agreed. The more options we have should something go wrong, the better."

Tristan rubbed his face with both hands and took a deep breath. After a few seconds, he exhaled and looked back at us. "Let's get started then."

"Mm. Tristan, don't stop petting me," Ara murmured, then giggled. "It feels so nice."

Keke snickered, and Cannoli squeaked behind a deep blush. Ceres smiled knowingly while Ravyn groaned and rolled her eyes.

I cleared my throat, and Ara's eyes snapped open. She pushed herself to sitting and quickly brushed her fingers through her hair.

"O-oh! You're back." Ara coughed and smoothed her skirts. "Excuse me. I must have lost track of time." Her face turned a deep red, and she slowly rose to her feet. "So, erm, do you have the potions?"

Ravyn crossed her arms over her chest. "We do."

"Wonderful. Can we proceed?" Ara didn't wait for an answer. Instead, she pushed between Keke and me, making her way to the staircase.

"She's so cute," Cannoli whispered.

"She really is." Tristan chuckled beneath his breath as he watched her quickly ascend the stairs. There was a lot he wasn't saying behind that stare. But I had to give him points for holding it together. He shook his head and stood, rubbing his hands on his jeans. "Well, let's start with Lynn, then?"

"As you wish." Ceres nodded and followed Ara to the staircase.

Ravyn caught my sleeve and held me back once Keke and Cannoli had gone. Her eyes were cold, and her lips formed a small, hard line.

"What's up?" I asked.

"This won't be pretty, Matt," she whispered. "No matter what happens, you need to trust us."

"I do trust you," I replied, if a little incredulously.

Her frown deepened. "I'm serious. Complete trust. Without question. If Ceres or I tell you to jump off the roof, you do it. Understood?"

The tight knots in my stomach returned, but I nodded. "Yes. I promise."

"Alright." Without another word, she accompanied the others to Lynn's room. I gathered my thoughts and did the same.

Keke and I stood in the doorway, out of the way from the three working on Lynn. Cannoli and Ravyn flanked Lynn's bed while Ceres drew back the curtains, spreading more light into the dim room. Tristan and Ara stood in the far corner, Ara's trembling hand entwined with his. Keke glanced at Tristan and Ara, then slid her hand into mine.

"It'll be okay," Keke murmured, squeezing my hand.

"I hope so."

"First, we'll start with the salve." Cannoli set her [Cat Pack] on the bed next to Lynn, fishing out one clay jar of ointment and one glass bottle of the violet potion. She twisted the cap free and lathered her hands with the balm before passing it to Ravyn. "We should apply it everywhere we can since we don't know where she's hurt."

Ravyn accepted the container and coated her palms. "This smells really strong," she noted.

Cannoli nodded. "Keke and I doubled the intensity. She knew a heating trick that upped the potency without using more ingredients." She smiled as she gingerly applied it to Lynn's arm. "She's a lot better at [Alchemy] than she says."

Keke grumbled, "I'm standing right here."

Ceres took the jar after Ravyn and started on Lynn's leg. "I wish to learn more of this art from the three of you. If you are open to teaching me, of course."

"I would love to!" Cannoli replied. "I can show you around Granny Nauka's lab, and we can make potions together! Ravyn even knows how to—"

"Cannoli. Focus," Ravyn chided gently.

"O-oh! Right. Sorry." Cannoli chewed her lower lip and set back to work.

There were hushed affirmations between the three girls as they continued to cover Lynn in the numbing agent. I hadn't realized how tightly I was squeezing Keke's hand until she glanced up at me and touched her head to my shoulder.

"That should be good. Let's start feeding her the potion," Cannoli said.

Ceres gently slid one arm beneath Lynn's neck, supporting her head as she lifted her up from the bed. Cannoli parted Lynn's lips and tilted the purple brew into her mouth. Ceres tipped her chin upward, and they poured a slow, measured stream down Lynn's throat.

"Start the spell, Ravyn," Cannoli instructed.

"[Disenchant]," Ravyn whispered, holding her hand against Lynn's forehead. A warm, white aura surrounded her hand, and she closed her eyes.

I counted ten heartbeats before Cannoli said, "Alright, that's about all we can give her until she's awake." She drew the bottle away and set it on the table beside the bed.

Ceres held Lynn steady, and Ravyn continued casting. Five more seconds passed, and the glow disappeared.

A soft groan hummed from Lynn's lips.

"That's our cue, Matt." Ravyn stepped away from the bed and tugged my shirt. "Further back, boy."

Keke, Ravyn, and I moved outside of the room, watching the procedure through the open door. Ara and Tristan stepped forward, standing beside Ceres and opposite Cannoli. I could still see slivers of what was happening between their bodies, and I held my breath.

Lynn's groaning escalated into panicked whimpers.

Ara reached for her hand. "Lynn. Lynn, it's me, Ara. I'm right here."

"No...*No!*" Lynn cried. "Please! Not again!"

"I'm right here, love. You're safe," Ara continued, dropping to her knees.

"I don't know anything!" Lynn mewled, sobs wracking her chest. "I-I told you! I don't— I don't!" Then she screamed.

Keke huddled closer to me and grabbed my arm. Ara and Tristan repeated soft words and kind phrases. Ceres and Cannoli held Lynn at the shoulders while she writhed in pain. *She's feeling everything all at once.* Every renewed howl sounded as if we were witnessing the beatings in real time.

Hell wasn't deep enough for what Celestia deserved.

"Lynn, sweet, I need you to drink this. Please," Cannoli said, reaching for the bottle on the table. "It'll help. I promise you."

Ceres helped stabilize Lynn as Cannoli put the potion to her lips again, forcing her to drink it between sobs.

The cries sank to desperate whimpers and violent coughing. Lynn blinked wildly, her hands writhing beside her. Violent coughs wracked her throat, and her breathing sped to shallow gasps.

"She's going into shock," Ravyn murmured. "Cannoli, you have to calm her down."

"I'm trying my best," Cannoli replied, her face maintaining the same concentrated disposition of a surgeon. "Lynn, everything's alright."

Tears streaked Ara's face and she touched her forehead to Lynn's hand. She stole a shuddering breath, then started to sing. *"Dry your tears, my precious one, 'tis only shadows o'er the sun. Feel the warmth upon your face and recognize its sweet embrace."*

The rapid rising and falling of Lynn's chest gradually slowed, and her eyes became focused.

"See the flowers in the trees, scent their petals on the breeze," Ara continued. *"And if e'er you find yourself afraid—"*

"—Look 'round at our world that Saoirse's made," Lynn whispered in harmony. "A...Ara?"

Ara bit her lip and nodded. "I'm here, Lynn. I'm right here." She laughed with relief before she was overcome once more with emotion.

"Welcome back, Lynn," Tristan murmured, brushing long strands of damp hair from her face.

Keke buried her head against my arm, her tears soaking my sleeve.

Ravyn looked up at me, tinges of anxiety still evident in her features. She set her jaw, then smacked her lips. "One down."

Cannoli Pro Tip: Lynn is through the worst of it. She'll still need plenty of time to heal, and I'm so glad Ara will be with her.

Chapter 50

Where No Carnation Fades

The remainder of the afternoon was harrowing. Once Lynn had settled, we tended to Destiny and Lara immediately afterward. They similarly screamed and flailed as if an invisible force was tormenting them. Thankfully, their plights weren't as desperate as Lynn's, and the fear of going into shock didn't come up again. In the meantime, we offered kind words, nurturing hands, and some light soups to get some of their strength back when it was over.

Ravyn had assured us that we'd done all we could, but the periodic fits of whining, crying, and screaming had me wishing there was more we could do. She explained that the girls' perception of time may be warped, and it would take a few days to work itself out. For the life of me, I couldn't understand how Celestia could treat people like this and still maintain her composure. There was no excuse for the way she acted. I ground my teeth any time I thought about her.

At first, Destiny, Lara, nor Lynn could speak in complete sentences, which was jarring, to say the least. Ara spent the majority of her time at Lynn's side but took breaks to accompany Ravyn, Cannoli, and Tristan on their half-hour rounds to check in on the girls. She and Tristan were tight-lipped for a good part of the day. Sometimes I'd catch Tristan staring wistfully out of a window, pacing the kitchen, biting his nails. All questions I tossed to him were answered with very few words, and he seemed stuck inside his own head. I didn't want to bother him. He had me worried.

It was hard to fall asleep that night, even with Keke by my side. Even when I did, it was shrouded by nightmares.

To my relief, I was greeted by Cannoli's cheery smile when Keke and I left the room the next morning.

"Matt, Keke!" Cannoli had deep bags under her eyes, but the light in them said she was too excited to care.

"What's up?" I asked.

"The girls are talking! They can speak again with coherence!"

Keke and I exchanged looks before I breathed a heavy sigh. "That's great to hear."

"Come on, come on! Ara's talking to Lynn right now!" Cannoli snatched up our wrists before we had a chance to protest, then led us to Lynn's room.

Cannoli stopped in front of the door, knocked, then put a hand to her ear. "Come in," came Ara's voice.

"Hold on," I said as I put a hand on Cannoli's shoulder. "Should I really go in there right now? What if she freaks out?"

Cannoli shook her head. "Lynn understands what happened—Ravyn's talking to her right now. Besides, I got permission from Ara herself!"

Keke seemed as uncomfortable as I was about it.

"Well, if you're sure," I said, running a hand through my hair.

Cannoli gave one of her trademark nods of approval, then pushed the door open. "We're here," she hummed.

Ara and Tristan were sitting on the left of Lynn's bedside, while Ravyn and Ceres had the side opposite. Lynn was propped up by a handful of pillows, her hair in two braids over her shoulders. She turned her head to see us, albeit slowly, blinked twice, then offered a slight bow.

"Please, you don't have to move. How are you feeling?" I asked.

Lynn's eyes went wide. "The other man who was staying here." Her voice cracked, and she coughed into her fist. She held a small cup of tea in her spare hand while Ara rubbed her back. "Y-you *are* the one Celestia was looking for."

"I'm very sorry," I said immediately. I know I couldn't take full responsibility, but I couldn't deny that a big part of why this happened to her was because of us. The least I could do was apologize.

"Matt," I heard Keke whisper.

"I'm sure you've had the situation explained to you already, but I feel you deserve at least that much." I was struggling to make eye contact with her. It was one thing to see her asleep or hear her writhing in pain as she woke up. But it was an entirely different thing to look directly at her while she was conscious. The gravity of the situation weighed heavy on my chest, and if this was even half of what Tristan was feeling, then I could suck it up and give her the respect she deserved.

Lynn's lips formed a straight line. "I understand that Celestia has been replaced."

Ara nodded. "Yes, sister." She took one of Lynn's hands in her own. "I will see to it that what Celestia did never occurs here again. You have my word."

"And mine," murmured Tristan. "I will play my part here. Celestia will see justice by the hands of the Queen."

"I see," said Lynn.

An uncomfortable silence swept the room for a while. My toes began to squirm, so I thought to ask about the other girls. "How're Destiny and Lara doing?"

"They're awake," Ravyn said with crossed arms. "They're coherent for the most part, but we'll still need to watch over them for a couple of days."

"Alright."

My situation felt awkward, out of place. Much of what was happening was outside my jurisdiction. Unless it had any direct effect on my Party, then this was really none of my business. Even so, I wanted Tristan and Ara to know we'd be here if they needed anything. There was no reason for them to shoulder this burden alone.

"If there's anything I can do to help, just let me know," I said. "Anything at all."

"Thanks, Matt." Tristan finally smiled, but that was the end of it.

The next couple of days continued to improve. Cannoli, Ravyn, and Ceres could get more sleep than before, and the color in the girls' skin was starting to come back. Ravyn and I stayed out of sight for the most part. Lynn's mannerisms reminded me a lot of Cannoli in some ways now that I wasn't on guard—exceptionally understanding, kind, and soft-spoken. All the more reason why Ravyn and I stayed out of sight most of the time. Even if she wasn't about to admit it, we got the feeling that we were making her uncomfortable.

Destiny and Lara were about the same. From what Tristan and Ara told us, they were still a bit uneasy about us. Understandable, seeing as we'd drugged them and left them at the mercy of Celestia. Just an apology wasn't going to get me very far. But there wasn't much for us to do until they were back to full health, so Keke, Ravyn, and I spent some time wandering the town.

Tristan, Ara, and Ceres spent a lot of the hours while the girls were sleeping to try and ease the tension in the town, expressing that the Defiled threat was a false alarm. From what I heard, Tristan and Ara were completely upfront about the situation. Some girls expressed disdain for her departure, but their tune changed when the circumstances behind her expulsion were explained. Gradually, the curtains and shops opened, and girls filled the streets. It was good to hear the hum of conversation again.

A few days had passed before Lynn, Destiny, and Lara came downstairs in freshly laundered maid uniforms. They wore bright smiles, and Destiny was on the verge of tears.

"I-I can't thank you enough," said Destiny.

"Thank you for coming back for us," said Lara.

Both of the girls curtsied.

Can take the girls away from Shi Island but can't take Shi Island away from the girls.

Ravyn stared blankly, then clicked her tongue. "We had to set things right. *Mou ii.*"

Tristan beamed. "It's as she says. I speak for myself, but I know Ara and everyone else here feel the same way. Something had to be done about Celestia. About Shi Island. I'm so sorry that I didn't realize how bad things were on the island sooner."

"*Eheheh.*" Destiny waved her hands through the air and shook her head. "I-It's nothing you did wrong. W-we believed in Celestia."

"I didn't," Lara said, one brow furrowed. "I won't lie. I fantasized about trapping her in a gaol of rock and letting her starve." She stood her ground when she got wide-eyed looks from everyone except her sister. "Those daydreams kept me going through the day."

I admit it was nice to see one of them speaking so frankly.

Destiny clasped her hands in front of her. "We were never proper maids."

"You were always proper maids," Tristan corrected with his lips pursed and his brow furrowed. "It's Celestia's loss that she never saw that. I don't want her indoctrination to poison your mind, Destiny." He looked at Lara. "You either, Lara. I want each of you to be your own person. Please."

A soft smile tugged at Destiny's lips. "Thank you, Tristan."

Lara put a hand to her mouth. "You address him by name."

"A-ah! Slip of the tongue! Haha!" Destiny's face went beet red. "Guess he's just bringing out the most natural parts of me!"

The late-night visits die hard, I see.

Lynn put the tips of her fingers to her lips and smiled knowingly. "Oh, my."

Ara cleared her throat, and the room quieted. "I think it would be best if we discussed what occurs from here."

"Are you coming with us?" Cannoli asked, grabbing hold of Lynn's hands.

Lynn shook her head. "I will remain here with my sister. However," Lynn gestured to Destiny and Lara, "these two have agreed to accompany you."

"Assuming you're okay with a pair from Leche," said Lara.

"Your origin doesn't dictate your importance," Tristan said. "I would love your company."

"You're an [Alchemist] and a [Conjurer], right?" I asked, despite knowing the answer.

Destiny and Lara nodded enthusiastically, then mirrored each other with matching peace signs across their faces as if on cue. "The [Alchemist] and [Conjurer] duo, at your service!" they said in unison.

Lynn giggled. "It's been a while since I've seen that. I'm glad to see you're back to your old selves."

"Mostly," Lara said in a barely audible mutter as she stared to one side. "N-not my idea."

"We learned it from Tr—err, the young master!" said Destiny. "He said that girls in his old world did this sorta thing all the time at his school!"

You sly devil.

A pink hue decorated Tristan's cheeks, and Ara raised a brow. "Is that so?"

"Hey, Ara, it's not really *that* important," Tristan said. "It was, uh, a long time ago."

Then, Ara swung her hips to the side, imitating the same peace sign across her face we saw moments earlier. "[Rogue] Ara! At your service!" There was a pause as she held the position. Her face distorted to all sorts of expressions I'd never seen before.

Keke covered her mouth and began to snicker.

Ara drew a deep breath, then straightened her back. "Perhaps I will leave such actions to those more capable than I."

"That was really cute, Ara," Lynn said, giggling.

The room filled with laughter. I would've never thought that Ara would become such a household name for our group. It felt wrong to leave her here on the island while Tristan departed. But such was the duty of a man from Nyarlea.

Destiny and Lara were sure to make great companions. With Tristan and our Party's help, I was convinced we could move mountains.

I was sure that time and the vast deserts of Ichi would put us all to the test.

To Be Continued...

Special Thanks

It takes so many hands to build a project like this one.

An enormous thank you to Catherine LaCroix for editing and formatting this book. Cat and her husband, R. A. Hollatz also stream as Ravyn and Matt on Twitch as ravynthecave.

Thank you Maon, my merchandise artist. Without you, the world of Nyarlea would be so much less colorful. Another enormous thank you to Kiora, the designer and creator of the pixel art and the menu interfaces. Thanks GBSartworks for the stunning cover, Racknar Teyssier for the gorgeous title logo, and Comt216 for the phenomenal illustrations inside. Also, thanks to Lienae2day for the Ai chibi.

Thank you to my beta readers, Shneekey, Alex Voigt, Sky, Queen Toast, Stefani, King Jerkera, Michael, Sir Galahad II, Jack, and Stan Hutchings for helping me polish this paperback to the best it can be.

To my Patrons, it's thanks to you that I've been able to continue this ride for two years.

And thank you, dear reader. I hope you enjoyed the story and I look forward to reading your review on Amazon. No matter what brought you here, your support means the world to me.

See you soon,

DoubleBlind

Everyone's a Catgirl! [Volume Four] Preview

Releasing 2024
Pre-Order Now on Amazon

Chapter 1

Rhododendrons and Heather

Leaving Shi Island was bittersweet. Tristan and Ara must've shared at least half a dozen farewells and promises before we finally departed, and I am proud to say I remained silent the entire time. I wasn't about to get in their way and ruin the moment. Ara had her work cut out for her, to be sure. Between her, Lynn, and many of the other capable catgirls on the island, I was confident that Tristan would return to an island he'd be proud of.

Portia snaked across the crowded sloop, grumbling and muttering curses that closely resembled the ones I'd hear out of the mouths of sailors back in my old world. She'd gone above and beyond the call of duty, and I made sure I thanked her for all the work she did. I'd have to make it up to her later.

From the moment we left until the dock was finally out of sight, Ara and Lynn never moved. Tristan watched them the entire time, and I pretended not to notice. I couldn't imagine the thoughts going through Tristan's head, and I didn't try to. Instead, I figured it was best to look at the future and not dwell on what could have been or what we could've done better. What was done was done, and we still had one more man to collect. For better or worse.

"Do we need to pick up anything for either of you?" I asked, passing glances between the twins.

Destiny put a finger to her lips. "I think I got everything I need in my [Cat Pack]."

"You'd better," Ravyn said with a raised brow. "[Alchemist]s are an expensive Class." She shifted the weight from one curvy leg to the other. "You're not going to run out in the middle of a fight, are you?"

Destiny blinked. "Well, we certainly won't be fighting all that much."

Uh oh. She's making some dangerous assumptions there.

"Even if that may or may not be the case," Keke said with her beautiful back turned to us, "we want to make sure we're prepared. Cannoli, Matt, Ravyn, and I are all experienced with [Alchemy]."

"Some of us more than others," Ravyn commented.

Keke glared over her shoulder, then turned back to the rope she was fastening. "It's good, Portia!"

"Thanks a ton! The wind is rough today!" Portia called.

"Wind's in a bit of a mood, I believe," Lara said.

Well, that was a weird comment to make.

"Oh! And Destiny is a great [Alchemist]," Lara continued excitedly. "She helps people all the time!"

To be honest, I had my doubts. Though I struggled to remember the exact details, I was pretty sure I remembered them being somewhat despondent when it came to their maidly duties. Then again, perhaps my mere presence was the main culprit for how they reacted. Celestia did have a strong collar on these girls, it seemed.

"Okay, so then you're fine. But I do have to warn you, we've seen a good share of Encroachers and Defiled, so I just wanted to make sure you're prepared. We can always go and collect materials," I said.

"Oh, I, uh, I couldn't ask you to do that," Destiny said as she played with a lock of her hair.

Tristan parted the girls, seating himself between them. "Did I miss anything?"

I shook my head. "Not at all. We're just making sure we're all prepared. How are you holding up?"

Tristan took a few seconds to reply. "I'm doing okay. I trust Ara with my life, and I think she'll do a great job. I'm sad I can't be there to help her, but...from what you've told me, I can see the reason in assembling the men." He reached for my hand. "I want to thank you for helping me see what was really going on, and at the same time, I want to offer any assistance that I can. We shouldn't be struggling alone."

I reciprocated without a second thought. "I'm with you, man."

We shared a smile, and I caught Ravyn rolling her eyes within my peripheral vision. When our hands parted, I looked at Lara. "So how does [Conjurer] work?"

Lara tilted her head. "Meaning?"

Tristan laughed. "I'm quite curious myself. I'm still delving into the magical arts, so I'd like to get to know both of you a little more." Perhaps it was just my imagination, but I was sure he shot a look in Destiny's direction at the end. "Think you could help me out?"

Lara blinked. Her eyes wandered for some time like she was thinking about it. "[Conjurer] is good at three Elements. Water, Wind, and Earth."

"Oh, so you summon nature?" asked Tristan.

"Uh, sorta? More like, I plead with it and ask for help, and then I hope it listens. Like a kitten, really."

How awfully honest of you. I hope Mother Nature doesn't frown upon your word choice.

I gawked and inched closer. I caught a gentle whisper from behind me and made room for Cannoli. She sat down beside me and listened in.

"So, what do you mean exactly? I haven't touched any magic-related Classes, so I'm still learning." I heard Ravyn snicker, and I shot her a glare.

"Erm, I'm having a hard time finding a way to explain this." Lara scratched her ear and bowed her head. "Let's see, it's kind of like riding a bike. You can't really explain it to someone, but when you do it, it just makes sense."

Silence fell upon us. The calm wind blew through our hair, and a salty smell entered my nostrils. Lara's explanation made no sense whatsoever. Considering it might just be a modern perspective of mine, I looked at Keke, Ravyn, then turned around to look at Cannoli beside me. Each of them wore bewildered stares.

"I am unsure what you mean by that," Ceres admitted a few feet from behind me. She'd been standing next to Portia the entire time, and I assumed she heard in on the conversation. "Could you please elaborate?"

Lara thought again, taking her time to respond. "So, like, if I start talking to Wind, or Earth, or Water, I ask them for favors. If they like me, then they do stuff for me."

I opened my mouth to speak but quickly shut it. Each time Lara spoke, I found myself more confused. "You…talk to the land?"

Destiny nodded. "Yeah. When they're on good terms, the Elements respond, and then they'll do her favors." She shrugged. "I have no idea how it works. I understand potions and tonics much better. But it's true!" She elbowed her sister playfully. "Show 'em, sis!"

"The Elements are kind of shy, though. I'm not sure any of them will listen to me right now," Lara admitted.

"Oh, go on! Give it a try!"

Lara turned her head to the never-ending ocean. "Okay, I'll try." She put her left palm out toward the sea. "Water, can I ask for your help for a bit?" A pause followed. "I know, but I have some new people with me, as you can see… right, no, I know that, but I… uh huh. Okay? But I might have to fight." Lara's frown deepened. "I know, but Earth isn't around right now. I'm out in the middle of the ocean, so I'm asking you." Lara sighed. "I understand. Will you come when I need you in a fight? Yeah, but… okay. But if they need healing, and I mean some strong healing, I can depend on you, right?" Lara's shoulders slumped. "I'll ask Wind, then."

I'm not sure how familiar Tristan was with Lara, but based on what I'd seen, I was beginning to have second thoughts about taking her with us. Was this a typical trait for all [Conjurer]s?

"So, can [Conjurer]s normally talk with the Elements like you do?" I asked. I had to know. It was the burning question that would keep me up at night if I didn't get answers.

"Some of them," said Lara.

That's not a good look for you, Lara.

Tristan put a hand on her shoulder. "So, what are you going to do now? Sounds like the water was having issues?"

Lara shrugged, then whipped her long, blonde hair behind her. "Water's in a weird mood right now. I know I shouldn't say that out loud, but Water tends to get upset with me. Something about attunement and not being proper for the situation."

"The elements don't talk." Ravyn crossed her arms and rolled her eyes.

I raised my hand. "So, then, you can't talk to the elements, Ravyn?" The look she gave me could kill most men. "I'm sorry. Please continue, Lara."

Lara made several noises resembling a hissing cat, shooting a glare at Ravyn all the while. "Yes. They can." She puffed out her cheeks, then snapped her head back around. "I'll ask Wind, then."

Is this going to be the process every time there's a fight? This does not bode well.

"Before you do, you said the elements are shy." I met Lara's eyes. "Does that mean the elements have personalities?"

"Yes! Absolutely! Hang on, let me converse with Wind."

Here we go.

Lara raised both hands into the air. I was half-expecting lightning bolts to strike the tips of her fingers. "Wind, can you hear me?" After a pause, Lara flinched. "How are you doing? Ahh, I'm sorry to hear that. Is she okay?" Lara's expression continued to change, and I wished I could hear what was going on between her and, uh…Wind. "That's horrible! Well, don't listen to her. She's wrong about you. In every way I can imagine. Uh-huh. Yep! So, I'm sorry to interrupt you, but can you do me a quick favor?"

"Tristan, were you aware of this?" I asked.

He swallowed and scratched the back of his neck. "Y-yeah!"

I see.

"Thank you!" Lara clapped her hands together, then began to whip her right arm through the air. The wind wrapped around her wrist in ribbons of green light. As she continued, more and more of the strange winds began to tighten and converse around her, enveloping the entirety of her arm. There was a sudden popping noise, and then the currents converged into a single ball of wispy air with a gentle light in the middle. The sphere did nothing on its own, just rotated around her head. "I now have Wind with me! Now Wind will perform an action I ask of it. Wind is kind, understanding, and exceptionally creative, so her and I often see eye-to eye."

So, there *was* some reasoning behind what she was doing.

"What can you do now?" I asked.

Lara rose to her feet, then looked off into the distance where we couldn't see a thing. She turned her head to Portia. "Your name is Portia, right?"

Portia nodded. "Yeah, what's up?"

"Can you stop the boat for a moment?"

"Sloop," she corrected. "And yeah, hold on."

The sloop slowed, and the waves became gentler with the reduction in speed. After a couple of minutes, the sloop came to a halt, and Lara offered her one of Shi Island's curtsies.

"Thank you so much, Portia," said Lara. She directed her attention back to the ocean and held out her hand. "Observe the power of nature!"

I'm watching.

"I command you, spirit of nature! [Whirlwind]!" A whistle soared past my ears. It was loud enough that it almost hurt. Above us, a dark cloud formed, and lightning and thunder roared within. The orb of wind that Lara had summoned disappeared, and shortly after, a gust of wind blew past us, forming a miniature tornado some distance away from us from below the cloud. Before I could even register what happened, the cloud disappeared, and with it, the wind. Lara fell to one knee, panting. "That's— Hold on for just a second." She heaved, then rested back into a cross-legged position. "She wasn't in the best of moods right now, so it was a little weak. But that's a small example of what [Conjurer] can do!"

I had no idea what to say. On the one hand, it appeared to have a ton of potential. However, if it was so fickle, then I had my concerns.

Is nothing ever easy?

Lara Pro Tip: I can hear Fire, Lightning, and Ice, but they won't help me out. Well, not yet, I think.

Now Connecting to [User DoubleBlind]...

Social Media:

Twitter: @DDoubleBlinDD
Instagram: @ddouble.blindd
Discord: discord.gg/doubleblind
Linktree: linktr.ee/doubleblind

Support:

Patreon: patreon.com/ddoubleblindd
Merchants of Nyarlea: doubleblind.bigcartel.com

Made in the USA
Middletown, DE
21 February 2024